His Ultimate Demand

MAYA BLAKE

DANI COLLINS

VICTORIA PARKER

First Published in Great Britain 2016
By Mills & Boon, an imprint of HarperCollins*Publishers*
1 London Bridge Street, London, SE1 9GF

HIS ULTIMATE DEMAND © 2017 Harlequin Books S. A.

The Ultimate Playboy, *The Ultimate Seduction* and *The Ultimate Revenge* were first published in Great Britain by Harlequin (UK) Limited.

The Ultimate Playboy © 2014 Maya Blake
The Ultimate Seduction © 2014 Dani Collins
The Ultimate Revenge © 2014 Victoria Parker

ISBN: 978-0-263-92948-5

05-0117

Maya Blake fell in love with the world of the alpha male and the strong, aspirational heroine when she borrowed her sister's Mills & Boon at the age of thirteen. Shortly thereafter the dream to plot a happy ending for her own characters was born. Writing for Mills & Boon is a dream come true. Maya lives in South East England with her husband and two kids. Reading is an absolute passion, but when she isn't lost in a book she likes to swim, cycle, travel and Tweet!

You can get in touch with her
via e-mail, at mayablake@ymail.com,
or on Twitter: www.twitter.com/mayablake

To David and Peter.
Life would be so much duller without you two!

CHAPTER ONE

New York

NARCISO VALENTINO STARED at the box that had been delivered to him. It was large, made with the finest expensive leather, trimmed with velvet rope, with a horseshoe-shaped clasp made of solid twenty-four-carat gold.

Normally, the sight of it brought anticipation and pleasure.

But the ennui that had invited itself for a long-term stay in his life since he'd turned thirty last month leached excitement from him as the stock market leaked money after a juicy disaster.

Lucia had accused him of turning into a boring old man right before her diva exit out of his life two weeks ago.

He allowed himself a little grin of relief. He'd celebrated her departure with a boys' weekend ski trip to Aspen where he'd treated himself to a little palate cleanser in the form of a very enthusiastic Norwegian ski instructor.

But much too quickly, the jaded hollowness had returned.

Rising from his desk, he strode to the window of his seventieth-floor Wall Street office and stared at the New York skyline. Satisfaction eased through him at the thought that he owned a huge chunk of this city.

Money was sexy. Money was power. And The Warlock of Wall Street—as the newspapers had taken to calling him—never denied himself the pull of power and sex.

The opportunity to experience two of his favourite things lay within the package on his desk.

Yet it'd remained unopened for the last hour…

Shrugging off the lethargy, he returned briskly to his desk and flipped the clasp.

The half mask staring up at him from a bed of black satin was exquisite. Pure silver edged with black onyx and Swarovski crystals, its intricate design and flawless detail announced the care and attention that had gone into creating it. Narciso appreciated care and attention. It was what had made him a millionaire by eighteen and a multibillionaire by twenty-five.

His vast wealth was also what had gained him admission into *Q Virtus,* the world's most exclusive gentlemen's club, whose quarterly caucus invitation was the reason for the mask. Two four-inch-long diamond-tipped pins held the mask in place. Pulling them out, he flipped it over to examine the soft, velvet underside, which held the security microchip, his moniker—The Warlock—and the venue, *Q Virtus,* Macau. He ran his thumb over the smooth surface, hoping to summon a little enthusiasm. Failing miserably, he set the mask down and glanced at the second item in the box.

The List.

Zeus, the anonymous head of *Q Virtus,* always provided club members with a discreet list of business interests who would be attending the caucuses. Narciso had chosen not to attend the last two because he'd already dealt with those lists' major players.

His gaze skimmed the heavily embossed paper and his breath caught. Excitement of a different, dangerous kind sizzled through him as the fourth name jumped out at him.

Giacomo Valentino—*Daddy dearest.*

He perused the other names to see if anyone else on the list would make his attendance worthwhile.

His lips twisted. Who the hell was he kidding?

One name and one name only had become *the* deciding factor. There were one or two business interests worth cultivating

during the two-day event, but Giacomo was who he intended
to interact with.

Although perhaps *interact* was the wrong word.

Setting the list down, he fired up his computer. Entering
the security codes, he pulled up the file he kept on his father.

The report his private investigator updated on a regular basis
showed that the old man had rallied a little from the blow Narciso had dealt him three months ago.

Rallied but not fully recovered. Within minutes, Narciso
was fully up to speed on his father's latest business dealings.

He didn't fool himself into thinking it gave him any sort of
upper hand. He knew his father kept a similar file on him. But
the game wouldn't have been this interesting if advantages had
been one-sided. Nevertheless Narciso gained a lot of satisfaction from knowing he'd won three of their last four skirmishes.

He was contemplating the latest approach to his annihila-
tion campaign when his phone buzzed.

Allowing the distraction, he thumbed the interactive surface
and read the message from Nicandro Carvalho, the closest thing
he had to a best friend.

Still caught in premature midlife-crisis mode, or are you ready
to shake off that clinging BOM image?

Boring old man. A corner of his mouth lifted as his gaze
slid to the list and his father's name. Suddenly energised, he
whipped back a response.

BOM has left the building. Care to get your ass whopped at
poker?

Nicandro's response—Dream on but bring it on—made him
laugh for the first time in weeks.

Powering down his laptop, he slammed it shut. His gaze
once again fell on the mask. Picking it up, he stashed it in his
safe and shrugged into his suit jacket.

Zeus would receive his RSVP in the morning, once he'd devised exactly how he was going to take his father down once and for all.

The internet was a scary place. But it was an invaluable tool if you wanted to hunt down a slippery son of a bitch.

Ruby Trevelli sat cross-legged on her sofa and stared at the blinking cursor awaiting her command. That she was reduced to online trawling for a solution to her problem spiked equal measures of irritation and frustration through her.

She'd made it a point to avoid anything to do with social media. The one time she'd foolishly typed her name into a search engine, the sheer volume of false information she'd discovered had scared her into never trying again.

Of course, she'd also found enough about her parents to have scarred her for life if she hadn't already been scarred.

Tonight, she had no choice. Because despite thousands of pages featuring Narciso Media Corporation, every effort to speak to someone who could help her had been met with a solid stone wall. She'd already wasted a solid hour discovering that a thirty-year-old billionaire named Narciso Valentino owned NMC.

She snorted under her breath. Who on earth named their child *Narciso* anyway? That was like inviting bullies and snark-mongers to feast on the poor child. On the flip side, his unique name had eased her search.

Sucking in a breath, she typed in her next request: *Narciso's New York hangouts.* There were over two million entries. Awesome.

Either there were millions of men out there named Narciso or the man she sought was indecently popular.

Offering up a Hail Mary, she clicked the first link. And nearly gagged at the graphic burlesque images that popped up.

Hell no!

She closed it and sat back, fighting the rising nausea.

Desperate was fast becoming her middle name but Ruby

refused to accept that the answers to her woeful financial predicament would be found in a skin den.

Biting her inside lip, she exhaled and typed again: *Where's Narciso Valentino tonight?*

Her breath caught as the search engine fired back a quick response. The first linked the domain of a popular tabloid newspaper—one she'd become rudely acquainted with when she'd received her first laptop at ten, logged on and seen her parents splashed over the home page. In the fourteen years since then, she'd avoided the tabloid, just as she avoided her parents nowadays.

Ignoring the ache in her chest, she clicked on the next link that connected to a location app.

For several seconds, she couldn't believe how easily she'd found him. She read the extensive list of celebrities who'd announced their whereabouts freely, including one attending a movie premiere right now in Times Square.

Grabbing the remote, she flipped the TV channel to the entertainment news station, and, sure enough, the movie star was flashing a million-dollar smile at his adoring fans.

She glanced back at the location next to Narciso Valentino's name.

Riga—a Cuban-Mexican nightclub in the Flatiron District in Manhattan.

Glancing at the clock above the TV, she made a quick calculation. If she hurried, she could be there in under an hour. Her heart hammered as she contemplated what she was about to do.

She despised confrontation almost as much as her parents thrived on it. But after weeks of trying to find a solution, she'd reached the end of her tether.

She'd won the NMC reality TV show and scraped together every last cent to come up with her half of the hundred-thousand-dollar capital needed to get her restaurant—Dolce Italia—up and running.

Any help she could've expected from Simon Whittaker, her

ex-business partner and owner of twenty-five per cent of Dolce Italia, was now a thing of the past.

She clenched her fist as she recalled their last confrontation.

Finding out that the man she'd developed feelings for was married with a baby on the way had been shock enough. Simon trying to talk her into sleeping with him despite his marital status had killed any emotion she'd ever had for him.

He'd sneered at her wounded reaction to his intended infidelity. But having witnessed it up close with gut-wrenching frequency in her parents' marriage, she was well versed in its consequences.

Cutting Simon out of her life once she'd seen his true colours had been a painful but necessary decision.

Of course, without his business acumen she'd had to take full financial responsibility of Dolce Italia. Hence her search for Narciso Valentino. She needed him to stand by his company's promise. A contract was a contract....

A gleaming black limo was pulling up as she rounded the corner of the block that housed the nightclub. The journey had taken an extra half-hour because of a late-running train. Wincing at the pinch of her high heels on the uneven pavestones, she hurried towards Riga's red-bricked façade.

She was navigating her way around puddles left by the recent April shower, when deep male laughter snagged her attention.

A burly bouncer held open the velvet rope cordon as two men, both over six feet tall, exited the VIP entrance in the company of two strikingly beautiful women. The first man was arresting enough to warrant a second look but it was the other man who commanded Ruby's interest.

Jet-black hair had been styled to slant over the right side of his forehead in a silky wave that flowed back to curl over his collar.

Her steps faltered as the power of his presence slammed into her, and knocked air out of her lungs. His aura sent a challenge to the world, dared it to do its worst.

Dazed, she documented his profile—winged eyebrow, beautifully sculpted cheekbone, a straight patrician nose and a curved mouth that promised decadent pleasure—or what she imagined decadent pleasure looked like. But his mouth promised it and, well, this guy looked as if he could deliver on whatever sensual promises he made.

'Hey, miss. You coming in any time this century?'

The bouncer's voice distracted her, but not for long enough to completely pull her attention away. When she looked back, the man was turning away but it wasn't before Ruby caught another quick glimpse of his breathtaking profile.

Her gaze dropped lower. His dark grey shirt worn under a clearly bespoke jacket was open at the collar, allowing a glimpse of a bronzed throat and mouth-watering upper chest.

Ruby inhaled sharply and pulled her coat tighter around her as if that could stem the heat rushing like a breached dam through her.

The drop-dead gorgeous blonde smiled his way. His hand dropped from her waist to her bottom, drifted over one cheek to cup it in a bold squeeze before he helped her into the car. The first man shouted a query, and the group turned away from Ruby. Just like that, the strangely intimate and disturbing link was broken.

Her insides sagged and she realised how tight a grip she'd held on herself.

Even after the limo swung into traffic, Ruby couldn't move, nor could she stem the tingling suspicion that she'd arrived too late.

The bouncer cleared his throat conspicuously. She turned. 'Can you tell me who that second guy was who just got into that limo?' she asked.

He raised one *are-you-serious?* eyebrow.

Ruby shook her still-dazed head and smiled at the bouncer. 'Of course you can't tell me. Bouncer-billionaire confidentiality, right?'

His slow grin gentled his intimidating stature. 'Got it in one. Now, you coming in or you just jaywalking?'

'I'm coming in.' Although the strong suspicion that she'd missed Narciso Valentino grew by the second.

'Great. Here you go.' The bouncer placed a Mayan-mask-shaped stamp on her wrist, glanced up at her, then added another stamp. 'Show it at the bar. It'll get you your first drink on the house.' He winked.

She smiled in relief as she entered the smoky interior. If her guess had been wrong and she hadn't just missed Narciso Valentino, she could nurse an expensive drink while searching him out.

She'd worked in clubs like these all through college and knew how expensive even the cheapest drinks were. Which was why she clutched an almost warm virgin Tiffany Blue an hour later as she accepted that Narciso Valentino *was* the man she'd seen outside.

Resigned to her fruitless journey, she downed the last of her drink and was looking for a place to set the glass down when the voices caught her attention.

'Are you sure?'

'Of course I am. Narciso will be there.'

Ruby froze, then glanced into one of the many roped-off VIP areas. Two women dripping in expensive jewellery and designer dresses that would cost her a full year's salary sat sipping champagne.

Unease at her shameless eavesdropping almost forced her away but desperation held her in place.

'How do you know? He didn't attend the last two events.' The blonde looked decidedly pouty at that outcome.

'I told you, I overheard the guy he was with this evening talking about it. They're both going this time. If I can get a job as a *Petit Q* hostess, this could be my chance,' her red-headed friend replied.

'What? To dress in a clown costume in the hope of catching his eye?'

'Stranger things have happened.'

'Well, hell will freeze over before I do that to hook a guy,' the blonde huffed.

Statuesque Redhead's lips pursed. 'Don't knock it till you try it. It pays extremely well. And if Narciso Valentino falls in my lap, well, let's just say I won't let that life-changing opportunity pass me by.'

'Okay, you have my attention. Give me the name of the website. And where the hell is Macau anyway?' the blonde asked.

'Umm…Europe, I think?'

Ruby barely suppressed a snort. Heart thumping, she took her phone from her tiny clutch and keyed in the website address.

An hour and a half later, she sent another Hail Mary and pressed send on the online forms she'd filled out on her return home.

It might come to nothing. She could fail whatever test or interview she had to pass to get this gig. Heck, after discovering that she was applying to hostess for *Q Virtus,* one of the world's most exclusive and secretive private clubs, she wondered if she didn't need her head examined. She could be wasting money and precious time chasing an elusive man. But she had to try. Each day she waited was another day her goal slipped from her fingers.

The alternative—bowing to the pressure from her mother to join the family business—was unthinkable. At best she would once again become the pawn her parents used to antagonise each other. At worst, they would try and drag her down into their celebrity-hungry lifestyle.

They'd made her childhood a living hell. And she only had to pass a billboard in New York City to see they were still making each other's lives just as miserable but taking pleasure in documenting the whole thing for the world to feast on.

The Ricardo & Paloma Trevelli Show was prime-time viewing. The fly-on-the-wall documentary had been running for as long as Ruby could remember.

When she was growing up, her daily routine had included

at least two sets of camera crews documenting her every move along with her parents'.

TV crews had become extended family members. For a very short time when it'd made her the most popular girl at school, she'd told herself she was okay with it.

Until her father's affairs began. His very public admission of infidelity when she was nine years old had made ratings soar. Her mother publicly admitting her heartbreak had made worldwide news. Almost overnight, the TV show had been syndicated worldwide and brought her parents even more notoriety.

The subsequent reunion and vow renewal had thrilled the world.

After her father's second admission of infidelity, millions of viewers had been given the opportunity to weigh in on the outcome of Ruby's life.

Strangers had accosted her on the street, alternatively pitying and shaming her for being a Trevelli.

Escaping to college at the opposite end of the country had been a blessing. But even then she hadn't been able to avoid her roots.

It'd quickly become apparent that she had no other talent than cooking.

The realisation that the Trevelli gene was truly stamped into her DNA was a deep fear she secretly harboured. It was the reason she'd cut Simon out of her life without a backward glance. It was also the reason she'd vowed never to let her parents influence her life.

Which was why she needed a ten-minute conversation with Narciso Valentino. A tingle of awareness shot through her as she replayed the scene outside Riga.

With a spiky foreboding, she recalled the dark, dangerously sensual waves vibrating off him; those bronzed, sure fingers drifting over the blonde's bottom, causing unwelcome heat to drag through Ruby's belly.

God, what was she doing lying in bed thinking of some stranger's hand on his girlfriend's ass?

She punched her pillow into shape and flipped off her bedside lamp. She couldn't control the future but she could control the choice between mooning over elegant hands that looked as if they could bring a woman great pleasure or getting a good night's sleep.

She was almost asleep when her phone pinged an incoming message.

Exhaling in frustration, she grabbed the phone.

The brightness in the dark room hurt her eyes, but, even half blinded, Ruby could see the words clearly. Her CV had impressed the powers that be.

She'd been granted an interview to become a *Petit Q*.

CHAPTER TWO

Macau, China, One Week Later

THE RED FLOOR-LENGTH gown sat a little too snugly against Ruby's skin, and the off-the-shoulder design exposed more cleavage and general flesh than she was comfortable with. But after two gruelling interviews, one of which she'd almost blown by turning up late due to another delayed train, the last thing she could complain about was the expensive designer outfit that spelt her out as a *Petit Q*.

She was careful now to avoid it getting snagged on her heels as she walked across the marble floor of her hotel towards the meeting place, from where they'd be chauffeured to their final destination. In her small case were two carefully folded, equally expensive outfits the management had provided.

An examination had shown that they, too, like the dress she wore, would be tight...everywhere. It was clear that someone, somewhere in the management food chain had got her measurements very wrong.

She'd already attracted the attention of an aging rock star in the lift on the way to the ground floor of her Macau hotel. It didn't matter that he'd seemed half blind when he'd leered at her; attracting *any* attention at all made her stomach knot with acid anxiety.

She'd let her guard down with Simon, had believed his interest to be pure and genuine, only to discover he wanted nothing more than a bit on the side. The idea that he'd assumed because she was a Trevelli she would condone his indecent proposal, just as her mother continued to accept her father's, had shredded the self-esteem she'd fought so hard to attain when she'd removed herself from her parents' sphere.

She wasn't a coward, but the fear that she might never be able to judge another man's true character sent a cold shiver through her.

Pushing the thought away, she straightened her shoulders, but another troubling thought immediately took its place.

What if she'd made a huge mistake in coming here?

What if Narciso didn't show? What if he showed and she missed him again?

No, she had to find him. Especially in light of the phone call she'd received the morning after she'd signed on to be a *Petit Q*.

The voice had been calm but menacing. Simon had sold his twenty-five-per-cent share of her business to a third party. 'We will be in touch shortly about interest and payment terms,' the accented voice had warned.

'I won't be able to discuss any payment terms until the business is up and running,' she'd replied, her hands growing clammy as anxiety dredged her stomach.

'Then it is in your interest to make that happen sooner rather than later, Miss Trevelli.'

The line had gone dead before she could say anything more. For a moment, she'd believed she'd dreamt the whole thing, but she'd lived in New York long enough to know loan sharks were a real and credible threat. And Simon had sold his share in her business to one of them.

Panicked and angry with Simon, she'd been halfway across the Indian Ocean before she'd read her *Petit Q* guidelines and experienced a bolt of shock.

No doubt to protect its ultra-urban-legend status, the *Q Virtus* Macau caucus was to be a masked event at a secret location in Macau.

Masked, as in *incognito.* Where the chances of picking out Narciso Valentino would be hugely diminished.

The memory of broad shoulders and elegant fingers flashed across her mind. Yeah, sure, as if she were an expert in male shoulders enough to distinguish one from the other.

Her fingers clenched around her tiny red clutch. She'd come all this way. She refused to admit defeat.

The redhead from Riga turned towards her and Ruby fought not to grit her teeth as the other woman dismissed her instantly.

As the door to the Humvee limo slid shut behind them another jagged stab of warning pierced her. Every cell in her body screamed at her to abandon this line of pursuit and hightail it back home.

She could use the app to find out when Narciso returned to New York. She could confront him on home turf where she was more at ease, not here in this sultry, exotic part of the world where the very air held a touch of opulent magic.

But what if this was her last chance? A man who would fly thousands of miles for a highly secretive event could disappear just as easily given half a chance. She'd been lucky to be in the right place to find out where he'd be at this point in time.

Fate had handed her the opportunity. She wasn't going to blow it.

The limo hit a bump, bringing her back to reality.

Despite the glitzy lights and Vegas-style atmosphere, the tiny island of Macau held a charisma and steeped-in-history feel that had spilled over from mainland China. She held her breath as they crossed over the Lotus Bridge into Cotai, their final destination.

Bicycles raced alongside sports cars and nineteen-fifties buses in a spectacular blend of ancient and modern.

Less than ten minutes later, they rolled to a stop. Exiting, she looked around and her trepidation escalated. The underground car park was well lit enough to showcase top-of-the-line luxury sports cars and blinged-out four-by-fours next to stretch limos.

The net worth in the car park alone was enough to fund the annual gross domestic product of a small country.

The buzz of excitement in her group fractured her thoughts and she hurried forward into waiting lifts. Like her, the other nineteen hostesses were dressed in red gowns for the first evening, and the ten male hosts dressed in red jackets.

Six bodyguards accompanied them into the lifts and Ruby stemmed the urge to bolt as the doors started to close. Five seconds later it was too late.

The doors opened to gleaming parquet floors with red and gold welcoming carpet running through the middle of the vast, suspended foyer.

On the walls, exquisite tapestries of dragons flirting with maidens were embellished with multihued glass beads. Red and gold Chinese-silk cloth hung in swathes from the tapered ceiling to the floor, discreetly blacking out the outside world.

Two winged staircases led to the floor below where a sunken section in the middle had been divided into twelve gaming tables, each with its own private bar and seating area.

All around her, masked men in bespoke tuxedos mingled with exquisitely clad women dripping with stunning jewellery that complemented their breathtaking masks. Granted, the number of women was marginally less than men, but from the way they carried themselves Ruby suspected these women wielded more than enough power to hold their own against their male counterparts.

A tall, masked, jet-haired woman wearing a sophisticated-looking earpiece glided forward and introduced herself as Head Hostess. In succinct tones, she briefed them on their roles.

Ruby tried to calm her jangling nerves as she descended the stairs and headed for the bar of the fourth poker table.

A bar she could handle.

Nevertheless, she held her breath as the first group of men took their places at the table. They all wore masks in varying degrees of camouflage and design. As she mixed her first round of drinks and delivered it to the table, Ruby tried to glean if any of them resembled her quarry.

One by one, she dismissed them. Eventually, they drifted off and another group took their place.

A grey-haired man—the oldest in her group—immediately drew her attention. He carried himself with command and control, but he was too old to be Narciso Valentino and his frame was slightly stooped with age.

He snapped his fingers and threw out an order for a glass of Sicilian red. Ruby pursed her lips and admonished herself not to react to the rudeness. Five men took their places around the table, leaving only one other space to be filled.

Safely behind the bar after delivering their drinks order, she watched their bets grow larger and bolder.

Music pumped from discreet loud speakers, and through a set of double doors guests took to the dance floor. It wasn't deafening by any means but Ruby felt the pulse of the provocative music through the soles of her feet.

She swallowed down the mingled distaste and latent fear as she noticed things were beginning to get hot and heavy as guests began to loosen their inhibitions.

She could do this. Just because she was a Trevelli didn't mean she would lose sight of her goals. Decadence and excess were her parents' thing. They needn't be hers…

The lights overhead dimmed.

A door to one side of the lift labelled The Black Room swung open and two men stepped onto the gangway.

One wore a gold half-mask that covered him from forehead to nose. The aura of power that radiated from him raised the very temperature of the room.

But the moment Ruby's eyes encountered the second man, her belly clenched.

The head hostess drifted towards him but he raised a hand and waved her away. At the sight of those slim fingers, recognition slammed into her. She watched, dry-mouthed, as he sauntered down the steps and headed for her side of the room.

He stopped in front of her bar.

Silver eyes bore into hers, drilling down hard as if he wanted to know her every last secret. The smile slowly left his face as he continued to stare at her, one eyebrow gradually lifting in silent query.

His silver and black onyx mask was artistically and visually stunning. It revealed his forehead and the lower part of his face and against its brilliance his olive skin glowed in a way that made her want to touch that chiselled jaw.

Piercing eyes drifted over her in a lazy sweep, pausing for a long second at her breasts. Her breath hitched in her throat as her body reacted to his probing gaze.

Narciso Valentino. If she'd had two dollars to rub together she'd have bet on it.

Her mouth dried as she looked into his eyes and lost every last sensible thought in her head.

'Serve me, *cara mia*. I'm dying of thirst.' His voice was raw, unadulterated sin, oozing what Ruby could only conclude was sex appeal.

At least she thought so because the sound of it had transmitted a tingling to parts of her body she hadn't known could tingle just from hearing a man's voice. And why on earth had her hands grown so clammy?

When his brow arched higher at her inactivity, she scrambled to think straight. 'W-what would you like?'

His eyes moved down again, paused at her throat, where her pulse jumped like a frenzied rabbit.

'Surprise me.'

He turned abruptly and all signs of mirth leached from his face.

Across the small space between the bar and the poker table, he speared the silver-haired man with an unforgiving gaze.

The man stared back, the part of his face visible beneath his mask taut despite his whole body bristling with disdain.

Animosity arced through the air, snapping coils of dangerous electricity that made Ruby's pulse leap higher. Her gaze slid back to the younger man as if drawn by magnets. She told herself she was trying to decipher what sort of drink to make him but, encountering those broad shoulders again, her mind drifted into impure territory, as it had outside the nightclub in New York.

Focus!

The older man had requested a Sicilian red but instinctively she didn't think the man she'd concluded was Narciso would go for wine.

Casting her gaze over the bottles of spirits and liqueurs, she quickly measured the required shots, mixed a cocktail and placed it on a tray.

Willing her fingers not to shake, she approached the poker table and placed his drink at his elbow.

He dragged his gaze from the older man long enough to glance from the pale golden drink to her face. 'What is this?' he asked.

'It's a…*Macau Bombshell,*' she blurted out the name she'd come up with seconds ago.

One smooth brow spiked as he leaned back in his seat. 'Bombshell?' Once again, his gaze drifted over her, lingered at the place where her dress parted mid-thigh in a long slit. 'Would you place yourself in that category, too? Because you certainly have the potential.'

Right, so really he was one of those. A Playboy with a capital *P*.

A man who saw something he coveted and went for it, regardless of who got hurt. The clear image of his hand on another woman made her spine stiffen in negative reaction, even as a tiny part of her acknowledged her disappointment.

Irritated with herself, she pushed the feeling away.

Now she knew what sort of man she was dealing with, things would proceed much smoother.

'No, I wouldn't,' she said briskly. 'It's all about the drink.'

'I've never heard such a name.'

'It's my own creation.'

'Ah.' He sipped the champagne, falernum, lemon and pineapple mix. Then he slowly tasted the cocktail without taking his eyes off her. 'I like it. Bring me one every half-hour on the button until I say otherwise.'

The implication that she could be here for hours caused her teeth to grind. She looked from the dealer to the other players at the table, wondered if she could ask to speak to Narciso privately now.

'Is there a problem?' he queried.

She cleared her throat. 'Well, yes. There are no clocks in this place and I don't have a watch, so…'

The silver-haired man swore under his breath and moved his shoulders in a blatantly aggressive move.

'Hold out your hand,' Narciso said.

Ruby's eyes widened. 'Excuse me?'

'Give me your hand,' he commanded.

She found herself obeying before she could think not to. He removed an extremely expensive and high-tech-looking watch from his wrist and placed it on her right wrist. The chain link was too large for her but it didn't mask the warmth from his skin and something jagged and electric sliced through her belly.

When his hand drifted along the inside of her wrist, she bit back a gasp, and snatched her hand back.

'Now you know when I'll next need you.'

'By all means, keep me waiting as you try out your tired pickup lines,' the older man snapped with an accent she vaguely recognised.

Silver Eyes shifted his gaze to him. And although he continued to sip his cocktail, the air once again snapped with dark animosity.

'Ready for another lesson, old man?'

'If it involves teaching you to respect your betters, then I'm all for it.'

The resulting low laugh from the man next to her sent a shiver dancing over her skin. On decidedly wobbly legs, she retreated behind the bar and forced herself to regulate her breathing.

Whatever she'd experienced when those mesmerising eyes had locked into hers and those long fingers had stroked her was a false reaction. She refused to trust any emotion that could lead her astray.

Focus!

She glanced down at the watch. The timepiece was truly exquisite, a brand she'd heard of and knew was worth a fortune.

Unable to stop herself, she skated her fingers over it, her pulse thundering all over again when she remembered how he'd looked at her before slipping the watch on her wrist. She shifted as heat dragged through her and arrowed straight between her legs.

No!

She wasn't a slave to her emotions like her parents. And she wasn't the gullible fool Simon had accused her of being.

She had a goal and a purpose. One she intended to stick to.

Exactly half an hour later, she approached, willing her gaze not to trace those magnificent shoulders. Up close they were even broader, more imposing. When he shifted in his seat, they moved with a mesmerising fluidity that made her want to stop and gawp.

Keeping her gaze fixed on the red velvet table, she quickly deposited his drink on the designated coaster and picked up his almost-empty one. He flicked a glance at her.

'*Grazie.*'

The sound of her mother tongue on his lips flipped her stomach with unwanted excitement. She told herself it was because she was one step further to confirming his identity but Ruby suspected it was the sheer sexiness of his voice that was the bigger factor here.

'*Prego,*' she responded automatically before she could stop herself. She bit her lip and watched him follow the movement. A deeply predatory gleam entered his eyes.

'I want the next one in fifteen minutes.' His gaze returned

to his opponent, who looked a little paler since the last round of drinks. 'I have a feeling I'll be done by then. Unless you want to quit while you're behind?' he asked, sensual lips parted in a frightening imitation of a smile.

The older man let out a pithy response that Ruby didn't quite catch. Two players quickly folded their cards and left.

The two men eyeballed each other, pure hatred blazing as they psychologically circled one another.

Narciso laid down his cards in a slow, unhurried flourish. His opponent followed suit with a move that was eerily similar and made Ruby frown. The connection between the two men was unmistakable but she couldn't quite pin down why.

When the older man laughed, Ruby glanced down at his cards. She didn't know the rules of poker, but even she guessed his cards were significant.

She held her breath. Not with so much as a twitch did Narciso indicate he'd just lost millions of dollars.

'Give it up, old man.'

'Mai!' Never.

Ten minutes later, Narciso calmly laid down another set of cards that won him the next game. Hearing Giacomo's grunt of disbelief was extremely satisfactory. But it was the indrawn breath of surprise from the woman next to him that drew his attention.

He didn't let himself glance at her yet. She'd proven a seriously delicious distraction already. He had plans for her but those plans would have to wait a while longer.

For now, he revelled in Giacomo's defeat and watched a trickle of sweat drip down his temple.

They were barely an hour in and he'd already divested him of several million dollars. As usual, Giacomo had been lured in by the promise of trouncing his son, enabling Narciso to lay the bait he knew wouldn't be resisted.

The last game had won him a midsize radio station in Anaheim, California.

It would be a superb addition to his already sizeable news

and social media portfolio. Or he could shut it down and declare it a loss.

It didn't matter either way.

What mattered was that he had Giacomo's financial demise within his grasp. How very fitting that he should be in the perfect place to celebrate once he'd hammered the last nail into the coffin.

His gaze flickered to the stunning woman in red who regarded him with a touch of wariness and a whole lot of undisguised interest.

The silky cognac-coloured hair begged to be messed with, as did that sinful, pouting mouth she insisted on mauling every time he won a hand.

But her body, *Dio!* Her dress was a little too tight, sure, but even the fact that it made her assets a little too in your face didn't detract from the fact that she was a magnificent creature.

A magnificent creature he would possess tonight. She would be the cherry on his cake, one he would take the utmost pleasure in savouring before he devoured.

But first…

'Do you yield?' he asked silkily, already anticipating the response. In some ways they were so very similar. Which wasn't surprising considering they were father and son.

Although a father and son who detested the very ground each other walked on put an interesting twist on their *relationship*.

'Over my dead body.' Giacomo snapped his fingers at the dealer and threw his last five-million-dollar platinum chip in the middle of the table.

Beside him, his hostess's mouth dropped open. The sight of her pink tongue sent a spike of excitement through his groin.

Sì…he would celebrate well tonight. For a while there, he'd begun to suspect that beating Giacomo would be his only source of entertainment in Macau. Which was why he'd sought the old man out instead of leaving him to squirm a little longer. He'd wanted to be done and out of here as soon as possible.

The other deals he'd come to negotiate had taken the necessary leap forward and he'd believed there was nothing left.

But now…

His groin hardened as he watched her mouth slowly press shut and her eyes dart to his with the same anticipated excitement that flowed within him.

He let his interest show, let her see the promise of what was to come.

Heat flared up her delicate neck and flawless skin into a surprisingly innocent face that could've graced a priceless painting.

Dio, she was truly entrancing. And yet she was in a place like this, where the likelihood of being hit on, or more, was very real.

He gave a mental shrug. He'd stopped trying to reason why people took the actions they took well before he'd grown out of long socks.

Otherwise he'd have driven himself mad from trying to decipher why the father whose DNA flowed through his veins seemed to hate every single breath he took.

Or why Maria's betrayal still had the power to burn an acid path in his gut—

No.

That train had long left the station. Giving it thinking room was a waste of time and his time was extremely precious.

Keeping his eyes on his hostess, he downed his drink and held out his empty glass.

'I'm thirsty again, *amante.*'

With a nod, she sashayed away in her too-tight dress and returned minutes later with his drink.

When she started to move away, he snagged a hand around her waist. The touch of warm, silk-covered flesh beneath his fingers short-circuited his brain for a few moments. Then he realised she was trying to get away from him.

'Stay. You bring me luck when you're near.'

'Shame you need a woman to win,' Giacomo sneered.

Narciso ignored him and nodded to the dealer. He wanted this game to be over so he could pull this magical being tighter into his arms, feel her melt against him, his prize for emerging triumphant.

Giacomo threw his chip defiantly into the fray. Narciso's chest tightened with the anger that never quite went away. For as long as he remembered, his father had treated him like that chip—inconsequential, easily cast aside. Underneath all the anger and bitterness, a wound he'd thought healed cracked open.

Ignoring it, he calmly plucked his cards from the table.

'Let's up the stakes.'

Eyes that had once been similar to his own but had grown dimmer with age snapped at him. 'You think you have something I want?'

'I *know* I do. That tech company you lost to me last month? If I lose this hand, I'll return it to you, along with all of this.' He nodded to the pile of chips in front of him, easily totalling over thirty million dollars.

'And if I lose?' His voice held a false confidence Narciso almost smiled at. *Almost.*

'You hand over the other five-million chip I know is in your pocket and I'll let you keep your latest Silicon Valley start up.'

Giacomo sneered but Narciso could see him weighing up the odds. Thirty million against ten.

He waited, let the seductive scent of his hostess's perfume wash over him. Unable to resist, he slid his hand lower. The faintest sensation of a thong made his groin tighten. Again, she tried to move away. He pulled her back towards him and heard her breath catch.

'My offer expires in ten seconds,' he pressed.

Giacomo reached into his tuxedo pocket and tossed the second chip onto the table. Then he laid out cards in a flourish.

Four of a kind.

Narciso didn't need to glance down at his own cards to know *he'd* won.

And yet…the triumph he should've experienced was oddly missing. Instead, hollowness throbbed dully in his chest.

'Come on, then, you coward. It's your turn to answer this—do you yield?'

Narciso breathed in deep and fought the tight vice crushing his chest. Slowly, the hollowness receded and anger rushed into its place. 'Yes, I yield.'

His father's bark of victorious laughter drew attention from other tables but Narciso didn't care.

His hand was tightening over her waist, anticipation of a different sort firing his body. He was about to turn towards her when Giacomo reached for the cards Narciso had discarded.

A straight flush. A winning hand more powerful than his father's.

The evidence that he'd been toyed with registered in Giacomo's shocked eyes. *'Il diavolo!'* He lunged across the table, his whole body vibrating with fury.

Narciso stood, his eyes devoid of expression. *'Sì,* I am the devil *you* spawned. You'll do well to remember that next time we meet.'

CHAPTER THREE

I AM THE devil you spawned.

Had he meant that literally?

Ruby glanced at the man who had her imprisoned against his side as he steered her towards…

'Where are you taking me?' she demanded in a rush as electrifying fingers pressed more firmly into her skin. Who knew silk was an excellent conductor of heat?

She burned from head to toe and he wasn't even touching her bare skin.

'First to the dance floor. And then…who knows?'

'But my duties…behind the bar—'

'Are over,' he stated imperiously.

Despite the alien emotions swirling through her, she frowned. 'Can you do that?'

'You'll find that I can pretty much do anything I want.'

'You deliberately lost thirty million dollars two minutes ago. I think doing what you want is pretty obvious. What I'm asking is, am I risking my job by deserting my post?'

He ushered her into the lift, took hold of her wrist and held the smartwatch against the panel. When it lit up, he pressed the key for the floor below. 'You're here to serve the members of this club. I require your services on the dance floor. There, does that ease your anxiety?' He asked the question with a thread of cynicism that made her glance closely at him.

The tic throbbing at his temple and tense shoulders indicated that he hadn't shrugged off his encounter at the poker table.

'Who was that man you were playing with?' she asked.

Silver eyes hardened a touch before they cleared and he smiled. Ruby forced herself not to gulp at the pulse-destroying transformation his smile achieved.

'No one important. But you—' he faced her fully as the lift stopped and the doors glided open '—are much more fascinating.'

One hand brushed her wrist and slid up her arm. The shiver when he'd first touched her returned a hundredfold, sending soul-deep tremors through her.

What on earth was going on? She'd believed herself in love with Simon, enough to come within a whisper of making a fool of herself, and yet he'd not triggered an iota of what she was feeling now.

Chemistry.

The word fired alarm bells so loud in her head she jerked backwards. Her back hit the lift wall and panic flared high as he stepped closer. Heat waves bounced off his hard-packed, unapologetically male body straight into hers.

'I'm not fascinating. Not in the least,' she said hurriedly.

He laughed, a deep, husky sound that sent warning tingling all over her body.

Was this how helpless prey felt within the clutches of a merciless predator? She was nobody's prey; nonetheless she couldn't deny this man's seriously overwhelming presence.

'You're refreshingly naïve, too.' His gaze probed, then his smile slowly faded. Although the hunger didn't. 'Unless *that's* the ploy?' he queried in the same silky tone he'd used at the poker table.

Ruby's breath caught as the unmistakable sense of danger washed over her again. 'There's no ploy. And I'm not naïve.'

His fingers had reached her shoulder. They skated along her collarbone, perilously close to the pulse jumping at her throat.

The doors started to slide shut. His fingers stopped just shy of touching her pulse, then returned to grasp her wrist. With a tap on the smartwatch the doors parted again.

'Come and dance with me. You can tell me how un-naïve and un-fascinating you are.'

He led her to the middle of a dance floor much larger than the one upstairs. Over a dozen guests graced the large space, moving to the beat of the sultry blend of Far Eastern music and western jazz.

They could've danced apart. In fact Ruby was counting on the brief reprieve from close contact. But he had other ideas.

He caught her close, one arm around her waist and the other catching her hand and imprisoning it against his chest as he began to sway. The fluidity with which he moved, his innate sensuality, told her that this man knew a lot about sex and sexuality. Would know how to take a woman and leave her utterly replete but desperate for more.

'I'm waiting for you to enlighten me.'

For a second she couldn't get her brain to work. Sensations she'd never felt before crashed through her as his hard thighs brushed hers.

'About what?'

'About why you think you're not fascinating. Those impure thoughts running through your head we'll leave for later.'

She sucked in a shocked breath. 'How…? I wasn't…'

'You blush when you're flustered. As endearing as that is, you'd make a lousy poker player.'

'I don't gamble. And I don't know why I'm having this conversation with you.'

'We're performing the requisite mating dance before we… mate.'

She stopped dead. 'In your dreams! I'm not here to be your, or anyone's, appetiser.'

'Don't sell yourself short, sweetheart. I'd place you more as a deliciously forbidden dessert than an appetiser. But one I intend to devour nonetheless.'

She was on a dance floor thousands of miles away from home, immersed in a debate about which food course she was.

Surreal didn't even begin to cover the emotions coursing through her as she glanced up at him and encountered that blatantly masculine square jaw and those hypnotic eyes.

'Look, Mr...?'

He raised a brow. 'You're at a masked event, shrouded in secrecy, embroiled in intrigue and mystery, and you want to know my name?' he asked cynically.

Damn, how could she have forgotten? 'Why do I get the feeling that all this bores you rigid?'

His eyes gleamed. 'How very intuitive of you. You're right—it does. Or it did, until I saw you.'

Her heart gave a little kick. One she determinedly ignored. 'You were fully engaged when you played your game. And *that* had nothing to do with me.'

Again that reminder hardened his eyes. 'Ah, but I lost thirty million dollars so I could make what's happening between us happen sooner.'

'There's nothing happening—'

'If you believe *that* then you really are naïve.'

Another couple danced closer. The flash of red hair distracted Ruby enough to make her look. *Redhead* was in the arms of another man but her hungry eyes were fixed squarely on Narciso.

Irrational irritation jerked up Ruby's spine.

Pursing her lips, she tilted her chin at the redhead. 'Why don't you help yourself to her? She definitely wants you.'

He didn't bother to glance where Ruby indicated. He merely smiled and shrugged. 'Every woman wants me.'

'Wow, you're not the shy type at all, are you?' she snapped.

He leaned forward, and a swathe of luxurious black hair fell over his forehead to curl over the top of his mask. 'Are those the types that turn you on?' he whispered.

The image of shy, self-effacing...*duplicitous* Simon fleeted across her mind. She stiffened. 'We're not discussing my tastes here.'

'I've clearly hit a nerve. But if you don't tell me what your tastes are, how will I know how to please you?' His mouth was a hair's breadth from her ear.

Ruby fought to breathe. Her chest was a mere inch from his but her lower body was plastered against his in a way that made his body's response blatant and unmistakable.

He was aroused. And he meant her to know it.

Her abdomen clenched so forcefully, she lost her footing and stumbled.

Strong hands righted her and began to pull her back into his arms but Ruby quickly stepped back.

'You can start by buying me a drink.'

He reluctantly dropped his hand from her waist. Expecting overwhelming relief, Ruby frowned when it didn't arrive.

A white-jacketed waiter hovered nearby. 'Champagne?'

She shook her head. 'No. Something else.'

Something that would take several minutes to make and give her time to get her perplexing emotions under control.

'State what you wish,' he said.

She almost blurted her reason for being in Macau there and then. But this wasn't the right time. She needed to get him alone, in a place where he couldn't blow her off as easily as his employees had these past weeks.

Casting her gaze around, she pointed to the far side of the room. 'There.'

'The ice-vodka lounge? Is this a delaying tactic?'

'Of course not. I really want a drink.'

He watched her for several seconds, then he nodded.

This time her relief was tangible. But the reprieve didn't last long. His arm slid possessively around her waist as he led her off the dance floor.

She was suppressing the rising tide of that damned *chemistry* when he leaned in close. 'You're only trying to delay the inevitable, *tesoro*.'

'I have no idea what you mean.'

His laughter drew gazes and turned heads. Ruby had a feeling everything this man did compelled attention. And not just of the female variety.

Powerful men stepped aside as he steered her towards the vodka lounge. A faux-fur coat appeared as if by magic and he draped it over her shoulders before they entered the sub-zero room. She headed for an empty slot at the bar, near an ice sculpture carved in the shape of a Chinese dragon.

The bartender glanced at her unmasked face with a frown.

'I'd like a *Big Apple Avalanche*, please. Heavy on the apple.' She needed a clear head if she intended to stay toe to toe with Narciso Valentino.

The bartender didn't move. 'I don't think you're allowed—'

'Is there a problem?' The hard rasp came from over her shoulder.

The bartender snapped to attention. 'Not at all, sir.' He grabbed the apple mixer and the canister of top-range vodka.

'I'll take it from here.' Narciso took the drinks from him and waved him away.

Despite the warmth of her coat, she shivered when he turned to her.

'Ready?'

God, this wasn't going well at all. Far from feeling under control, she felt her thoughts scatter to the wind every time he looked into her eyes.

'Yes,' she said as she inserted the specialised drinking spout into the ice outlet and brought her lips to it.

Her eyes met molten silver ones and fiery heat rushed into her belly. He slowly tipped the canister and icy vodka and apple pooled into her mouth.

Cold and heat simultaneously soothed and burned their way down her throat but the power of the decadent drink came nowhere close to the potent gleam in his eyes.

Before discovering Simon's duplicity, sex had been something she'd imagined in abstract terms; something she'd accepted would eventually happen between them, once the trust and affection she'd thought was growing between them was solid enough to lean on.

Sex just for the sake of it, or used as a weapon the way she'd watched her parents use it, had made being a virgin at twenty-four an easy choice.

But looking into Narciso's eyes, she slowly began to understand why sex was a big deal for some women. Why they dwelled on it with such single-minded ferocity.

Never had she wanted to drown in a man's eyes. Never had she wanted to kiss sensually masculine lips the way she wanted to kiss him right now. She wanted to feel those arms around her again, holding her prisoner the way they'd held her on the dance floor. She wanted to spear her fingers through his luxurious hair, scrape her nails over his scalp and find out if it brought him pleasure.

'Have another one,' he commanded huskily. He raised the sterling silver mixer, his gaze riveted on her mouth.

He wanted to kiss her badly. The same way she wanted to kiss him. Or would have if she didn't know from painful experience how treacherous and volatile sexual attraction could be.

'No, thanks. It's getting late. I need to go.'

One beautifully winged brow rose. 'You need to go.'

'Yes.'

'And where *exactly* do you intend to go?'

She frowned. 'Back to my hotel, of course.'

He slowly lowered his arm. 'I thought you understood your role here,' he murmured coolly.

Icy foreboding shivered down her spine. 'What's that supposed to mean?'

'It means, the moment the last guest arrived, the whole building went into lock down. You're stuck here with me until tomorrow at six.' He discarded the canister and stepped closer. 'And I have the perfect idea of how we can pass the time.'

* * *

Narciso watched a myriad expressions dart over her face.

Excitement. Anxiety. Suspicion.

Two of those three weren't what he expected from a woman when he announced they were effectively locked in together. Most women would be salivating at the thought and making themselves available before he changed his mind.

Not this one.

Even the hint of excitement was fading. Now she just looked downright frightened.

He frowned. 'I expected a more enthusiastic response.'

Her gaze went to the watch—his watch—then back to his face. Narciso decided not to think about why the sight of his large watch on her delicate wrist pleased him so much.

He would gift it to her. She could keep it on during sex. Once he'd dispelled that unacceptable look from her face.

'You just told me I can't leave. And you expect me to be excited?'

'You have some of the world's richest and most influential men gathered in one place. Everyone who attends these events has the same agenda—network hard and party harder, especially the *Petit Qs*. You, on the other hand, are acting as if you've received a prison sentence. Why?'

Her eyelids lowered and she grabbed the lapels of her coat.

Faint alarm bells rang at the back of his mind. Going against a habit of a lifetime, he forced himself to ignore it as she raised those delicate lids to lock gazes with him.

Her sapphire-blue eyes held a combination of boldness and shyness that hugely intrigued him. She wanted something but wasn't quite sure how to get it.

He had every intention of showing her how to get exactly what she wanted once he got her to his suite upstairs. He might even tempt her into using the velvet ropes that held back his emperor-size bed's drapes…

Desire slammed into him with a force he hadn't experienced

in years…if ever. The strength of it struck him dumb for a few seconds before he realised she was speaking.

'…knew about the club, of course, and that my hostessing gig was for two days. I didn't know I'd be staying here for the duration.'

'Ah, one small piece of advice. Always read the small print.'

Her delicious mouth pursed. He had the sudden, clamouring urge to find out if it tasted as succulent as it looked. Her narrowed-eyed glare stopped him. Barely.

'I always do. I can't say the same for other people though. Especially people who have the small print pointed out to them and still wilfully ignore it.'

The alarm bells grew louder. 'That's decidedly…pointed. Care to elaborate?'

She opened her mouth, then shut it again. 'I'm cold. Can we leave?'

'That's an excellent idea.' He walked her to the door of the ice bar and helped her out of her coat.

The sight of her hardened nipples—an effect of the sub-zero temperature—fried a few million brain cells. That clawing hunger gutted him further, making him fight to remember whether he was coming or going.

Going. Definitely. Up to his allocated suite with this woman who sparked a reaction within him that left him reeling, and wanting more. He hadn't wanted anything this badly for a long time. Not since his eleventh birthday…

He shut off his thoughts and walked her to the lift, absurdly pleased when she didn't protest. Perhaps she'd accepted the inevitable.

They were meant to be together. Here in this place where the events of earlier this evening with Giacomo had nearly soured his experience.

She would take away the bitterness for a while. Take away his unsettling hollowness when he'd held the old man's financial demise in his grasp but hadn't taken it.

All would be better in the morning.

For tonight, he intended to seek the most delicious oblivion.

'Should I bother to ask where you're taking me now?'

His smile felt tight and his body on edge. 'No. Don't bother. What you should ask is how many ways will I make you like what's coming next.' He activated the electronic panel. When the chrome panel slid back to reveal the row of buttons he selected the fiftieth floor for his penthouse suite.

'If you're planning to throw a few more millions away, then I'd rather not watch.' Again there was that censorious note in her voice that strummed his instincts.

From experience he knew women always had hidden agendas, be it the urge to make themselves indispensable in his life the moment he so much as smiled their way or to take advantage of his power and influence—as well as his body—for as long as possible.

But the woman in front of him was exhibiting none of those traits. And yet there was something... Narciso didn't like the mixed signals he was receiving from her.

'Have we met before?' he demanded abruptly, although he was sure he would have remembered. She had an unforgettable body, and that mouth... He was absolutely certain he would have remembered that mouth.

'Met? No, of course not. Besides, I don't know who you are, remember?'

'If you don't know who I am then how do you know we haven't met before?'

Her eyes shifted away from his. 'I...don't know. I just think a man like you...I'd have remembered...that's all.'

He smiled at her flustered response, deciding he definitely liked her flustered. 'I like that you think I'm unforgettable. I aim to make that thought a permanent reality for you.'

'Trust me, you already have,' she quipped.

Narciso got the distinct impression it wasn't a compliment.

He stepped forward. She stepped back. Her eyes widened when she realised she was trapped against the wall of the lift.

His pulse thundered when her gaze darted to his mouth and then back to his eyes.

'Somewhere along the line, I seem to have made a bad impression on you. Normally I wouldn't care but...' He stepped closer, until the warmth of her agitated exhalations rushed over his chin. Her scent hit his nostrils and he nearly moaned at the seductive allure of it.

'But...?' she demanded huskily.

'But I find myself wanting to alter that impression.'

'You want me to think you're a good guy?'

Laughing, he slid his hand around her trim waist. 'No. *Good* is taking things a touch too far, *amante*. I haven't been *good* since...' he blunted that knife of memory again '...for ever.'

Her darkened eyes dropped to his mouth again and Narciso barely stopped himself from groaning. But he couldn't stop his hands from tightening on her waist. In contrast to her lush hips, her waist was so tiny, his hands spanned it easily.

'Then what do you want from me?'

Before he could succinctly elaborate, the lift doors slid open. The double doors leading into his suite beckoned. Beyond that the bedroom where he intended to make her his.

He grasped her wrist and tugged her after him. Using the smartwatch to activate the smaller panel, he pressed his thumb against the infrared scanner and pushed the doors open. He didn't bother to shut it because the doors were automatic. Security was exemplary at all *Q Virtus* events, especially the private suites. He had the whole floor to himself and no one would disturb them unless he wanted them to.

And he had no desire for any interruptions—

He noticed she'd stopped dead and turned to find her staring at him.

'You've brought me to your suite,' she blurted.

The pulse pounding at her throat could've been excitement. Or more likely it was the trepidation he'd seen earlier.

'Very observant of you.'

'Know this now—I won't be indulging in anything…illicit with you.'

'Since we haven't established exactly what it is we'll be doing I think we're getting a little ahead of ourselves.'

'I wish you'd stop toying with me.'

His shoulders moved with the restlessness that vibrated through his whole being. He couldn't remember the last time he'd had to work this hard to get a woman to acknowledge her interest in him. 'Fine. Do you deny that there's something powerful and undeniable happening between us?'

'I don't want—'

'If you really don't want to be here, say the word and I'll let you leave.' That wasn't strictly true. First he'd use his infinite skills to convince her to stay. Arrogance didn't come into his awareness that he was attractive to most women, and, despite her mixed signals, this woman was as attracted to him as he was to her.

She might need a little more work than usual—and the thought wasn't unpleasing—but he was more than up to the task.

He watched her debate with herself for an endless minute. Then she turned towards the window.

Narciso forced himself to remain still, despite his every cell screeching at him to grab her. Picking up a control device, he pushed the button that allowed the glass windows to turn from opaque to transparent.

Macau City lay spread before them in a cascade of lights, glittering water and awe-inspiring ancient Portuguese, Chinese and modern architecture.

Since he'd started doing business here, his fascination with the city had grown along with his bank balance.

But right now his fascination with her was much more paramount.

'Tell me you'll stay.' His voice emerged rougher than normal.

The thought that he wanted her badly, alarm bells or no alarm bells, made him frown. He'd trained himself not to want anything he absolutely could not have. It was why he calculated his every decision with scalpel-like precision.

That way he avoided disappointment. Avoided…heartache…

She turned from the window, arms crossed at that tiny waist. Her response took a minute, two at a stretch, but they were the longest minutes of Narciso's life.

'I'll stay…for a little while.'

He swallowed and nodded. Suddenly, his fingers itched to remove the pins in her hair, to see its silky dark gold abundance cascade over her shoulders.

'Take your hair down,' he instructed. The time for playing was over.

Her eyes widened. 'Why?'

'Because I want to see it. And because you're staying.'

Her fingers touched the knot at the back of her head. Anticipation spiked through him only to be doused in disappointment when she lowered her hand.

'I prefer to keep it up.'

'If you're trying to keep me hyped up with interest, trust me, it's working.'

'I'm not, I mean… My hair is no big deal.'

'It is to me. I have a weakness for long hair.'

Her head tilted to one side, exposing a creamy neck he longed to explore. 'If I take my hair down, will you take your mask off?'

As much as he wanted to rip his mask off, something told him to delay the urge. 'No,' he replied. 'My house, my rules.'

'That's not fair, is it?'

'If life was fair you'd be naked and underneath me by now.'

A blush splashed up her exquisite throat and stung her cheeks. Molten lust rushed into his groin and spread through his body. Feeling restricted and seriously on edge, he shrugged off his tuxedo jacket and flung it over the long sofa. Next came the bow tie. He left that dangling to tackle the top buttons of his shirt and looked up to find her gaze riveted on him.

Good, he was not alone in this. Sexual desire pulsed from

her in drenching waves. Which made the reticence in her eyes all the more intriguing.

Enough!

In three strides, he stood in front of her. She made a high, surprised noise as he tugged her close. Without giving her a chance to protest further, he swooped down and took her lips with his.

She tasted glorious. Like a shot of premium tequila on a sultry night. Like warm sunshine and decadent, sticky desserts. Like jumping off the highest peak of an icy mountain with nothing beneath him but air and infinite possibilities.

Narciso's lids slid shut against the drugging sensation of her lips.

Madre di Dio! He was hard. Harder than he'd ever been. And he'd only been kissing her a few seconds.

She made another sound in her throat and her lips parted. Her tongue darted out to meet his and he plunged in, desperate for more, desperate to discover her every secret.

He deepened the kiss and groaned as her hands slid up his biceps to entwine around his shoulders. In a curiously innocent move, she tentatively caressed his nape before boldly spiking her fingers into his hair.

The scrape of her fingers against his scalp made him shudder with escalating arousal. Raising his head, he gazed down into eyes darkened with desire. '*Amante,* you already know what pleases me.'

Shock clouded her expression, as if what she'd achieved had stunned her.

Without giving her a chance to speak, he took her luscious mouth again. The highly potent sound of their kisses echoed in the room as they devoured each other.

Pulling her even closer, he finally touched the pulse that had taunted him all evening. It sang beneath his touch, racing with her excitement.

She inhaled deeply, and her breasts smashed against his

chest. He cupped one, glorying in the weight and perfect fit of it as his thumb brushed across one rigid nub.

She jerked and her teeth sank into her bottom lip. With a rough sound, she pulled away.

Narciso continued to play with her nipple as they stared at each other. Her mouth, wet and slightly swollen, parted as she sucked in panicked breaths.

'You like the way I make you feel?' He brought his other hand up from her waist and cupped her other breast, attending to the equally stiff and aching peak. 'I promise I will make you feel even better. Now take your hair down and show me how gorgeous you really are.'

The words pulled Ruby from the drugged stupor she was drowning in. Reality didn't rush in, it trickled in slowly.

Blinking eyelids heavy with desire, she tried to focus on something other than his arrestingly gorgeous face—the part not covered by his mask.

First, she noticed the stunning chandelier. Then a repeat of that bold dragon motif from downstairs on the wall behind his shoulder. Reality rushed in faster. Stunningly designed black velvet sofas, including an authentic French chaise longue perfect for reclining in…

Then her focus drew in closer. She glanced down at the powerful hands cupping her breasts.

The sight was so erotically intoxicating it nearly knocked her off her feet.

Sensation shot between her thighs, stinging so painfully, she wanted to place her hand there, seek some sort of relief.

'Take your hair down for me,' he insisted again.

She came plunging back down to earth. 'No!'

Telling herself she didn't care about the jaw that tightened in displeasure, she took several steps away from his hot, tempting body.

Focus, Ruby!

The last time she'd mixed business with pleasure, she'd almost ended up becoming the one thing she despised above all else—a participant in infidelity. It didn't matter that she hadn't known Simon was married. The very thought of what could've happened made shame lodge in her belly.

She was here to get Narciso Valentino to honour his deal with her, not to get pulled into the same dangerous vortex of emotions that led to nothing but pain and heartache.

Her father's inability to limit his sexual urges to his marital bed and her mother's indecision whether to fight or turn a blind eye had made her childhood a living hell. It'd been the reason why she'd slept most nights with her headphones on and music blaring in her ears. Even then she'd been unable to block out the blistering rows or her mother's heart-wrenching sobs.

And after her experience with Simon, there was no way would she allow herself to jump on that unpredictable roller coaster.

She took another step back, despite the magnetic pull of desire dragging her to Narciso. Despite the soul-deep notion that sex with him would be pulse-poundingly breathtaking. Despite—

Despite nothing!

Her treacherous genetic make-up didn't mean she would allow herself to fall into the same trap as her mother just because an unrepentant, unscrupulous playboy like Narciso Valentino crooked his wicked finger.

But she couldn't risk alienating him before she got what she'd come here for. Licking tingling lips, she forced her brain to track.

She cast her gaze around the large, luxuriously appointed suite. Seeing the extensive, well-stocked bar on the far side of the room, she made a beeline for it. 'Here, let me get you another drink.'

'You don't need to get me drunk to have your way with me, *amante*.'

She flushed and stopped, whirling to find him directly behind her. The sheer size of him, the arousal stamped so clearly in his eyes, made her breath fracture. 'Stop calling me that.'

A small smile played around his exquisite mouth. 'You know what it means.'

She nodded. 'Yes, I'm Italian.'

'And I'm Sicilian. Big difference, but we will speak your language for now.'

'Whatever language we speak, I don't want you referring to me as a…as your…'

'Lover?'

'Yes. I don't like it.'

'What do you want me to call you?'

'Just call me Ruby.' She didn't mind telling him her name. In order to explain her presence here, she would have to disclose who she was.

So no harm done.

'Ruby.'

Definitely lots and lots of harm done. The way he said her name—wrapped his mouth and tongue around it in a slow caress—made her pulse leap crazily.

'Ruby. It suits you perfectly,' he murmured.

Against her will, his response drew her interest. 'How do you mean?'

'Your name matches the shade of your mouth after I've thoroughly kissed it. I imagine the same would apply to other parts of your body by the time we're done.'

Her flush deepened. *'Seriously?'*

He laughed but the hunger in his eyes didn't abate. 'Too much?'

'*Much* too much.'

He shrugged and nodded to the bar. 'I'll give you the reprieve you seek. But only for a little while.'

She dived behind the bar and gathered the first bottles that came to hand. Almost on automatic she replicated one of her favourite creations and slid it across the shiny surface.

He picked it up and sipped without taking his eyes off her.

He rolled the drink in his mouth before his eyes slowly widened. 'You're very talented.'

Pleasure rushed through her. 'Thank you.'

'Prego.' He threw back the rest of the drink and set the glass down with a decisive click. 'But enough with the foreplay, Ruby. Come here.'

Heart pounding, with nowhere to hide, she approached him.

'Give me what I want. Now.'

She debated for a tense few seconds. Then, figuring she had nothing to lose, she complied.

Her hair was thick, long and often times unmanageable. She'd spent almost an hour wrestling it into place tonight and in the end had chosen to wear it up. Her effort to straighten it would've worn out by now, and she couldn't help but fidget when his gaze raked over the golden-brown tresses once, twice and over again.

'You're exquisite,' he breathed after an endless moment during which her stomach churned with alien emotion. 'Your skin is flawless and I want to drown in your eyes, watch them light up with pleasure when I take you.'

Ruby couldn't believe mere words could create such heat inside her. Hell, everything about him made her hot and edgy.

She needed to nip this insanity in the bud before it went any further. 'I'm sorry if I gave you the impression that something more was going to happen between us. You won't be... taking me.'

'Will I not?' he asked silkily, his finger drifting down her cheek to settle beneath her chin. 'And what makes you say that?'

'Because you don't really want me.'

His laugh was rich, deep and incredibly seductive.

'Every nerve in my body disagrees with that statement. But if you need proof...' He bent low, scooped her up and threw her over his shoulder.

His laughter increased at her outraged squeal. 'Put me down!'

The hallway passed in a blur as he took her deeper into the

suite. Her hair entangled with his long legs as he strode with unwavering purpose.

'I don't know what the hell you think you're doing but I demand you put me down right—' Her breath whooshed out of her lungs as she was dumped on a bed. A very large emperor-size bed with slate-coloured sheets and over a dozen pillows.

'You were saying?'

She brushed her hair out of her eyes and saw him tugging off his shoes. When he unhooked his belt, she scrambled off the bed.

He caught her easily and placed her back in the centre. 'Are you going to be a good girl and wait for me?' Silver eyes speared her.

'Wait for… Hell, no!'

He stepped forward and caught her chin in his hand. When his head started to descend, she jerked away. 'What the hell do you think you're doing?'

'Capturing your attention for a moment. You don't need to be frightened, *dolce mia*. Nothing will happen in this room without your consent.'

Oddly, she believed him. 'You don't need to kiss me to capture my attention.'

Slowly he straightened and dropped his hand. 'Shame. Let me remind you of some ground rules before we proceed. We're not supposed to reveal ourselves to each other. However, since you've done me the honour of revealing your name to me, I'll grant you the courtesy of removing my mask. But you'll give me your word that it will stay between us, *si?*' He started unbuttoning his shirt, revealing mouth-watering inches of golden skin.

Heat slammed into her chest and she sucked in a gulping breath.

Crunch time. Time to get this dangerously bizarre situation over and done with.

'There's no need. I already know who you are. You're Narciso Valentino. You're the reason I'm here in Macau.'

CHAPTER FOUR

HE FROZE AT her announcement. A second later, he drew the mask over his head, and Ruby got her first full glimpse of Narciso Valentino.

He was breathtakingly gorgeous. With a definite edge of danger that sent her already thundering pulse straight into bungee-jump mode.

She watched his face grow taut. Watchful…condemning.

'You know who I am.' His words were icily precise, the warmth in his tone completely gone.

Licking dry lips, she nodded. His other hand dropped from his belt, leaving her curiously disappointed.

'You're American.'

'Yes, I live in New York, same as you. That's where I came from.'

'And you followed me all the way to Macau. Why?' The clipped demand came with eyes narrowed into cold slits.

A mixture of anger and trepidation rushed through her, propelling her from the bed.

He caught her easily. 'Move again and I'll be forced to restrain you.'

Panic flared through her. Tugging at his hands, she fought to free herself. Before she could fathom his intentions, her wrists were bound to the bedpost with velvet rope he'd pulled from the side of the bed.

She looked from her wrists to his face, unable to believe what was happening. He tossed his mask on the bed, whipped the unbound tie from his neck and flung it across the room, barely suppressed fury in the movement. 'Okay, fine, you've made your point. But you can't keep me prisoner for ever.'

'Watch me.'

'I could scream, you know.'

Nice, Ruby. Nice.

'You could. And I can turn you over to the management and let them deal with what can only be regarded as a security breach. Trust me, breaches aren't taken lightly.'

She tugged at her bound wrists. 'I can't believe you tied me up.'

'You left me no choice. Now start talking before I call security.'

Her breath caught as images tumbled through her head of being stuck in a foreign prison. Aside from her roommate, Annie, no one knew her whereabouts. And even if Annie tracked her down to Macau, she wouldn't have the first clue where to find her.

'Tell me what you want to know,' she offered in a rush.

'Is Ruby really your name?' he asked, his gaze dropping to her lips.

Remembering what he'd said about her mouth, she felt heat spike through her belly again.

'Yes.'

'And your earlier assurance that we hadn't met before?'

'Is true. Although we almost did…last week.'

One sleek brow shot upward. 'How?'

'I tried to find you at a nightclub—Riga—but you were leaving when I arrived.'

He prowled closer to the bed, and a fresh load of anxiety coursed through her system. Hands poised on lean hips, he stared down at her.

'I've had women do…unexpected things to get my attention but I don't think I've had the privilege of a full-blown crazy stalker before.' His eyes raked her from head to toe. 'Perhaps I should've made it happen sooner.'

'I'm not a crazy stalker!' She yanked at the restraints and only succeeded in tightening them.

'Of course not. Because those ones readily admit to their charges.'

'Look, I can explain. Just…untie me.'

He ignored her and leaned down, placing his palms flat on the bed so his face was level with hers. 'We could've had so much fun, *amante*. Why did you have to spoil it?' There was genuine regret in his tone, but bitterness had crept in with the iciness.

'I have a genuine reason for being here.'

'For your own sake, I hope so. I don't take lightly to being manipulated.'

Her mind flashed to earlier in the evening. Watching him toy with his opponent had shown her just how dangerous this man was. Despite the outward charm and spellbinding magnetism, he could become lethal on the turn of a dime.

He turned and prowled to the window. With jerky movements, he tore off his expensive shirt, sending cufflinks she was almost certain were made with black diamonds pinging across the room.

Tossing the shirt the way his bow tie had gone, he shoved his hands into his pockets.

The movement contracted his bronzed, strongly muscled back. Among the electrons firing crazily in her brain came the thought that this was the first time she'd come this close to a semi-naked man worth looking at.

He turned and the sight of his naked torso was almost too much to bear. A light smattering of hair grew outward from the middle of his sculpted chest and arrowed down to disappear into his waistband.

Heat intensified as her gaze landed on his flat brown nipples. A decadent shudder coursed through her. She grasped the sturdy, intricately carved bedpost made of highly polished Chinese cedarwood, pulled herself closer to the edge of the bed and peered closer at the intricate knots that bound her.

'Where do you think you're going?' he rasped.

'I can't stay trussed up like a Thanksgiving turkey all night long.'

'Answer my questions and I'll consider freeing you.'

'You'll *consider* it?'

'Have you forgotten already that I hold all the cards here?' He sauntered back and stopped in front of her.

Suddenly, Ruby wished she'd stayed put in the middle of the bed. *This* close the heat emanating from his satin-like skin blanketed her. The urge to move her fingers just that little bit and touch the skin covering his ribcage was immense.

'Go ahead,' he invited softly. Silkily.

Flames leapt through her bloodstream. 'Excuse me?'

'You want to touch me. Go ahead. We can pick up this conversation in a moment once you've satisfied your craving.'

'I... You're wrong. I don't want to touch you. There's no craving. What I want is to be set free—'

Her words froze when he placed large hands on her hips and pulled her into his body.

'Well, despite you ruining my evening, I *still* have a craving for you.'

He smothered her protests by capturing her mouth again. It was as potent as before but this time there was a rough demand in his kiss that spoke of his fury beneath all that outward calm.

But rough didn't mean less pleasurable. Her lips parted, welcoming the jagged thrust of his tongue and the domineering pressure of his kiss.

She moaned before she could stop herself, flexing fingers that wouldn't obey their order to stay put, and touching the velvety smoothness of his neck and collarbone.

By the time he lifted his head, they were both panting. He slowly licked his lips, savouring her taste. The sight of his wet tongue sent liquid fire straight to that raging hunger between her thighs.

Ruby shut her eyes in shuddering despair and opened them to find him sliding off her shoes.

'God, will you please stop doing things like that?' she snapped.

'I'm into kinky when the occasion calls for it, but I don't generally risk puncturing a lung with stiletto heels unless the payback is worth it.' He flung her shoes away. 'Do you need help with your dress?'

'No! Why on earth would I want that?' She edged away from him, the fear that her emotions wouldn't be as easy to control around this man spiking through her.

'It's nearly two a.m. And we're yet to have our little tête-à-tête. But if you want to keep cutting off your circulation in that restricting dress, suit yourself. Tell me why you're here,' he bit out, as if he wanted to be done with the conversation.

'Release me first,' she insisted.

'I released you three minutes ago.'

Shocked, Ruby glanced down at her wrists. Sure enough, the velvet rope was loose enough to free herself. She'd been too spellbound by his kiss to notice.

She met his hard, mocking gaze. Rubbing her right wrist, she encountered his watch. She pulled it off and held it out to him.

He didn't take it. 'I'm waiting for an answer.'

'My name is Ruby Trevelli.'

He continued to stare at her. 'Should that mean anything to me?'

Despite knowing how self-absorbed he was, that flippant question hurt. She flung his watch on the bed. He calmly retrieved it, took hold of her wrist, slipped it back on, and returned to his predator-like position.

'What—?'

'Answer me. Should your name mean anything to me?'

'Yes. I was recently voted Élite Chef.'

His lips twisted. 'My apologies. I don't keep up with pop culture,' he said.

'Well, you should. Your TV company sponsored the show.'

He frowned. 'I have over sixty media companies scattered

all over the world. It would be impossible to keep up with every progamme that's aired through my networks. So you're here to collect some sort of prize—is that it?' The disappointment she'd heard earlier was back, accompanied this time by a flash of weariness that disappeared as quickly as it'd arrived.

'You make it sound like a whimsical endeavour. I assure you, it's not.'

'Enlighten me, then, Miss Contest Winner. Why have you flown thousands of miles to accost me?'

Put like that it *did* sound whimsical. Except this was her life and livelihood they were talking about, the independent life she'd worked hard for so she wouldn't be pulled into her parents' damaging orbit. The life that was being threatened by a loan shark.

'I want your company to honour its agreement and pay me what I'm owed.'

His face hardened into a taut, formidable mask of disdain. 'You came after me because of *money?*' His sneer had thickened.

Ruby couldn't really dwell on that. She needed to state her purpose and leave this room, this suite. He was close, so tantalisingly close, the warmth of his skin and the spicy scent of his aftershave made stringing words together an increasingly difficult task. He smelled like heaven. And she wanted to drown in it.

'Prize money, yes.'

His eyes narrowed. 'But why come after me? Why not go after the man I've put in place to head NMC?'

'You think I haven't tried? No one would take my calls.'

'Really? No one in a company with over a thousand employees?'

'No. Trust me, I have the phone bill to prove it.'

'Well, clearly, I need to hire better staff.'

'I don't like your tone,' Ruby snapped. She sidled towards the edge of the bed.

He caught her and placed her back in front of him, keeping her captive with one large hand on her waist.

'What tone do you mean?' Silver eyes gleamed with cynical amusement.

With every breath she took, the imprint of his hand seared her skin. 'You obviously don't believe me. Why would I travel thousands of miles unless it was because I'd hit a brick wall?'

'Or you'd hoped an extra tight dress and body that won't quit would get you an even better deal?'

The image his words conjured up made blood leach from her face. It was one she'd vowed never to portray. 'I understand you don't know me, Mr Valentino, but I've never used sex or my sexuality to further my career. You can be as offensive and as delusional as you want. The simple fact is Nigel Stone never took my call in the two dozen times I tried to reach him.'

His eyes narrowed at her furious words but he kept silent.

'We can resolve this very quickly. Call him now, get him to talk to me. Then I'll get out of your hair.'

'It's Saturday morning back in the States. I make it a point never to disturb my employees during the weekend.'

Anger stiffened her spine. 'Yeah, right.'

His cynical smile widened. 'You don't believe me?'

'I believe you do exactly what you want when you want. If it suited you, you'd be on the phone right now.'

His shrug outlined sleek muscle beneath his skin. He moved with an innate grace that made Ruby's pulse race shamefully. 'Fine. I admit I ride my employees hard when I have to. But I also recognise their need for down time the same way I recognise the need for mine.'

'You're telling me you need your beauty sleep to function?' she snapped.

'Down time doesn't necessarily mean sleep, *amante*. Tonight, I was counting on wild, unfettered sex,' he delivered smoothly.

She flung herself away from him, from the temptation his words dredged up inside her, before that Trevelli gene she so feared could be fully activated.

Far too often since she'd clapped eyes on him, she'd found herself imagining what sex would be like. Her roommate had referred to the best sex as sheet-clawing, toe-curling. At the time Ruby had silently scoffed at how anything besides the best, decadently prepared dessert would feel that great.

Now she couldn't stop herself from wondering…

Disgust at herself propelled her off the bed. She refused to sink into the quagmire of rampant promiscuity.

Her feet hit the luxurious carpet, bringing a much-needed return to reality. She darted out of the door and hurried along the long hallway towards the main suite doors.

With relief, she grasped the door handle and yanked it down. Nothing happened. She pulled harder.

Glancing around wildly, she spotted the electronic panel and pressed the most obvious-looking button.

Nothing.

'You can't get out unless I allow you out.'

She whirled. He casually leaned one shoulder against the hallway wall. The sight of him standing there, looking sexily tousled and half naked, made panic flare anew inside her.

'Then let me out.'

'I could. But once I do, any hope of a discussion about why you're here ends. My company, if it's liable as you say, owes you nothing the minute you walk out of here.'

'That's preposterous! I signed a contract. *You* signed a contract. You can't just back out on a whim.'

'Think about it, Ruby. You've travelled thousands of miles to get my attention. I intend to give you that attention. Do you think it prudent to walk out now, when you could be so close?'

'I…' She sucked in a breath as overwhelming feelings swamped her. 'Why can't we discuss it now?'

'Because I don't like to discuss business without a clear head. And since you've plied me with exquisite cocktails all evening, I'd be making those decisions under severe influence.' He tilted his head again in that alarmingly endearing way and a lock of hair fell over his eyes.

Dear God. This man was truly lethal. He oozed sex and sensuality without so much as lifting a finger.

'You didn't ply me with all those drinks in order to take advantage of me, did you? Because that would be horrifyingly disappointing.'

Outraged, she gasped. 'I most certainly did not.'

Slowly, he extended a hand to her. 'In that case, Ruby Trevelli, there's no earthly reason not to stay. Is there?'

Narciso was doing his best to stop his fury from showing. The same way he was doing his best to keep from kicking himself for ignoring the alarm bells.

Usually he could spot chancers and gold-diggers a mile away, be they tuxedo-clad or dressed in designer gowns that looked too small for them.

For a moment he wished she'd kept her mouth shut until after he'd slept with her to make her avarice known. He would've been a lot more generous than he was feeling now.

He would also have felt used.

Fury mounted and his frustrated erection threatened to cut him in half as she stayed out of his reach. Out of his arms.

Recalling her responsiveness, the gut-clenching potency of her kiss, he nearly growled.

She kissed as if she were born for it. Narciso wondered how many men she'd kissed like that in the past and felt a red haze wash over his fury.

Dio, what was wrong with him? He should find the nearest phone and report her to management.

Zeus, his host and owner of the club, had so far excelled in keeping people like Ruby away from *Q Virtus* guests. Sure, most *Petit Qs* would accept a generous gift from a guest, but blatant stalking wasn't tolerated.

Except, his stalker seemed eager to get *away* from him, her catlike blue eyes apprehensive as she glanced at his outstretched hand.

'Come here,' he commanded.

She swayed towards him, then abruptly halted her forward momentum. 'If you're too drunk to talk, what other reason is there for me to stay? And don't mention wild sex. Because that's not going to happen.'

Contrary to what he'd said, his mind was as clear and as sharp as a fillet knife. And it sensed a curious dichotomy in her words and actions. The dress, make-up and screw-me stilettos said one thing. Her words indicated another.

He intended to burrow until he found the truth.

Nice choice of words, Narciso, he thought as arousal spiked higher in his blood. Lowering his hand, he turned abruptly.

'I'm returning to the bedroom. If you're not there within the next minute, I'll take it that our business is concluded,' he said over his shoulder.

'Wait! You can't do that…'

Narciso smiled with satisfaction at her frustration. Whether she followed him or not, there was no way he was letting her out of his suite tonight. Not until he'd had her checked out thoroughly and satisfied himself what sort of threat she posed.

He recalled the circumstances of their meeting. Of all the tables she could've been hostessing, she'd been at Giacomo's table.

This time he didn't ignore the churning in his gut. Giacomo had played that game before…

He turned and found her two steps behind him but any satisfaction was marred by the new set of questions clamouring for answers.

'Why are you really here, Ruby? Did the old man send you?'

Fresh trepidation flared in her eyes at his harsh tone. 'Who… Oh, that guy you were playing with? No, I have no idea who he is and I'd never met him before tonight.'

He tried to read her. Surely, even seasoned liars couldn't look him straight in the eye as she was without flinching?

'Be warned, if I find that to be untrue, there'll be hell to pay.'

'I'm telling you, I don't know him.' Her fingers meshed together and she began to fidget. But not once did her stare waver from his.

Narciso decided to be satisfied. For now. He entered the bedroom and crossed to the en suite.

'So I'm here. Now what?' she asked.

'I'm going to take a shower. You do whatever you want. As long as you don't leave this room.'

'God, this is nuts,' he heard her mutter as he entered the bathroom. Despite the volatile emotions churning through him, he smiled. From the corner of his eye, he watched her head once more to the stunning view of Macau City.

Silhouetted against the view, her body was so perfectly stunning, his mouth dried. Disappointment welled in his chest but he suppressed it as he undressed.

The cold shower was bracing enough to calm his arousal but not enough to wash away the bitterness as he replayed his evening.

Giacomo was bent on trying to take Narciso down.

Well, that suited Narciso fine. Although Narciso could've destroyed him with that last move, the notion of leaving him dangling a little bit longer had been irresistible.

The opportunity would present itself again soon enough. Giacomo was predictable in his hatred for him, if for nothing else.

And at thirty, exactly ten years after his father's most cutting betrayal, the need for vengeance burned just as brightly in Narciso's veins.

For as long as he'd been old enough to retain his memories, Narciso had known that Giacomo bore him a deep, abiding hatred. As a child he'd been bewildered as to why nothing he did pleased or satisfied the man he once called Papa.

On his eleventh birthday, a whisky-soaked Giacomo had finally revealed to him the reason he detested the sight of his son. At first, even reeling from the shock of the discovery, Narciso had stupidly believed he could turn things around, make his father, if not love him, at least learn to cohabit peacefully with him. He'd made sure his grades were perfect, that he was quiet and obedient and exemplary in all things.

Narciso's mouth twisted. That had lasted all of a year before he'd accepted he was flogging a dead horse. When his thirteenth birthday had come and gone without so much as a single lit candle on a store-bought birthday cake, he'd finally admitted that war was the only way forward.

He'd suppressed whatever heartache had threatened to catch him unawares in the dead of night and used animosity to feed his ambitions to succeed. He'd won scholarships to the best colleges in the world. His head for figures had seen him attain his first million by eighteen. By twenty he'd been a multi-millionaire.

Twenty…also the age he'd met Maria, the unexpected tool his father had used against him. The wound gaped another inch.

With a sharp curse, he shut off the shower. Snapping up a towel, he tied it around his waist.

Maria was dead to him, but, in a way, he was pleased for her transient presence in his life ten years ago. She'd reinforced his belief that lowering his guard, even for a moment, was fool-hardy. That even fake love came at a steep price.

Money and sex were the two things he thrived on now. Emotions…connections, hell, *love,* were a complete waste of his time.

He entered the bedroom and found Ruby reclining on the bed, legs crossed, one bare foot tapping in agitation. She shot upright at his entry. After that one quick look, Narciso barely glanced in her direction as he walked to the connecting dressing room.

The whole evening was screwed up. His thwarted efforts to bed her, and now his unexplained trip down memory lane had left him in an edgy mood. Snatching at his fast-dwindling control, he reached for the rarely used silk pajama bottoms and dropped his towel.

The choking sound made him glance over his shoulder through the open door. She sat frozen on the bed, her eyes wide with astonishment.

'Something wrong?' he asked as he stabbed one leg into the garment. At her silence, he started to turn.

She shut her eyes and jerked away from him. He pulled the bottoms on and entered the bedroom. 'Open your eyes. It's safe to look now.'

She opened her eyes but kept her gaze averted.

'Come on, now, the way you're acting you'd think I was the first naked male you'd ever seen.'

That gurgling sound came again and Narciso shook his head. 'I have very little interest in virgins, *amante*. If you hope to snag my attention, I suggest you drop that particular act.'

She inhaled sharply. 'It's not an—' She bit off the rest of her answer as he drew back the sheets.

Four of the six pillows he threw to the floor before he got in. The sight of her sitting so stiffly made his jaw tighten. Reaching across, he pulled her into the middle and pulled the sheet over them.

'You were saying?'

She shook her head. 'Nothing. Are you really going to sleep?'

'Yes. I suggest you get some sleep too even though I fear for your circulation in that dress you're wearing.'

'I'm fine.'

'If you say so.' He relaxed against the pillows. Sleep would be elusive with her so close. For a moment he wondered why he was torturing himself like this.

Keep your friends close and your stalkers closer?

He suppressed a grim smile, grabbed the remote and doused the light in the bedroom. But with one sensory factor taken away, her erratic breathing became amplified.

Good. If he was to be tortured with images of what sex between them would be like, it was only fair she experienced the same fate.

'What happens tomorrow?' she asked quietly.

'Tomorrow we talk. And by talk I mean you come clean, completely, as to why you're here. Because if you hold anything back from me, I won't hesitate to throw you to the wolves.'

CHAPTER FIVE

RUBY WOKE WITH the distinct feeling that something had changed. It took a millisecond to realise what that *something* was.

'You took my clothes off?' she screeched, her fingers flying to the hem of the black T-shirt that had miraculously appeared on her body.

The man who lay so languidly beside her, his head propped up on his hand, nodded.

'I feared you'd suffocate in your sleep in that dress. Despite your dubious reasons for being here, even I would find it difficult to explain death by designer gown to the authorities. You were quite co-operative. I think it was the only time you've been co-operative since we reached my suite, which tells me you were as uncomfortable as I suspected.'

She licked her lips and struggled not to squirm under his scrutiny. At least her bra and panties were intact. But the fact was she didn't recall what had happened. And there was only one worrying explanation for that. 'I was tired,' she bluffed.

'Right.' Silver eyes bore into her until she felt like a fly hooked on a pin.

His gaze dropped to her twisting fingers, and she abruptly stilled the movement. 'Tell me what happened. *Exactly.*'

One brow rose at her firm directive but Ruby was desperate to know what had happened during the night. She'd tossed and turned in agitation until sheer exhaustion had finally pulled her under some time before dawn.

'You tried to escape a few times. I brought you back to bed.'
God. No. It'd happened again…

Definitely time to leave. She tried to move, and felt a snag on her foot. Shoving aside tangled sheets, she stared in horror at the rope tied around her ankle.

'You tied me up again! Do you have a thing for bondage?'

His eyes gleamed. 'Until last night, I'd never needed to tie a woman to keep her with me.'

'Oh, well, lucky me. Did you tie me before or after you took off my dress?'

'After the second time you tried to take the door off its hinges to make your escape, we came back here and I relieved you of your suicidal gown and put the T-shirt on—' A deep frown slashed his face. 'Are you saying you don't remember any of this?'

She sucked in a slow breath and looked away.

He caught her chin in his hand and forced her to look at him, his steady gaze demanding an answer. '*Dio,* you really don't remember?'

Ruby had no choice but to come clean. 'No. sometimes I… sleepwalk.'

His brows hit his hairline. 'You *sleepwalk?* How often is sometimes?'

'Not for a while, to my knowledge. It only happens when I'm…distressed.'

His frown intensified. 'You found last night distressing?'

'Being tied up and kept prisoner? No, that was a picnic in the park.' She tugged at her ankle restraint. 'And now I'm tied up again.'

'It was for your own good. After I put the restraint on, you stopped making a run for it. I think secretly you liked it.' His fingers caressed along her jaw, his eyes lowering to her lips.

Instantly the mood changed, thickened with sensual promise. 'I'm *not* into bondage.' Or sex with playboys, or anyone for that matter!

'How do you know? Have you ever tried it?'

'No. But I've never jumped off a cliff either, and I'm certain I wouldn't enjoy that experience.'

'Fair point. For the record, I have. With the right equipment, all experiences can be extremely enjoyable. Exhilarating even.'

She watched, terrified and mesmerised, as his head started to lower. 'What are you doing?'

'I'm kissing you *bon giornu, bedda*. Relax.'

That was easier said than done when every nerve in her body was strained in anticipation of the touch of his mouth on hers. She told herself she was sluggish because she was sleep deprived. But it was a lie.

As much as she yearned to deny it, she wanted the pressure of his demanding kiss and the heady racing of her blood through her veins.

His moan as he deepened the kiss echoed the piercing need inside her.

One hand clamped on her hip, drew her sideways into him. At the sensation of his sleep-warmed body against hers, she moaned. The fact that she was clothed from neck to hip and he was clothed from hip to ankle didn't alter the stormy sensation of their bodies meshing together.

Nipples, stung to life at the touch of his mouth on hers, peaked and ached as they brushed his chest.

When his hand moved under the T-shirt and skimmed over her panties, Ruby jerked at the vicious punch of desire that threatened to flatten her.

She was drowning. And she didn't want to be rescued.

'*Dio mio,* you're addictive, *bedda,*' he murmured against her mouth before plunging back in. His tongue shot between her lips to slide against hers. He staked his claim on her until she couldn't think straight. Even when his mouth left hers to nibble along her jaw, she strained closer, her hand sliding up his chest in a bold caress that shocked and thrilled her at the same time.

When her nail grazed his nipple, he hissed. Stunned at the surge of power that action gave her, she flicked her nail again.

'Careful, *amante,* or I might have to repay the kindness.'

Lost in a swirl of desire, she barely heeded the warning. Bringing up her other hand between them, she flicked both flat nipples at once.

'*Maledizione!*' He pushed her back onto the bed and yanked up her T-shirt.

Danger shrieked in her head a second before his mouth closed over her nipple. Tonguing, licking, he pulled the willing flesh deep into his mouth.

Sensation as she'd never felt before tore through her. Between her legs where her need burned fiercest, liquid heat fuelled her raging desire.

Her fingers curled up and spiked into his hair as he transferred his attention to her other nipple. A little rougher than before, he used his teeth this time.

Her tiny scream echoed through the bedroom as her head slammed back against the pillow.

Feeling his thick arousal against her thigh, she moved her leg, eager to rub closer against the potent evidence of his need.

The snap of the ankle rope broke through her haze. The reality of what she was doing hit Ruby with the force of a two-by-four.

'No!' She pushed at his shoulders until he lifted his head. The sight of her nipples, reddened and wet from his ministrations, made dismay slither through her in equal measures. She was nothing like her parents. Nothing—

'What's wrong, *bedda?*' he grated huskily.

'What's wrong? Everything!'

'Everything is a huge undertaking. Narrow it down for me a little. I'll take care of it.'

She pushed harder. 'For a start. Get. Off. Me.'

His nostrils flared with displeasure and his fingers bit into her hip. 'You were moaning your willingness a moment ago.'

'Thankfully, I've come to my senses. Get off me and take off that…shackle you've placed on my ankle.'

He slowly levered himself off her but not before she got

another sensation of his thick arousal. Flames rushed up her cheeks.

Back in his previous position, he dropped his gaze from hers to her breasts. Realising she was still exposed, she yanked her bra cups into place and tugged down the T-shirt. A T-shirt that bore his unique scent, which chose that moment to wash over her again. As if she weren't suffering enough.

'I don't like women who blow hot and cold, *tesoro*.'

'Where I come from a woman still has the right to say no.'

'A stance I fully respect. Except your actions and your words are at direct variance with each other. You crave me almost as much as I crave you. I can only conclude that this is a ploy to string me along until I'm too whipped to put up much protest against your demands.'

Again his description of her behaviour struck painfully close to the bone, pushing all her fears to the fore. Struggling to hide it, she raised an eyebrow.

'Wow, you really have a low opinion of yourself, don't you? Or is that a high opinion on my sexual prowess?'

'Unlike you, I'm not afraid to admit my desire for you. It's almost enough to tempt me to tell you to name your price so we can be done with this…*aperitivo* and get to the main course.' There was a hard bite to his voice that instinctively warned her to do that would be a mistake.

'I only want you to hear me out. You said we'd talk this morning.'

He got up from the bed in a sleek, graceful move that brought to mind a jungle creature.

The unmistakable evidence of his arousal when he faced her made her swallow. He showed no embarrassment in his blatant display of manhood. Even in thwarted desire, Narciso Valentino wore his male confidence with envy-inducing ease. Whereas she remained cowering beneath the sheets, afraid of the sensual waves threatening to drown her.

'And so we will. Come through to the kitchen. Caffeine is a

poor substitute for sex but it'll have to do.' With that pithy pronouncement, he walked out of the bedroom.

She lay there, floundering in a sea of panic and confusion. If anyone had told her she'd be in Narciso Valentino's bed mere hours after meeting him, she'd have laughed herself hoarse. Particularly since she'd vowed never to mix business with pleasure after what had happened with Simon.

But what Narciso had roused in her just now had frightened and excited her. Kissing him had been holding a live, dangerous firework in the palm of her hand. She hadn't been sure whether she would experience the most spectacular show of lights or blow herself to smithereens with it.

And yet she'd been almost desolate when the kiss ended. Which showed how badly things could get out of hand.

Squeezing her eyes shut, she counted to ten. The earlier she finished her business with Narciso and got on the plane back to New York, the better.

Throwing off the sheet, she glanced at the velvet rope around her ankle. Twisting her body into the appropriate position, she tugged on the double knot, surprised when it came loose easily.

Again, the realisation that she could've freed herself at any time made her view of him alter a little. Her fingers lingered on the rope warmed from her body.

Bondage sex. Until now, the scenario had never even crossed her mind. But suddenly, the thought of being tied down while Narciso laid her inhibitions to waste took up centre stage in her mind.

Heat flaming her whole body, she jumped from the bed. Upright, his T-shirt reached well past her knees, and covered her arms to her elbows.

She glanced at her gown, laid carefully over the arm of the chaise longue, and made up her mind. She would dress after they'd had their talk. She couldn't bear being restrained in the too-tight dress just yet. Ditto for her heels.

Stilettos and a T-shirt in the presence of a dangerously sexual man like Narciso Valentino evoked an image she didn't want to tempt into life now, or ever.

For some reason, her body turned him on. She wasn't stupid enough to bait the lion more than he was already baited.

Barefoot, she left the bedroom and went in search of the kitchen.

He stood at a centre island in a kitchen that made the chef in her want to weep with envy. State-of-the-art equipment lined the surfaces and walls and through a short alcove a floor-to-ceiling wine rack displayed exquisite vintages.

'You get all this for a two-day stay?'

He jerked at her question. Before he could cover his emotions, Ruby glimpsed a painfully bleak look in his eyes.

A second later, the look was gone as he shrugged. 'It suits my needs.'

'Your needs... I'd kill for a kitchen like this in my restaurant.'

'You own a restaurant?' he asked.

She concluded her survey of the appliances and faced him. 'Not yet. I would've been on my way to opening Dolce Italia by now if NMC had honoured its commitments.'

'Ah, the sins of imaginary corporate sharks.'

The coffee machine finished going through its wake-up motions. He pressed a button and the beans started to churn.

'Not imaginary.' Ruby stepped forward when she realised what he was doing. 'Wait, you're doing it wrong. We're in a warm climate. The coffee beans expand in warm weather so you need to grind them looser to extract the maximum taste. Here let me do it.' Even though stepping closer would bring her dangerously close to his sleek frame, she seized the opportunity to make herself useful and not just stare at his broad, naked back. A back she could suddenly picture herself clawing in the heat of desire.

Just as she tried not to stare when he leaned his hip against the counter and crossed his arms over his bare chest.

'How are you at multitasking?' he asked.

'It's essential in my line of business.' Content with the setting, she pressed the button to resume the grinding and went to the fridge. She grabbed the creamer, and forced herself not to gape at the mouth-watering ingredients in there.

'Good, then you can talk while you prepare the coffee. Tell me everything I need to know.' His brisk tone was all business.

Quickly, she summarised the events of the past two months.

'So you entered this competition as a chef?' he asked.

'Yes, I have a degree in hospitality management and a diploma in gourmet cuisine and I'm an approved board-certified mixologist.'

He grinned. 'You have to go to college to mix drinks?'

'You have to go to school to wash dishes right these days or someone will sue your ass.' She started to grin, then stopped herself. 'I mean…if you don't want to be sued for accidentally poisoning someone. Besides, I plan to make my cocktail bar accessible to allergy-sufferers, too, so I need to know what I'm doing.'

'Which of your drinks is your favourite?' he fired back.

The question threw her for a second. Then she shrugged. 'They're all my favourite.'

'Describe the taste of your signature drink,' he pressed.

She went in search of coffee cups, opening several cabinets before she located them. She had to reach up to grab them and the cool air that passed over the backs of her legs reminded her how exposed she was.

'Umm, I don't actually like cocktails that much,' she blurted to distract herself from her state of undress.

'You're a mixologist who doesn't like her own creations? How do you know you're not poisoning the general population?'

'Because nobody's died yet sampling my drinks. And as to how I know my drinks rock? I try them out on my roommate.'

'You want me to invest…how much does my company owe you?'

'Two hundred thousand dollars to help towards construction and advertising costs for Dolce Italia.'

'Right, two hundred thousand dollars, based on your room-mate's assessment of your talent?'

She poured and passed him a cup, forcing herself not to react to the spark of electricity when their fingers brushed. 'You threw away thirty million last night without blinking but you're grilling me over two hundred thousand?'

He stiffened. 'That was different.' His voice held icy warning.

She heeded it. *'Anyway,'* she hurried on, 'thousands of people voted for me to win *your* show based on three of my best dishes and cocktails.'

His gaze drifted over her, lingered at her breasts then down her legs before he came back to her face. 'Are you sure that's the only reason they voted?'

The sudden tremble in her fingers made her set the cup down. 'You're an ass for making that inference.' Again, much too close to home. Too many times her mother had been ridiculed for using her sexuality to boost ratings, a fact Ruby had burned with humiliation for every single time.

'What inference?' he asked with a sly grin.

'The stupid sexist one you're making. Are you saying they voted for me because I have boobs?' Her rough accusation finally got his attention. The smile slid from his face but not the stark hunger in his eyes.

'Very nice ones.'

Despite her annoyance, heat rushed through her. 'Yeah, well, two of the other contestants had boobs, too.'

'I have no interest in theirs,' he returned blandly.

She picked up her cup and started to blow on her coffee, noticed his intense gaze on her mouth and thought better of it. 'Are you really that shallow?'

'Sì, I am.'

'No, you're not.'

'You wound me.'

'You wound yourself. You're clearly intelligent—'

'Grazie—'

'Or you wouldn't be worth billions. I fail to see why you feel the need to add this to the equation.'

'Tell me, sweet Ruby, why is it sexist to state that I appreciate an attractive body when I see it?'

Her mouth tightened. 'It's sexist when you imply I got where I am by flaunting it when you couldn't be more wrong.'

'Point taken.' He said nothing further.

'Is that supposed to be an apology?'

'Yes, I apologise unreservedly for making observations about your body.'

'That's almost as bad as saying "I apologise if your feelings are hurt" instead of "I'm sorry for hurting your feelings".'

'Let's not dwell on the pedantic. You have my unreserved apologies.' His gaze was steady and clear.

Ruby chose to believe he meant it. 'Thank you.'

'Good. I tried to reach Stone. I've been informed he's on vacation and can't be reached.'

She took a huge gulp of coffee and nearly groaned at the superb taste. Then his words broke through. 'Right. I wasn't born yesterday, you know.'

The seriously gorgeous grin returned. 'I know, and I'm very grateful for that.'

'Get to the point, *please*.'

'Stone is trekking in the Amazon for the next three weeks.'

Alarm skated through her. 'I can't wait another three weeks. I'll lose everything I've poured into getting the restaurant off the ground so far.'

'Which is what exactly?'

'Simon secured the rent but I put up my own money for the conversion of the space and the catering equipment.'

He froze. 'Who is Simon?' he asked in a silky tone threaded with steel.

'My ex-business partner.'

'Enlighten me why he's your ex,' he said in that abrupt, imperious way she'd come to expect.

The ache from Simon's betrayal flared anew. 'We didn't see eye to eye so we parted ways.'

Narciso's eyes narrowed. 'Was he your lover?'

She hesitated. 'Almost,' she finally admitted. 'We met in college, but lost touch for a while. A year ago we met again in New York. I told him about opening my restaurant and he offered to become my partner. We got close…'

He tensed. 'But?'

'But he neglected to tell me he had a pregnant wife at home and…I almost slept with him. He almost made me an accomplice in his infidelity.' The thought sent cold anger through her.

'How did you find out?'

Her hand tightened around her coffee cup. 'We were on our way to Connecticut for a romantic getaway when his wife called to say she'd gone into labour. I trusted him, and he turned out to be no better than…' She shook her head angrily and jumped when his fingers touched hers. Looking up, her eyes connected with his surprisingly gentle ones.

'I think you'll agree he takes the douche-bag crown, no?'

She swallowed the lump in her throat. 'Yes.'

He remained silent for several minutes, then he drained his cup. 'So my company's contribution is to help finish your restaurant?'

'That and the advertising costs for the first six months.'

'Do you have any paperwork?'

'Not with me, no. I couldn't exactly bring a briefcase to the job last night. But Nigel can prove it…'

'I'm taking over from Nigel,' he said abruptly.

'Excuse me?'

He set his cup down. 'As of now, I've relieved him of his duty to you. You'll now deal with me and me alone.'

That felt a little too…sudden… Ruby assured herself it was the reason why her heartbeat had suddenly escalated. She refused to let hope rise until she'd read the small print in his words. 'So…you'll sign over what NMC promised me?'

His eyes gleamed as he regarded her. 'Eventually,' he said lazily.

'Ah, there it is. The big, fat catch. What does *eventually* mean?' she demanded.

'I need proof that you're as good as you say you are. I don't endorse mediocre ventures.'

'Wow, are you always this insulting in the morning?'

'Sexual frustration doesn't sit well with any man, *amante,* least of all me.'

'And you think bringing your sexual frustration into a business discussion is appropriate?'

Silver eyes impaled her where she stood. 'You followed me thousands of miles and inveigled yourself into my company under false pretenses. You wish to discuss who holds the monopoly on what's appropriate right now?'

'What other choice did I have? I couldn't lose everything I've worked for because your employee is chasing orangutans in the Amazon.'

'I may be way off the mark but I don't think there are any orangutans in the Amazon. Borneo, on the other hand—'

'I didn't mean it literally. I meant…' She sighed. 'Bottom line is, NMC agreed to help me launch my business and it's reneging on the deal.'

'And I'm giving you a chance to get things back on track.'

'By making me jump through even more hoops?'

'I employ the best people. There must be a reason why Stone delayed in honouring the agreement.'

'And you think the fault is mine?' Irritation bristled under her skin. He stood there, arrogant and nonchalant as she flailed against the emotional and professional sands shifting under her feet.

'I'm trying to meet you in the middle.'

'All you have to do is review the show's footage. There were world-renowned food critics who judged my cuisine and cocktails the best. I won fair and square.'

'So you keep saying. And yet I'm wondering if there's something else going on here. If everything was above board, why didn't you use lawyers to hold my company to account? Why the very personal touch?'

'I don't have the kind of money it takes to involve lawyers. Besides, I was hoping you'd be reasonable.'

He moved towards her, his gaze pinned on her face. Danger blazed from his eyes. Along with hunger, passion and a need to win at all costs.

Her heart hammered as she forced herself to return his stare.

'You lied in order to get close to me. And you continued to lie until we were alone together. Having caught a glimpse of who I am, Ruby, how reasonable do you think I am?' His tone was silky soft, but she wasn't fooled. Underneath the lethally thrilling charm and the man who'd shown a surprising gentle side moments ago lay a ruthless mogul who ate amateurs for breakfast.

During her internet trawl she'd come across his moniker— The Warlock of Wall Street.

It took a special kind of genius to reach multibillionaire status by twenty-five and even more to attain the kind of wealth and influence Narciso Valentino wielded by his thirtieth birthday. If she didn't tread carefully, she'd leave Macau the same way she'd arrived—with nothing.

'I'm not unwilling to renegotiate our terms, Mr Valentino...' she ventured.

'I've had my mouth on parts of your body that I believe have earned me the right to hear you say my first name.'

Her blush was fierce and horrifyingly embarrassing. 'Fine! You can have thirty per cent,' she blurted.

His eyebrows shot up. 'Thirty per cent of your body?'

'What are you talking about? God, you think I'm renegotiating with my *body?*' She gasped in shocked horror. 'I'll have you know that I'd rather *die* than do something like that!'

His discomfiture was evident as he slowly straightened and spiked a hand through his hair. 'I'm...sorry,' he murmured.

A touch of warmth dispelled the ice. 'Apology accepted.'

'*Per favore,* enlighten me as to what you meant.'

'Part of the deal for winning was that you'd help with the cash prize and advertising and I'd give you a twenty-five-per-cent share in my business for the first three years. After that I'd have the option to buy it back from you. I'm willing to go up to thirty per cent.'

His shook his head. 'I have a new proposal for you. Agree to it and you can keep your extra five per cent.'

'Do I have a choice?'

'There's always a choice, *cara.*'

'Okay, let's hear it.'

'Convince me of your talent. If you're good enough, I'll hire you to cater my upcoming VIP party. If you're better than good, I'll recommend you to a few people. Now, the only thing you need to decide is if it's a choice you wish for yourself.'

'But I've already proved I deserve this by winning the show.'

'Then this should be a doozy.' He raised an eyebrow. 'Do you agree to my terms?'

The sense of injustice burned within her, the need to stand her ground and demand her due strong.

But from what she'd seen of him so far he could destroy her just as easily as he'd offered to help her. He'd rightly pointed out that she'd sought him out under false pretences. She should be thanking her lucky stars he hadn't turned her over to the security guards.

The small print in her *Petit Q* contract had warned of serious repercussions if she breached confidentiality or behaved inappropriately towards a *Q Virtus* member.

So far she'd breached several of those guidelines. It was therefore in her interest to stay on the right side of Narciso Valentino.

If he could throw away thirty million dollars with the careless flick of those elegant fingers, surely it was worth her while to endure this small sacrifice to prove herself to Narciso. Getting her restaurant opening back on track would also send her parents the message once and for all that she had no intention of bowing to their pressure to join the family business.

She sucked in a breath, which hopelessly stalled when his eyes darkened. 'Yes, I agree to your terms.'

He didn't move. He just stood there staring at her. Ruby had the weird sensation he was weighing her up, judging her...

Unable to stand his stare, she started to turn away. His eyes dropped to her bare legs, heat flaring in his gaze. The power of it was so forceful she took a step back. Then another.

'Stop,' he rasped.

'Why?'

'I need you.'

Her heart hammered. 'What?'

His nostrils flared as he reached and captured her arm. Strong fingers slid down her elbow to her wrist. Ruby's pulse raced harder under the pressure of his fingers as he raised her right arm.

The electronic beep as he activated the smartwatch on her wrist knocked her out of her lust haze. Biting the inside of her cheek to bring her down to reality worked for a few seconds, until he started to speak.

Sicilian wasn't in any way similar to the language she'd learnt growing up, but she managed to pick up a few words that had her frowning.

'You're not returning to New York?'

'Not yet. My plan was to take a long-needed vacation after Macau.'

Her heart sank. 'So I still have to wait until you come to New York to finalise this agreement.'

'Not at all, Ruby. I leave for Belize tonight. And you're coming with me.'

The sight of her open-mouthed was almost amusing. Almost. Had he not been caught up in the maelstrom of severely thwarted desire, Narciso would've laughed at her expression.

As it was, he couldn't see beyond the need to experience again the sensational taste of those lips.

Pure sin. Wrapped in sweet, angelic deliciousness.

He'd never kissed lips like hers. Or tasted nipples like hers. In fact, so far Ruby Trevelli was proving disconcertingly unique in all aspects. Even the confession of her bastard of an ex's betrayal had touched him in a way he most definitely did not desire.

The flash of pain he'd seen had made his insides clench with an alien emotion that had set even more alarm bells clanging.

He hadn't intended to go to Belize till after the party he'd planned for when his Russian deal was completed.

But he was nothing if not adaptable.

'Belize?' Astonishment blazed from her stunning blue eyes.

'Yes. I have a yacht moored there. We'll sail around along the coast, dive in the Blue Hole. And in between, you'll stun me with your culinary delights. But be warned, nothing short of perfection will satisfy me.'

'I've never provided anything short of that. But…' She hesitated, again displaying that reticence he'd sensed in her earlier. If she wanted to play hard to get, she was going about it the right way. He wanted her…hard. But he was no pushover.

'But what?'

'We need to agree on one thing.' Her pulse throbbed under his thumb. He wanted to stop himself from caressing the silky, delicate skin but he couldn't help himself.

'*Sì?*'

'From now on things remain strictly business between us. The next time we have a discussion, I'd rather do it without the need for ropes.'

The hard tug of arousal the image brought almost made him groan out loud. 'I guarantee you, *amante,* the next time I tie you up, it'll be because you beg me to.'

She snatched her wrist from his grasp.

'Okay. And Superman rides on a unicorn, right?'

'I have no idea about that. Ropes, on the other hand—'

'Will play no part in our interaction for the duration I'm to prove myself to you. Unless, of course, you're bringing your girlfriend along. In which case, what you get up to with her is your business.'

Irritation fizzed inside him. Having the attraction he knew she reciprocated dismissed so casually stuck like a barb under his skin. 'I'm currently unattached. But I don't think I'll stay that way for much longer,' he said.

Her eyes widened but her lips pursed. Again arousal bit deep.

Suddenly, he wanted to leave Macau. Wanted to be alone with her so he could probe her deeper. The double entendre brought a grim smile.

Veering away from her, he stalked out of the kitchen.

The case he'd asked his personal butler to fetch was standing by the sofa in the living room. She spotted it the same time he did.

'You had my things removed from my room?' The incredulity in her voice amused and irritated him at once.

'I don't believe in wasting time when my mind is made up.'

'And what about *my* mind? You didn't know what choice I would make!'

'That's where you're wrong. I did. I'm very familiar with the concept of supply and demand. You want something only I can provide. You wanted it enough to hop on a plane on the strength of an eavesdropped conversation between complete strangers. I wagered on you being ambitious enough to agree to my demands.'

'You make me sound so mercenary.'

'On the contrary. I like a woman who states what she wants upfront. Subterfuge and false coyness are traits I actively despise.'

'Somehow I don't believe that.'

'You think I like liars?'

Her gaze slid away. 'I didn't say that.'

He forced himself to turn away, resume his path towards his bathroom and another cold shower. *Maledizione!*

'As for your case, I had it brought here to avoid any awkwardness. Or would you rather have answered questions as to why you've been absent from your duties for the last several hours?'

She groaned. 'Oh, God! What will they think?'

'They'll think the obvious. But you're with me, so no one will question you about it.'

'I…I…'

'The words you're looking for are *thank you*. You can use the second bedroom suite to get ready. I have a brunch meeting in the Dragon Room in half an hour.'

'And you want me to come with you?'

'Of course. From here on in, you serve no one but me.' His words echoed in his head and his fists clenched.

For the second time in less than ten minutes another unwanted emotion sideswiped him. *Possessiveness.*

Just as he'd trained himself not to trust, he'd trained himself not to become attached. Possessiveness suggested an attachment to something…*someone.*

Narciso didn't *do* attachment. And yet—

'What happens after your meeting?'

He forced nonchalance into his voice. 'We return here to indulge in…whatever we please. Tomorrow when the lock down is lifted, we leave.'

CHAPTER SIX

THE REST OF the morning turned out to be a study in how the very rich and influential operated. Having grown up in relative wealth and seen the lengths to which people went to keep what they had, Ruby had imagined she knew how power and influence were wielded.

Watching Narciso Valentino command a room just by walking into it took her education to a whole different level. People's attitude transformed just by him entering their presence, despite his mask now being back firmly in place.

Although dressed more casually than he'd been last night, he exuded the same authority and attention as he moved from room to room, chatting with other well-heeled guests. The brief time he left her to attend his meeting, Ruby was left with a floundering feeling in her stomach that irritated and shocked her at the same time.

She was finishing her buttered brioche and café Americano when she sensed a gaze on her. Anticipating another of the speculative looks she'd been on the receiving end of since she came downstairs with Narciso, she stemmed her apprehension and raised her head.

The man who'd played against Narciso last night and won thirty million dollars was watching her with stormy grey eyes.

He moved forward and pulled out a chair. 'May I join you?' He sat down before she could stop him.

'Sure. It's a free country, I think.'

His smile didn't quite reach his eyes. He steepled his fingers together and stared at her. 'Where's my... Where's your companion?'

'At a meeting...' She paused and stared down at his wrist. 'I thought those smartwatches could tell you where each guest is. Why are you asking me?'

'Perhaps I just wanted a conversation opener.'

'Needing an opener would mean you have something specific to discuss with me. I don't see what that could be.' Her discomfort grew underneath that unwavering, hostile stare. She started to put her flatware down, thought better of it and hung on to the knife.

His gaze went to it and swung back to hers. 'You won't be needing that.'

'I'll be the judge of that. Now, can I help you with something?' As she'd thought last night, there was something vaguely familiar about him. But like every single guest present, his mask was back on and nothing of the rest of his features was enough to pinpoint where she might have seen him before, and she was not going to commit another faux pas by asking him his name.

'I merely came to offer you a warning. Stay away from The Warlock.'

'Considering you won over thirty million dollars from him last night, I'd have thought you'd be in a better frame of mind, perhaps even celebrating your huge windfall, not wasting your time casting aspersions on someone you defeated.'

'He thinks he has bested me but he'll soon learn the error of his ways.'

'Right. Okay...was that all?' she asked, but his eyes had taken on a faraway look, as if he were somewhere else entirely.

'He's been poison ever since...' His mouth tightened and his eyes grew colder. 'For as long as I've had to deal with him, he's been nothing but trouble. He was given his name for a reason.'

'The Warlock?'

His hand fluttered in a dismissive gesture. 'No, I meant his real name. Take my advice and remember that once he tells you who he really is.'

'I'm not supposed to know who he is, so what you're saying means less than nothing to me.'

'Or you could understand perfectly what I mean.' His upper lips twisted. 'Unless spreading your legs for him has robbed you of all common sense.'

The barb struck too close to home. 'How dare you?' She jerked back at the sheer hatred pouring from him. Ice-cold sensation drenched her veins at the same time as warm hands cupped her shoulders.

'Ruby?' Narciso clipped out her name. 'What's going on here?' The question was quite rhetorical because she was sure he'd caught part of the exchange.

Certainly, his flint-hard gaze and tense jaw made her think of her earlier assessment of just how dangerous an opponent he could be.

For whatever reason, the man sitting across from her spewing vitriol had wronged Narciso Valentino on a very deep level. The skin around his mouth was white and the hands curved over her shoulders were a little less than gentle.

Ruby carefully set her knife down and took a deep breath. 'Nothing. He was just leaving. Weren't you?'

The older man smiled and took his time to rise. His eyes locked on Narciso's and for a moment Ruby thought she understood the connection, then dismissed it. What she was imagining couldn't be possible.

Pure visceral hate existed between these two men. It coloured the air and crawled over her skin.

In her darkest days before she'd actively distanced herself from her parents, her father's behaviour had permeated every single corner of her existence and she'd imagined she hated him. She could never accept the way Ricardo Trevelli lived his life, or the careless way he treated her mother. But she'd never encountered hate this strong. It was a potent, living thing.

She shivered. Narciso felt it and glanced down at her before refocusing on her unwanted guest.

'Do I need to teach you another lesson, old man?'

'Keep your money, hotshot. I understand the need to brag in front of your woman. Shame it had to cost you so much last night.'

'It was worth it to see your face. If you need a refresher on how to win, I can accommodate you.'

The old man sneered. 'The time is coming when I'll wipe that smug look off your face once and for all.'

Narciso's smile was arctic. 'Do it quickly, then. I'm growing tired of your empty promises.'

Ruby sucked in a shocked breath at the blatant taunt. With a thick swear word that would singe the ears off a Sicilian donkey, the old man swivelled on his heel and walked away.

Narciso pulled back her chair, caught her up and swung her around to face him. 'What did he say to you?' he demanded, his nostrils pinched hard with the anger he was holding back.

'Oh, he was educating me on the real meaning of your name, albeit very cryptically. Who is he anyway?'

He looked after the departing man and visibly inhaled.

'I told you—he's no one important. But I want you to stay away from him.'

'That would be difficult since I don't even know who he is.'

Tucking her arm through the crook of his elbow, he led her out of the dining area styled with large, exquisitely scrolled Chinese screens. She'd heard one of the guests comment that the stands holding up the scrolls were made of solid gold. *Q Virtus,* its mysterious owner, Zeus…in fact this whole place was insane with its surrealistic extravagance, secrecy and decadence.

'You're an intelligent woman, hopefully equipped with enough of that intuition you women are so proud of. Use it and stay clear of him.'

'Funny, he said the same thing about you. And why does that sound suspiciously like a threat?'

He led her into another express lift and used his thumbprint and her smartwatch to activate the panel before pressing the button for the sub-basement.

'Because it is one.'

'So we've graduated from ropes to threats?' Her attempt at humour fell flat when his face tightened further.

'Don't tempt me. I'm this close to breaking point.' He held two fingers together for emphasis.

She froze when the arm imprisoning hers drew her closer to his warm body. 'Did something go wrong with your meeting? A deal fall through or something?'

'What makes you ask that?'

'Aside from the confrontation just now, you seem to be in a foul mood. Did something happen?'

'No, sweet Ruby. The "network hard" part of my day is ticking along nicely. It's the "play harder" part that has failed miserably.'

So she was partly to blame for his disagreeable mood.

Time for a subject change.

'Where to now?'

'The champagne mixer in the Blue Dungeon. Then we're leaving,' he clipped out.

'I thought we couldn't leave until the lock down was lifted tonight?'

'I've asked for a special dispensation from Zeus,' he said, his gaze on the downward-moving arrow. They were sinking deeper into the bowels of the building. Ruby felt as if she were disappearing into Alice's Wonderland. 'The dispensation should be coming through on your smartwatch any minute now. Let me know when it does.'

'The owner's name really *is* Zeus. Seriously?'

'You don't find my moniker incredulous.'

'That's because...' She paused, unwilling to voice the thought rattling through her head.

'Because?'

She shrugged. 'The Warlock suits you, somehow.'

He faced her fully, his gaze raking her face in that intensely raw way that made her feel vulnerable, exposed.

'In what way does it suit me?' he asked silkily.

Because you mesmerise me with very little effort. Ruby cleared her throat.

'You're obviously a genius at what you do.'

'And you think my success stems from sorcery?'

She shrugged. 'Not in the chicken bones and goat sacrificing sense but in other ways.'

One hand rose, trailed down her jaw to rest on the pulse pounding at her throat. 'And will I be able to sway you into my bed with this potent magic of mine?'

'No.'

His smile this time was genuine. And devastating to her senses. 'You sound so very sure.'

'Because I am. I told you, I don't mix business and pleasure.'

His smile dimmed. 'Would this have anything to do with your ex-almost-lover?'

'I believe it's a sound work ethic,' she answered.

Once Narciso had left her on her own, she'd replayed the events of last night and this morning. Shame at her behaviour had charged through her, forcing her to quickly reinforce her crumbling self-control.

Letting her feelings run wild and free was not an option. Heartache and devastation could be the only result if she didn't get herself back under control.

'So you intend to let him win?' Narciso queried softly.

'This is *my* choice.'

'If you say so.'

She had no chance to respond before the doors opened and they entered the most surreal room Ruby had ever seen. Blue lights had been placed strategically on the floors, walls and ceilings of a huge cavern. And bottles of champagne hung on wires, their labels combined with the words *QV Macau*.

'What does *Q Virtus* mean?' she asked.

His smile was mysterious. 'I could tell you but I'd have to—'

'Oh, never mind.' She turned as an excited murmur went through the crowd.

Six acrobats clad in LED-lit costumes swung from tension cables from one end of the room to the other.

She couldn't help her gasp of wonder at their movement. 'Oh, my God.'

'So *that's* what it'll sound like.' The wicked rasp was for her ears alone. His warm breath tickled her ear, sending a tingle right to her toes.

'What *what* will sound like?'

'Your gasp of wonder when I'm deep inside you.' His lips touched her lobe and she jerked at the electric sensation.

'Since that's never going to happen, you'll just have to keep guessing,' she replied.

He merely laughed and plucked two glasses off a sterling-silver tray that dropped down from the ceiling as if by magic. 'Champagne?' He passed her a glass.

She took it simply for something to do besides staring at his gorgeous face, which had transformed dramatically from his earlier formidable demeanour. He clinked glasses with her and raised his in a toast. 'To the thrill of the challenge.'

'I won't participate.'

'Too late. You threw the gauntlet. I accepted. Drink your champagne. That's a five-thousand-dollar glass you're holding.'

She stared down into the golden liquid before answering. 'I don't really drink that much.'

'I guessed as much. Another souvenir from the ex?'

The pain of the memory scythed through her before she could guard herself against it. She shook her head.

'Why don't you drink, Ruby?' His voice was hypnotic, pulling on a cord deep inside that made her want to reveal everything to him.

'I don't like the loss of control it gives me.'

Silver eyes narrowed. 'Something happened to you?'

'You could say that.'

'Something bad?'

'Depends on your definition of bad. Someone upset me. I thought getting drunk would solve the problem. It didn't. It made it worse.'

'Who was it?'

'My father—' She stopped as she realised how much she was revealing to him.

'Ah, *sì*. Fathers. It's such a shame they're necessary for evolution, isn't it?' Although his words were light, his eyes had taken on that haunted look she'd glimpsed this morning in his kitchen.

Out of nowhere came the overwhelming urge to take his pain away. 'I can't believe we're standing in one of the most spectacular rooms I've ever seen, discussing our daddy issues.'

'You're discussing *your* daddy issues. I have none.'

She frowned. 'But you just said—'

His mouth tightened. 'I merely expressed a view on evolution.' He took a large slug of his drink and set the glass aside. 'Come, the show's about to begin.'

He walked her deeper into the room, to an even larger space where a stage was brightly lit in hues of blue and green.

Several more acrobats struck different poses from their ropes but as the oriental-themed music filled the room they started to perform as one. Immediately she recognised the world-renowned group whose exclusivity was reserved to royalty and the crème de la crème of A-listers.

The fluidity of their movement and sheer talent taken to hone such an awe-inspiring performance kept Ruby mesmerised for several minutes, until she noticed Narciso's renewed tension. A glimpse at his profile showed a tense jaw and tightly pursed lips.

She debated for a second, then took a breath.

'It's okay if you don't want to admit to having daddy issues. I lived in denial myself for a long time,' she whispered, aware several guests stood close by.

'Excuse me?' he rasped.

'I could apologise but I thought we were…you know…sharing.'

'I don't *share,* Ruby. At least not in that way.'

'Listen—'

'You're missing the show,' he cut across her.

Forced to curb her reply, she resumed watching the show, aware that he grew tenser with every passing minute.

A particularly daring acrobat surged right over their heads. Narciso's hand tightened around hers. Thinking he was reacting to the spectacular display, she glanced at him, to find his gaze fixed across the stage, on the man who'd confronted her less than an hour ago.

In that instant, the resemblance between them struck her hard. Their similar heights, their silver eyes, the proud, arrogant way they viewed the world. How could she not have seen it until now?

'Oh, my God, he's your father.'

He stiffened and glanced down at her with cold, grim eyes. 'He's a man whose DNA I happen to share. Nothing more.'

Applause broke through the crowd as the show finished in a crescendo of dives and leaps choreographed so fabulously, she couldn't help but clap despite her shocking discovery.

They were father and son. And they hated each other with a passion that was almost a separate being every time they were within feet of each other.

She wanted to know what had placed such a wide divide between them but she held her tongue. She had no right to pry into anyone's life. Her own baggage was enough to be dealing with. After fighting for so long and so hard to get away from the noxious environment her parents chose to inhabit, the last thing she wanted was for someone like Narciso Valentino to dredge it all up.

The smartwatch on her wrist beeped twice.

Narciso glanced down at it. 'We're leaving.'

Her heart climbed into her throat, and she fought the snap of excitement fizzing through her. What on earth was wrong with her? She couldn't be secretly thrilled with the thought of being alone with this man.

Could she?

Within minutes their cases were being loaded into the trunk of the stretch limo that stood idling in the underground car park, with a smartly dressed driver poised at the door. She slid in and Narciso joined her.

The moment the door shut, she wanted to fling it open and dive out. She'd thought she was venturing into the unknown by coming to Macau.

By agreeing to go to Belize with The Warlock of Wall Street, she was really stepping into an abyss.

'I…don't think I can…' She stopped. What was she doing? She'd forced herself to endure a TV show after Simon had convinced her it was the only way she could fund Dolce Italia.

She'd plunged herself into the very environment she'd grown up in and actively detested just so she could establish her independence. Now she stood on the threshold of seeing it pay off.

'Having second thoughts?' he asked as the car rolled up a ramp and exited into bright mid-afternoon sunshine.

'No. I'm not,' she insisted more to herself than to him.

'Good.'

The smartwatch emitted several discreet beeps. 'What's it doing?'

'It's erasing the evidence of my activities here.'

'Wow, you're not part of the CIA, are you?'

'I could be if spies are your thing.' He gave another of those wicked smiles and her mouth dried.

'I'll pass, thanks. Although I'm curious what you have to do to belong to a club like that.' She took the watch off and examined its multifaceted detail.

'It involves a lot more than chicken bones and goat sacrifices, I can assure you.'

Against her will, a smile tugged at her mouth. Letting go, she laughed. He joined her, his perfectly even teeth flashing in the sunlight. The deep sound echoed in the enclosed space and wrapped itself around her.

Danger! Her senses screamed again. But it was a seductive

danger, akin to knowing that extra mouthful of rich, decadent mousse was deadly for you but being unable to resist the taste.

· And she'd quickly discovered that if she let herself fall under his spell, he would completely bypass her hips and go straight to her heart.

'Here, take this back.' She held out his watch, stressing to herself that she didn't miss having something of his so close to her skin.

'Keep it. It's yours.'

'Are you serious?' she gasped. 'But what about its value—'

'I wasn't thinking of its monetary value when I offered it. And if you're thinking about pawning it, think twice.'

'I meant its sentimental value to you, of your visit here? And I'd never pawn a gift!'

'I'm happy to hear it. As for sentiments, I prefer mine to be warm-blooded.' He took off his mask and laid it on his knee. 'Luckily, I have you.'

The statement sent equal parts of apprehension and excitement through her. She slowly slid the watch back onto her wrist, and watched as they approached the Pearl River. Luxury super yachts in all shapes and sizes lined the marina.

The limo drew to a stop beside a sleek speedboat and Narciso helped her out. The driver held out a leather case, its velvet inside carved in the exact shape of his mask. Narciso placed the mask inside, shut the case and handed it to the driver.

Seconds after their luggage was loaded, the pilot guided the boat towards the open river.

'I've spent a lot of time asking you where we're going but I need to ask you one more time.'

'Don't you trust me?' he asked with a mockingly raised brow.

'No.'

He laughed again. And again, the sound tugged deep inside.

'We're heading to the airport. My private jet will fly us to Belize.'

Nodding, she watched the disappearing skyline of Macau City. It'd earned its name, Vegas of the East, but there was also soul in this place, and in other circumstances Ruby would've loved to explore a lot more.

She turned to find him watching her. The hunger was back in his eyes, coupled with a dangerous restlessness.

'What?' she demanded when she couldn't stand his intense scrutiny any longer.

'I came here for a purpose. You succeeded in swaying me from that purpose. I intend to find out why.'

'Was that purpose to destroy your father?' she asked before she thought better of it.

He immediately stiffened. The breeze rushing over the water ruffled his hair. He slowly scythed his fingers through it without taking his eyes off her.

'Among other things.'

'But you decided to spare him at the last minute.'

'A very puzzling notion indeed.'

Her heart hammered as his speculative gaze rested on her lips.

'I don't think it's puzzling at all. I think you knew exactly what you were doing.'

His eyes narrowed. 'And what would that be, O Wise One?'

'You were extending the thrill of the chase, delaying the gratification of the kill blow.'

'How very astute of you.'

'So what were the other things?'

'*Perdono?*'

'You said among other things.'

His gaze drifted down the neckline of her black tube dress, again a tighter fit than she would've preferred. 'What do you think?'

'According to online sources you have an IQ of a hundred and forty-eight.'

'It's closer to one-fifty but who's counting?'

Her mouth pursed. 'It also says you're a rampantly rabid playboy who thinks about nothing else but the next woman he intends to sleep with. It's a shame you've chosen to use *all* hundred and fifty to chase skirts.'

He grinned. 'No, I only use one hundred and forty-eight. I need the other two to walk and talk.'

She rolled her eyes even though the corners of her mouth curved. The boat pulled up to a jetty, beyond which she could see several planes parked on tarmac.

Narciso's plane was the same silver shade as his eyes, with a black trim that made it stand out among the other jets.

He lived a life of extreme luxury and decadence, while making people like her jump through hoops to claim what was rightfully theirs.

'What's wrong? You're frowning.'

'You're asking me to spend time and energy claiming something that should be already mine. I'm trying to see the fairness in that.'

'Something about going the extra mile? Doing whatever it takes?' he mocked, but his eyes held a flash of warning. 'Get on the plane, Ruby.'

'Or what?'

'Or you lose everything. Because I won't renegotiate and I despise being thwarted.'

Her feet remained leaden. Her instinct warned her she wouldn't emerge unscathed if she went with him.

'Is this how you do business? You strike a deal, you renegotiate, then you renege?' he demanded.

'Of course not. I'm only here because *your* company reneged on the deal it struck with me!'

'A fact I'm yet to verify. The quicker you get on the plane, the quicker this can be resolved.'

She had no argument against that. And the reality was she'd come too far to turn back. And there was the small problem of Simon's loan shark lurking in the background.

Taking a deep breath, she started to mount the steps. Recalling something he'd said, she twisted and nearly collided with his lean, muscular frame. The steadying hand he threw around her waist burned through to her skin. This close, without the hindrance of his mask, she could see how his envy-inducing cheekbones and long eyelashes framed his impossibly handsome face.

'What did you mean about being thwarted?'

'Sex, Ruby. I meant sex. We're going to have it together. It's going to be spectacular and, yes, I know you're going to protest. But it will happen. So prepare yourself for it.'

She was still reeling from the raw, brazen words hours later as she tried to doze in her fully reclined seat two rows from where he conducted a teleconference call.

She had no idea how long the flight to Belize would take. She had no idea what the temperature would be this time of year.

In fact, her mind was empty of everything but the words Narciso had uttered to her on the steps of his plane.

Punching her pillow, she silently cursed herself for dwelling on it. It was *never* going to happen. She'd have to be ten kinds of fool to repeat what she'd nearly gone through with Simon—

'If you punch that pillow one more time, it'll give up its secrets, I'm sure of it.'

She twisted around and found him standing beside her seat, one hand held out.

'Sleep is eluding you. Let's spend some time together.'

'No, thanks.'

He dropped his hand and shoved it into his pocket. Ruby tried not to stare at the way his shoulders flexed under the snow-white T-shirt he'd changed into. 'Please yourself. But if you end up serving me food that I find abhorrent because you haven't done your homework, you'll only have yourself to blame.'

The challenge had the desired effect. Pushing aside the cashmere throw the stewardess had provided, she went after him.

He smiled mockingly and waved her into the club chair opposite his.

Ruby smoothed her dishevelled hair down, and activated her tablet. 'Okay, shoot. What's your favourite food?'

'Life offers such vast richness. Having favourites is severely restricting.'

She sighed. 'This isn't going to be easy, is it?'

He shrugged. 'I take entertainment where I can get it.'

'Okay, next question. Any food allergies?'

'Peanuts and avocado.'

Her head snapped up. 'Seriously?'

'I don't joke with my health, *amante*.'

She noted it on her tablet. 'How do you feel about Sicilian food?'

'I'm completely indifferent.'

She looked up in surprise. 'Really? Most Sicilians are passionate about everything to do with their homeland.'

'Probably because they have a connection to be passionate about—' He stopped suddenly and his jaw clenched.

She watched him try to rein in his control and her chest tightened. 'And you don't?'

Tension gripped his frame. 'Not for a long time.'

Her tablet dimmed, but she didn't reactivate it. The flash of anguish in his eyes snagged her attention.

'Because of your father?' she pushed.

His eyes narrowed. 'Why does this interest you so much?'

The question took her aback, made her ask herself the same thing. 'I...I thought we were making conversation.'

'This is one subject I prefer to steer clear of. *Capisce?*'

'Because you find it upsetting.'

He cursed under his breath and raked back his hair as that stubborn lock fell over his forehead again. 'Not at all. The subject of my father fires up my blood. I just prefer not to discuss it with near strangers.'

Despite cautioning herself to stick to business, she found herself replying, 'Haven't you heard of the saying make love not war?'

'Why do I need to choose one when I can have both? I'll make love to you and I make war with Giacomo.'

'For how long?'

'How long can I make love to you? Is that another challenge to my manhood?'

'I meant your father, and you know it.'

'I intend to keep going until one of us is in the ground.'

She gasped. 'You don't really mean that, do you?'

Again that flash of pain, gone before it'd even formed. '*Sì*, I do.'

'You know, he called you poison.'

This time the anguish stayed for several seconds, shattered his expression. Her heart fractured at the pain she glimpsed before his face settled into neutral indifference. 'He's right. I am poison.'

His unflinching admission made her heart contract. 'What happened between you two?'

'I was born.'

Narciso watched her try to make sense of his reply. She frowned, then shook her head. 'I don't understand.'

He wanted to laugh but the vice gripping his chest every time he thought of Giacomo made that impossible. He rose and walked to the bar at the mid-section of his plane. Pouring two glasses of mineral water, he brought one to her and gulped down the other. 'That's because you're trying to decipher a hidden meaning. There is none. I was born. And Giacomo has hated that reality ever since.'

'He hates being a father?'

He paused before answering, unwilling to utter the words he hadn't said aloud for a very long time, not since he'd wailed it as a pathetic little boy to the housekeeper who'd been the closest thing he'd known to a mother.

'No. He hates me.'

Shock darkened Ruby's eyes.

He sat back down abruptly, and willed back the control he'd

felt slipping from him since he'd walked into the poker den in Macau last night. He glanced up and saw sympathy blazing from Ruby's face. The rawness abated a little but, no matter how much he tried, he couldn't shake off the unsettling emptiness inside him.

He swallowed his water and set the glass down.

'Enough about me. Tell me about *your* father.'

She stiffened. 'I'd rather not.'

'You were ready to *share* just a little while ago.' He settled deeper into his seat and watched her face. And it was a stunning face. The combination of innocence and defiance in her eyes kept him intrigued. She didn't hide her emotions very well. Right now, she was fighting pain and squirming with a desire to change the subject.

The sudden urge to help her, to offer the same sympathy she'd just exhibited, took him by surprise.

Dio, what was wrong with him?

This woman who'd flown thousands of miles after him was an enigma. An enigma with daddy issues. He should be staying well clear.

He leaned forward. 'Since you seem shocked by the depth of my…feelings towards Giacomo, I'm assuming your feelings towards your father are much less…volatile?'

Those full lips he wanted to taste again so badly pressed together for a moment. 'I don't hate my father, no. But I prefer to keep my distance from them.'

'Them?'

She fidgeted. 'You're going to find out anyway. My parents are Ricardo and Paloma Trevelli.'

Her stare held a little defiance and a whole load of vulnerability. 'Sorry, you lost me.'

A delicate frown marred her perfect skin. Again his fingers ached to touch. Soon, he promised himself.

'How come you own several media companies and yet have no clue what goes on in the world?'

'My line of work doesn't mean I compromise my privacy. So your parents are famous?'

Her eyelids swept down to cover her expression. 'You could say that. They're famous celebrity TV chefs.'

'And their fame disgusts you?' he deduced.

Blue eyes flicked to his. 'I didn't say that.'

'Your voice. Your eyes. Your body. They all give you away, Ruby Trevelli.' He loved the way her name sounded on his lips. He wanted to keep saying it… 'So you despise them for being famous and cashing in on it. Isn't that what you're doing?'

'No! I'd never whore myself the way—' She stopped and bit her lip.

'Do they know you have this view of them?' he asked.

She shrugged. 'They've chosen a lifestyle I prefer not to be a part of. It's that simple.'

'Ruby…' he waited until her eyes met his '…we both know it's not that simple.'

Shadows chased across her face and her mouth trembled before she firmed it again. Before he could think twice, he reached out and touched her hand.

She swallowed hard, then pulled her tablet towards her. 'How many people will I be catering for at your event?'

He told himself he wasn't disappointed by her withdrawal. 'Are we back to all business again?'

'Yes. I think it's safer, don't you?'

Narciso couldn't deny the veracity of that. Dredging up his past was the last thing he'd intended when he'd boarded his plane. And yet, he resented her switch to all-business mode.

'If you say so,' he replied. 'You think you can handle a VIP dinner?'

'I believe in my talent as much as you believe in your abilities as the Warlock of Wall Street. If I say I'll rock your socks off, I will.'

A reluctant smile tugged at his lips. 'A confident woman is such a turn-on.'

She glared at him. 'If you say so,' she replied sweetly. 'Is there a guest of honour that I should pay particular attention to?'

'Vladimir Rudenko. I'm in the last stages of ironing out a deal with him. He's the VIP guest.'

She started to make another note when her tablet pinged. He heard her sharp intake of breath before she paled.

'What is it?'

'It's nothing.'

The blatant lie set his teeth on edge. 'Don't lie to me.' He reached for the tablet but she snatched it off the table.

'It's a private thing, all right?'

'A private thing that's obviously upset you.' He watched her chest rise and fall in agitation and experienced that disconcerting urge to help again.

'Yes, but it's my problem and I'll deal with it.'

Before he could probe further, she jumped up. 'You said I could use the bedroom if I wanted. I'll go finish making my notes now and get some sleep, if that's okay?'

It wasn't okay with him. Nothing had been okay since he met Ruby Trevelli. But short of physically restraining her, an action sure to bring brimstone upon his head, he let her go.

'We won't be landing for another six hours. I'll wake you before we do.'

She nodded quickly. 'Thanks.'

He watched her walk away, her short, tight black dress framing her body so deliciously, his groin hardened. He couldn't suppress his frustrated growl as the bedroom door shut after her.

The image of her lying in his bed haunted him. But those images were soon replaced by other, more disturbing ones as his thoughts turned to their earlier conversation.

His father.

He shoved a hand through his hair. He'd come so close to revealing the old, bottled-up pain. Hell, he'd even contemplated spilling his guts about Maria.

Maria. The tool his father had used to hammer home how much he detested his son.

His laptop beeped with an incoming message. Casting another glance at the bedroom door, Narciso pursed his lips.

The next six hours would be devoted to clearing his schedule.

Because once they were in Belize, he would devote his time to deciphering the code that was Ruby Trevelli and why she had succeeded in getting under his skin.

CHAPTER SEVEN

SHE WAS WARM. And comfortable. The steady sound drumming in her ears soothed her, made her feel safe from the erratic dreams that still played in her mind.

But she wanted to get warmer still. Wanted to burrow in the solid strength surrounding her.

The heart beating underneath her cheek—

Ruby jerked awake.

'Easy now, tigress. You'll do yourself an injury.'

'What the hell…? What are you doing here?'

'Sharing the bed. As you can see, once again I managed to restrain myself. And this time we're both fully clothed. That means I win brownie points.'

'You win nothing for letting yourself into my bed uninvited.'

'Technically, this is my bed, Goldilocks. Besides, you were muttering in your sleep and tossing and turning when I looked in on you. I had to make sure you didn't sleepwalk yourself out of an emergency exit in your agitation.'

Ruby tried to pry herself away from the inviting length of his warm body, but the arm clamped around her waist refused to move. 'I wasn't that agitated.'

Silver eyes pinned hers. 'Yes, you were. Tell me what upset you.' His voice was cajoling, hypnotic.

She wanted to tell him about the undeniable threat in the email that had made a shaft of ice pierce her nape and shimmer down her spine. The loan shark had stepped up his threat level, implicating her mother.

Ironic that Narciso, the world-famous playboy and media mogul, had no idea who her mother was but some two-bit loan shark who inhabited the dregs of society knew who Paloma Trevelli was enough to threaten to break her legs if Ruby didn't reply with a timescale of payment.

Her reply had bought her a few more days but there was no way she intended to tell Narciso what was going on.

'I told you. It's my business to handle.'

'Not if it will potentially impede your ability to perform your job.'

'I can cook blindfolded.'

'That I would pay good money to see.' He pulled her closer, wedging his thigh more firmly between hers so she was trapped. Some time during sleep, she'd curled her hand over his chest. Now, firm muscles transmitted heat to her fingers, making them tingle.

Awareness jolted through her when his lips drifted up her cheek to her temple. 'If we weren't landing in less than thirty minutes, I'd take this a step further, use other means to find out what's going on.'

'You're operating under the assumption that I would've permitted it.'

He laughed, then sobered. 'It wasn't your father, was it?'

'No, it wasn't.'

He stared down at her for a long time, then nodded. 'I did some research while you were asleep. I know about your parents.'

'Oh?' She couldn't help the wave of anxiety that washed over her.

His eyes narrowed. 'Has it always been like that with them?'

That mingled thread of pain and humiliation when she thought of them tightened like a vice around her heart. 'You mean the crazy circus?'

He nodded.

'Until I went to college, yes. I didn't return home afterward. And I have minimal contact these days. Any more and it gets… unpleasant.'

'For whom?'

'For everyone. My father is a serial adulterer who doesn't understand why I won't condone his behaviour. My mother doesn't understand why I don't forgive my father every time he strays. They both want me to join the family business. The same business for which they shamelessly exploit their fame, their family, their friends—' She ground to a halt and tried to breathe around the pain in her chest.

His hand stroked down her cheek. 'You hate yourself for the way you feel.'

Feeling exposed, she tried to pull away. He held her firmer. 'Ruby *mio*, I think you'll agree we went way past business when we spent the night together in my bed. Talk to me,' he coaxed.

She drew in a shaky breath and reassured herself that they were talking. Just talking. 'I hate that my family is broken and I can't see a way to fix it without being forced to live my life in a media circus.'

'And yet you chose that avenue to fund your business.'

'Believe me, it wasn't my first choice.'

'Then why did you do it?'

'We'd tried getting loans from the banks with no success. Simon heard about the show and convinced me to enter. Taking three weeks out of my life to be on the show felt like a worthy sacrifice.'

'So you returned to the thing you hate the most in order to achieve your goal.'

'Does that make me a fool?'

'No, it makes you brave.'

The unexpected compliment made her heart stutter. Silver eyes rested on her, assessing her so thoroughly, she squirmed. Of course the movement made her body rub dangerously against his.

He emitted a leonine growl and the arm around her waist

tightened. One hand caught her bent leg and hitched it higher between his legs. The bold imprint of his erection seared her thigh. Heat flared between them, raw and fervent.

'So you don't think it's wrong to do whatever it takes to achieve one's dreams?'

His eyes darkened. 'No. In fact, it's a trait I wholeheartedly admire.'

Her throat clogged at the sincerity in his voice. The barriers she'd tried so hard to shore up threatened to crumble again. A pithy, mocking Narciso was bad enough. A gentle, caring Narciso in whose eyes she saw nothing but admiration and praise was even more dangerous to her already fragile emotions.

Scrambling to regroup, she laughed. 'Dear God, am I dreaming? That's two compliments within—'

'Enough,' he snapped. Then he kissed her.

Ruby's heart soared at the ferocity of his kiss. Desire swept over her, burying the volatile memories under even more turbulent currents of passion as he mercilessly explored her mouth with a skill that left her reeling.

Narciso could kiss. She already had proof of that. But this time the sharper edge of hunger added another dimension that made her heart pump frantically, as she saw no let-up in the erotic torrents buffeting her.

When he sank back against the pillows and pulled her on top of him, she went willingly. Strong, demanding hands slid up her bare thighs to cup her bottom, press her against that solid evidence of his need.

Unfamiliar hunger shot through her belly to arrow between her legs. Desperate to ease it, she rocked her hips deeper into him.

His thick groan echoed between their fused lips. He surged up to meet her, thrusting against her in an undeniable move that made her blood pound harder.

With her damp centre plastered so firmly and fully against him, she moaned as the beginnings of a tingle seized her spine. Hunger tore through her as rough fingers bit into her hips, keeping her firmly in place as they found a superb synchronicity that needed no words.

The first wave of sensation hit her from nowhere. She cried out, her fingers spiking into his hair as she grasped stability in a world gone haywire.

'*Dio!* Let go, baby. Let go.'

The hot words, crooned in her ear from a voice she'd found mesmerising from the very first, were the final catalyst. With a jagged moan, Ruby gave into the bliss smashing through her. She melted on top of him, giving in to the hands petting down her back as her shudders eased.

'I don't know whether to celebrate for making you come while we're both fully dressed or spank you for your appalling timing.'

Slowly, the realisation of what she'd just done pierced her euphoria.

Beneath her cheek, his heart raced. She could feel his erection still raging, strong and vital.

She'd orgasmed on top of Narciso Valentino and he hadn't even needed to undress her.

'*Oh, God.*'

Narciso held himself very still. He had to, or risk tearing her clothes off and taking her with the force of a rutting bull.

'God isn't going to help you now, naughty Ruby. You have to deal with me.'

'I... That shouldn't have happened.'

He nodded grimly. 'I agree.'

Wide blue eyes locked on his. 'You do?'

He swallowed hard. 'It should've happened when I was inside you. Now I feel woefully deprived.' Unable to stop himself, he moved his hands up and down her back. He tensed as her breathing changed. Desire thickened the air once more. Sensing her about to bolt, he flipped her over and trapped her underneath him. 'But I have you now.'

She tried to wriggle away but all she did was exacerbate the flashflood of desire drowning them both.

'No, I can't… We can't do this.'

He stiffened. 'Why not?'

'It won't end well. Simon—'

His eyes narrowed into warning slits. 'Was a cheating low-life who didn't deserve you. You and I together…we're different. We deserve each other.'

Narciso speared his fingers into her soft hair. But instead of kissing her, he grazed his lips along her jaw and down her throat to the pulse racing crazily there. He drew down her sleeves, exposing her breasts to his mouth. His mind screamed at him to stop before it was too late, but he was already sliding his tongue over one nipple.

Dio! He'd never known a woman to smash so effortlessly through his defences.

Her nails raked his nape and he groaned in approval. By the time he turned his attention to her other nipple, her whimpers were adding fire to his raging arousal.

She tugged on his shirt and he gave in to her demand. With a ragged laugh, he helped her reef it over his head and divested her of her dress.

Stark hunger consumed him as he took a moment to feast his eyes on her exposed body. 'You're so beautiful.' He drifted a hand down her chest and over her stomach to the top of her panties.

That disconcerting throb of possessiveness rocked through him again. He didn't want to know who else she'd been with but, in that moment, Narciso was glad her ex-business partner had failed to make her his. He settled himself over her, taking her mouth in a scorching kiss that obliterated words and feelings he didn't want to examine too closely.

His hand slid over her panties, hungrily seeking the heart of her. Her breath caught as his fingers breached her dampness and flicked over her sensitive flesh.

She jerked and squeezed her eyes tightly shut.

'Open your eyes, *amante*,' he commanded. He wanted…no, *needed* to see her, to assure himself that she was sliding into insanity just as quickly as he was. When she refused to comply, he applied more pressure. 'Do it or I'll stop.'

Eyes full of arousal slowly opened. His breath fractured at the electrifying connection. His whole body tightened to breaking point and he mentally shook his head.

What the hell was happening here?

Her delicate shudder slowed his flailing thoughts. Absorbing her reaction, he inserted one finger inside her, drinking in her hitched cry as she shuddered again.

'*Dio,* you're so tight.' He waited until she'd adjusted, then pressed in another finger.

Narciso was unprepared for her wince.

Instantly alert, he asked, 'What's wrong?'

She shook her head but he could see the trepidation in her eyes.

Those now familiar alarm bells shrieked. 'Answer me, Ruby.'

Nervously, she licked her lips. 'I'm…a virgin.'

Shock doused him in ice. For several seconds he couldn't move. Then the realisation of how close he'd come to taking her, to staking a claim on what he had no right to, hit him like a ton of bricks.

He surged back from her, reefing a hand through his hair as he inhaled sharply.

'You're a virgin,' he repeated numbly.

Raising her chin, she stared back at him. 'Yes.'

Several puzzle pieces finally slotted into place—the touches of innocence he'd spotted, her bolshiness even as she seemed out of her depth.

Her trepidation.

What had he said a moment ago—they *deserved* each other? Not any more.

Regret bit deep as he forced himself off the bed. 'Then, *cara mia,* this is over.'

Ruby came out of the bathroom of her cabin and slowed to a stop. Glancing around her room, she tried again to grapple with the sheer opulence around her. The three-decked yacht, complete with helicopter landing pad, had made her jaw drop the first time she'd seen it two days ago.

But the inside of Narciso's yacht was even more luxurious.

Black with a silver trim on the outside, it was an exact reverse on the inside. Silver and platinum vied with Carrara marble mined from the exclusive quarries north of Tuscany.

Her suite, complete with queen-size bed, sunken Jacuzzi bath and expensive toiletries, was the last word in luxury.

But all the opulence couldn't stem the curious emptiness inside her.

Since her arrival in Belize, she'd barely seen Narciso. The only times she saw him was when she served the list of meals he'd approved the day they'd boarded *The Warlock*.

At first the studied consideration with which he'd treated her after she'd blurted her confession had surprised her. Who knew he was the sort of playboy who treated virgins as if they were sacred treasures?

But then she'd seen the look in his eyes. The regret. The banked pain. Her surprise had morphed into confusion.

She was still confused now as she tugged off her towel and headed for the drawer that held her meagre clothes. Only to stop dead at the sight of the monogrammed leather suitcase standing at the bottom of the bed.

She opened it. Silk sarongs, bikinis, sundresses, designer shoes and slippers fell out of the case as she dug through it, her stomach hollowing out with incredulity.

Dressing in the jeans and top she'd travelled to Macau in and taken to wearing since her arrival simply because the three evening gowns were totally out of the question, she went in search of the elusive Sicilian who seemed hell-bent on keeping her permanently off balance.

She found him on the middle deck, after getting lost twice. He wore white linen shorts and a dark blue polo shirt. The early evening sun slanted over jet-black hair, highlighting its vibrancy and making her recall how it had felt to run her hands through the strands.

The sight of his bare legs made her swallow before she reminded herself she wasn't going to be affected by his stunning physique any longer. He'd pointedly avoided her for two whole days. She was damned if she'd let him catch her drinking him in as if he were her last hope for sustenance.

She was here to do a job. Whatever closeness they'd shared on his plane was gone, a temporary aberration never to be repeated. Her focus now needed to be on what she'd come here to do. But before that…

'You bought me clothes?' she asked.

He turned around, casually shoving his hands into his pockets. When his eyes met hers, she couldn't read a single expression in the silver depths. The Narciso who'd alternately laughed, mocked and devoured her with his eyes was gone. In his place was a coolly remote stranger.

'The size of your suitcase suggested you'd packed for a short stay. This is a solution to a potential problem. Unless you plan on wearing those jeans every day for the next week?'

True, in the strong Belizean sun, they felt hot and sticky on her skin. Not to mention they were totally inappropriate for the job she was here to do. When she cooked, she preferred looser, comfortable clothes.

But still. 'I could've sorted my own wardrobe.'

'You're here on my schedule. Making time for you to go shopping doesn't feature on there.'

'I wouldn't have—'

'It was no big deal, Ruby. Let's move on. It's time to step up your game. I want to see how you fare with a three-course meal. Michel will assist you if you need it.' He glanced at his watch. 'I'd like to eat at seven, which gives you two hours.'

The arrogant dismissal made her hackles rise. The distance between them made her feel on edge, bereft.

She assured herself it was better this way. But deep down, an ache took root.

Michel, Narciso's chef, greeted her with an openly friendly smile when she entered the kitchen.

'What do you have in mind for today for *monsieur?*' the Frenchman asked. Deep blue eyes remained contemplative as he stared at her.

'He wants to eat at seven so I was thinking of making a special bruschetta to start and chicken parmigiana main if we have the ingredients?'

'Of course. I bought fresh supplies this morning from town.'

The mention of town made her wonder when Narciso had bought her clothes. Had he shopped for them himself or given instructions?

Shaking her head to dispel the useless wondering, she followed Michel into the pantry. 'Oh…heaven!' She fell on the plump tomatoes and aubergines and squealed when she saw the large heads of truffles carefully packed in a box.

Freshly sliced prosciutto hung from specially lined containers that kept it from drying out and Parma ham stayed cool in a nearby chiller.

Michel took out the deboned chicken breast in the fridge. 'Would you like me to cut it up for you?'

'Normally, I'd say yes, but I think it's best if I do everything myself.' She smiled to take the sting out of the refusal.

He shrugged. 'Shout if you need anything.' After helping himself to a bottle of water, he left her alone.

Ruby selected the best knife and began chopping garlic, onions and the fresh herbs Michel kept in the special potted containers in the pantry.

The sense of calm and pure joy in bringing the ingredients together finally soothed the unsettled feeling she'd experienced for the last forty-eight hours.

Time and anxiety suspended, and her thoughts floated away as she immersed herself in her one salvation—the joy of cooking.

She started on the caviar-topped bruschetta with ricotta and peppers while the parmigiana was in the last stages of cooking.

Setting it out on a sterling-silver tray, she headed upstairs to where the crew had set the table.

Her feet slowed when she saw the extra place setting, then she stopped completely at the intimacy created by the dim lighting and lit candles. Her stomach fluttered wildly as steel butterflies took flight inside her.

'Are you going to stand there all evening?' Narciso quipped from where he sat on a sofa that hugged the U-shape of the room.

'I...thought I was cooking for just you.'

'You thought wrong.' He stood, came over and pulled out her chair. 'Tonight we eat together.' His gaze took in her jeans. 'Right after you change.'

'I don't need to change.'

'One rule of business is to learn to let the little things slide. Standing on principle and antagonising your potential business partner doesn't make for a very good impression.'

'I really appreciate you helping me out but—'

'I would personally prefer not to eat with a dinner companion wearing clothes smeared with food.'

Ruby glanced down and, sure enough, a large oily streak had soiled her vest top.

He'd gone to the trouble of providing new clothes for her comfort. Would it hurt to show some appreciation? In a few days, she'd be back in New York, hopefully with a contract firmly in her pocket. He'd made it clear she was no longer attractive to him in the sexual sense, so she had nothing to fear there.

'I'll go and change,' she murmured around the disquiet spreading through her.

'*Grazie,*' he replied.

Returning to her suite, she quickly undressed and selected a soft peach, knee-length sundress with capped sleeves. Slipping her feet into three-inch wedged sandals, she tied her hair back and returned to the deck.

His gaze slid over her but his face remained neutral as he pulled out her chair.

'Sit, and tell me what you've made for us.'

The intimate *us* made her hand tremble. Taking a deep breath, she described the first course. He picked up a piece of bruschetta, slid it into his mouth and chewed.

The process of watching him eat something she'd made with her two hands was so strangely unsettling and erotic her fingers clenched on her napkin.

'Hmm, good enough.' He picked up another piece and popped it in his mouth.

When she found herself staring at his strong jaw and throat, she averted her gaze, picked up a piece and nibbled on the edge. 'Damned with faint praise.'

'The cracked pepper adds a zing. I like it.'

Heady pleasure flowed through her. 'Really?'

'I always mean what I say, Ruby.' His grave tone told her they weren't talking about just food.

'O…okay,' she answered. 'I have to check on the parmigiana in ten minutes.'

'That's more than enough time for a drink.'

Abandoning her half-eaten bruschetta, Ruby headed for the extensive bar, only to stop dead.

'We're no longer moored?' The bright lights of the marina had disappeared, leaving only the stunning dark orange of the setting sun as their backdrop.

'No, we're sailing along the coast. Tomorrow morning, I intend to dive the Blue Hole. Do you dive?' he asked.

She continued to the bar, her nerves jumpier than they had been a minute ago. 'I did, a long time ago.'

'Good. You'll join me.'

'Is that a request or a demand?'

He'd ignored her for the past two days. The idea that he now wanted to spend time with her jangled her fraying nerves. As she recalled what had happened on the plane heat and confusion spiked anew through her.

'It's a very civilised request.'

And yet…

Regardless of what Narciso was requesting, the last thing she needed to be doing was anticipating spending any time in his company. He made her lose control. She only had to look into his eyes to feel herself skating close to emotional meltdown.

The last thing she'd wanted when she met Narciso was to give in to the attraction she'd felt for him. But perversely, now he'd made it clear he intended to give her a wide berth, her mind kept conjuring up scenarios of how things could be between them.

She'd been wrong to compare Narciso to Simon, or even to her father. Despite the playboy exterior, she'd glimpsed a core of integrity in her potential new business partner that was markedly absent from the men she'd so far encountered.

Potential new business partner…

Therein lay her next problem. Whether active or passive, if she passed his test, Narciso would own a share in her business. They'd have a *business* relationship.

Which meant, nothing could be allowed to develop between them personally.

She worked almost absent-mindedly and only realised the drink she'd made after she opened the cocktail shaker. Aghast, she stared into the bold red drink.

'Are you going to serve…what is that anyway?'

Flames surged up her cheeks. 'Allow me to present the *Afrodisiaco.*'

One brow cocked; a touch of the irreverence she'd become used to darted over his features. 'Is there a message in there somewhere?'

That she'd produced one of the most suggestive cocktails on her list made her pulse jump as she poured it. 'It's just a name.'

He immediately shook his head. 'I've learned that nothing is ever what its face value suggests.' He sipped the cocktail, swirled it around in his mouth. 'Although now I've tasted this, I'm willing to alter that view.'

'Narciso…' The moment she uttered his name he froze. Another crack forked through the severely compromised foundation of her resistance as she watched his eyes darken.

'No, Ruby *mio,* you don't get to say my name for the first time like that.'

She paused. 'I'm sorry, but you need to explain to me what the last two days have been about.'

'*Basta*…' His voice held stark warning.

'*Non abbastanza!* I didn't ask you to seduce me on your plane. In fact, I made it very clear I wanted to be left alone because I knew— I wasn't… Look, whatever experiences you've had in the past are your own. But you told me you didn't like women who blew hot and cold. Well, guess what, that's exactly what you're doing!'

'Are you quite finished?' he grated out, his face a mask of taut control.

She gripped the counter until her knuckles whitened and she stared down at her dress. 'As a matter of fact, I'm not. Thank you for buying the clothes. If I appeared unappreciative before it was because I've learnt that nothing comes for free.'

'You're welcome,' he replied coolly. 'Now am I allowed to respond to that diatribe?'

'No. I have to check on the chicken parmagiana. The last thing I want to do is jeopardise my chances by serving you burnt food.' She rounded the bar and walked past him.

He grasped her wrist, easily imprisoning her.

Instantly, heat and electricity flooded through her. 'Let me go!'

'I haven't been blowing hot and cold.'

'You've certainly made avoiding me an art form.'

'I was trying to save us both from making a mistake, *tesoro.*'

The realisation that she didn't want that choice made for her sent a bolt of shock through her. Sheer self-preservation made her raise her chin. 'Well, you needn't have bothered. In fact you did me a favour back on your plane.'

His hand tightened. 'Really?'

'Yes. You reminded me that you're not my type.'

His nostrils flared. 'And how would you know what your type is considering your lack of experience?'

'I don't need experience to know playboys turn me off.'

His mouth flattened. 'You didn't seem turned off when you climaxed on top of me, then proceeded to writhe beneath me.'

The reminder made her pulse skitter. The hungry demand that hadn't abated since then made her pull harder. He set her free and she retreated fast. 'Maybe I wanted to see what the fuss was all about. Whatever. You helped me refocus on the reason I'm here on your boat. Now if you'll excuse me, I have to check on the main course.'

Narciso watched her go, furious that he'd allowed himself to be drawn into her orbit again.

The way he'd operated the last two days had been the best course.

So what if he'd climbed metaphoric walls while locked in his study? He'd sealed two deals and added to his billions, and he'd even managed to stop thinking about Ruby Trevelli for longer than five minutes.

But then his investigator had presented him with another opportunity to finish off Giacomo. And once again, Narciso had walked away, unable to halt the chain reaction inside that seemed to be scraping raw emotions he'd long ago suppressed; unable to stop his world hurtling towards a place he didn't recognise.

That his first thought had been to seek out Ruby and share his confusion had propelled him in the opposite direction.

His reaction to her continued to baffle him. In the last two days, he'd expended serious brainpower talking himself out of tracking down the woman who kissed like a seductress but whose innocence his conscience battled with him against tainting.

Dio, when the hell had he even *grown* a conscience?

With a growl, he grabbed the last of the canapés and munched on it. Delicate flavours exploded on his tongue.

The past two days had shown him how talented Ruby was in the kitchen and behind the bar. Her skill was faultless and she'd risen to his every challenge. In that time, while he'd locked himself in his study to resist temptation, he'd also reviewed the TV show footage and seen why she'd won the contest.

Her skittishness every time the camera had focused on her had also been made apparent.

She hated being under the spotlight. And yet she'd forced herself to do it, just so she could take control of her life.

His admiration for her had grown as he'd watched the footage even as he'd cursed at the knowledge that she was burrowing deeper under his skin.

He looked up as she entered, a silver-topped casserole dish in her hand. The flourish and expertise with which she set the dish down spoke of her pride in her work. He waited until she served them both before he took the first bite.

His hand tightened around his fork. 'Did you cook this for Simon?'

She visibly deflated. 'You don't like it.'

He didn't just like it. He loved it. So much so he was suddenly jealous of her sharing it with anyone else. 'I didn't say that. Did you cook it for him?'

Slowly, she shook her head.

Relief poured through him. 'Good.'

'So, you like it?' she asked again.

'*Sì,* very much,' he responded, his voice gruff.

The pleasure that lit up her face made his heart squeeze. He wanted to keep staring at her, bathe in her delight.

Dio, he was losing it.

He reached for the bottle to pour her a glass of chilled Chablis.

'No, thanks,' she said.

His hand tightened around the bottle. 'You have nothing to fear by drinking around me, Ruby.'

She raised her head and he saw a mixture of anguish and sadness displayed in her eyes. In that moment, Narciso wanted to hunt down the parents who'd done this to her and deliver unforgettable punishment.

'I know, but I'd like to keep a clear head, all the same.'

He set the wine aside and reached for the mineral water. 'Well, getting blind drunk on my own is no fun, so I guess we're teetotalling.'

She rolled her eyes and smiled, and his gut clenched hard.

'We haven't discussed wines yet. When we're done meet me at the upper deck. And wear a swimsuit. The sun may have gone down but you'll still boil out there in that dress.'

The tension in his body eased when she nodded.

After dinner, he made his way up to the deck. They could do this… They could have a conversation despite the spiked awareness of each other. Or the hunger that burned relentlessly through him—

Five minutes later, she mounted the stairs to the deck and his thoughts scattered.

Madre di Dio!

The body he could see beneath the sarong was spectacular. But he couldn't see enough of it. And he wanted to, despite the *off limits* signs he'd mentally slapped on her.

Seeing doesn't mean touching.

'Drop the sarong. You don't need it here.'

She fidgeted with the knot and his temperature rose higher. It loosened as she walked over to the lounger. She finally dropped it, sat down, and crossed her legs. Minutes ticked by. She recrossed her legs.

'Stop fidgeting.'

She blew out a sigh. 'I can't stand the tension.'

'Well, running away won't make it go away.'

'I wasn't planning to run,' she replied. 'You wanted to talk about wines, remember?'

He nodded, although he'd lost interest in that subject. Forcing himself to look away from the temptation of the small waist that flared into very feminine hips and long, shapely legs, he stared at the moon rising over the water.

'Or I could easily return to my cabin and we can continue to treat each other like strangers.'

He considered the idea for exactly two seconds before he tossed it.

'What the hell, Ruby *mio*, let's give civility a try.'

She exhaled, sat up and poured a glass of mineral water from the jug nearby. 'Okay, first, I have to ask—what the heck is up with your name, anyway?'

He smiled despite the poker-sharp pain in his gut. 'You don't like it?'

'It's…different.'

'It was Giacomo's idea of a joke. But I've grown into it, don't you think?' Despite his joviality, the pain in his chest grew. Her eyes stayed on him and he saw when she noticed it. For some reason, revealing himself in that way didn't disturb him as much as he'd thought it would. In fact, talking to her soothed him.

'You've never wanted to change it?'

'It's just a name. I'm sure a few people will agree I can be narcissistic on occasion. I have no problems in pleasing number one.'

Her eyes gleamed with speculative interest. 'It really doesn't bother you, does it?'

'It may have, once upon a time,' he confessed. 'But not any more.'

Sympathy filled her eyes. 'I'm sorry.'

He tried to speak but words locked in his throat. Two simple words. Powerful words that calmed his roiling emotions. *'Grazie,'* he murmured.

His eyes caught and held hers. Something shifted, settled between them. An acknowledgement that neither of them were whole or without a history of buried hurt.

'The email on the plane. What was that about?' he asked abruptly.

She slowly inhaled. 'Before I tell you, promise me it won't

affect the outcome of this test run.' Her imploring look almost made him reply in the affirmative.

He hardened his resolve when he realised she was doing it again. Getting under his skin. Making a nonsense of his common sense.

'Sorry, *amante,* I don't make blind promises when it comes to business.'

Her lips firmed. 'Simon sold his share of the business to a guy who doesn't see eye to eye with my business plan.' In low tones, she elaborated.

He jerked upright. 'You're being threatened by a loan shark?'

'Yes.'

'And you didn't think to inform me?' he demanded.

'Would you have believed me? Especially in light of how I approached you?'

'Perhaps not right then, but...' The idea that he was prepared to give her the benefit of the doubt gave him a moment's pause. 'What's his name?'

'I don't know—he refused to tell me. All he wants is his money.'

'So I own twenty-five per cent of your business and a loan shark whose name you don't know another twenty-five per cent?'

'Yes.'

He slowly relaxed on his lounger and stared at her. 'You do realise that our agreement is transforming into substantially more than a talent-contest-prize delivery, don't you?'

A flush warmed her skin. 'I'm not sure I know what you mean.'

'What I mean, Ruby *mio,* is that in order to realise my twenty-five-per-cent investment, it seems I have to offer my business expertise. Writing you a cheque after next week and walking away is looking less and less likely.'

Why that thought pleased him so much, Narciso refused to examine.

CHAPTER EIGHT

'I DON'T REMEMBER the last time I sunbathed.'

'I can tell.'

Blue eyes glared at him and his pulse rocketed. Narciso tried to talk himself calmer. No one else was to blame since *he'd* invited her to go scuba-diving with him. *After* another sleepless night battling unrelenting sexual frustration.

'How can you tell? And don't tell me it's because you're a warlock.'

'I don't need otherworldly powers, *cara*. Your skin is so pale it's almost translucent and there are no visible tan lines.'

She glanced down at herself. 'Oh.'

'Here.' He grabbed the sun protection, started to move towards her, changed his mind at the last minute and tossed it to her.

'Thanks.' She sat on the same lounger as last night. But this time, the smell of her skin and the drying sea water made his blood heat.

'Where did you learn to dive?' he asked to distract himself from following the slim fingers that worked their way up her leg.

She smiled. 'I spent a few summers working at a hotel in Florida when I was in high school. I worked in the kitchens and got to dive in my spare time.'

'Have you always known you wanted to be a chef?'

Her smile immediately dimmed and he cursed himself for broaching a touchy subject.

'I knew I had my parents' talent but I resisted it for a long time.'

'I've seen the footage of the contest. You're not a natural in front of the camera.'

One brow rose. 'Gee, thanks.'

'What I mean is, you can easily prove to your parents that they're wasting their time trying to recruit you.'

'It won't stop them from trying.'

He shrugged. 'Then tell them you have a demanding new business partner.'

She shook her head. 'I'd rather not.'

'You want to keep me your dirty little secret, *tesoro?*'

She smiled but the light in her eyes remained dim. 'Something like that. What about you? Have you always known you wanted to be a warlock?'

He laughed, experiencing a new lightness inside. When her lips curved in response, he forcibly clenched his hands to stop from reaching for her. 'Ever since I made my first million at eighteen.'

'Wow, that must have brought the girls running.'

He shrugged, suddenly reluctant to dwell on past conquests. 'It gave me the ammunition I needed…'

She frowned slightly. 'Ammunition. To fight your father?'

'To fight Giacomo, yes.'

'Why do you call him Giacomo?'

He exhaled. 'Because he was never a *father* to me.'

She paused and that soft look entered her eyes. The realisation that he didn't mind talking to her about his past shocked him. He tried to tell himself it meant nothing, but he knew he was deluding himself.

'What about your mother? Is she alive?'

Sharp pain pierced his chest. 'My poor mama is what started this whole nasty business.'

'What do you mean?'

'She died giving birth to me. I was so determined to make

a quick entrance into the world, I caused her to bleed almost to death by the roadside before an ambulance could arrive.'

Her gasp echoed around the sun-dappled deck. 'Surely, you don't think that's your fault?'

'Giacomo certainly seems to think so.'

It occurred to him that Ruby was the first woman he'd actively conversed with. Normally, any conversation was limited to the bedroom. But with sex off the table it seemed *talking* was the next best thing.

'That's why there's so much animosity between you two. He blames you for your mother's death?'

'It may have started out that way, but our *relationship* has evolved…mutated.'

'Into what?'

He started to answer then stopped. 'Into something that's no longer clear-cut.' Shock rolled through him as he accepted the truth. He'd started out wanting to destroy his father. Along the way, and especially lately, the urge to deliver the kill blow had waned. Even toying with his father now no longer held any interest for him.

'So what are you going to do about it?'

Sì, what was he going to do?

Call it a day and cut off all ties with Giacomo? The sudden ache in his gut made him stiffen and jerk upright.

'Enough about me. You have an exceptional talent. I'm officially hiring you to cater my dinner party.'

The compliment brought a smile to her lips. Again, he forced himself not to reach out and caress the satin smoothness of her determined jaw. The urge was stronger because he needed something to blot out his confused thoughts of his father.

'Thank you.' She put the sun protection down and glanced at him. 'Can I get you anything?'

He shook his head. 'No more cocktails.'

Her smile widened. 'Then I have the perfect thing.'

She stood and walked to the chiller behind the bar. To his

surprise she returned with an ice-cold beer. 'Sometimes a beer is the perfect solution to thirst.'

Narciso twisted off the cap with relish and took a long swig, and looked over to find her eyes on his throat. The feel of her eyes on him made his temperature shoot sky-high.

'Aren't you having a drink?'

She indicated the glass of water on the table next to her lounger.

'That must be warm by now.'

Wordlessly, he held out the bottle to her. Her eyes met his and sensation skated over him. Their attraction was skittering out of control but he couldn't seem to apply the brakes.

'You're thirsty. Take it.'

Slowly, she took the bottle from him. Her pink tongue darted out to caress the lip of the bottle before she took a small swig.

She held it back out to him. 'Thanks.'

'So beers are an exception to your don't-drink-much rules?'

'A small drink doesn't hurt.'

'Aren't you afraid you'll lose control with me?' he asked roughly.

'We established that anything between us would be a mistake, remember?'

He stepped deeper into quicksand, felt it close dangerously over him but still he didn't retreat.

Eyes on her, he took another swig of beer. 'Perhaps that no longer holds true.'

Her breath audibly hitched. 'Why? Tell me and I'll remind you when things threaten to get out of hand.'

He couldn't stop the laughter that rumbled from his chest. 'You mean as some form of shock therapy?'

'If it's what works for you.'

His gaze slid down her body. Skin made vibrant by the sun and the exertions of their dive this morning offered temptation so strong it was no wonder he could think straight.

'Don't worry, *tesoro,* I'll try and curb my uncontrollable urges.'

'I'm glad you can. I'm not so sure about myself,' she blurted.

For a moment, he thought his hearing was impaired. 'What did you just say?'

She shut her eyes and cursed as he'd only heard a true New Yorker curse. 'I feel as if I'm skidding close to the edge of my control where you're concerned. After Simon—'

'I am *not* Simon,' he grated out.

She trembled. 'Believe me, I know. But even though I keep telling myself what a bad idea this is, I can't stop myself from… wanting you.'

The blunt delivery made his eyes widen. 'You realise how much power you're giving me by telling me?'

'Yes. But I'm hoping you won't take undue advantage of it.'

Slowly, he set the bottle down. 'Come here.'

'Did I not just mention undue advantage?'

'Come here and we'll see if the advantage is undue or not.'

Ruby stood slowly and stepped towards him, fighting for a clear breath as he loomed large, powerful and excruciatingly addictive before her. Her skin burned where he cradled her hips in his palms.

'What do you want, Ruby?' he rasped.

She looked into his face and every self-preservation instinct fled.

She'd never met a man like Narciso Valentino before. Everything she'd found out about him in the last few days had blown her expectations of him sky-high.

His name might indicate self-absorption but she was learning he was anything but. He could've reported her to Zeus when he'd found out she'd applied to be a *Petit Q* under false pretences. He could've sent her packing after she told him about his company owing her. Stopping himself from seducing her and his generosity with the clothes coupled with his easy companionship this morning as they'd scuba-dived at one of the most beautiful places in the world had shown her that Narciso could be nothing like his name.

Little by little, the traits she'd discovered had whittled at her defences.

And now…

'As crazy and stupid as it is, I want to kiss you more than I want to breathe.'

Dear God, what was wrong with her?

'*Dio mio.*' He sounded strained…disarmed, as if she'd knocked his feet from under him.

She ought to pull back, retreat to the safety of her cabin. Instead, she took his face in her hands, leaned forward and kissed him.

His grunt of desire slammed into her before he seized her arms. Leaning back against the lounger, he tugged her on top of him. Strong arms imprisoned her as he moulded her body to his.

The evidence of arousal against her belly was unmistakable, gave her strength she hadn't known existed. She plunged her tongue into his mouth, felt the stab of pleasure when he jerked beneath her and groaned long and deep.

Firm hands angled her head for a deeper penetration that made her pulse thud a hundred times faster.

He made love to her with his mouth, lapping at her lips with long strokes that pulled at the hot, demanding place between her legs.

Her hands hungrily explored his warm, firm muscle and hair-roughened chest. When her fingers encountered his nipple, she grazed her nail against it, the way she knew drove him mad.

He tore his mouth from hers, his eyes molten grey as he gazed up at her.

'*Cara mia,* this will not end well for either of us if you don't stop that.'

Brazenly, she repeated the action. And watched in fascination as it puckered and goose bumps rose around the hard disc. Before she could give in to the urge to taste it, Narciso was moving her higher, stark purpose on his face.

'One bad turn deserves another.' Roughly, he tugged at her

bikini string and caught one plump breast in his mouth as they were freed from the garment.

The sight of him feasting on her in the dimming light was so erotic, Ruby's nails dug into his chest.

Her hips bucked against his hardness, that hunger climbing even higher as she rubbed against his full, heavy thickness. The thought of having that power inside her made her whimper. When his teeth tugged at her in response, her moan turned into a cry.

Foolish or not, dangerous or not, she wanted him. More than she'd ever wanted anything in her life. For the first time, Ruby understood a little bit of the passion that drove her parents. Of the need that forced two people wholly unsuited to stay together. If it was anywhere near this addictive, this mad, she could almost sympathise…

'Narciso…please…'

One hand splayed over her bottom, squeezed before grabbing the stretchy material of her bikini. He pulled, sending a million stars bursting behind her closed eyelids as the pressure on her heated clitoris intensified her pleasure. At her shocked gasp, he pulled tighter. Liquid heat rushed to fill her sensitive flesh. Almost immediately, she needed more, so much more that her body was threatening to burst out of her skin. She sank her hands into his hair and bit down on the rough skin of his jaw.

He cursed and froze, hard fingers gripping her hips. When the sensation slid from pleasure to a hint of pain, she lifted her head to gaze drowsily at him.

'What…?'

'Before this goes any further I need to be sure you want this,' he rasped.

She looked down, saw her state of undress, saw his hard, ready body.

Instinctively she went to adjust her clothes, her face flushing with heat. 'God, what's wrong with me?'

He stopped her agitated movements with steady hands. 'Hey,

there's *nothing* wrong with you. You're a sensual creature, with natural needs just like—'

'My father?' she inserted bleakly.

Surprisingly gentle hands framed her face. 'If you were like him you wouldn't still be a virgin. Do you get that?'

Tears prickled her eyes. 'But…I…'

'No, no more excuses. You stopped being their puppet a long time ago—you just forgot to cut the strings.'

Her breath stalled and her vision blurred. He brushed away her tears and she fought to speak. 'What does that say about me?'

His jaw clenched. 'That we sometimes spend too much time looking in the rear-view mirror to see what's ahead.'

She moved on top of him because, despite everything going south, her hunger hadn't abated one iota. His hands clamped down harder on her hips.

'What's in your rear-view mirror?' she asked him softly.

'Too much. Much too much.'

His answer held a depth of anguish that cut to her soul. Heart aching for him, she started to lean down but he caught and held her still.

'No.'

She looked into his face and saw his slightly ashen pallor. 'You don't want me to kiss you?'

His chest heaved and he glanced away.

The realisation hit her like a bolt of lightning. 'You stopped us making love on the plane and just now because you don't think you're worth it, do you? Why not? Because your father told you you weren't?'

'Ruby, stop,' he warned.

She ignored him, the need to offer comfort bleeding through her. She caressed his taut cheek. A pulse beat so hard in his jaw, her fingers tingled from the contact.

'*Cara,* I'm a man on the edge. A man who wants what he shouldn't have. Get off me before I do something we'll both regret, *per favore.*'

Fresh tears prickled her eyes, stung the back of her throat.

If anyone had told her a week ago she'd be lying on top of the world's most notorious playboy, baring her soul to him and catching a glimpse of his ragged soul in return, she'd have called them insane.

Her hands shook as she slowly removed them from his face. Levering herself away from him was equally hard because her knees rebelled at supporting her in her weakened state.

Snatching at her bikini top, desperately trying to ignore his silent scrutiny, she tied the strings as best she could and secured the sarong over her chest.

Her hair was an unruly mess she didn't bother to tackle. What had just happened had gone beyond outer appearances.

She looked down at him and he returned her look, the torture unveiled now. She floundered, torn between helping him and fleeing to examine her own confused emotions. Eventually, she chose the latter. 'I have a few things to take care of in the kitchen before I go to bed. *Bona notti.*'

Slowly, he rose to tower over her, and in the fading daylight she saw his bunched fists at his sides.

His smile was cut from rough stone. 'I've awakened too many demons for me to have a restful night, *tesoro*. But I wish you a good night all the same.'

I've awakened too many demons...

Ruby lay in bed a few hours later, wracked with guilt.

She'd pushed him to relive his past, to rake over old wounds because she'd wanted to know the real man underneath the gloss.

To reassure herself he wouldn't hurt or betray her?

Shame coiled through her as she acknowledged that she'd been testing him. But then deep down, ever since he'd turned away from her on the plane, she'd known Narciso was nothing like her father. Or Simon.

And still she'd pushed...

She reared up and gripped the side of her bed. Her head

cautioned her against the need to find out if she'd pushed him too far, if the demons were indeed keeping him awake. But her heart propelled her to her feet.

She went down the hallway and knocked on his door before her courage deserted her.

The evidence that he was indeed up came a second later when the door was wrenched open. He was dressed in his silk pajama bottoms and nothing else.

'What the hell are you doing here, Ruby?' he flung at her.

She struggled to look up from his chest. 'I…wanted to make sure you were okay. And to apologise for what happened earlier. I had no right to push you like that.'

His eyes narrowed for several seconds before he turned and strode back into the bedroom. 'I'm learning that warlocks and demons keep good company.' He picked up a crystal tumbler of Scotch, raised it to her and took a sip.

Ruby found herself moving forward before she'd consciously made the decision to.

Her hand closed over the glass and stopped his second sip.

He stepped back away from her but, hampered by the bed, he abruptly sank down. She took the glass from him and set it on the side table.

'Drinking is not the answer. Trust me, I know.'

Strong hands gripped the sheets as if physically stopping himself from reaching for her and he exhaled harshly.

This close, the beauty of him took her breath away. His chest heaved again, the movement emphasising his stunning physique and golden skin.

Fiery desire slammed into her so hard she reeled under the onslaught.

Before she could stop to question herself, she slid her hands over his biceps. Warm muscles rippled under her touch.

'What the hell are you doing?' His voice was rough and gritty with need.

Her face flamed but a deeper fire of determination burned

within her. 'I have a feeling it's called seduction. I don't know because I've never done this before.'

She leaned in closer. He groaned as her hardened T-shirt-covered nipples grazed his chest. *'Per amore di Dio,* why are you doing it now?'

She placed a finger over his lip and felt a tiny jolt of triumph when it puckered slightly against her touch. 'Because it's driving me as insane. And because I don't want to live in fear of what I might become if I let go. So this is me owning my fear.'

He cursed again and he shook his head. Knowing he was about to deny her, she pushed him onto the bed and sealed her mouth over his.

He groaned and accepted her kiss with a demanding roughness that threatened to blow her away. Encouraged by that almost helpless response, she threw one leg over him and straddled his big body.

Immediately, his already potent arousal thickened, lengthened, found the cradle between her legs. Before she lost her mind completely, Ruby reached out to both sides of the bed and loosened the ties she needed, then she worked quickly before he could stop her.

He wrenched his mouth from hers, and glanced up. Silver eyes darkening in shock, then disbelief. *'Hai perso la tua mente?'*

'No, I haven't lost my mind.'

'Clearly, you have.' He yanked on the binds but they only tightened further. 'Release me, Ruby.'

'Nope. What goes around comes around, *tesoro.'*

Feeling a little bit bolder now she knew he wouldn't easily overpower her or dismiss her, she took a deep breath, drew her T-shirt over her head and flung it away.

'Ruby…' Warning tinged his low growl.

She wavered but the look in his eyes stalled her breath—hunger, anger, a touch of admiration, that little bit of wonder and vulnerability she'd seen earlier on the deck all mingled in his hypnotic eyes.

'I would, but the look in your eyes is scaring me right now. What's to say you won't devour me the minute I set you free?' She trailed a finger down his chest and revelled in his hitched breathing.

'I won't,' he bit out.

She shivered again at the menace in his voice. 'Liar, liar.'

'*Madre di Dio,* do you really want to lose your virginity so badly?'

She shook her head and her hair came free from the loose knot she'd put it into. 'No, it isn't actually that important to me. What I want, what I crave, is to make love with you.'

His eyes darkened. 'Why?'

She tamped down on what she really wanted to say. That he'd shown her another way to view herself. Another way that didn't make her skin crawl for feeling sensual pleasure.

'Do I have to have some noble reason? Isn't crazy chemistry enough? I was absolutely fine before you touched me. You woke this hunger inside me. Now because of some stupid principle, you're trying to deny me what I want. What we both want. I won't let you.'

His chest heaved. 'I won't let you either. Not like this.' The roughness in his tone gave her pause. When she looked into his eyes, that bleakness she'd spotted in the kitchen on their first morning in Macau was back. 'If you want me, release me.'

She wanted to kiss that look away, to utterly and totally eradicate it so it never returned. Leaning down, she did exactly that, luxuriating in the velvety feel of his warm lips. He kissed her back but she could sense the agitation clawing under his skin and she drew back a little. Caressing his chest and shoulders, she touched her lips to his again in a gentle offer of solace from whatever demons were eating him alive.

A rough sigh rumbled from his chest.

'Narciso…'

His lips trembled against hers. 'Release me, Ruby.'

Heart in her throat, she repeated the words he'd said to her in Macau. 'I already have.'

Shocked eyes darted upward. A split second later he was flipping her beneath him, ripping away her panties and flinging them over his shoulder.

Molten eyes speared her as he tugged off his pyjamas, his gaze settling possessively on her damp, exposed sex. 'Sorry, Ruby *mio,* I lied.'

'About what?' Her voice trembled.

'About not devouring you.'

Hot, sensual lips grazed down her cleavage to her navel, the rasp of his growing stubble sending electrifying tingles racing through her body. His tongue circled her navel, then strong teeth bit the skin just below.

Her shudder threatened to lift her off the bed.

One large hand splayed on her stomach and the other parted her legs wider. Watching him watch her was the most erotic experience of her life so far.

She didn't need a crystal ball to know there was more, so much more in store for her.

He bypassed her most sensitive place, lifted one leg to bend it at the knee. Hot kisses trailed down her inside thigh. Again the graze of his stubble added a rough, pleasurable edge that made her breath come out in agitated gasps.

Nibbling his way down, he soothed his bites with open-mouthed kisses that sparked a yearning for that mouth at her core.

But he took his time. Leisurely, he kissed his way down her other thigh, all the while widening her thighs, those molten eyes not leaving her heated sex.

Ruby wondered why she wasn't dying with embarrassment. But seeing the effect the sight of her had on him—nostrils flared as he breathed her in, his fingers trembling slightly as he gripped her knee—she had little room for anything but desire.

'Lei è sfarzoso,' he muttered thickly.

She *felt* gorgeous, a million miles from what she'd always feared she would feel when it came to sex. She blinked back tears and cried out as sublime pleasure roared through her.

Lips, tongue, teeth. True to his words Narciso devoured her with a singular, greedy purpose.

From far away, she heard her cries of ecstasy, smelled the heat of his skin coupled with the scent of her arousal as she writhed with bliss beneath him.

Just when she thought she would burst out of her skin, he raised his head.

'I'd had this thought in my head that the first time I took you I'd torture you for hours with pleasure.' Still holding her down, he pulled open the beside drawer and grabbed a condom. Impatiently, he ripped it open with his teeth. 'But I can't wait one more second, *amante*.'

'I don't want you to.'

Hooded eyes regarded her. 'I can't promise it will be gentle. I could hurt you.'

The slight note of apprehension washed away when she recalled what had happened on the deck earlier this evening. Despite the volatile emotions that had raged between them, he'd never hurt her.

She laid her hand over the one he'd flattened on her belly. 'I'm ready.'

He leaned back and she saw him, really saw him for the first time. The erection that sprang from his groin was powerful and proud. Another testament to how well his name suited him. Judging from the size of him, he had a lot to crow about in that department, too.

Holding himself in one fist, he rolled on the condom and settled stormy eyes on her. 'Are you sure about this?' he rasped.

'Right this moment, my confidence is wavering a little,' she confessed, her voice shaky with the knowledge that he would soon be inside her.

He inhaled deeply. 'I promise to go as fast or as slow as you desire,' he said in a deep solemn voice.

Unable to speak, Ruby nodded. In a slow, predatory crawl he surged over her. Dark hair fell over his forehead in that careless way she found irresistible. She had a second to weave her fingers through it before he was kissing her again.

By the time he lifted his head hers was swimming. The flush that scoured his cheekbones signalled his fast-slipping control. His erection pulsed against her thigh and the very air crackled with sensual expectation so thick, all her confidence from minutes ago oozed out of her like air from a balloon.

'What do I do now?'

He glanced down to where her hunger raged, to the glistening entrance to her body. 'Open wider for me,' he breathed.

Every single atom in her body poised with tingling expectation as she complied with his command and spread her thighs wider. 'Now what?'

Silver eyes returned to hers. 'Now…you breathe, Ruby *mio*.' He took her lips in a quick, hard kiss. 'This will be no fun at all if you pass out.'

Reeling from the sensation coursing through her, she sucked air through her mouth.

'That's it. Eyes on me and don't move,' he instructed.

The first push inside her threatened to expel the air she'd fed her starving lungs. From head to toe, Ruby was soaked in indescribable sensation.

'Oh!' She breathed out again, her hands tightening on his shoulders as her craving escalated. 'More.'

He shut his eyes for a split second, then he pushed in further, carefully gauging her reaction as he deepened the penetration.

The need clawing through her sharpened, deepened. Unable to lie still, she twisted upward to meet him.

'*Dio!* Don't do that.'

'But I like it.' She twisted higher, then gave a cry as pain ripped through her pelvis.

'*Per amore di…* I told you not to move.' His lips were tension-white and sweat beaded his forehead.

He started to withdraw but the pain was already fading. Quickly she clamped her legs around his waist.

'No.' He levered his arms on either side of her in preparation to remove himself from her body. The knowledge that he was holding himself back so forcefully sent a different sensation through her.

Her hand trailed up his throat to clutch his nape, holding him prisoner. 'Yes.'

Tightening her grip, she forced her hips up. He slid deeper to fully embed himself within her and she cried out in pleasure.

'Ruby…'

'Make love to me, Narciso,' she pleaded, because she knew that whatever she was feeling right now, there was so much more to come. 'Please.'

With a groan, he sealed his body fully with hers.

Sizzling pleasure raced up her spine as he set a thrusting rhythm designed to drive her out of her mind. Considering she was already halfway there, it didn't take long before Ruby stopped breathing again, poised on the edge of some unknown precipice that beckoned with seductive sorcery.

Against her lips, Narciso murmured thick, hot words in native Sicilian. Those that she understood would've made her blush if her whole body wasn't already burning from the fierce power of his possession.

His lips grazed along her jaw, down her throat to enslave one nipple in his mouth. His tongue lapped her in rhythm with his thrusts, adding another dimension to the sensations flowing through her.

One hand hooked under her thigh, spreading her even wider. He groaned at the altered angle just as she began to fracture.

He raised his head from her breast and locked his gaze on hers. The connection, deep, hot and direct, was the final straw.

Convulsions tore through her, rocking her from head to toe with indescribable bliss that wrenched a scream from the depths of her soul.

Lost in the maelstrom of ecstasy, she heard him groan deeply before long shudders seized his frame.

His damp forehead touched hers, then his head found the

curve of her shoulder. Hot, agitated breaths bathed her neck as his heartbeat thundered in tandem with hers.

In that moment, she experienced a closeness she'd never experienced with another human being. She told herself it was a false sensation but still she basked in it, unable to stop the giddy, happy feeling washing over her. Her arms tightened around him and she would gladly have stayed there for ever but he moved, turning sideways to lie on the bed.

'I don't want to crush you.' His voice was thick, almost gruff.

'Don't worry, I'm stronger than I look.'

He half growled. 'I guessed as much earlier. Where did you learn to make ties like that?'

'Tying up chickens and turkeys for roasting.'

He grimaced. 'I'm flattered.'

'Don't worry, Narciso. I'll never mistake you for a chicken.'

His laughter caused her heart to soar, the simple pleasure of making him laugh lifting her spirits.

Resting her chin on his chest, she looked into his eyes. *'Grazie.'*

He caught a curl and twisted it around his finger. *'Per quello che?'*

'For making my first so memorable.'

'It was a first for me, too, after a fashion.'

A thousand questions smashed through her brain but she forced herself to push them away. 'Hmm, I guess it was.'

They lay in replete silence for several more minutes. And then the atmosphere began to change.

She started to move but his arm tightened around her. A deep swallow moved his Adam's apple.

'Tomorrow, we'll talk properly, *sì?*'

Heart in her throat, she nodded. *'Sì.'*

'Good. Now I get to show you my favourite knot.'

CHAPTER NINE

'*Ciao.*'

The deep voice roused her from languor and she opened her eyes to find Narciso standing over her lounger, cell phone in one hand.

The midmorning sun blazed on the private deck outside his bedroom suite and Ruby squirmed under his gaze as it raked her.

'*Ciao.* I can't believe I let you convince me to sunbathe nude.'

'Not completely nude.' He eyed her bikini bottoms.

Heat crawled up her neck and she hurriedly changed the subject. 'Was your call successful?'

'*Sì,* but then all my negotiations are,' he said with a smug smile.

'Your modesty is so refreshing. I guess making a million dollars by age eighteen tends to go to one's head.'

'On the contrary, my head was very clear. I had only one goal in mind.'

Despite the sun's blaze, she shivered. 'So it started that long ago, this feud between you two?'

He tossed his phone onto the table and stretched out on the lounger next to hers. Ruby fought not to ogle the broad, firm expanse of skin she'd taken delight in exploring last night. The grim look on his face helped her resist the temptation.

'Believe it or not, there was a time when I toyed with the idea of abandoning it.'

Surprise scythed through her. 'Really?'

'*Sì,*' he replied, almost inaudibly.

'What happened?'

'I graduated from Harvard a year early and decided to spend my gap year in Sicily. I knew Giacomo would be there. And I knew he couldn't throw me out because the house he lived in belonged to my mother and she'd willed it to me when I turned eighteen. I…hoped that being under the same roof again for the first time in five years would give us a different perspective.'

'It didn't?'

The hand on his thigh slowly curled into a fist. 'No. We clashed harder than ever.'

She couldn't mistake the ragged edge in his voice. 'If he hated you being there so much, why didn't he leave?'

'That would've meant I'd won. Besides, he took pleasure in reminding me I'd killed my mother on the street right outside her home.'

Ice drenched her veins. 'What happened to her?'

'She suffered a placental abruption three weeks before I was due. She'd gone for a walk and was returning home. By the time she dragged herself up the road to the house to alert anyone, she'd lost too much blood. Apparently, the doctor said he could only save one of us. Giacomo asked him to save my mother. She died anyway. I survived.'

Ruby reached out and covered his fist with her hand. He tensed for a second, then his hand wrapped around hers.

'How can anyone in their right mind believe that something so tragic was your fault?'

'Giacomo believed it. That was enough. And he was right to demand that the doctor save my mother.'

She flinched. 'How can you say that?'

'Because he knew what I would become.'

'A wildly successful businessman who donates millions of dollars each year to fund neo-natal research among other charitable organisations?'

He jerked in surprise. 'How do you know that?'

A blush crept up her cheeks. 'When I did a web search on you a few things popped up.'

He shrugged. 'My accountants tell me funding charities is a good way to get tax breaks. Don't read more into the situation than there is, *amante*.'

Lowering her gaze, she watched their meshed fingers. The feel of his skin against hers made her heart skip several beats. 'I think we're past the point where you can convince me you're all bad, Narciso,' she dared.

He remained silent for so long she thought he'd refused to pick up the thread of their conversation. Then his breath shuddered out. 'Giacomo believes that.'

'Because you perpetuate that image?'

His smile was grim but it held speculation. 'Perhaps, but it's an image I'm growing tired of.'

Her breath caught.

His eyes met hers and he reached across and took her hand. 'Does that surprise you? That I'm thinking it's time to end this vendetta?'

'Why the change of heart?' she asked.

His casual shrug looked a little stiff. 'Perhaps it's time to force another mutation of our relationship,' he said obliquely.

'And if it fails?'

His eyes darkened before his lashes swept down to veil his expression. 'I'm very good at adapting, *amante*.' He stood up abruptly and pulled her up. 'Time for a shower.'

She waited until they were both naked in the bedroom before she spoke.

'All that with Giacomo. I'm sorry it happened to you.'

His nostrils flared as bleakness washed over his face. Then slowly, he reasserted control.

Intense silver eyes travelled over her, lingering on her bare breasts with fierce hunger that made her nipples pucker. 'Don't be. Our feud brought me to Macau. Macau brought you to me. I call that a win-win situation, *amante*.'

He lunged up and grabbed her. Swinging her up in his arms, he crossed the suite and entered the adjoining bathroom.

'Wait, we haven't finished talking.'

'*Sì*, we have. I've revealed more of my past to you than to any other living soul. If I'm The Warlock you should be re-named The Sorceress.'

Demanding hands reached for her, propelled her backwards into the warm shower he'd turned on.

'But I don't know you nearly enough.'

He yanked the shower head from its cradle and aimed the nozzle in the curve of her neck. Water set to the perfect temperature soothed her and she allowed her mind to slide free of the questions that raced through her thoughts.

Understanding the boy he'd been, caught in the hell of a father who hated the very sight of him, Ruby found it wasn't a stretch to understand why he'd closed himself off.

But she'd seen beneath the façade, knew the playboy persona was just a defence mechanism. His relationship with Giacomo meant more to him than he was willing to admit.

As if reading her thoughts, he sent her a narrow-eyed glare. 'Don't try and *understand* me, Ruby. You may not like what you discover.'

'What's that supposed to mean?'

His eyes met hers and she glimpsed the dark river of anguish. 'It means there may never be enough underneath the surface to be worth your time.'

'Shouldn't I be the judge of that?'

He stepped forward and aimed the shower right between her thighs. Ruby gasped as sensation weakened her knees. She reached out for something to steady her and got a handful of warm, vibrant flesh. He angled the showerhead and she let out a strangled moan.

'No. This conversation is over, *amante*,' he growled. 'Now, open wider for me.'

Despite his clipped words of warning and the blatantly sexual way he chose to end their conversation, Narciso proceeded to wash her with an almost worshipful gentleness that undid her. When he sank down in front of her and washed between her legs, tears prickled her eyes.

Hell, she was losing her mind. Right from the beginning, she'd primed herself to hate this skilled playboy for his shallow feelings and careless attitude towards women and sex.

Instead she'd discovered that beneath the glossy veneer lurked a wounded soul, hurting from a tortured past.

She wanted to touch him the way he'd touched her. She reached out, but he grasped her hand in his, surged upright and set the showerhead back in its cradle. Beside the expensive gels and lotions a stack of condoms rested. Her heart lurched as she saw him reach for one and tear it open.

Grasping her waist, he whirled her around, then meshed his fingers through hers before raising them to rest above her head.

'*This* is the only conversation I want to continue. Are you ready?' he rasped low in her ear.

His thickness pressed against her bottom. Recalling the pleasure she'd experienced before, she could no more stop herself from answering in the affirmative than she could stop herself from breathing.

He slid slowly into her, leaving her ample time to adjust to his size. Pleasure shot through her, imprisoning her in its merciless talons.

Her groan mingled with his as steam rose around and engulfed them in a cocoon of rough kisses and wet bodies.

Narciso let pleasure wash over him, erasing, if only temporarily, the cutting pain of the past rehashed. The raw agony of recollection eased as he surged deeper into her and, even though he refused to acknowledge that her touch, her warmth and soft words eased his pain, he hung on to the feel of being in her arms.

She rewarded him by crying out as her muscles tightened around him.

Dio mio, she was unbelievable! And she'd got under his skin with minimum effort. But he'd get his control back.

He had to.

Because this unravelling, as much as it soothed the deep wound in his heart, couldn't continue. For now, though, he intended to lose his mind in the most spectacular way. He slid his hands down her sides, glorying in her supple wet skin. Encircling her tiny waist, he threw his head back and let desire roar through his body.

She woke to a silent room and a half-cold bed.

Ruby didn't need a crystal ball to know regret played a part in Narciso's absence. She felt equally exposed and vulnerable in the light of day at how they'd bared their pasts to each other.

But as much as she wanted to stay hidden beneath the covers, she forced herself to leave Narciso's bed. Shoving her hand through her hair, she picked up the T-shirt she'd brazenly discarded during her seduction routine. Her ripped-beyond-redemption panties she quickly balled up in her fist.

Luckily, she met no one on the way to her own cabin.

Ten minutes later, and freshly showered, she dressed in white shorts and a sea-green sleeveless top, and opened her door to find a steward waiting outside.

'Mr Valentino would like you to join him for breakfast on the first deck.'

Her pulse raced as trepidation filled her.

Yesterday morning hadn't really counted as *the morning after* because after their shower they'd returned to bed and spent the rest of the day making love.

She entered the salon that led to the sun-dappled dining space on the deck.

Fresh croissants, coffee, juices and two domed dishes had been neatly laid out. But her attention riveted on the man flicking his finger across his electronic tablet.

'Morning,' she said, her voice husky.

His gaze rose and caught hers. 'Feeling rested?'

She managed a nod and glanced around. 'Where are we?' The day before they'd moored at the Bay of Placencia after leaving the spectacular Blue Hole.

'We're just coming into Nicholas Caye. Mexico is just north of us.'

'It's beautiful here,' she said, nerves eating her alive at the intense look in his eyes.

'Sit down and relax, Ruby. It will be hard but I can just about stop myself from jumping on you and devouring you for breakfast.'

Heat shot into her cheeks. 'That wasn't what I was thinking,' she blurted, then pursed her lips and pulled out a chair.

Lifting the dome, she found her favourite breakfast laid out in exquisite presentation. Along with her preferred spear of asparagus. 'You made me Eggs Benedict?' Why the hell was her throat clogged by that revelation?

'I didn't make it myself, *tesoro*. I'm quite useless in the kitchen.'

But he'd taken note somewhere along the way that this was her favourite breakfast meal. 'I… Thank you.'

He snapped shut his tablet, shook out his napkin and laid it over his lap. 'Don't read anything into it, Ruby.'

'You keep saying that. And yet you can't seem to help yourself with your actions.'

He picked up his cutlery. 'I must be losing my edge,' he muttered.

'Or maybe you're rediscovering your human side?'

He smiled mockingly. 'Now I sound like a reformed comic villain.'

'No, that would require a lot of spandex,' she quipped before taking a bite of the perfectly cooked eggs.

He laughed, the sound rich and deep. Ruby barely stopped the food from going down the wrong way when she glimpsed the gorgeously carefree transformation of his face. 'You don't think I'd look good in spandex?' he asked drily.

'I think you'd look good in anything. And I also believe you can do anything you put your mind to.'

He tensed and slowly lowered his knife. 'Is there a hidden message in that statement?'

'No…maybe. This is my first morning-after conversation. I may say things that aren't thought through properly.'

Her gaze connected with his. An untold wealth of emotions swirled through his eyes and her stomach flipped her heart into her throat. 'Now you're selling yourself short. You're one of the most talented, intelligent people I know,' he delivered. 'And the waters are treacherous for me, too.'

'Really?' she whispered.

His lids lowered, breaking the connection. '*Sì*. I think we both know we're under each other's skin. It's up to us to decide what we do with that knowledge. What's your most prized ingredient?'

'The white Alba truffle, hands down,' she blurted, reeling at the abrupt question. 'Truffles make everything taste better.'

He slowly nodded. *'Bene.'* He said nothing else and resumed eating.

Ruby felt as if she'd fallen down the rabbit hole again. The conversation felt surreal. 'Why is that important?'

His jaw clenched slightly. 'I need a truffles day to make me feel better.'

'Why?'

'Because I can't wrap my mind around the things I spilled to you yesterday.'

'I didn't force anything out of you, Narciso.'

'Which makes it even more puzzling. So I need a minute and you're going to give it to me,' he stated blatantly.

'How?'

'We're going to spend the day together. And you're going to tell me every single thought that jumps into your head.'

Her brows rose. 'You want to use me to drown out your thoughts? You realise how unhealthy that sounds, right?'

His grimace was pained. 'Yes, I do, but I'll suffer through it this once in the hope I emerge unscathed.'

'And if you don't?'

Silver eyes darkened as they swept over her. The message in

them when they locked on her lips punched heat into her belly.
'Then I'll have to find a different solution.'

Six hours later, Narciso was wondering if he'd truly lost his
mind. Although he'd learned everything about Ruby from the
moment she'd learned to speak to the present she'd received
from her roommate, Annie, on her last birthday, he yearned
to know more.

Never had he taken even the remotest interest in a woman
besides her favourite restaurant and what pleased her in bed.
The fact that he wanted to know Ruby Trevelli's every thought
sent a shiver of apprehension down his spine.

He was unravelling faster than he could keep things under
control.

Every emotion he'd tried to lock down since that summer
in Sicily threatened to swamp him. He gritted his teeth and
watched Ruby surge out of the turquoise sea. She walked towards him, clad in the minuscule bikini he'd supplied her with.
Her body—supple, curvy and dripping with water—made his
mouth dry. When she dropped down next to him on the deserted beach they'd swum to, he burned with the need to reach
for her. *Dio,* with the amount of sex they'd had how could he
still be this hungry for her?

'So, is the inquisition over?' she asked playfully.

'*Sì,*' he growled. 'It's over.'

Her gaze darted to his and he saw her tense at the coolness
in his voice.

'Something wrong?'

'Why would anything be wrong?'

'Because you won the swim race from the yacht and you're
not crowing about it. And you're not firing questions at me
any more.'

'Perhaps I've had my fill for now.'

'Right. Okay,' she said.

He couldn't dismiss the hurt he heard in her voice. Turning,
he watched her slim fingers play with the sugary white sand

next to her feet. The desire to have those hands on his body grew until it became a physical pain.

Abruptly, he leaned forward and opened the gourmet picnic basket that had been delivered by his crew. He bypassed the food and reached for the chilled champagne. Popping the cork, he poured a glass and handed it to her.

'What are we celebrating?'

'The end of our beautiful down time. We leave for New York in the morning.'

Her eyes widened. Hell, he was more shocked than she was. His plan had been to stay for a full week. But the restlessness that had pounded through him all day wouldn't abate and he needed to find some perspective before it was too late.

At least once they returned to New York, back into the swing of things, everything would make sense again.

'You've asked my every thought for the last six hours. I think it's my turn now.'

He thought of sparing her the chaos running through his head. Then he mentally shrugged. 'I'm thinking why the thought of being free of you gives me no satisfaction.'

'Wow, you really know how to make a woman feel special, don't you?'

'I don't believe in sugar-coating words.'

'Please, spare me the macho stance. You know how to be gentle. What's going on here, Narciso? Why are you suddenly angry with me?'

He met her cloudy gaze and every thought disappeared but one. 'I'm finding how much I despise the thought of you ever taking another lover.'

Shocked blue eyes darted back to his. 'Narciso—'

'Now I've felt you shatter in my arms, the thought of you with another man makes my head want to explode.'

She gasped. 'Did you really just say that?'

He gave a harsh laugh and shook his head, as if testing his own sanity. '*Sì*, I just did.'

Beautifully curved eyebrows rose. 'And I'm guessing that's the first time you've admitted that to a woman?'

'It's the first time I've *felt* that way about any woman.' He shoved a hand through his hair.

Dio mio, he was like a leaking tap! Yesterday, he'd bared his past and his soul as if he were under the influence of a truth serum; today he was contemplating the future and the ache of not having Ruby Trevelli in it.

He knocked back the rest of his drink and surged to his feet. The crew member manning the launch a few dozen metres away looked his way and Narciso beckoned him over.

'It's time to go.' Reality and the cut and thrust of Wall Street would bring some much-needed common sense.

Unlike when they'd donned their swimming gear and laughingly dived from the side of the boat half an hour ago, silence reigned on the way back to *The Warlock.*

When he helped her up from the launch onto the floating swim deck at the back of the yacht, he forced himself to let her go, to stop his hands from lingering on her skin. As much as he wanted to touch her, weave his fingers through the damp hair curling over her shoulders, he couldn't give in to the spell threatening to pull him under.

'I have work to do. I'll catch up with you later.' With his insides twisting into seething knots, he walked away.

Ruby watched him walking away, a giant chasm opening up where pleasure had been half an hour ago. Things had been perfect. So much so, she'd pinched herself a couple of times to make sure the combination of sun, sea and drop-dead-gorgeous companion who'd laughed at her jokes and insisted on knowing every thought in her head was real.

She hadn't told him every thought, of course. For instance, she hadn't admitted that every time he'd touched her she'd heard angels sing to her soul. *That* would've been nuts. As would've been the admission that she was dying to make love with him again.

No chance of that now...

The hard-assed, enigmatic Narciso Valentino of three days ago hadn't made a comeback—and Ruby hoped against all hope the Narciso who chose to smother away his pain was gone for good—but a new Narciso had taken his place. One who fully recognised his vulnerabilities but then ignored them.

The need to go after him was so strong, she locked her knees and gripped the steel banister. He needed time.

Heck, *she* needed time to grapple with the mass of chaotic emotions coursing through her.

Scrambling for control, she went into her cabin and showered off the seawater. Clad in a long, flowered dress with a long slit down one side, she returned to the bar and lined bottles on the counter. Work would take her mind off her unsettling thoughts about Narciso Valentino.

She was measuring a shot of tequila into a shaker when one of the crew members approached.

'Can I get miss anything to eat?'

She shook her head. He smiled and turned to leave. 'Wait.' He paused. 'Have you seen my phone? I've been looking for it everywhere.'

He smiled. 'Oh, yes. One of my colleagues found it in the kitchen yesterday and handed it to Mr Valentino.'

Narciso had her phone? 'Thank you,' she murmured. She slowly screwed the top back on the bottle she'd opened and put the lemon wedges back in the cooler. Wiping her hands on a napkin, she left the deck.

His study was on the second level, past a large room with a sunken sitting area perfect for a dinner party. Like the rest of the vessel, every nook and cranny screamed bespoke and breathtaking luxury.

He growled admittance after her tense knock.

Seated in a leather armchair behind a large antique desk, he watched her enter with a frown. 'Is something wrong?'

'As long as you can adequately explain why you've commandeered my phone, no.'

'You're expecting a call?' he asked.

'Whether I am or not is beside the point.' She shut the door and approached his desk. 'You've had it since yesterday. Why didn't you hand it over?'

He shrugged. 'It must have slipped my mind.'

Somehow she doubted that. But watching him, seeing his face set in those stern, bleak lines she'd recognised from before made her heart stutter. She'd seen that look before.

She stepped closer, looked down and saw the pictures and papers strewn on his desk. The date stamp on the nearest one—showing that very morning—made ice slide down her spine. 'This is the business you had to take care of?'

He slowly set down the document in his hand. 'No. Believe it or not, I intended to scrap all this.'

'But?'

'But something came up.'

She glanced down at the photos. All depicted Giacomo. In one of them, the one Narciso had just dropped, he was dining with a stunning woman in her late twenties.

'Is that the *something?*' she asked, telling herself the pain lancing her chest wasn't jealousy.

His mouth tightened. 'We're not having this conversation, Ruby.'

'What happened to the man who was going to try to find a better way than this need to destroy and annihilate?'

His head tilted. 'That means the same thing.'

'Excuse me?'

'Destroy and annihilate—same meaning.'

'Really? That's all you have to contribute to this conversation?'

His jaw tightened. 'I told you I was good at adapting, *cara*. So why are you surprised that I'm adapting to the situation I find myself in? And seriously, screwing my brains out does not entitle you to weigh in on this.' He waved to his desk.

'Then why did you share it with me?' she replied.

For a moment he floundered. The clear vulnerability in his eyes made her breath catch. 'A misjudgment on my part.'

'I don't believe you.'

Shock widened his eyes. It occurred to her that she was probably the only person who'd dared challenge him this way.

Slowly, his face transformed into an inscrutable mask. Hell, he was so expert at hiding his feelings, he didn't need a mask at his next ball, she thought vaguely.

'I don't care whether you believe me or not. All I care about, what *you* should care about, is whether you can deliver on our agreement. I can easily find a replacement for you if you wish to terminate it when we get back to New York. Believe that.'

'Oh, I believe you. I also believe you think you can hide behind hatred and revenge to find the closeness you seek.'

'*Madre di Dio.* When I suggested you tell me every thought that came into your head, I had no idea you were a closet pop psychologist or I'd have thought twice. I unequivocally revoke that request, by the way.'

Listening to him denigrate what had been a perfect few hours in her life made anger and pain rock through her. Stepping back from the desk, she glanced at the picture, pain slashing her insides.

'I'll leave you to your machinations.' She rushed out and hurried up the stairs, swiping at the foolish tears clouding her vision.

If Narciso wanted to bury himself in the past, he was welcome to do so.

CHAPTER TEN

'THERE'S A NEW recipe I want to try. Care to join me?'

Ruby looked up as Michel approached the counter she'd been working at for the last two hours.

Her mood had vacillated between anger and hurt, undecided on which emotion had the upper hand. Certainly, the piece of meat she'd been hammering was plenty tenderised.

She set it to one side, went to the sink to wash her hands, and rested her hip against the granite trim. 'As long as it's nothing Sicilian. I've had my fill of Sicilians for the foreseeable future.'

Michel cast her a curious glance, then gave a sly smile. 'No, what I'm thinking of is unapologetically French.'

She wiped her hand on her apron. 'Then count me in.'

'Excellent! It's a *sauce au chocolat* with a twist. You're making *croquembouche* for monsieur's dinner party in New York, *oui?*'

'Yes.' Although right now the thought of monsieur himself sautéed in a hot sizzling pan sounded equally satisfying.

'*Bien,* I thought instead of the caramel you could try using chillies.'

'Chilli chocolate? I love the idea. I always convince myself the heat burns away half the calories.'

He gave a very Gallic shrug. 'In my opinion, you do not need to worry about calories, *'moiselle.'*

The compliment took her by surprise. 'Umm, thanks, Michel.'

He shrugged again and started grabbing ingredients off the

shelves. They worked in harmony, measuring, chopping, straining until the scent of the rich chocolate sauce bubbling away in the pan filled the kitchen.

On a whim, she asked, 'Do you have any fresh vanilla pods? I want to try something.'

He nodded. Opening his spice cabinet, he grabbed the one long pod and handed it to her. Ruby cut it open and scraped out the innards. Then, slicing a few strips, she dropped them into the sauce. 'Let that infuse for a few minutes, and we'll try it.'

He rubbed his hands together with a childlike glee that made her laugh. After two minutes he grabbed a clean spoon and scooped a drop of the sauce. 'As the last ingredient was your idea, you sample it first.' He blew on it and held it to her lips.

She tasted it, shut her eyes to better feel the flavours exploding on her tongue. The decadent taste made her groan long and deeply.

'Ruby.'

Her name was a crack of thunder that had her spinning round.

Narciso stood in the doorway, the look on his face as dark and stormy as the tension thickening the air. For several seconds, everyone remained frozen.

Then silver eyes flicked to the Frenchman. 'Leave.'

Michel's eyes widened at the stark dismissal. Narciso took a single step forward to allow the chef to sidle past before he slammed the door shut behind him.

The sound of the lock turning made her nerves scream.

Slowly, Narciso walked towards her. With his every step she willed her feet to move in the other direction, away from the imposing body and icy fury bearing down on her. But she remained frozen.

She held her breath as he stopped a whisper from her.

'My intention was to find you and explain things better, perhaps even apologise for what I said in my study.'

Her heart lifted, then plummeted again when she deciphered his meaning. 'Well, I'm waiting.'

'Oh, you won't be getting an apology from me *now, amante*.'

He leaned over and looked into the copper pan bubbling on the stove. Picking up a spoon, he scooped up some sauce and sampled it.

'Not half bad. What is it?'

'Oh, I thought you'd recognise it, Narciso. This sauce I've named The Valentino Slimeball Special. It'll taste divine with the freshly made Playboy's Puffballs I'm planning on serving them with. You'll love it, trust me.'

Slowly, he lowered the spoon and speared her with those icy silver eyes. 'Say that again.'

'I'm pretty certain there's nothing wrong with your hearing.'

He tossed the spoon into the sink and leaned closer, bracing his hands on either side of her so she was locked in. 'Say it again anyway. I like the way that pretty mouth of yours pouts when you say *puffballs*.'

Despite his indolent words, his eyes glinted with fury. Her instinct warned her to retreat, but caged in like this, watching the erratic pulse beating at his throat, she knew any attempt at escape would be futile.

He was hanging on to his control by a thread. The sudden urge to shatter it the way he seemed to shatter hers so very easily made her stand her ground.

'You'll have to beg me if you want that.'

'Ah, Ruby, shall I let you in on personal insight?'

'Can I stop you?'

'I think you delight in pushing my buttons because you know it'll get you kissed. Am I right?'

'You're wrong.'

'Then why are you licking your lips like that? Anticipation has you almost insane with desperation right now.'

'You have a ridiculously high opinion of yourself.'

'Prove me wrong, then.'

'I won't play your stupid games.'

'Scared?'

'No. Uninterested.'

'Believe me, Ruby, this isn't a game.' When his hands went to undo the tie holding her dress together, she batted them away.

'Stop. What's wrong with you?'

His laugh was filled with bitter incredulity. 'I walk in here to find you moaning for another man and you ask *me* what's wrong with me?'

'You're *jealous?*'

Right before her eyes he seemed to deflate. His hold on her dress ties loosened. And the eyes that speared hers held hellish agitation.

'Yes! I'm jealous. Does that make you happy?'

Her senses screamed yes. Jealousy meant that she mattered in some way to him. The way he'd come to matter to her. 'Why did you come in here, Narciso?'

He sucked in a breath. 'I told you, to apologise.'

'Because my feelings are hurt or because *you* hurt me?'

He lifted a hand and trailed his fingers down her cheek. 'Because I hurt you,' he rasped deeply.

The breath shuddered out of her. 'Thank you for that.'

'Don't thank me, Ruby. What I'm feeling…what you make me feel, I don't know what to do with it. It may well come back and bite us both.'

'But at least you're acknowledging it. So what happened in your study?' she asked before she lost her nerve.

His lips firmed. 'That woman in the picture you saw. Her name is Maria.'

She bit her lip to stem the questions flooding her.

'She's Paolina's—my housekeeper's—granddaughter. I met her that summer ten years ago. She came to visit from Palermo. Paolina brought her to the house and we hung out. By the second week I'd convinced her to stay for the whole summer. I believed myself…infatuated with her.' His lips pinched until the skin showed white. 'I was young and naïve and respected her see-but-don't-touch edict. Until I found out she was giving it up to Giacomo.'

Shock rocked through her. 'She was *sleeping* with your father?'

'Not only sleeping with him. He'd convinced her to make a sex tape, which he forced me to watch on the last day of my stay in Sicily.' Something in the way he said it made her tense.

'What do you mean *forced?*'

His teeth bared in a parody of a smile. 'He had two of his bodyguards hold me down in a chair while the video played on a super-wide screen, complete with surround sound. It was quite the cinematic experience.'

Her mouth gaped. '*Oh, my God.* That's vile!'

'That's Giacomo,' he said simply.

'So, what is he doing with her in New York now?'

His jaw clenched. 'I don't know. The reason I opened the file in the first place was to tell my investigator to toss the case.'

'But now you think he's plotting something?'

'She's broke. Which means she's the perfect pawn for Giacomo.'

Ruby wanted to ask him how he knew that, but the forbidding look in his face, coupled with the anguish lurking in his eyes, changed her mind.

With the evidence of the two people who'd betrayed him before him, he'd have to have been a saint to remain unaffected. Hell, the thought of the double blow of betrayal made her heart twist in pain for him.

'I'm sorry I condemned you. I didn't know.'

Mingled fury and anguish battled in his eyes. 'What about this, Ruby *mio*? Do you know *this?*' he muttered roughly.

He parted her dress and his fingers were drifting down the bare skin of her belly, headed straight for her panty line, before she could exhale. Warm, sure fingers slid between her thighs before Ruby knew what had hit her.

Her cry of astonishment quickly morphed into a moan of need as his thumb flicked against her clitoris.

'Narciso!'

'*Dio,* how can I crave you this badly when I didn't know you a week ago?'

Need rammed through her and she clung to him. 'I don't know. You forget that I should hate this, too. I should hate you.'

He leaned in close, until his hot mouth teased her ear lobe. 'But then that would mean you were conforming to some lofty image you have in your head of your ideal man. You'd be denying that our little tiffs make you so wet you can barely stand it. I turn you on. I heat up your blood and make you feel more alive than you've ever felt. I make you crave all the things you've denied yourself. I know this because it's what you make me feel too. Close your eyes, Ruby.'

'No.' But already her eyelashes were fluttering down, heavy with the drugging desire stealing over her.

The next moment, his breath whispered along her jaw. 'Do you want me to stop?'

She groaned. 'Narciso…'

'Say no and I'll end this.'

She whimpered. 'You're not being fair.'

He laughed again. 'No, I'm not, but I never claimed I was a fair man. And when I feel as if my world is unravelling, halos don't sit well on my head.'

His fingers worked faster, firing up sparks of delight in her that quickly flared into flames.

'Oh! Oh, God.'

He kissed her hard and deep, then nibbled the corner of her mouth as she shattered completely. He ran his free hand down her back in a roughly soothing gesture as she floated back down. The mouth at her ear lobe feathered kisses down her jaw to her throat, then back up again.

'I'm sorry that I hurt you, Ruby. But I'm not sorry that I make you feel like this.'

The New York she'd left just days ago to travel to Macau was the same. Ruby knew that, and yet it was as though she were seeing it for the first time.

As they travelled through midtown towards Narciso's penthouse on the Upper East Side, the sights and sounds appeared more vibrant, soulful.

Part of her knew it was because she was seeing it through different eyes. The eyes of a woman who'd been introduced to passion and intense emotion.

She wanted to push that woman far away, deny all knowledge that she existed. But self-delusion had never been her flaw.

She'd slept for most of the four-hour flight from Belize City, a fact for which she was thankful. Awake and in close proximity to Narciso, she didn't think she could've avoided letting him see her confusion.

Their intense encounter in the kitchen on his yacht had been highly illuminating. Very quickly after granting her most delicious release, he'd walked away, leaving her replete and alarmingly teary.

She'd stood in the kitchen long after he'd left, clutching the sink and fighting a need to run after him and offer him comfort.

But how could she have when his words echoed in her ears.

I hurt you...I'm sorry...I crave you...

With each word, her heart had cracked open wider, until she'd been as raw as his voice had been.

As raw as she was now...

The need to run from her thoughts was very tempting. Giving in, she activated her returned phone. Several voice and text messages flooded into her inbox.

Three were from the same number. One she didn't recognise but suspected its origin.

She answered Annie's query as to when she would be returning and declined her invitation to a girls' night out when she was back from the West Coast. She wasn't ready to face anyone yet, least of all her perceptive roommate, when her emotions felt as if they'd been through a shredder.

The second message was from her mother, asking her to get in touch. She tensed as she listened to the message again. On the surface, it sounded innocuous, a mother asking after her child.

But she heard the undercurrents in her mother's voice and the hairs on her neck stood up. The other messages forgotten, she played the message a third time.

'What's wrong?' Narciso's deep voice cut across her flailing emotions.

'Nothing.'

'Ruby.'

She glanced at him, and her heart lurched. 'Don't look at me like that.'

'Like what?'

'Like you care.'

'I care,' he stated simply.

She sucked in a breath. 'How can you? You told me there was nothing beneath the surface, remember?'

She knew she was probably overreacting but the thought that her mother was reaching out to her because her father had in all likelihood had another affair made her stomach clench in anger and despair.

But unlike the numerous times before when she'd been angry with her parent, Ruby was realising just how harshly she'd misjudged her mother.

From the cocoon of self-righteousness, it'd been easy to judge, to see things in black and white. But having experienced how easy it was to lose control beneath the charisma and magnetism of a powerful man, how could she judge her mother?

Sure, she was aware that part of the reason her mother had stuck around was because she craved the fame that came with being part of a power couple. But Ruby also knew, deep down, her mother could be a success on her own.

A strong, warm hand curled over hers. Her gaze flew up to collide with silver eyes. 'I know what I said but I want to know what's going on anyway.'

His concern burrowed deep and found root in her heart. 'My mother left me a message to call her.'

He nodded. 'And this is troubling?'

'Yes. Normally she emails. She only calls me when some-thing…bad happens.'

'Define bad.'

'My father…sleeping with a sous chef, or a waitress, or a member of their filming crew. That kind of *bad*.'

He swore. 'And she calls you to unburden?'

'And to put pressure on me to join their show. She seems to think my presence will curb my father's wandering eyes.'

His gaze remained steady on hers. 'You don't seem angry about it any more.'

Because he'd made her see herself in a different light: one that didn't fill her with bitterness.

Warmth from his hand seeped through, offering comfort she knew was only temporary.

'I've come to accept that sometimes we make choices in the hope that things will turn out okay. We take a leap of faith and stand by our choices. My mother's living in hope. I can't hate her for that.'

A flash of discomfort altered his expression. 'How very ac-commodating of you.'

'Accommodating? Hardly. Maybe I'm just worn out. Or maybe I'm finally putting myself into someone else's shoes and seeing things from their point of view.'

'And your father?'

'I can't forgive any man who toys with my…a woman's feel-ings. Who exploits her vulnerabilities and uses them against her.'

His sharp glance told her the barb had hit home. 'If you're referring to what happened in the kitchen—'

'I'm not.' A lance speared her heart. 'I think it's best we for-get about that, don't you?'

I think it's best we forget…

He had no idea why that statement twisted in his gut but it did long after they'd reached his underground car park and entered the lift to his penthouse. Beside him Ruby stood stiffly, her face turned away from him.

He'd expected her to protest when he'd demanded she stay with him until after his VIP dinner party.

Instead, she'd agreed immediately.

The idea that she couldn't be bothered to argue with him made another layer of irrational anxiety spike through him.

Roughly he pushed the feeling away, meshed his fingers with Ruby's and tugged her after him when the lift doors opened.

Paolina exited one of the many hallways of his duplex penthouse to greet him.

Despite being in her late sixties, his housekeeper was as sprightly as she'd been when he was a boy.

'Ciao, bambino. Come stai?'

He responded to the affectionate greeting, let himself be kissed on both cheeks; allowed himself to bask in the warmth of her affection. But only for a second.

Catching Ruby to his side, he introduced her, noting her surprise as he mentioned Paolina's name.

She turned to him as Paolina took control of their luggage and headed to the bedrooms. 'Would this be the same Paolina who's related to Maria?'

His smile felt tight. *'Sì.'*

'I…I thought…'

'That I was a complete monster who cut everyone out of my life because of one incident? I'm not a complete bastard, Ruby.'

'No, you're not,' she murmured.

Her smile held none of the vivacity he'd come to expect. To *crave*. He wanted to win that smile back. Wanted to share what plans he'd put in place before they left Belize. But unfamiliar fear held him back.

Would she judge him for doing too little too late?

He watched her turn a full circle in the large living room, her gaze taking in and dismissing the highly sought-after pieces of art and exclusive decorative accessories most guests tended to gush over. The location of his apartment alone—on a thirtieth floor overlooking Central Park—was enough to pull a strong reaction from even the most jaded guest.

Ruby seemed more interested in the doors leading out of the room. 'Do you mind showing me to the kitchen? I'd like to see where I'll be working and if there's any equipment I need to hire. I should also have the final menu for you shortly. If there's anything you need to change I'd appreciate it if you let me know ASAP.'

Again he felt that unsettled notion of unravelling control. But then…when it came to Ruby, had he held control in the first place?

It certainly hadn't felt like it when he'd walked in on Ruby and Michel. Hearing her moan like that had been a stiletto wound to his heart.

In his jealousy and blind fury had he taken things too far? He tried to catch her eye as he walked beside her towards the kitchen but she refused to look at him.

He'd never had a problem with being given the silent treatment. But right now he wanted Ruby to speak, to tell him what was on her mind.

'What I've seen so far of the menu's fine. It's the perfect blend of continental Europe and good old-fashioned Italian. The guests will appreciate it.'

Her only reaction was to nod. They reached the kitchen and she moved away from him.

She inspected the room with a thoroughness that spoke of a love for her profession. Her long, elegant fingers ran over appliances and worktops and he found his disgruntlement escalating.

Dio, was he really so pathetic as to be jealous of stainless-steel gadgets now? He shook his head and stepped back. 'I'm leaving for the office. We will speak this evening.'

Four hours later, he was pacing his office just as he had been last week.

Only this time there was no sign of the ennui that had

gripped him. Instead, a different form of restlessness prowled through him, one that was unfamiliar and mildly terrifying.

He laughed mirthlessly and pushed a hand through his hair. Narciso wasn't afraid to admit so far he wasn't loving being thirty. He seemed to be questioning his every action. He was even stalling on the deal with Vladimir Rudenko. Did he really need to start another media empire in Russia?

Going ahead with it would mean he'd have to spend time in Moscow. Away from New York. Away from Ruby. *Dio,* what the hell was she doing in his head?

Gritting his teeth, he strode to his desk and pressed the intercom that summoned his driver.

The journey from Wall Street to his penthouse took less than twenty minutes but it felt like a lifetime. Slamming the front door, he strode straight into the kitchen. He needed to tell her of his plans. Needed her to know he'd chosen a different path…

She was elbow deep in some sort of mixture. She glanced up, eyes wide with surprise. 'You're back.'

'We need to talk.'

'What about?'

'About Giacomo—' he tensed, then continued '—about my father.'

Her eyes grew wider. 'Yes?'

'I've decided to end—'

A phone beeped on the counter. A look of unease slid over her features as she wiped her hands and activated the message. A few seconds later, all trace of colour left her cheeks. 'I have to go.'

He frowned. 'Go where?'

'Midtown. I'll be back in an hour.'

'I'll drive you—'

'No. I'll be fine. Really. I've been cooped up in here all afternoon. I need the fresh air.'

'Fresh air in New York is a misnomer.' He continued to watch her, noting her edginess. 'Is it your parents?'

Her fingers twisted together. 'No, it's not.' Sincerity shone from her eyes.

He nodded. 'Fine. I just wanted you to know, you have my backing one hundred per cent. After the party, I'll have the papers drawn up to provide the funds you need for the restaurant.'

'Th-thank you. That's good news.' The definite lack of pleasure on her face and voice caused his spine to stiffen. She reached him and tried to slide past.

Unable to help himself, he caught her to him and kissed her soft, tempting mouth. She yielded to the kiss for a single moment before she wrenched herself away.

'Amante—'

'I have to go.'

Before he could say another word she snatched her bag from the counter and walked out of the door.

Narciso stood frozen, unable to believe what had happened. By the time he forced himself to move, Ruby was gone.

CHAPTER ELEVEN

RUBY ENTERED THE upscale restaurant at the stroke of six and gave her name.

A waiter ushered her to a window seat. It took seconds to recognise the man at the table. Shock held her rigid as she stared at him.

Without his mask, Giacomo Valentino bore a striking resemblance to his son. Except his eyes were dull with age and his mouth cruel with entrenched bitterness.

'I knew I recognised you from somewhere, Ruby Trevelli,' Giacomo Valentino said the moment she sat down. 'The wonders of modern technology never cease to amaze me. A few clicks and I had everything I needed to know about you and your parents.'

She tensed. 'What do you want?'

'A way to bring my son down. And you will help me.'

She rushed to her feet. 'You're out of your mind.'

'I met with your loan shark today,' he continued conversationally. 'As of three hours ago, I own twenty-five per cent of your yet-to-be-built restaurant. If you walk out of here, I'll call in the debt immediately.'

Heart in her throat, she slowly sank back into her seat. 'Why are you doing this?'

His face hardened. 'You saw how he humiliated me in Macau.'

'Yes, and since then I've also heard what you did to him. And I know you met with Maria yesterday.'

A flash of fear crossed his face but it was quickly smothered. 'So Narciso knows?'

'Yes.'

The old man visibly paled.

'Give it up, Giacomo. You're out of options because there's no way I'll help you further your vendetta against your own flesh and blood.'

The flash came again, and this time she saw what it was. Deep, dark, twisted pain. 'He's a part of me that should never have come into being.'

She shook her head. 'How can you say that?'

'He took away from me the one thing I treasured most in this world. And he struts around like the world owes him a living.'

Ruby heard the black pain behind his words and finally understood. Deep down, Giacomo Valentino was completely and utterly heartbroken over losing his wife.

A part of her felt sympathy for him. But she could tell Giacomo was too set in his thinking to alter his feelings towards his son.

Narciso, on the other hand, wasn't. Ruby had seen gentleness in him. She'd seen compassion, consideration, even affection towards Paolina, the grandmother of the woman who'd betrayed him. He had the capacity to love, if only he'd step back from the brink of the abyss of revenge he was poised on.

And will you be the one to save him?

Why not? He'd helped her come to terms with her own relationship with her parents. She'd called her mother this afternoon, and, sure enough, her father had strayed again. But this time, Ruby had offered her mother a shoulder to cry on. They'd spoken for over an hour. Tears had been shed on both sides. An hour later, she'd received a text from her mother to say she'd contacted an attorney and filed for a divorce from her husband.

Ruby knew the strength it'd taken for her mother to break free. Taking a deep breath, she looked Giacomo in the eye. 'You probably don't want my advice but I'll give it anyway. You and Narciso both lost someone dear to you. You were lucky enough to know her. Have you spared a thought for the child who never knew his mother?'

'Ascolta—!'

'No, you listen. Punishing a baby for its mother's death went out with the Dark Ages. Do you have any idea how much he's hurting?'

Pale silver eyes narrowed. 'You're in love with my son.'

Her heart lurched, then hammered as if fighting to get away from the truth staring her in the face. Her fingers tightened on her bag. 'I won't be a party to whatever you're cooking up.'

'You disappoint me, Miss Trevelli. Before you go, I should tell you that your loan shark provided me with an extensive file on you, which details, among other things, a building on Third and Lexington.'

Panic flared high. *'My parents' restaurant?'*

Giacomo gave a careless nod.

'I swear, if you dare harm them I'll—'

Giacomo put a hand on her arm. 'My request is simple.'

She wanted to bolt but she remained seated.

His speculative gaze rested on her. 'My son is taken with you. More than he has been with any other woman.'

Her insides clenched hard. 'You're wrong—'

'I'm right.' He leaned forward suddenly. 'I want you to end your relationship with him.'

Her mouth dried. 'There is no relationship.'

'End it. Sever all ties with him and I'll make sure your parents' livelihood remains intact. I'll even become your benefactor with your restaurant.'

Frantically she shook her head. 'I don't want your charity.'

His eyes narrowed. 'Do you really want to risk crossing me? I urge you to remember where my son inherited his thirst for revenge from.'

Feeling numb, she rose. This time he didn't stop her.

Her thin sweater did nothing to hold the April chill at bay

as she blindly struck through the evening crowd. She only realised where she was headed when the subway train pulled into
the familiar station.

Her apartment was soothingly quiet. Dropping her bag, she
went to the small bar she'd installed when she moved in.

Blanking her thoughts, she went to work, mixing liqueurs
with juices, spirits with the bottle of champagne she'd been
gifted on her birthday. Carefully she lined up the mixtures that
worked and discarded the rest. She was on her last set when she
heard the pounding on the door.

Breath catching, she went to the door and glanced into the
peeper.

Narciso loomed large and imposing outside her door. Jumping back, she toyed with not answering.

'Let me in, Ruby. Or so help me, I'll break this door down.'

With shaking hands, she released the latch.

He took a single, lunging step in and slammed the door behind him. 'You said you'd be an hour, tops.' Silver eyes bore
into her, intense and frighteningly invasive.

She forced a shrug. 'I lost track of time.'

'If you wanted to return here all you needed was to say.'
There was concern in his voice, coupled with the vulnerability
he'd been unable to hide on the yacht.

Knowing what had put that vulnerability there, knowing
what his father's lack of love had done to him, made her chest
tighten. She so desperately wanted to reach for him, to soothe
his pain away.

But in light of what she faced, there was only one recourse
where Narciso was concerned. 'I didn't realise I had to answer
to you for my movements.'

He frowned and speared a hand through his hair. The way
it fell made her guess he'd been doing it for a while. Swallowing hard, she forced her gaze away and walked into the small
living room.

He followed. 'You don't,' he answered. 'But you said you'd
come back. And you didn't.'

'It's no big deal, Narciso. I wanted to return home for a bit.'

'Are you ready to return now?' he shot back, his gaze probing.

The need to say yes sliced through her. 'No. I think I'll spend the night here.'

He started to speak. Stopped, and looked around. She didn't even bother to look at her apartment through his eyes. Annie had used the term shabby chic when they'd picked up knick-knacks from flea markets and second-hand shops to furnish their apartment. The plump sofas were mismatched, as were the lamps and cushions. The pictures that hung on the walls were from sidewalk artists whose talent had caught Ruby's eye.

'Why are you here, Narciso?'

Narciso walked over to a lampshade and touched the bohemian fringe. 'I tried to tell you earlier. I've called off the vendetta with my father.'

Shock rocked through her, followed swiftly by sharp regret. 'Why?'

He shoved his hand into his pockets and inhaled. 'In a word? *You.* You're the reason.' Again that vulnerability blazed from his eyes. Along with a wariness as she remained frozen.

'I shouldn't be the reason, Narciso. You should do it for yourself.'

He shrugged. 'I'm working my way to that, *amante.* But I need your help. You set me on this road. You can't walk away now.'

Oh, God!

She choked back a sob and fled to the bar. He followed and saw the drinks lined up on the counter.

'You were working?'

'I never stop.'

'What have you come up with?' There was a genuine interest in his tone. For whatever reason, he wanted to know more about her passion.

His softening attitude towards her sent her emotions into panicked freefall. Belize had warned her she was at serious risk of developing feelings for Narciso Valentino. Seeing him in her home, touching her things, making monumental confessions, made her want to rush to him and burrow into his chest, hear his heart pounding against her own. But she couldn't. Not now.

She shoved her hands into her jeans pockets and shrugged. 'This and that.'

He flicked a glance at her. Then he picked up the nearest drink and took a sip. 'What's this one called?'

Push him away!

She took a deep, frantic breath. '*Sleazy Playboy.* The one next to it is *The Studly Warlock,* the blue one is the *Belize Bender,* and the pink one I've termed *The Virgin Sacrifice.*'

He stiffened.

'There's a black Sambuca one I'm intending to call *Crazy, Stupid Revenge*—'

'Enough, Ruby. I get the message. I've upset you. Again. Tell me how to make it better.' He looked over at her and his eyes held a simple, honest plea.

Dear God. Narciso wasn't all gone at all. In fact, right at that moment, he was the single, most appealing thing in her life.

Heat and need and panic and lust surged under her skin as his gaze remained steady on hers. With every fibre in her being she wanted to cross the room and launch herself into his arms.

Giacomo's face flashed across her mind.

'There's nothing to make better because there's nothing between us.'

His eyes widened. *'Scusi?'*

'We had what we had, Narciso. Let's not prolong it any further.'

His eyes slowly hardened. In quick strides, he crossed the room and jerked her into his body. The contact threatened to sizzle her brain. Throwing out her hands against his chest, she tried to break free. He held tight.

'Let me go!'

'Why? Scared I'll prove you wrong?'

'Not at all—'

He swooped down and captured her mouth. His kiss was raw, possessive and needy.

'What the hell's happening, Ruby?' he whispered raggedly against her mouth.

Again her heart skittered.

Briefly, she thought to come clean, tell him where she'd been. Panic won out.

'Dammit, Ruby, kiss me back!' he pleaded raggedly against her lips.

She couldn't deny him any more than she could deny herself what would surely be her last time of experiencing this magic with him.

Desperate hands grazed over his chest to his taut stomach. Grasping the bottom of his T-shirt, she pulled it up. He helped her by tugging it over his head and flinging it away. Eyes blazing with an emotion she was too afraid to name met hers. Stepping forward, she placed an open-mouthed kiss on his collarbone.

His hiss of arousal echoed around the room. Emboldened, she used her teeth, tongue and mouth to drive them both crazy. When he stumbled slightly, she realised she'd pushed him towards the sofa. With a hard push she sent him sprawling backwards. Within seconds he was naked, his perfect body beckoning irresistibly. Driven by guilt and hunger, she stripped off her T-shirt and bra and unsnapped her jeans.

With a shake of his head, he covered her hands with his. 'Let me.'

The slow slide downward was accompanied by hot, worshipful kisses that brought tears to her eyes. Afraid her emotions would give her away, she hurriedly stepped out of the jeans and pushed him back down again and resumed the path she'd charted moments before.

His groan when her lips touched the tip of his shaft was ragged and raw. But encouraging hands speared through her hair, holding her to her task.

Boldly, she took him in her mouth. '*Dio,* Ruby!'

She looked up at him. His eyes were closed, his neck muscles taut from holding on to his control. Taking him deeper, she lost herself in the newfound power and pleasure, her heart singing with an almost frightening joy at being able to do this, one last time.

Tomorrow would bring its own heartache but for now—

'Basta!' he rasped. 'As much as I'd love to finish in your mouth, my need to be inside you is even greater.'

He pulled her up and astride him. Reaching for his discarded jeans, he took a condom from his back pocket.

The thought that he'd come prepared dimmed her pleasure for a second. But realising what the alternative would've meant, she took the condom from him, tore it open and slipped it on his thick shaft, experiencing a momentary pang at how big he was.

Silver eyes gleamed at her. 'We fit together perfectly, *tesoro,* remember?' he encouraged gently.

Nodding, she raised her hips and took him inside her.

Delicious, sensational pleasure built inside her, setting off fireworks in her body. His face a taut mask of pleasure, his hands settled on her thighs and he allowed her to set the pace. But this new, deeper penetration was her undoing. Within minutes, her spine tingled with impending climax. She had no resistance when Narciso reared up, sucked one nipple into his mouth and sent her over the edge.

She surfaced from the most blissful release to find their positions reversed. Narciso's fingers were tangled in her hair and his mouth buried in her throat.

When he raised his head, the depth of emotion on his face made her breath catch.

'I need you, Ruby,' he repeated his earlier statement. Only this time, she was sure he didn't mean sexually.

The knowledge that things would never be right between them sent pure, white-hot pain through her heart.

Unable to find the right words to respond, she cradled his face. Locked in that position, his eyes not leaving hers, he surged inside her and resumed the exquisite, soul-searing lovemaking. Eventually, he groaned his release and took her mouth in a soft, gentle kiss, murmuring words she understood but refused to allow into her heart.

Tears sprang into her eyes and she rapidly blinked them away, glad that he was rising and putting his clothes back on.

'I can stay here, or we can return to my place.' Although his tone wasn't as forceful as before, she knew he wouldn't accept a third choice.

'I'll come back with you.' Despite all that had happened, she still had his dinner party to cater for.

They dressed in silence and she studiously avoided the puzzled glances he sent her way.

When he caught her hand in his in the lift on the way to the ground floor, she let him. When he brought the back of her hand to his lips and kissed it, she sucked in a deep breath to stop the tears clogging her throat from suffocating her.

In his car, he pulled her close, clamped both arms around her and tucked her head beneath his chin. In the long drive back to the Upper East side, neither of them spoke but he took every opportunity to run gentle hands down her arms and over her hair.

Unable to stop herself, she felt tears slide down her cheeks. *Dear God,* what the hell had she done? Of all the foolish decisions she could've made, she'd gone and fallen in love with Narciso Valentino.

'Qualunque cosa che, oi facevo io sono spiacente,' he murmured raggedly in her ear. *Whatever I did, I'm sorry.*

The tears fell harder, silent guilty sobs racking her frame.

He led her to the shower the moment they returned to his penthouse. Again, in silence, he washed her, then pulled a clean T-shirt of his over her head. Pulling back the covers to his bed, he tugged her close and turned out the lights.

'We'll talk in the morning, Ruby. Whatever is happening between us, we'll work it out, *sì?*'

She nodded, closed her eyes and drifted off to a troubled sleep.

She jerked awake just after 5:00 a.m., fear and anguish

churning through her body. The need to tell Narciso the truth burned through her.

She needed to tell him about the meeting last night. Needed to let him know that Giacomo's thirst for revenge burned brighter than ever.

Her fear for her parents had blinded her to the fact that she was stronger than Giacomo's blackmail threats. There was no way Ruby would do as Giacomo asked.

She loved Narciso, and, if there was any way he reciprocated those feelings, she didn't intend to walk away.

But she had to warn him that Giacomo might come at him by a different means once he found out Ruby had no intention of walking away.

Turning her head, she watched Narciso's peaceful profile as he slept. Her heart squeezed and she sucked in a breath as tears threatened.

She'd never have believed she could fall in love so quickly and so deeply. But in less than a week she'd fallen for the world's number-one playboy.

But there was far more to Narciso than that. And if there was a chance for them…

Vowing to speak to him after the party, she slid out of bed, dressed without waking him and left the bedroom.

Armed with the black card he'd given her yesterday, she went outside and hailed a taxi. The market in Greenwich was bustling by the time she arrived just before six. For the next hour, she lost herself in picking the freshest vegetables, fruit and staples she needed for the dinner party.

Next, she stopped at the upmarket wine stockist.

Narciso had enough wine and vintage champagne so she only selected the spirits and liqueurs she needed for her cocktails.

She was leaving the shop when her phone buzzed. Heart jumping into her throat because she knew who it would be, she answered.

'You left without waking me,' came the quiet accusation.

'I needed to get to the market before sunrise.'

He sighed. 'I'm sorely tempted to cancel this event but I have several guests flying in specially.'

'Why would you want to cancel it?'

'Because it's coming between me and what I want right now.'

Her heart thundered. 'Wh-what do you want?'

'You. Alone. A proper conversation with no disturbances. To get to the bottom of whatever last night was about.'

'I'm sorry, I should've told you...' She stopped as a phone rang in the background.

'*Scusi,*' he excused himself, only to return a minute later. 'I need to head to the office but I'll be back by five tonight, *si?*'

'Okay, I'll see you then.'

He paused, as if he wanted to say something. Then he ended the call.

Ruby was glad for the distraction of getting everything ready for the dinner party. By the time Michel showed up midafternoon, she'd almost finished her preparations.

They talked through the recipes she'd planned and settled on the timing.

'Monsieur tells me you'll be manning the bar tonight?'

'The idea is to divide my time between the bar and the kitchen. I know I can trust you to hold the fort here?'

'Of course.' He peered closer at her. 'Is everything all right?'

She busied herself placing large chunks of freshly cut salmon in its foil wrappings.

'It will be when the evening's over. I always get the jitters at these events.'

His knowing glance told her he hadn't missed her evasiveness. Thankfully, Paolina entered the kitchen and Ruby sighed with relief.

The planning team arrived at four. After that, deliveries flooded in. Flowers, a DJ and lighting specialists who set up on the terrace.

But the most unexpected delivery came in the form of a couture designer bearing a zipped-up garment bag, which she handed over and promptly departed. The note pinned to the stunning powder-blue floor-length gown was simple—*a beautiful gown for a beautiful woman*.

Joy burst through her heart, made her smile for the first time that day.

For the job she had to do tonight, it was severely impractical, as were the silver shoes almost the exact shade as Narciso's eyes, but as she walked into Narciso's bedroom and hung up the dress she knew she would wear it.

Narciso was late. He arrived barely a half-hour before his guests were due to arrive and walked into the bedroom just as she was putting finishing touches to her upswept hair.

He froze in the doorway, and stared. 'You look gorgeous, *bellissima*.'

She turned from the mirror, a cascade of love, trepidation and anxiety smashing through her. How would he take the news of his father's continued scheming?

Remember where my son inherited his thirst for revenge...

Forcing down the shiver of apprehension, she murmured, *'Grazie.'*

His eyes darkened with pleasure. 'You need to speak more Italian. Or better still Sicilian. I'll teach you,' he said as he shrugged off his jacket and tugged at his tie.

Then he strode to where she stood. Snaking a large hand around her nape, he pulled her in for a long, deep kiss. Then with a groan he stepped back.

'Give me fifteen minutes and I'll be with you.'

'Okay.'

'Dio, I must be growing a conscience, *bellissima,* since I keep dismissing the idea of calling this party off.'

She forced a laugh. 'You must be.'

Shaking his head, he entered the bathroom. She stood there until the sound of the shower pulled her from her troubled thoughts.

She was behind the bar, pouring the first of the cocktails into glasses, when he emerged.

The sight of him in a superbly cut grey suit and a blue shirt that matched her dress made her heart slam into her throat. He'd taken a single step towards her when the doorbell rang.

He rolled his eyes dramatically, then his gaze drifted over her in heated promise before he nodded for the butler to answer the door.

For the next two hours, Ruby let her skills take over, serving food that drew several compliments from the dinner guests.

She declined when Narciso invited her to join them at the dinner table. Although his eyes narrowed in displeasure, there was very little he could do about it, much to her relief.

She was preparing a round of after-dinner cocktails when she looked up and gasped.

Giacomo was framed in the penthouse doorway.

Her gaze swung to Narciso; frozen, she watched his head turn and his body tense as he saw his father.

For several seconds, they eyed each other across the room.

Giacomo sauntered in as if he belonged. Several guests, sensing the altered atmosphere, glanced between father and son.

'Hey, watch it!'

She jerked and looked down to find she'd overfilled a glass and the lime-green cocktail was spilling over the counter.

Setting the shaker down, she grabbed a napkin.

'*Bona sira,* Ruby,' came the mocking voice. 'How lovely you look.'

Her head snapped up and connected with Giacomo's steely gaze. Surprise that he hadn't headed straight for his son held her immobile. Long enough for him to calmly reach across the counter, take her hand and press a kiss on her knuckles.

She tried to snatch her hand away but he held on tight, a triumphant smile playing about his lips. 'Play along, little one, and all your problems will go away,' he said in a low voice.

'I have no intention of playing along with anything.'

'It doesn't matter one way or the other. Narciso is infatuated with you. He'll see what I want him to see.'

With the clarity of a klaxon, everything fell into place.

She'd been played. Giacomo had always intended *this* to be his revenge. By meeting with him last night, she'd only given him more ammunition.

Heart shattering, she glanced over to where Narciso stood stock still, his eyes icy lakes of shock.

CHAPTER TWELVE

'Narciso—'

'Don't speak.'

Narciso paced in his office, marvelling at how his voice emerged so calm, so collected, when his insides bled from a million poisonous cuts.

'Listen to him, *bedda*. He's prone to childish tantrums when he's upset. Just look at how he threw out all his guests a few minutes ago—'

'Shut up, old man, or so help me I'll bury my fist in your face.'

Giacomo shook his head and glanced at Ruby in a *what-did-I-say?* manner.

'What the hell are you doing here?'

'Ruby told me you were having a party. I decided to invite myself.'

'I didn't—!'

'*Ruby* told you? When?' Narciso's gaze swung to her, then returned to his father.

'Last night, when she met me for dinner.'

'He's lying, Narciso.' He heard the plea in her voice and tried to think, to rationalise what was unfolding before him. Unfortunately his brain seemed to have stopped working.

From the moment he'd seen Giacomo take her hand and kiss it, time had jerked to a stop, then rewound furiously, throwing up old memories that refused to be banished.

Forcing himself into the present, he stared at Ruby. The gorgeous firecracker who'd got under his skin. The woman who'd made love to him last night in her apartment as if her soul belonged to him.

Waking up this morning to find her gone had rocked him to his soul. The realisation that he wanted her in his bed and in his arms every morning and night for the rest of his life had been shocking but slowly, as the idea had embedded itself into his heart, he'd known it was what he wanted.

He loved her. He, who'd never loved anything or anyone in his life, had fallen in love…

With a woman who would meet with his father and not tell him…allow Giacomo to put his hand on her.

No! He couldn't have made the same mistake twice.

Ruby was different…

Wasn't she? Reeling, he watched Giacomo stroll to the large sofa in the room and ease himself into it. His attitude reeked a confidence that shook Narciso to the core.

He forced himself to speak. 'Ruby, is this true?'

She shook her head so emphatically, tendrils fell down her graceful neck. 'No, it's not. I only—'

'You have a spy following me around. I know you do. He reports to you twice a week. Today is one of those days, I believe,' Giacomo said.

Narciso's fists tightened. 'Not any more.'

Surprise lit the old man's eyes. 'Really? You must be going soft. Luckily, I had my own pictures taken.'

Giacomo reached into his pocket and threw down a set of photos on the coffee table.

Narciso felt his body tremble as he moved towards the table. For the first time in his life, he knew genuine fear. He glanced up to see Ruby's eyes on his face.

'Please, Narciso, it's not what you think. I can explain.'

He took another step. And there in Technicolor was the woman he loved, with the man he'd believed until very recently he hated most in his life.

Ironically, it was Ruby who'd made him look deeper into himself and acknowledge the fact that it wasn't hate that drove him but a desperate need to connect with the person who should've loved him.

His legs lost the ability to support him and he sank into his chair. Vicious pain slashed at his heart and he fought against the need to howl in agony.

'Leave,' he rasped.

'I warned you you would never best me,' his father crooned.

Slowly, Narciso raised his head and looked at his father. Despite his triumph, he looked haggard. The years of bitterness had taken their toll. It was what he'd risked becoming…

'She insisted on saving you, do you know that?'

Ice filled his gut. *'Scusi?'*

Giacomo's gaze scoured him. 'Your *mamma.* She had a chance to live. The doctor who arrived could only save one of you. She had a chance and she chose you.' Bitterness coated every word.

'And you've hated me for it ever since, haven't you?'

Giacomo's face hardened. 'I never wanted children. She knew that. If she'd only listened to me, she'd still be alive.' He inhaled and surged to his feet. 'What does it matter? Come, Ruby. You're no longer wanted here.'

Narciso snarled. 'Lay another finger on her and it's the last thing you'll ever do.'

His father jerked in shock, then his face took on a grey hue. Narciso watched, stunned, as Giacomo clutched his chest and began to crumple.

'Narciso, I think he's having a heart attack!'

For several seconds Ruby's words didn't compute. When the meaning spiked, poker hot, into his brain, he reached out and caught Giacomo as he fell.

Behind him he heard Ruby dialling and speaking to emergency personnel as he tore open his father's shirt and began chest compressions.

'Madre di Dio, non,' he whispered, the fear clutching his chest beginning to spread as his father lay still.

The next fifteen minutes passed by in a blur. The ER helicopter landed on the penthouse roof and emergency personnel took over.

He sagged against a wall when they informed him Giacomo was still alive but would need intensive care immediately.

'He'll pull through. I'm sure of it.'

He looked up to find Ruby in front of him, holding out a glass of whisky. He took it and knocked it back in one gulp.

It did nothing to thaw the ice freezing his heart.

'Leave.' He repeated the word he'd said what seemed like a lifetime ago.

Shock rushed over her face.

'Narciso—'

He threw the glass across the room and heard it shatter. 'No. You don't get to say my name. Never again.'

He took satisfaction in seeing tears fill her eyes. 'I can explain—'

'It's too late. I told you this thing between Giacomo and I was over. I'd trusted your counsel, taken your advice and abandoned this godforsaken vendetta. But where was your trust, *tesoro mio*? You knew this was coming. And you said nothing!'

'He threatened my parents!'

His expression softened for a split second. Then grew granite hard. 'Of course he did. But his threats meant more to you than your belief that I would help you. That we could fight him together!' He couldn't hide the raw pain that flowed out of his voice.

'I didn't want to fight! And I was going to tell you. Tonight after the party.'

'We'll never know now, will we?' he said scathingly.

'Narciso—'

'Your actions spoke clearly for you. Unfortunately for you, you made the same mistake Maria did. *You chose the wrong side.*'

* * *

Ruby smoothed her hand down the sea-green dress and tried to stem the butterflies.

In less than half an hour, the grand opening of Dolce Italia would be under way.

Two months of sheer, sometimes blessedly mind-numbing, hard work. She'd volunteered for every job that didn't require specialist training in the blind hope of drowning out the acute pain and devastation of having to live without Narciso. Her success rate had been woefully pathetic...

'Are you ready yet, *bella bambina?* The paparazzi will be here in a minute.' Her mother entered, wearing an orange silk gown that pleasantly complemented her slim figure. Despite being in her late forties, Paloma looked ten years younger. With her divorce from her philandering husband firmly underway, she appeared to have acquired a new lease on life. The spring in her step had grown even bolder when Ruby had allowed her to take a financial stake in the restaurant.

She stopped in the middle of the small room they'd converted to a dressing room at the back of the two-storey restaurant and cocktail bar in the prime location in Manhattan.

'Oh, you look stunning,' she said, then her eyes darkened with worry. 'A little on the thin side, though.'

'Don't fuss, Mamma.'

'It's my job to fuss. A job I neglected for years.'

Knowing she was about to lapse into another self-recriminating rant, Ruby rushed forward and hugged her. 'What's done is done, Mamma. Now we look forward.'

Her mother blinked brown eyes bright with unshed tears and nodded. 'Speaking of moving forward, the most exquisite bouquet of flowers arrived for you.'

Ruby's breath caught, then rushed out in a gush of pain. 'I don't want them.'

Her mother frowned. 'What woman doesn't want flowers on the most spectacular night of her life?'

'Me.'

'Are you sure you're all right? Last week you sent back that superb crate of white Alba truffles, the week before you refused the diamond tennis bracelet. I wish you'd tell me who all these gifts are from.'

'It doesn't matter who they're from. I don't want any of them.' She fought the rising emotions back. She'd shed enough tears to last her a lifetime.

Not tonight. With her mother as her new business partner, she'd paid off Giacomo's loan and closed that chapter.

Tonight, she would push Narciso and his in-your-face gifts out of her mind and bask in her accomplishment.

'I'm ready.'

They entered the large reception area to find a three-deep row of photographers and film crew awaiting them. In the time she'd decided to open the restaurant with her mother, Paloma had guided her in how to deal with the press. Where her reaction to them had been led by fear and resentment, now she used banter and firmness to achieve her aim.

With the press conferences and TV junkets taken care off, her mother passed her the scissors and she moved to a large white ribbon.

'Ladies and gentlemen, my mother, Paloma, and I are proud to declare Dolce Italia open—'

At first she thought she was hallucinating. Then the face became clearer.

Narciso stood to one side of the group, his silver eyes square on her face.

'Ruby?' she heard her mother's concerned voice from far away as the heavy scissors slipped from her grasp.

'Ruby!'

She turned and fled.

'Ruby.' He breathed her name as if it were a life-giving force, pulling her from the murky depth of pain. 'Open the door, *per favore.*'

She snatched the door she'd slammed shut moments ago

wide open. 'You ruined my opening. Weeks of preparation, of breaking my back to make this perfect, and you swooped in with your stupid face and your stupid body and *ruined* it.' She found herself inspecting his face and body and tore her gaze away.

'*Mi dispiace.* I wanted…I *needed* to see you.'

'Why? What could you possibly have to say to me that you haven't already said?'

His jaw tightened. 'A lot. You returned all my gifts.'

'I didn't want them.'

He took a step into the room. 'And the NMC cheque? You returned it to me ripped into a hundred pieces.'

'I was making a point. Why did you keep sending me stuff?'

'Because I refused to contemplate giving up. I refused to imagine what my life would be like without the thinnest thread of hope keeping me going.'

She wanted to keep her gaze averted, but, like a magnet, it swung towards him.

He looked incredible, the five-o'clock shadow gracing his jaw making him look even more stunning. But a closer look pinpointed a few surprising changes.

'You've lost weight,' she murmured.

He shut the door behind him and she caught the faint snick of the lock. 'So have you. At least I have an excuse.'

'Really?'

'*Sì,* Michel threatened to quit. We agreed on a month-long vacation.'

'You don't deserve him.'

He grimaced. 'That's entirely true. He wasn't happy when he realised his culinary efforts were going to waste.' He threaded his fingers together and stared down at them. When he looked back up, his eyes were bleak, infinitely miserable. Her heart kicked hard. 'I can't eat, Ruby. I've barely slept since you left.'

'And this is my fault? I didn't *leave*. You threw me out, remember?'

He paled and nodded, his nostrils thinning as he sucked in

a long, ragged breath. 'I was wrong. So very wrong to believe even for a second that you were anything like Maria.'

'And you've suddenly arrived at this conclusion?'

'No. All the signs were there. I just refused to see them because I'd programmed myself to believe the worst.'

Her heart kicked again, this time with the smallest surge of hope. 'What signs?'

'Your determination to push me away when I came to your apartment. Your tears in the car on the way back home. Your clear distress when my father touched you. Why would you encourage me to reconcile with my father and turn round and betray me?'

'I wouldn't… I didn't.'

He shook his head. 'I know. I condemned you for something that never happened. Something you tried to tell me you would never do. But I was so bitter and twisted I couldn't see what was in front of me.'

'What was that?'

'The love I have for you and the probability that you could perhaps love me, too.'

Her breath caught. 'W-what?'

'I know I've blown all that now—'

'You mean you don't love me?'

He speared a hand through his hair and jumped up. 'Of course I love you. That's not the point here, I meant—'

'I think you'll find that's the whole point, Narciso,' she murmured, her heart racing.

He stopped. Stared down at her. Slowly his eyes widened. Ruby knew what he was seeing in her face. The love she'd tried for so long and so hard to smother was finally bursting out of her.

'*Dio mio,*' he breathed.

'You can say that again.'

'*Dio mio,*' he repeated as he sank onto his knees in front of her. 'Please tell me I'm not dreaming?'

'I love you, Narciso. Despite you being a horrible pain in the ass. There, does that help?'

With a groan, he rose, took her face in his hands and kissed her long and deep. 'I'll dedicate every single moment of the rest of my life to making you forget that incident.'

'That sounds like a great deal.'

'Can I also convince you to let me back Dolce Italia in any way I can?'

Despite the guilt she saw in his face, she shook her head. 'No. It's now a mother-daughter venture. I want to keep it that way.'

'What about your father?' he asked.

'He consults...from afar. We'll never be close but he's my blood. I can't completely cut him off.'

'*Prezioso,* you humble me with how giving you are.'

'You should've remembered that before you pushed me away.'

'I've relived the hell of it every single second since I lost you.'

'Keep telling me that and I may allow you to earn some brownie points.'

He smiled. 'Can we discuss accumulative points?'

'I may be open to suggestions.'

He kissed her until her heart threatened to give out.

'Wow, okay. That could work.'

'How about this, too?'

He reached behind him and presented her with a large leather, velvet-trimmed box. It was far too large to contain a ring but her heart still thundered as she opened it.

The mask was breathtaking. Bronze-trimmed around blue velvet, it was the exact colour of the waters of Belize. Peacock feathers sprouted from the top in a splash of Technicolor, and two lace ties were folded and held down by diamond pins.

'It's beautiful.'

'It's yours if you choose to accompany me on the next *Q Virtus* event.'

'I want to know more about your super-secret club.'

A sly smile curved his lips. 'I could tell you all the secrets,

but then I'd have to make love to you for days to make you
forget.'

'Hmm, I suppose I'd just have to suffer through it.'

He laughed, pulled her close and kissed her again. She pulled
away before things got heavy.

'Tell me what you've done to my mother.'

'She promised to hold the fort on condition I did everything
in my power to exit this room as her future son-in-law.'

Ruby gasped. 'She didn't! God, first you muscle in on my
opening, then you strike deals behind my back.'

'What can I say? She drives a hard bargain.' He pulled back
and stared down at her, a hint of uncertainty in his eyes. 'So
will you give me an answer?'

Her arms rose to curl over his shoulders. 'That depends.'

'On what?'

'On whether white Alba truffles come with the deal.'

He pulled her close and squeezed her tight. 'I'll keep you
supplied every day for the rest of your life if that's what it
takes, *amante*.'

Isla de Margarita, Venezuela

Narciso leaned against the side of the cabana and watched his
wife wow the crowd with her latest range of cocktails. Although her mask covered most of her face, he could tell she
was smiling.

Music pumped from the speakers strategically placed around
the pool area and all around him *Q Virtus* members let their
inhibitions fly musically and otherwise.

He raised his specially prepared cocktail to his lips and
paused as the lights caught his new wedding ring.

He'd wanted a big wedding for Ruby but she'd insisted on a
small, intimate ceremony at the Sicilian villa where he'd been
born.

In the end, they'd settled for fifty guests including her

mother, and Nicandro Carvalho and Ryzard Vrbancic, the two men he considered his closest friends.

Although they were working on their relationship, he and Giacomo had a way to go before all the heartache could be set aside.

'So…*last three bachelors standing* becomes two. How the hell are Nicandro and I going to handle all these women by ourselves, huh, my friend?'

Laughing, he turned to Ryzard. 'That's your problem. I'm willingly and utterly taken.' He glanced over and saw Ruby's eyes on him. He raised his glass and winked.

Ryzard shuddered. 'That's almost sickening to watch.'

'If you're going to throw up, do it somewhere else.'

Shaking his head, his friend started to walk away, then Narciso saw him freeze. The woman who had caught his attention was dancing by herself in a corner. Although she had a full mask over her face, her other attributes clearly had an effect on Ryzard.

Smiling, Narciso turned to watch his wife emerge from behind the bar and walk towards him, her stunning body swaying beneath her sarong in a way that made his throat dry.

She reached him and handed him another drink. 'What was that all about?'

'Just me bragging shamelessly on how lucky I am to have found you.'

She laughed. 'Yeah, about that. You might need to pull back on the gushing a bit. You're putting our friends off.'

He caught her around her waist, tugged her mask aside and kissed her thoroughly. 'I have no intention of pulling back. Anyone who dares to approach me will be told how wonderful and gorgeous my wife is.'

His pulse soared when her fingers caressed his collarbone. 'I love you, Narciso.'

'And I love that I've made you happy enough to keep you from sleepwalking lately.'

'That reminder just lost you one brownie point.'

He pulled her closer. 'Tell me how to win it back, *per favore,*' he whispered fervently against her lips.

'Dance with me. And never stop telling me how much you love me.'

'For as long as I live, you'll know it, *amante*. That is my promise to you.'

* * * * *

THE ULTIMATE SEDUCTION

BY
DANI COLLINS

Dani Collins discovered romance novels in high school and immediately wondered how a person trained and qualified for *that* amazing job. She married her high school sweetheart, which was a start, then spent two decades trying to find her fit in the wide world of romance-writing, always coming back to Mills & Boon Modern Romance.

Two children later, and with the first entering high school, she placed in Harlequin's *Instant Seduction* contest. It was the beginning of a fabulous journey towards finally getting that dream job.

When she's not in her Fortress of Literature, as her family calls her writing office, she works, chauffeurs children to extra-curricular activities, and gardens with more optimism than skill. Dani can be reached through her website at www.danicollins.com.

I've been lucky enough to work with a few different editors at Mills & Boon, London. They're all made of awesome, but I must send a huge shout of appreciation to my current editor, Laurie Johnson. Not only has she made my transition into her care utterly painless, but this is our first book completely midwifed from start to finish by her. No spinal block required! Writer and book are happy and doing well. Thanks, Laurie!

CHAPTER ONE

TIFFANY DAVIS PRETENDED she wasn't affected by the hard stare her brother and father gave her when she entered her father's office. It wasn't easy to let people she loved pass judgment on whether she'd used sufficient concealer on her scars. Sometimes she wanted to throw the bottle of liquid beige into the trash and scream, *There. This is what I look like now. Live with it.*

But her brother had saved her life pulling her from the fiery car. He felt guilty enough for putting her in it. He still grieved for her groom, his best friend, and everything else Tiffany had lost. She didn't have to rub salt in his wounds.

Good girl, Tiff. Keep biting back what you really want to say. It's not like that got you into these skin grafts.

She came to a halt and sighed, thinking it was probably time for another visit to the head doctor if she was cooking up that sort of inner dialogue. But her harsh exhale caused both men to tense. Which made her want to rail all the louder.

Being angry all the time was a character shift for her. Even she had trouble dealing with it, so she shouldn't blame them for reacting like this. But it still fed her irritation.

"Yes?" She clicked her teeth into a tight smile, attempting to hold on to her slipping patience.

"You tell us. What's this?" Christian kept his arms folded as he nodded at the large box sitting open on their father's desk. The lid wore an international courier's logo, and the contents appeared to be a taxidermist's attempt to marry a raven to a peacock.

"The feather boa you asked for last Christmas?" Lame joke, sure, but neither man so much as blinked. They only stared at her as if they were prying her open.

"Be serious, Tiff," Christian said. "Why is the mask for you? Did you request to go in my place?"

A claustrophobic band tightened around her insides. A year in a mask had left her vowing to never feel such a thing on her face again. "I don't know what you're talking about."

The frost in her voice made both men's mouths purse. *Why did all of this have to be so hard?* The touchiness between her and her family was palpable every minute of every day. If she was short, they were defensive. If she was the least bit vulnerable, they became so overprotective she couldn't breathe.

They'd nearly lost her. She got that they loved her and were still worried about her. They wouldn't relax until she got back to normal, but she would never be normal again. It made the situation impossible.

"Where is it you think I want to go?" she asked in as steady a tone as she could manage.

"Q Virtus," her father said, as if that one word sufficed as explanation.

She shook her head and shrugged, still lost. Did they realize she was in the middle of an exchange worth five hundred million dollars? She didn't have much, but she did have a job now. Seeing as it involved running a multibillion-dollar company, she tried to do it well.

"Ryzard Vrbancic," Christian provided. "We put in a request to meet him."

Pieces fell together. *Q Virtus* was that men's club Paulie used to talk about. "You want to meet a puppet leader at one of those rave things? Why? The man's a despot."

"Bregnovia is asking for recognition at the UN. They're a democracy now."

She snorted in disbelief. "The whole world is ignoring the fact he stole the last dictator's money and bought himself a presidency? Okay."

"They're recovering from civil war. They need the sort of infrastructure Davis and Holbrook can provide."

"I'm sure they do. Why go the cloak-and-dagger route? Call him up and pitch our services."

"It's not that simple. Our country hasn't recognized his yet so we can't talk to him openly, but we want to be the first number on his list when recognition happens."

She rolled her eyes. Politics were so fun. "So you've set up this clandestine meeting—"

"It's not confirmed. That happens when you get there."

"That would be the broad 'you,' right? Like the universal 'they'?"

Christian's mouth tightened. He lifted out the feathery contents of the box. It was actually quite beautiful. A piece of art. The blend of blue-black and turquoise and gold feathers covered the upper eyes and forehead and—significantly—splayed down the left side in an eerily familiar pattern. Ribbons tailed off each side.

It was like looking in the mirror, seeing that reflection of her scar. A slithery feeling inside her torso made her heart speed up. She shook her head. She wasn't going anywhere, especially in public, with or without a crazy disguise.

"You understand how *Q Virtus* works?" her brother prodded. "This mask is your ticket in."

"Not *mine.*"

"Yeah, Tiff, it is." He turned it around so she could see where her name was inscribed on the underside, along with *Isla de Margarita, Venezuela.* "See? Only you can attend."

His terse tone and shooting glance toward their father made it clear they'd spent some time pondering alternate solutions. Both men showed signs of deep frustration, a level of emotion usually reserved for when approval ratings were low. To see them so bent out of shape activated her don't-make-more-waves genes.

Your father is under a lot of pressure, dear. Do as he asks for now.

No, she reminded herself. She was living her life, not waiting for it to make everyone else's list of priorities. Still, she'd been raised to have civilized conversations, not be outright defiant. "I would think that taking off the mask to show your name defeats the purpose."

"There's a chip embedded. They know which mask belongs to which person, and as you can see, they only fit one face."

"They obviously know a lot about *me.* That's creepy. Doesn't it seem weird they would know how to cover my scars?"

"*Q Virtus* has an exceptional history of discretion and security," her father said, defending it with a kind of pompous grumpiness that surprised her. "Whatever they know about us, I'm sure it's kept very well protected."

A remarkably naive comment from a man who'd been in politics and business long enough to mistrust everyone and everything. Heck, he'd dragged her in here because he thought she'd undermined him with his brotherhood of secret handshakes, hadn't he?

"Dad, if you want to become a member—"

"I can't." He smoothed his tie, one of his tells when his ego was dented.

"Too old? Then Christian—?"

"No."

She was quite smart, had always had better marks than her brother, who fudged his way through just about everything, but she was missing something. "Well, Paulie was a member. What does it take?"

"Money. A lot of it. Paul Sr. was a member and once Paulie inherited, he had the means to pay the fee," her father said in a level tone.

Of course. Therein lay her father's envy and reverence. It must have eaten him alive that his best friend and rival for her mother's affections had possessed something he hadn't.

"When you were still in the hospital, I applied on your behalf, hoping to go as your proxy," Christian explained. "I didn't hear back until today." Glancing at their father, he added, "It is kind of creepy they know Tiff has finally recovered and taken over the reins of Davis and Holbrook."

"Everyone's talking about it. It's hardly a secret," her father dismissed with a fresh heaping of disapproval.

Tiffany bit back a sigh. She would not apologize for grappling her way into running the company now that she was well enough. What else would she do moving forward? Trophy wife and having a family was out of the question with this face.

Still, it was so *unladylike* to work, her mother reminded at every opportunity.

"I don't understand why they've accepted her. It's a men's club," her father muttered.

She eyed the mask, recalling the sorts of stories Paulie used to come home with after attending one of these *Q Virtus* things. "It's a booze-fueled sex orgy, isn't it?"

"It's a networking event," her father blustered.

Christian offered one of his offside grins. "It's a chance for the elite to let their hair down," he clarified. "But a lot of deals are closed over martinis and a handshake. It's the country club on a grander scale."

Right. She knew how that worked. Wives and daughters stood around in heels and pearls planning the Fourth of July picnic while husbands and fathers colluded to keep their money amongst themselves. Her engagement to Paulie, Jr. had been negotiated between the seventh and ninth holes of the top green, her wedding staged on the balcony by their mothers, her cake designed by the renowned chef, and all of it exploded into flames against the wrought-iron exit gate.

"This is all very interesting." It wasn't. Not at all. "But I'm in the middle of something. You'll have to sort this out yourselves."

"Tiffany."

Her father's stern tone was the one that made any good daughter spin, take a stance of dutifully planted feet, knees locked, hands knotted at her sides. She caught her tongue firmly between her teeth. "Yes?"

"Our friends in Congress are hoping for good relations with Bregnovia. I need those friends."

Because his hat was in the ring for the next election. Why was that always the only thing that mattered?

"I don't know what you expect me to do. Pitch our services while wearing a showgirl costume? Who would take that seriously? I can't go into a meeting without it, though. No one likes face-to-face interactions with this." She pointed at where her ear had been reconstructed and a cheekbone implant inserted.

Her father flinched and looked away, not denying that she was hard to look at. That hurt more than the months of screaming burn injuries.

"Maybe I could be your date," Christian said. "I don't know if members are allowed to bring an escort, but…"

"Bring my brother to the prom?" That certainly reinforced how far down the eligibility ladder she'd fallen. Her hands stayed curled at her sides, but mentally she cupped them around her tiny, shrunken heart, protecting it. *Love yourself, Tiff. No one else will.*

"Get me into the club and you won't have to leave your room until it's over," Chris said.

Hide the disfigured beast.

She had to close her eyes against her father's intense stare, the one that willed her to comply.

You weren't going to let yourself be a pawn anymore, she reminded herself.

"How long is this thing?" she heard herself ask, because what kind of family would she have, if not this one? Her friends had deserted her, and dating was completely off the table. Her life would be very dark and lonely if she alienated her parents and brother.

"We arrive at sunset on Friday night, and everyone is gone by Sunday evening. I'll make the travel arrangements," Christian said with quick relief.

"I wear this thing in *and* out. That's the deal, because I won't do this if I'm going to be stared at." Listen to her, talking so tough. She was actually scared to her toenails. What would people say if they saw her? She couldn't let it happen.

"As far as I know, everyone wears masks the whole time," Chris said, practically dancing, he was so elated.

"I'll be in my office," she muttered. *Searching for my spine.*

Ryzard Vrbancic abided by few rules beyond his own, but he left his newly purchased catamaran as the shadow of its mast stretched across the other boats in the Venezuelan marina. If he didn't climb the stairs before the red sky had inked purple, he would be locked out of the *Q Virtus* Quarterly.

Story of my life, he thought, but hoped that soon he'd be as welcome worldwide as the famous black credit card.

Security was its usual discreet step through a well-camouflaged metal detector that also read the chip in his mask. One of the red-gowned staff lifted her head from her tablet as he arrived and smiled. "We're pleased to see you again, Raptor. May I escort you to your room?"

She was a pretty thing, but the *petite q's* were off-limits, which was a pity. He hadn't had time to find himself a lover for weeks. The last had complained he spent more time working than with her, which was apparent from her spa and shopping bills. They were as high as his sexual frustration.

His situation should improve now, but he'd have to be patient a little longer. Like the music that set a vacation tone, the *petite q's* provided atmosphere. They could stroke an ego, dangle off an arm, flirt and indulge almost any reasonable request, but if they wanted to keep their job, they stayed out of the members' beds. Being smart and career minded along with attractive and engaging, the *petite q's* tended to side with keeping their jobs.

Such a pity.

His current escort set up his thumbprint for the door then stepped inside his suite for his briefing. "You have a meeting request from Steel Butterfly. Shall I confirm?"

"A woman?" he asked.

"I don't have the gender of our clients, sir."

And if she did know, she wouldn't say, either.

"No other requests?" He was hoping for a signal from international bodies that his petition to the UN was receiving a nod.

"Not at this time. Did you have any?"

Damn. He'd come here knowing he had a meeting request, hoping it would be a tip of the hand on his situation. Now he was under lockdown and liable to be taking a sales pitch of some kind.

"Not at present. I'll accept an introduction on that one, nothing longer." He nodded at her tablet.

"The time and location will be transmitted to your smartwatch. Please let us know if I can arrange anything else to ensure your satisfaction while you're with us."

He followed her out, confident that everything he'd preordered was in the suite. Zeus was exceptionally good at what he did. Ryzard had never had an issue of any kind while at *Q Virtus,* which made the exorbitant membership fee and elaborate travel and security arrangements worth the trouble.

Entering the pub-style reception lounge, he saw roughly thirty people, mostly men in tuxedos and masks. They stood with a handful of gorgeous *petite q's* wearing the customary red designer gowns.

He accepted the house drink for this session, rum over ice with a squeeze of lime and a sugared rim, then glanced at his watch. At his four o'clock, a collection of dots informed him the small conclave of men to his right included Steel Butterfly.

He had no idea where Zeus came up with these ridiculous nicknames, but he supposed Raptor was apt for him, coming from the Latin meaning to seize or take by force. The bones of several dinosaurs in that category had been uncovered in his homeland of Bregnovia, too.

Eyeing the group, he wondered which one was his contact. One accepted a drink from a *petit q* and handed her his watch. It didn't matter, he decided. He wasn't interested in beginning a conversation in public that he was scheduled to have in private tomorrow. He waited until he was out of range in the gambling hall to activate his identity on his own watch. This resulted in an immediate invitation to join the blackjack table.

He sat so he could read the screen mounted near the ceiling in the corner. It subtly manifested and dissolved with blurbs on presentations and entertainment to be held over the course of the *Q Virtus* Quarterly. Tastemakers, trendsetters and thought leaders were flown in to provide rich, powerful, political forces such as himself with the absolute cutting-edge information and samples of global economics and technology. Meanwhile, at tables such as this one, he would pick up the other side of the coin: gossip about a royal's addiction, a cover-up of a coup attempt on a head of state, a lie that would be accepted as truth to stem international panic.

He could only imagine what was said about him, but he didn't let himself dwell on what was likely disapproval and distrust. His people were free, his country independent. That was the important thing.

Still, thoughts of what it had cost him crept in, threatening to inject disappointment and guilt into an otherwise pleasant if staid evening. He folded his hand, left the table and lifted a rum off a passing waiter's tray as he moved outside in search of entertainment.

CHAPTER TWO

TIFFANY WAS STUCK and it was a sickeningly familiar situation, the kind she'd sworn she'd never wind up in again.

She'd love to blame Christian. He had urged her to step through the door when he'd been refused entry. *Go in and ask,* he'd hissed, annoyed.

Since her worst nightmare these days was being stared at, she'd forgone arguing on the stoop and stepped through the entranceway. Inside, pixies in designer nightgowns had fawned over the arriving men in masks. She'd looked around for a bell desk, and a stud named Julio had come forward to introduce himself as a *petite q.*

She, a seasoned socialite, had become tongue-tied over the strapping young man in a red footman's uniform. It was more than two years since she'd been widowed on her wedding day. Even without the scars, that would be bad mojo. Men didn't call, didn't ask her out. If she was in a room with a live one, they rarely looked her in the eye, always averting their gaze. She didn't exist for them as a potential mate.

Julio didn't attract her so much as astonish her. He didn't know what lurked beneath the mask and was all solicitous manners as he offered his services. "I see this is your first visit with us," he said after a brief glance at his tablet. "Please allow me to orient you."

She was completely out of practice with his type—the valet who never overstepped his station, but still managed to convey that he appreciated being in the presence of beauty. She'd haltingly fielded his questions about whether her travel had been pleasant as he smoothly escorted her into an elevator.

When he asked if she had any specific needs he could attend to while she was here, she'd come back to reality. "My brother needs a hall pass, or a mask. Whatever. Can you make that happen?"

"I'll send the request to Zeus, but the doors will be closing in a few minutes. Once we're in lockdown, no one comes or goes. Unless it's an emergency, of course." He'd lifted his head from tapping his tablet.

Lockdown? Alarmed, she'd tried to text Christian only to be informed that external service was cut off while inside the club.

"Cell phones and other cameras are discouraged, as is the sending of photos outside the club. Security will locate him and communicate his options," Julio assured her, then explained that if her requested meeting was accepted, the time and location would be sent to her Inspector Gadget watch.

"Where *are* we? A hollowed-out volcano?" she asked as he set up her thumbprint entry to her room.

"No, but we're working on obtaining one," he said, deadpan. "Now, you'll want to wear your watch throughout your stay. It tells a lot more than time. May I show you?"

Hearing that her scheduled meeting with the Bregnovian dictator wasn't a sure thing was a relief. Her father would be furious if she didn't go in Christian's place, but if the request was rejected, she would be off the hook. Still, she hoped her brother would be granted entry and save her worrying about any of it. She pressed Julio out of her suite with instructions to inform her about Christian as soon as possible.

Her suite was enough of an oasis to calm her nerves. Her

privileged upbringing had exposed her to some seriously nice digs, but she had to admit this was above and beyond. No expense had been spared on the gold fixtures, original art or silk bedding. The new clothes in the wardrobe were a pleasant distraction. Christian had said something about samples of prototypes being handed out to members. *If you don't want them, I do.*

She supposed he was referring to the spy watch Julio had shown her, but she was more interested in the designer gowns. Discreet labels informed her they were from the best of the best throughout South America, all in stunning colors and fabrics. Several were off-the-shoulder, figure-enhancing styles that would cover her scars.

Interesting.

Not that she had anywhere to wear them. She didn't intend to leave her room, but she would make the most of the in-suite amenities, she decided. Call it a vacation from her family. She'd work in peace for a few days.

Work, however, was next to impossible without Wi-Fi service to the external world, and besides, a calypso band was calling to her from below her open French doors. She *loved* dancing.

Full darkness had fallen, so she sidled into the shadows behind a potted fern on her balcony and gazed longingly at the party below, feeling rather like Audrey Hepburn in that old black-and-white. It was such a world beyond her. The pool's glow lit up ice sculptures on the buffet tables. Bartenders juggled open bottles, putting on a cocktail show as they poured fast and free while women in red gowns cha-cha'd with men in tuxedos and masks.

This whole mask thing was weird. As they'd flown south in the company jet, Christian had explained it allowed the world's elite to rub shoulders in a discreet way. Sometimes it was best for the biggest players to take their meetings in secret, so as not to cause speculative dips in the stock exchange. Certain celebrities stole these few days to relax without interruption by fans. *Q Virtus* catered to whatever the obscenely rich needed.

I need a new face, she thought sourly, but even the cavernous pockets her husband had left her weren't deep enough to buy a miracle.

She looked to where she'd left her mask dangling off a chair back's spire.

Despite her anxiety with the abrupt change of plans when she arrived, she had felt blessedly anonymous behind her mask as she had walked through the lobby and halls to her room. It had been an extraordinary experience to feel normal again. No one had stared. She had looked exactly like everyone else.

Hmm. That meant she didn't have to stay here like Rapunzel, trapped in the tower with the real world three stories below and out of her reach.

With her heart tripping somewhere between excitement and trepidation, she fingered through the gowns hanging in the wardrobe. The silk crepe in Caribbean blue would expose her good right leg, but not so high as to reveal where her grafts had been taken. After months of physiotherapy, she'd moved back into her old workout routine of yoga, weights and treadmill. She possessed all of her mother's vanity along with the genetic jackpot in the figure department. Only family saw her these days, and she hardly dressed to impress, but she was actually very fit.

Alone in the suite, she held the gown up to her body, then, without her mother there to discourage her, dared to try it on.

Whoever this Zeus guy was, he sure knew how to dress a woman. Especially one with defects to hide. The single sleeve went past her wrist in a point that ended in a loop of thread that hooked over her middle finger. The bodice clung to her waist and torso, plumping breasts that remained two of her best original features. She had to give her back-side the credit it deserved, too. When she buckled on new shoes that were little more than sky-high heels and a pair of saucy blue-green straps, it was like being hugged by old friends. She almost wept.

Filtering her image through her lashes as she looked in the mirror, she saw her old self. *Hi, Tiff. It's nice to see you again. 'Bout time, too.*

Makeup didn't completely cover her scars, nothing could, but she enjoyed going through her old ritual after using the concealer, taking her time to layer on shadow and liner, girling herself up to the max. By the time she was rolling spirals into her strawberry blond hair, she was so lost in the good ol' days, she caught herself thinking, *I wonder what Paulie will say.*

The curling iron tagged her cheek where she would never feel it, and she nearly broke down. *You're not Cinderella, anymore, remember? You're the ugly stepsister.*

No. Not tonight. Not when she felt confident and beautiful for the first time since her wedding day. Had she been happy then? She couldn't remember.

Don't go there.

Gathering the top half of her hair over her crown, she tied the mask into place, then let her loose curls fall to hide the strap that circled her skull. Oddly, the mask wasn't as traumatic to wear as she'd feared. It didn't suction onto her face and make her feel trapped in a body that writhed in agony. It stood cocked like a fascinator to cover the left side of her face, while the feathers arranged around her eyes gave an impression of overly long lashes that layered backward to cover her forehead and hairline. She had expected it to be heavy, but it was as light as, well, feathers. They tickled the edges of her scars, where her skin was extra sensitive, making her feel feminine and pretty.

Staring at herself in the full-length mirror, she allowed

that she *was* pretty. After painting on a coat of coral lipstick, she did a slow twirl and caught herself grinning. Smiling felt odd, as if she was using muscles that had atrophied.

She lifted the weighty watch on her wrist, the one that identified her as Steel Butterfly. More like a broken one. Her sides didn't even match.

It didn't have to make sense, she assured herself as she tossed her lipstick into her pocketbook then realized she didn't need either room key or credit card. Such freedom! For a few hours, she would be completely without baggage.

Taking nothing but lighthearted steps, she left to join the party.

Ryzard could drink with the best of them. He'd spent the older half of his childhood in Munich, had managed vineyards in France and Italy, and had lived in parts of Russia where not finishing a bottle of vodka was a gross insult to the host. He was restless enough to get legless tonight, but so far he'd consumed only enough to become mellow and hungry. The cashmere breeze and the scents of beach and pineapple and roasting pig aroused his appetite—all his appetites. He'd mentally stripped the nearest *petite q's* and was considering a pass at one of the female members currently being scouted by every other bachelor here—along with some of the married members.

Not Narciso, aka the Warlock of Wall Street, though. He chatted with his friend long enough to see the man wasn't just here with his wife, but besotted by her. Lucky bastard. Ryzard countered his envy by reminding himself that love was a double-edged sword. He wouldn't ruin his friend's happiness by saying so, but he had once looked forward to marital bliss. Luiza had died before they found it, and the anguish was indescribable. No matter how pleased he was for his friend, he would never risk that toll again.

He'd stick to the less permanent associations one found, enjoyed and left at parties such as this one.

Glass panels had been fitted over the lap pool, turning it into a dance floor that glimmered beams of colored light beneath the bouncing feet. People were having a lively time, keeping the band's quick salsa beat rapping. The drummer stared off to the left, however, his grin male and captivated.

Ryzard followed the man's gaze and his entire being crackled to attention.

Well beyond the pool's light, in a corner mostly blocked by a buffet table and ice sculpture, a woman undulated like a cobra, utterly fascinating in her hypnotic move-ments timed perfectly with the music. Her splayed hands slid down her body with sexy knowledge, her hips popped in time to the beat, and her feet kick-stepped into motion.

She twirled. The motion lifted her brassy curls like a skirt before she planted her feet wide and swayed her weight between them. The flex of her spine gave way to a roll of her hips, and she was back into motion again.

Setting down his drink, Ryzard beelined toward her. He couldn't tell if the woman had a partner, but it didn't mat-ter. He was cutting in.

She was alone, lifting her arms to gather her hair, eyes closed as she felt the music as much as heard it. She arched and stretched—

He caught her around the waist and used the shocked press of her hands at his shoulders to push her into accept-ing his lead, stepping into her space, then retreating, bring-ing her with him. As he moved her into a side step, she recovered, matching his move while her gaze pinned to his.

He couldn't tell what color her eyes were. The light was too low, her feathery mask shadowing her gaze into twin glinting lights, but he reacted to the fixation in them. She was deciding whether to accept him.

A rush of excitement for the challenge ran through him.

After a few more quick steps, he swung her into half pivots, catching each of her wrists in turn, one bare, one clad in silk, enjoying the flash of her bare knee through the slit of her skirt.

How had she been overlooked by every man here? She was exquisite.

Lifting her hand over her head, he spun her around then clasped her shoulder blades into his chest. Her buttocks—fine, firm, round globes as if heaven had sent him a valentine—pressed into his lap. Bending her before him, he buried his nose in her hair and inhaled, then followed her push to straighten and matched the sway of her hips with his own.

Tiffany's heart pounded so hard she thought it would escape her chest. One second she'd been slightly drunk, lost in the joy of letting the salsa rhythm control her muscles. Now a stranger was doing it. And doing it well. He pulled her around into a waltz stance that he quickly shifted so they grazed each other's sides, left, right, left.

She kicked each time, surprised how easily the movements came back to her. It had been years, but this man knew what he was doing, sliding her slowly behind his back, then catching her hand on the other side. He pushed her to back up a step, bringing one of her arms behind his head, the other behind her own. A few backward steps and they were connected by only one hand, arms outstretched, then he spun her back into him, catching her into his chest.

He stopped.

The conga beat pulsed through her as he ran his hands down her sides. Her own flew to cover his knuckles, but she didn't stop him. It felt too amazing. His fingertips grazed the sides of her breasts, flexed into the taut muscles of her waist and clasped her hips to push them in a hula circle that he followed with his own, his crotch pressed tight to her buttocks.

Sensual pleasure electrified her. No one touched her anymore. After being a genderless automaton for so long, she was a woman again, alive, capable of captivating and enticing a man. She nudged her hips into his, flashing a glance back at him.

He narrowed his eyes and held her in place for one deliberate thrust before he spun her into the dance, their energetic quick steps becoming an excuse to look at each other as he let her move to the farthest reach of his hand on hers.

She had been a bit of a tease in her day, secure in the knowledge everyone knew she was engaged. She'd been able to flirt without consequence, enjoying male attention without feeling threatened by it. This stranger's undisguised admiration was rain on her desert wasteland of feminine confidence. Climbing her free hand between her breasts to the back of her neck, she thrust out her chest then let the music snake up and down her spine as she flexed her figure for his visual pleasure.

His feral show of teeth encouraged her while his sheer male sexiness called to the woman in her, urging her to keep the notice of such a fine specimen. He might have started out his evening in a tux, but at some point he'd stripped down to the pants and the shirt, which was open at the collar and rolled back to his forearms at the sleeves. The mask he wore was vaguely piratical in its black with gold trim and wings at his temple, but the nose piece bent in a point off the end of his nose, suggesting a bird of prey.

A hunter.

And she was the hunted.

Her heart raced, excited by the prospect of being pursued. She wanted to be wanted.

Splaying her feet, she allowed her knees to loosen. The slit of her skirt parted to reveal her leg, and she made the most of it, watching him as she rolled her hips in a figure eight, showing off her body, enticing him with a come-hither groove.

He planted a foot between hers, surrounding her without touching her, hands raised as if he was absorbing energy from her aura. The sultry tropical air held an undertone of spicy cologne and musky man. Reaching out, she shaped the balls of his hard shoulders with her hands and climbed them to the sides of his damp neck, sidling close so they sidestepped back and forth, swaying together in time to the music, bodies brushing.

His wide hands flattened on her shoulder blades and slid with deliberation to the small of her back then took possession of her hips. As his unabashed gaze held hers, he pulled her in to feel the firm ridge of his erection behind his fly.

A flood of desire, not the trickles of interest she'd felt in the past, but a serious deluge of passion, transformed her limbs into heavy weights and flooded her belly with a pool of sexy heat. She became intensely aware of her erogenous zones. Her breasts ached and her nipples tingled into sharp, stinging points. Between her thighs, her loins pulsed with a swollen, oversensitive need.

As if he knew, he shifted and his hard thigh pressed into her vulnerable flesh. She gasped and her neck weakened as he bent over her. She dropped her head back and he followed, taking her body weight on his thigh. His nose grazed her chin, then her collarbone. His lips hovered between her breasts. Slowly he brought her up again and leaned his mouth close enough to tease her parted lips.

He was a stranger, she reminded herself, but her lips felt swollen and she desperately wanted the pressure of his mouth—

A clap of thunder exploded in the sky.

Jolted, she found herself smothered against his chest, his hard arms tight around her, one hand shielding the back of her head, fingers digging in with tension. Her mask skewed, cutting into her temple. Beneath her cheekbone, his heart slammed with power.

The claps and squeals and whistles continued and his arms relaxed enough she could fix her mask and look up. Fireworks painted the starscape in flowers and streaks of red and blue and green that dissolved into sparkles of silver and palms of gold.

As people moved into their space, he steered her away from the crowd, into a corner around a partition where they were hidden in an alcove. She set her hands on the concrete rampart and leaned back into the living wall he made behind her, eyes dazzled by the bursts of color reflected on the water as the fireworks continued to explode before and above them. The band switched to an orchestrated classic that matched the explosions, filling her with awe and visceral excitement.

Already fixed in the moment, they became one being, she and this stranger, their bodies pressed tight as they watched the pyrotechnics. His hands moved over her, absently at first, shaping her to his front. She responded, encouraging his touch by rubbing her buttocks into the proof that she could still arouse a man. When his hands cupped her breasts, bold and knowledgeable, she linked her own hands behind his neck, arching into his touch, reveling in the pressure of his palms and the thumbing of her nipples.

Dropping her head to the side, she turned her face and lifted her mouth, inviting his kiss with parted lips. He bent without hesitation, nothing tentative in the way he captured her mouth. Thorough and unhurried, he continued to caress her as he took sumptuous possession of her lips.

She ran her fingers into his hair, greeting his tongue with her own, inhibition melted by pure desire. Distantly she was aware this was out of character, but she wasn't Tiffany. Not the Tiffany of today and not the old one, either. Tonight she was the woman she wished she could have been. She was every woman. Pure woman.

Tonight she had no man to think about but this one. She didn't care that she didn't know him. She and Paulie hadn't known each other, either, not really, not the way a husband and wife should. Not in the biblical sense. She hadn't slept with him or any man.

But she wanted to. She had ached for years to experience sexual intimacy.

A strong male hand stroked down her abdomen and skimmed off to the top of her thigh, making her mewl in disappointment. Then he fingered beneath the slit of her skirt and she had to pull away from his kiss to draw in a gasp as he followed bare skin into the sensitive flesh at the top of her leg.

She stilled.

His arm across her torso tensed and the hand on her breast hesitated briefly before he continued caressing her, lightly and persuasively, both hands teasing her with the promise of continued pleasure.

A moan of craving left her and she shuddered in acceptance.

A streak of light shot skyward and his touch moved into her center, exploring satin and lace that were damp with anticipation. She couldn't help covering his hand with her own, pinning his touch where she ached for pressure.

He seemed to know what she needed more than she did. As he fondled her, her eyes drifted closed and her head fell back to rest against his shoulder. She bit her lip, ripples of delight dancing through her. Was she really doing this? Rubbing her behind into his erection, not caring they were in public, that she didn't know him, that this was all about her pleasure?

He started to draw his hand away and she turned her face to the side, a cry of disappointment escaping her, but he was only hooking her panties down her hip and returning to trace and part and seek and find.

She released a moan of pure joy.

He caught her chin in his other hand and tilted her face up for his kiss while his touch on her mound became deliberate and intimate and determined.

She let it happen. She held very still and kissed him back with naked passion, aware of the light breeze caressing where she was exposed to the shadows of the rampart and the velvety night air. She let him stroke her into delirious intensity, her awareness dimmed at the edges so she was focused on the pleasure he was delivering, plucking and teasing and bringing her closer.

Over the water, the biggest rockets exploded like thunder, sending shock waves through her that made her quiver in stunned reaction. The reverberations echoed inside her, sparking where he stroked, sending a wild release upward and out to the ends of her limbs. He pinched her nipple, and like a flashpoint, she was blind to everything but white light and astonishing pleasure. Glorious waves of joy crashed in, submerging her in tumultuous ripples that he seemed to control, pressing one after another through her with the rub of his fingertip.

As the fireworks dimmed to puffs of smoke surrounding a barge in the bay, her climax receded, leaving her a puddle of lassitude in his steely arms.

He adjusted her panties and started to turn her. She obeyed the command in his hands, wanting to kiss him, to thank him—

Without a word, he drew her across the balcony to a set of shallow stairs leading to the beach. She wobbled, partly because her legs were wet noodles, partly because her heels couldn't find solid purchase in the sand. He scooped her up, carrying her along with easy strength into a cabana encircled by heavy curtains.

Inside he set her on her feet and steadied her with one hand while he raked the cloth door closed behind them. Without a word, he scraped the mask off his face and yanked his shirt open, peeling it off his shoulders and throwing it aside.

She couldn't see his face, not really. It was barely a shade above pitch-black in here, but the glow of satin skin increased as he toed off his shoes and opened his fly, stripping without ceremony.

Sweet Lord, what a man. He stepped closer and she couldn't help reaching out to test the flat muscles of his abdomen, learning them by feel more than sight. Hot and damp, he reacted to her touch with a tense of muscles and a muffled curse, making her smile in the dark, pleased she had an effect on him.

Her hand bumped into his. He was applying a condom.

Curious, she lightly explored his latex-covered shape. As she did, the pressure of her mask shifted.

She knocked his touch away before she thought about what she was doing.

Stillness came over him.

She tried to penetrate the dark and read his face—which was what he was likely doing. He probably thought she was having second thoughts.

Hell, no. She might never have another chance to lose her virginity. Not like this, so caught up in desire she was shaking with it.

"Leave it on," she whispered.

His hands lowered to her shoulders, one skimming down the edge of her bodice under her arm. She knew what he was looking for.

"That, too." Catching his hand away from her zipper, she drew him toward the bed.

In the same way he'd taken her over on the dance floor, he took the lead. A tip of his weight, a knee in the bed and she was lifted and placed half under him in one smooth motion. Her startled exhale clouded between them as a hand sought beneath her skirt, catching at her panties then pausing.

She couldn't help chuckling, understanding the implicit question. Lifting her hips, she invited him to strip them off her. They caught on her shoe, and neither of them bothered to finish the job.

He hitched her skirt then tucked her neatly under him, his legs moving with practiced ease to part her knees wide.

More surprised than shocked, she stilled, bracing herself, wanting this, but not as lost in the moment as she'd been. That was okay. She'd had her fun and she wanted to remember everything about this encounter. Cataloguing the flex of his shoulders under the stroke of her hands, the weight of his hips, the roughened texture of his legs on her smooth inner thighs, she waited.

He teased her, rubbing the head of his erection against her and reawakening her senses. As she hummed a response, he kissed her, deeply, dragging her back into the well of desire she thought she'd left outside on the ramparts.

Sliding her knee up to his hip, she hooked her calf over his buttock and quite suddenly, it was happening. His flesh was pressing for entrance, stretching her. Oh, wow. It hurt, but not bad. She'd experienced pain way worse than this, but it was still very intimate. She bit her lip and concentrated on accepting him, breathing through the sting and countering her instinctive tension—

He swore and the hand in her hair tightened enough to pull, even though she suspected it wasn't intentional. His big body shook with tension.

"I'm hurting you," he said in a voice so gruff she couldn't discern what kind of accent he had.

"It's okay. It feels good. I like it." This was so primeval. Drinking in his scent, she licked his neck, wanting this delicious, mysterious man imprinted on her for all time.

Arching, she discovered there was more of him to take. Squeezing her leg to encourage him, she met resistance. Rather than press into her, he kissed her again, using his tongue, and lifted enough to sidle a hand between them, caressing where they joined. In moments he had her twisting in excitement, and a second later, he slid deep into her.

Ah, *this* was what it was all about.

Eyes wide open to the dark cabana, she hugged his rugged body and learned the dip in his spine and the shape of his buttocks. His tense muscles flexed as he retreated from her depths, pulling strings of sensations through her: echoes of sting, loss, but delicious friction, too. He smoothly filled her again, his big body trembling with strain as he controlled his movements. The smart was still there, but the pleasure was incredible.

Purring, she lifted her hips to his, clasping him with her inner muscles, kissing him with extravagant joy, telling him she loved everything he was doing to her.

For a second, he let her feel his full weight, the full power of his muscles as he caged her beneath him and pressed a hard, hungry kiss on her. The fingers tangled in her hair pulled again, and he held himself in stark possession of her. She could swear she felt him pulsing deep inside her.

Then his fingers massaged her scalp in gentle apology and he lifted slightly, withdrew and slowly began to thrust again. The music dimly entered her consciousness from far away as they danced, him leading her through the erotic steps as he lowered her zip and exposed her breast to his hand and mouth.

She sang breathy notes of acute pleasure and sensual agony, wanting this twisting, exciting play to go on for the rest of her life. But everything he did made the sweet pleasure intensify. Their lovemaking grew better and better, driving her up the scale of passion to exquisite heights. When he ran his hand up the bare thigh that bracketed his hip, and branded her buttock with his palm, lifting her into his quickening thrusts, she moaned in approval, needing that faster pace, that wild stimulation.

Climax arrived suddenly and more powerfully than the first. She clawed at him, stunned by the release, fixated by the intense sensation of his fullness inside her while she orgasmed. He cried out raggedly and shuddered over her and within her, pushing to take deep possession of her, holding them both on that place of ecstatic perfection.

Suffused with bliss, she didn't move afterward, just waited for her heart to slow and listened as his breath settled. In the distance, the music continued and voices rose in conversation and laughter.

At the first shift of his body to relax and leave hers, the first easing of his implacable lock of his hips against hers, she dropped her hands and removed her leg from his waist. Her long history with bandage changes gave her the knowledge that quick and ruthless was best, even though it hurt like hell.

He surprised her by merely shifting his weight off her a little before he pressed a kiss to the corner of her mouth then nuzzled his lips down her bare cheek to her ear. "That was incredible. Thank you."

She couldn't help the smile that grew unseen in the dark, or the way she warmed with pride and eye-stinging gratitude. "Thank *you*. I didn't expect anything like this to happen tonight," she confessed, even though she could hear the delight in her voice. He thought she was *incredible*.

"I'm pleased I could make your first time memorable."

Her heart stopped. "You could tell it's my first time?" She felt like the most gauche girl alive.

"I come to all of these. I know the regulars, and I've

never seen you before. I would have remembered," he added with another buss of warm lips against her cheekbone.

Oh, God, *that's* what he meant. She swallowed her relieved laughter, then stiffened as voices approached their cabana.

"We should go somewhere more private." He gently lifted off her, chivalrously flicking her skirt to cover her as he rolled away.

Everything in her protested, but she sat up on the other side of the narrow bed. As she tucked her breast back into her dress and closed the zipper, his hand curled around her upper arm, hot and commanding, drawing her into tipping back against him.

"I'm on the top floor. Are you closer?"

"I can't," she whispered with genuine regret, senses distracted by the musky scent surrounding him and the damp heat of his chest so close to her nose. She tilted her face to find his lips in a soft kiss of reluctant goodbye.

He didn't move his lips against hers except to say, "Why not?"

"It's complicated. I shouldn't have come out at all." Their breaths mingled. "I hope you *will* remember me," she admitted, feeling safe to reveal the bald longing here in the anonymous dark.

"I'll always wonder why, won't I?" he said with edgy dismay.

"And then you'll remember I wanted to keep this unspoiled by real life."

This time when she pressed her mouth to his, he kissed her back. Hard and thorough, so her heart rate picked up and her arms wanted to snake around his neck.

She wasn't about to hang around until the lights came on, though. She didn't want to see his face when he saw hers.

Pulling away, she stood and shook out her skirt, stepped her underwear off her heel and left them on the mat. Quite the cheeky Cinderella move. Her mother would never quit the slut-shaming if she knew.

Tiffany felt no guilt, however, no shame and no embarrassment as she slipped out of the cabana and up the stairs, past the pool and its raging party, toward the elevators and back to her room. Only sensual satisfaction and poignant *what-ifs* followed her steps.

CHAPTER THREE

RYZARD'S WATCH GAVE a muted beep, reminding him he had a meeting in ten minutes.

Annoyed, he rose from the small table where he'd sat for the last thirty minutes eating a meal he would have preferred to have taken in his room. He swept the breakfast room once more for a certain woman in a mask that made him think of a falcon's smoothly feathered head. A woman who was both gloriously uninhibited, yet had been so tight, he had feared as he entered her that she would call a halt.

A light sweat broke over him as he recalled possessing her, never having felt so—

He cut short the thought, stung by a dart of shame that he was on the verge of elevating a meaningless hookup past the only woman he would ever love. There was no comparison. Forget it all.

Good thing he hadn't allowed the *petite q* to send a message on his behalf. He'd been tempted, but the tight security here did him a favor, preventing him from a weak moment. All he'd had was a description of her mask, but when he had inquired to the nearest *petite q,* she had assured him she could deliver an invitation to the mysterious woman to join him at breakfast. She couldn't, however, divulge the member's name or moniker.

He'd declined, not wanting to look desperate. Not wanting to feel so desperate, but after the blood-chilling thought he'd just had, he *didn't* wish to see her again. Their some-what literal bumping of two strangers in the night was nothing significant. A letting off of steam. If it had seemed particularly intense, that had been leftover adrenaline from the false alarm when the fireworks had exploded. For a sec-ond he'd been back in the heat of Bregnovia's civil war, his life in danger along with the woman in his arms.

Shaking off that terrifying second of *not again,* he as-sured himself this urgency to see her again was merely his libido looking for another easy pounce and feed.

That's why he'd had to force himself to take his time rising and dressing in the cabana last night, despite a nag-ging desire to hurry. It wasn't that he'd wanted to catch another glimpse, to actually catch *her* and convince her to strip down completely and stay with him all night. No, he was merely still horny.

Wondering why she hadn't stayed was pointless. He'd never know. Everyone at *Q Virtus* had places to go and people they preferred not to be seen with. Did she know who *he* was, he wondered?

She hadn't been wearing a watch that he'd felt. He'd checked his own as she'd left, trying to read her identifier before she had moved out of range, but no luck. Perhaps she'd run off to rejoin her husband or lover.

That thought infuriated him. Waiting to marry Luiza until it was too late was one of his few regrets. When you did make a lifelong commitment, you didn't break it. If she had...

He refused to dwell on any of it. She was a wet dream and he was awake now. Time to move on. He had an in-troduction to suffer through—would in fact drag his feet getting there so as to use up most of their time.

Then he would put out feelers for the meeting he really wanted. Someone here would know what was being said in the UN about his country's chances for recognition. Whatever he had to do to bestow legitimacy on his people, he would. They were his priority. It was Luiza's dream. He owed it to all of them to stay focused on that.

Not on some easy piece he'd picked up for a few hours of distraction.

Until the accident, Tiffany had always been fashionably—some would say chronically or even rudely—late. Once she began working, she'd discovered how irritating it was to be on the other side of that. Nowadays she strove to be early, and to that end she followed the directions on her watch, only to come up against yet another set of sliding doors. Rolling her eyes, she watched the timepiece count down how long she'd have to wait until they opened.

"Come on, come on," she muttered, wanting this meeting over with.

She'd almost forgotten it completely and wished she had. Unfortunately, her watch had been returned to her with her breakfast. "It was left in the reception lounge last night," Julio had said. "You have a message. That's what the blue light means."

"It was heavy and men kept coming up to me, saying my watch indicated I was open to being approached," she complained.

"Excellent feedback on the weight. A woman's perspective is so valuable for the manufacturers. But please let me show you how to set your Do Not Disturb."

He'd also shown her how to follow the directions to her meeting.

"Can I wear my mask?" she'd asked, peering at him from behind her feathers while trying to keep them out of her orange juice.

"Of course. Members typically wear their masks the entire time they're here."

With her main argument for blowing off the meeting disintegrated, she'd managed only a quiet, "Thanks."

Biting her thumbnail after Julio left, she'd debated whether to risk leaving her room. What if she saw *him*?

Heated tingles awakened, hinting at how exciting it could be to bump into him, but she tamped down on the wild feelings. Her behavior last night had been a crazy combination of being away from the stifling proximity of her family and, well, she had been a little drunk on rum, having almost finished her second drink by the time she'd begun dancing.

With a stranger.

Her lover.

A burble of near-hysterical laughter almost escaped her as she walked, thinking of their incredible encounter. Part of her reaction was delight that she had it in her to be that bold and daring. Before the accident she might have fantasized about something like that, but it would never be something she could imagine actually doing. There was no such thing as impulse in her family. The consequences to Daddy's career always had to be considered.

The rest of her giddiness had a sharply disappointed edge. This was the sort of secret she might share with a close girlfriend, but she didn't have any. Her friends, some closer than others, had all continued on with their lives during her recovery, living the life she was supposed to have. Hers had stalled and taken a sharp left turn. She would never have much in common with them now except the good old days. That topic just invited pitying stares.

Work was what she had now. A career. She had Paulie's corporation and men in her life who loved her as a daughter and a sister. Last night had been exciting and fun, but she couldn't repeat it. What was she going to do? Come to these events every quarter and sleep with a different stranger each time? The alternative, to expose her scars and hope a lover could overlook them, made her shudder in appalled dread.

No, she had to stay serious and focused and do what she'd been sent here to do. Last night was her personal secret, something to keep her glowing on the inside through the cold years to come. Today she represented Davis and Holbrook, one of the largest construction firms in the world, thanks to her marriage merging her father's architecture firm with Davis Engineering. As the one person with claim to both those names, she supposed she could take ten minutes out of her life to hand over the letter of introduction her brother had prepared.

Even if she didn't entirely approve of this man they wanted to court.

At least she could hide behind her mask. Kinky was her new normal, apparently, since she was becoming really fond of it, but it rejuvenated her confidence.

These gopher burrows under the building she was less sure of.

"Am I in an abattoir?" she asked a *petite q* when she found one.

"Absolutely not," the perky young woman replied, obviously not paid to have a sense of humor. "To ensure complete privacy for our guests, the doors only open if the next hallway is empty. Several people are moving around at this time, causing minor delays. Your meeting room is at the end of this hall and will open to your thumbprint."

As she stepped into the empty meeting room, however, she had to admit that this particular man's world was astounding. Given the industrial decor she'd traversed to get here, she had expected more of the same with the conference rooms. Instead she was in an aquarium—a humanarium—in the bottom of the sea. Stingrays flew like sparrows across the blue water over the glass ceiling and a garden of tropical fish bobbled like flower heads in a breeze, poking from the living reef that fringed the glass walls.

Amazed, she set down her black leather folder on a table between two chairs in the center of the room and walked the curved wall, keeping one hand on it to maintain her equilibrium as the distorted image of swaying kelp made her dizzy. She reminded herself to breathe and oriented herself by turning back to the room to take in the pair of chairs on the white area rug. They faced the windows and were separated by the table that held a crystal decanter of ice water and two cut-crystal glasses.

As she leaned her back against the window, the door panel whispered open and *he* stepped in. Her stranger.

Shock ran through her in an electric current that held her fixed, stunned.

Yes, that was the mask from last night, and she recognized his powerful build even though he was dressed differently. His gray shirt was short-sleeved, tailored close to his muscled shoulders and accentuated his firm, tanned biceps. The narrow collar of his shirt was turned down in a sharply contrasting russet, drawing her eye to the base of his throat.

She watched him swallow and lifted her gaze to his green-gold eyes.

How had he found her?

Behind him, the door whispered closed. The noise seemed to prompt him into motion. He took a few laconic steps into the room, hands going into his pockets. He wasn't taken aback by their incredible surroundings. His eyes never left their lock on hers as he paused next to the chairs, lifted a hand and removed his mask. He dropped it into one of the chairs, still staring at her.

Barefaced, he was beautiful. Not pretty, not vulnerable, but undeniably handsome with his narrow, hawkish face and sharply defined cheekbones. His blade of a nose accentuated the long planes of his cheeks to the rugged thrust of his jaw, making his mouth appear sensual by comparison, even though his lips weren't particularly full.

They weren't narrow, either, and neither were his eyes, but the keen way he watched her spoke of focus and intelligence.

Don't think about last night, she ordered herself, fighting the inner trembling of reaction.

"You could have given me your name last night and saved us taking up a room when they're so highly in demand."

Her throat closed as she processed his thick accent first. It was more pronounced when he spoke above a whisper and charged his deep, stern voice with husked layers. Then his words sifted through her mind, allowing her first to absorb that he recognized her, but didn't know her name. How—? The criticism in his tone penetrated, distracting her. She was rather sensitive to being called thoughtless, willing to admit she'd been quite the spoiled brat before she'd learned that even charmed lives could be hexed.

Finally she grasped the whole of what he'd said, and it sounded as if he thought she had known whom she was messing around with last night. Which meant he hadn't come here because he was looking for her, but because…

Oh. My. God.

"Ryzard Vrbancic?" she managed faintly. Please no.

His gorgeous mouth twisted with ironic dismay. "As you can see. Who are you?"

Of course she could see. Now that her brain was beginning to function, it was obvious this was the self-appointed president of Bregnovia. The leader of a resistance movement turned opportunist who had claimed the national treasury—from a fellow criminal, sure, but claimed it for himself all the same—then used it to buy his seat in his newly minted parliament.

How did a name such as Ryzard go from being something vaguely lethal and unsavory to noble and dynamic simply by encountering the man in person? How had she not sensed or realized—

"There's been a mistake. I've made a mistake." Oh, gawd, she could never tell her family. Her *virginity?* Really? To this man?

And yet her body responded to being in his presence. Even though she wasn't drunk and no music seduced her, her feet didn't want to move and her eyes kept being dragged back to his wide chest, where a sprinkle of hair had abraded her palms. His arms flexed as she watched, forcing memories of being caught protectively against him when the fireworks had started then carried like a wilting Southern belle when sex had been the only thing on their minds.

His wide-spaced feet in Italian leather drew her gaze, making her recall the way he'd shed his shoes and the rest of his clothes so deftly last night. His burnished bronze skin had been anything but cold and hard. He'd been taut and alive.

And generous. He'd touched her with incredible facility completely devoted to her pleasure. She tried not to look for his hands, but she was fervently aware of the way he'd tantalized her so intimately toward orgasm. In public.

Mortified heat burned her to the core, especially because she yearned to know it all again. Everything about him called to her, feathering over her nerves like last night's velvety breeze, not just awakening her sensuality, but exciting her senses into full alert. Why? How? The rapid plunge back into sexual arousal was incredibly confusing. Disconcerting. She needed to get out of here.

Pushing off the glass wall, she took two steps and he took one, blocking her.

Her heart plummeted through the floor. This undersea

garden had suddenly become a shark cage, and she was trapped inside it with the shark.

Warily she eyed him. "I didn't know who you were last night."

"No?" His brow kicked up, dismissing her claim as a lie.

"No!"

"You sleep with strangers often?"

"Apparently you do, so don't judge me."

His head went back a fraction, reassessing her. "Who are you?"

She folded her arms, debating. If she left now, without telling him, Christian might salvage something. She, of course, could never show her face in public again, but she didn't intend to. Except—

Her gaze involuntarily went to the black dossier on the table, the one that held their letter of introduction and a background on the company. She jerked her gaze back to his, panicked that he might have followed her look, but trying not to show it.

His vaguely bored gaze traveled to the table and came back to hers. Intrigue lit his irises, turning their green-gold depths to emerald. A cruel smile toyed with his mouth.

"That's not for you," she said firmly. "I have to go." She took one step toward the table and he reached without hurry to pick the dossier up.

"I said—"

He only flashed her a dangerous look that held her off and opened it with an elegant turn of his long finger. *Don't think about those fingers.*

Leave, she told herself, but there was no point. She couldn't outrun this sizzling mortification, no matter where she went. Her stomach turned over as she waited for a sign of his reaction to what he read.

A muted bell pinged. "Your reserved time has reached

its limit," a modulated female voice said through hidden speakers.

Thank God. Tiffany let out her breath.

"Extend it," Ryzard commanded.

"Will another thirty minutes be sufficient?"

"I can't stay," Tiffany insisted.

Grim male focus came up to hold her in place, locking her vocal chords.

"Send a full report to my tablet on Davis and Holbrook, specifically their director, *Mrs.* Paul Davis. Thirty minutes is plenty."

"Very good, sir." The bell pinged again and Tiffany thought, *run.* The threat he emanated seemed very real, even though he didn't move, only stared at her with utter contempt.

Bunching her fists at her sides, she lifted her chin, refusing to be anything less than indignant if he was going to jump to nasty conclusions about her. *He* could be married for all she knew—which was a disgusting thought. Her brain frantically tried to retrieve knowledge one way or another. She was no poli-sci major, but she'd always kept up on headlines, usually knowing way more than she wanted to about world politics because of her father's ambitions. There were gaps because of the accident, of course, months of news she'd missed completely that coincided with the coup in Bregnovia.

She had no memory about his marital status, but something told her he wouldn't be nearly so scornful of her if he had his own spouse in the wings.

Ryzard tossed the folder into the empty chair and hooked his hands in his pockets to keep from strangling the woman who wanted to play him for a fool. Her being married was bad enough. She might shrug off little things like extramarital affairs, but he did not.

The fact she thought she could buy his business was even more aggravating, partly because he was so affected by last night. As much as he wished he wasn't, his body was reacting to her even though she was dressed very conservatively. Her loose, sand-colored pants grazed the floor over heeled sandals he'd glimpsed when she had moved. They were clunky-looking things, but their height elongated her legs into lissome stems he wanted to feel through the thin fabric of her pants. Her yellow top was equally lightweight and cut across her collarbone, hiding skin that had seemed powder white last night.

What he'd seen of it, anyway. He couldn't see much today and found that equally frustrating. He might have detected her nipples poking against the fine silk of her top, but while her flat green jacket nipped in to emphasize her waist, it also shielded her breasts from his view.

Nothing about her appearance hinted at the exciting, sensual woman he'd met last night. Even her wild curls had been scraped back, which might have been an elegant display of her bone structure if he could see her face.

"Take off your mask," he ordered, irritated that his voice wasn't as clear as he'd like.

"No."

The quietly spoken word blasted into his eardrums. It was not something he heard often.

"It's not a request," he stated.

"It's not open for discussion," she responded, body language so hostile he could practically taste her antagonism.

Curious.

No. He wouldn't allow himself to be intrigued by her. Pulling himself together, he did his best to reject and eject her from every aspect of his life in one blow.

Glancing away as if his senses weren't concentrated upon her every breath and pulse, he said dismissively, "Tell your husband you failed. My business can't be bought. He

might enjoy your second-rate efforts that offer no real pleasure, but I'm more discerning."

Her sharp inhale, as if she'd been stabbed in the lung,
drew his gaze back to her. Her lips were white and trembled
just enough to kick him in the conscience.

He forced himself to hold her hurt gaze, surprised how
effective his insult had been. Her startling blue eyes deepened to pools of navy that churned with angry hatred. He
didn't flinch from it, but instead held her gaze as if he was
holding a knife in a wound, ensuring he would fully sever
himself from a repeat performance of his weakness.

"How do you propose I tell him?" she asked with a bitterness that bludgeoned him, implacable and final. "Hire
a psychic? He's dead." She pivoted to the door.

A blinding flash, like white light, shot through him.
Not an external thing, but an inner slice of laser-sharp pain
that he felt as an echo of hers. He knew that sort of grief—

Before he realized what he was doing, he'd moved to
catch her arm and spin her around to him.

She used her momentum to bring her free hand up, sending it flying toward his face.

He caught her wrist and jerked back his head, his re-
flexes honed by war and a natural dominance that always
kept him on guard. Still, a heavy blanket of regret suffocated him as he held her while she wordlessly struggled.
He'd insulted her because he was angry, but he would never
wound someone by dangling such a loss over them. An
apology was needed, but holding on to her was like trying
to wrestle a feral cat into a sack.

"Stop fighting me," he ground out, surprised by her wiry
strength and unflagging determination.

"Go to hell!"

He got her wrists in one hand behind her back, her knee
scissored between his own tightly enough to prevent it ris-

ing into his crotch. Squeezing her enough to threaten her breathing, he loosened off as she quieted.

"Big man, overwhelming a helpless woman," she taunted in a pant.

"You're not that helpless," he noted, admiring her fighting spirit despite his inherent knowledge that he shouldn't like anything about her.

She was widowed. That was tremendously important, even though he refused to examine too closely why he was so relieved. Or why he was now determined to learn more about her. He'd been serious about not being corruptible, no matter how his body longed to be persuaded.

Her shaken breaths caused her breasts to graze his chest, increasing the arousal their struggle had already stimulated. She recognized his hardness and squirmed again, forcing him to pin her even closer to hang on to her.

"Let me go," she said in a furious voice that provoked more than intimidated.

"In a minute." He reached to remove her mask—

She tried to bite him. He narrowly snatched his fingers from the snap of her teeth.

"You little wildcat." He couldn't help but be amused by her streak of ferocity. Her bared teeth were perfect, her pinched nostrils as refined as a spoiled princess's.

"I'm reporting this assault," she told him.

"I have a right to see whose body I was in last night," he told her, unconsciously revealing with the low timbre of his voice how disturbed he was by the memory.

"No, you don't. I'm discerning about who sees any part of me. And maybe I didn't bring my best game last night because I was bored and wanted it over with. Did you think of that?"

"I suppose I deserved that," he murmured, but her insult still landed like a knee in the gut, making his abdominal muscles clench in offense.

Digging his fingers around the knot of her hair, he tugged lightly, deliberately overwhelming her with his strength, exposing her throat and making her aware she was at his mercy. Not because he got off on hurting women. Never. But she needed to understand that even though she was utterly vulnerable to him, he wouldn't harm her.

"Now we've both said something cruel, and neither of us will do it again."

Her outraged "Ha" warmed his lips, making him deeply conscious of the shape of her Kewpie-doll mouth with its peaks in her top lip over a fat strawberry of a bottom one. Her scent, like Saponaria, somewhere between dewy grass and sun-warmed roses, threatened to erase all thought but making love to her again.

"I only said what I did because I thought you were married. And you tricked me. I don't like your trying to take advantage of me. To even the playing field…" He reached for the tailing ribbon that held her mask.

"Noooo." The sharp anguish in her voice startled him. She was genuinely terrified, straining into a twist to escape his loosening of the mask.

He let go of the ribbon and her, horrified that he'd scared her so deeply, but he couldn't help reaching to steady her when she staggered as she tried to catch the falling mask. Her shaking hands fumbled it before her, turning it around and around, trying to right it so she could put it on again. A desperate sob escaped her.

It was too late. He'd seen what she was trying to hide, and the bottom dropped out of his heart. He touched her chin, wanting a better look.

She knocked his hand away and flashed a look of fury at him. With her jaw set in livid mutiny, she stopped trying to replace her mask and stared him down with the kind of aggression that would make him fear for his life if she'd been armed.

"Happy?" she charged.

Not one little bit.

As he took in the mottled shades of pink and red, all he saw was pain. He'd been in battle. He knew what bullets and flames and chemicals could do to the human body. That's why his world had stopped last night when he'd thought a bomb was landing on the ramparts of the club.

But these were healed injuries, as well as they'd ever get anyway. The ragged edge of the facial scar followed a crooked line like a country's border on a map, sharply defining rescued flesh from the unharmed with a raised pink scar. It hedged a patch from over her left eye into the corner of her lid—she might have lost her sight, he acknowledged, cold dread touching his internal organs. Under her eye, it cut diagonally toward her nose before tracing down to the corner of her mouth and under her jawline, and then wound back to her hair.

The side of her neck was only a little discolored, but the way the color fanned at the base of it made him suspect the scarring went down her arm and torso, too, maybe farther.

As he brought his gaze back up to her face, he met eyes so bruised and wounded, he was struck with shame at causing her to reveal herself. He hadn't been trying to humiliate her. This wasn't meant as a punishment.

The hatred in her eyes took it as such anyway, stabbing him with compunction.

"I wouldn't work for you if your country was knocked back into the Stone Age and we were overinventoried in animal fur and flint. I'm leaving. Now."

He didn't try to stop her, sensing he'd misjudged her on a grand scale.

She tied her mask into place without looking at him. When she pressed the button to open the doors, they didn't cooperate, remaining closed while she swore at her watch.

"Tiffany," he cajoled, pulling her name from what he'd read, but not sure what he would say if he could persuade her to stay.

"Die," she ordered flatly.

The doors opened and she walked out.

CHAPTER FOUR

FOR THE FIRST time in months, Tiffany cried. Really cried as she hugged her knees in the shower and released sobs that echoed against the tiles. They racked her so hard she thought she'd throw up. She hated her life, hated herself, hated him.

She'd still been processing his remark about her efforts being second-rate when he'd yanked back her curtain and looked at her as if she was an object of horror. As though he was repulsed.

Sex was not worth this. Men weren't. She was old enough, and educated enough, to know that having a husband and kids were not necessary ingredients to a woman's happiness. Why then was she so gutted every time she was forced to face that no man would ever want her? That a family life would never be hers?

It was self-pitying tripe, and she had to get over it.

Forcing her weak legs to support her, she turned off the shower and leaned against the wall, cold and dripping until she worked up the energy to pull on a robe. As she moved into her room, she felt empty. Not better, not depressed, just numb.

That was okay. She could live with numb.

Perching on the foot of the bed, she stared at her wrinkled fingers and wondered what she should do. Hide in her room until this ridiculous clubhouse opened its doors again? Fake appendicitis for a helicopter ride to the mainland? She felt sick. She was damp and feverish, aching all over, weak and filled with malaise.

A yawn took her by surprise and she thought, *Siesta*. One small thing in her favor. Crawling up to her pillows, she escaped into unconsciousness.

The sun crept around the edge of his balcony, likely to begin blistering his bare toes soon, but Ryzard was ready to stretch away the stiffness in his body anyway. He'd been motionless for over an hour as he read through the report he'd been provided by the *Q Virtus* staff.

Davis and Holbrook was an exceptional organization, very well regarded in the international construction industry. He could definitely do worse as he looked at rebuilding the broken roads and collapsed buildings in his city centers. They had wanted to land on his radar as he moved toward those sorts of goals, and now they were.

The rest of the report, about Mrs. Paul Davis, was even more interesting. She had started out as a wealthy society darling. Her marriage to a family friend had all the markings of a traditional fairy tale, right up to the wedding gown with a train and the multitiered cake.

Except a wedding gift from the bride's brother of a prestigious sports car had been more temptation than the drunken groom could resist. He'd taken it up to ninety between the courtyard and the gates of the golf and country club, detonating it against a low brick wall before the guests had stopped waving.

After a flurry of death and memorial announcements accompanied by touch-and-go mentions of the bride, the reports had dried up. Fast-forward two years and his widow was taking the reins of her dead husband's corporation. Her brother had held her power of attorney during her recovery, but his talents were better suited to hands-on architectural engineering. The plethora of awards he'd earned spoke to that very loudly.

All of this would have been flat information if it didn't reinforce to Ryzard that he'd made a mistake in assuming she'd been trying to influence him with sex. What reason would she have? Her company was flourishing—somewhat surprisingly, given that her credentials amounted to an arts degree and attitude, but her grades were exceptional. She was certainly intelligent.

And he could personally attest that she was a ballbuster, he allowed with irony. He had no doubt she was more than a figurehead. If she had a vision, quite likely one formed in her husband's name, she would achieve it.

Turning from that disturbing thought, he allowed that if Bregnovia had already attained recognition, she might have tried for an advantage while he had a wider playing field to draw from, but it would be a risky move until his government was recognized.

Did their interest in his business mean an acknowledgment for Bregnovia was in the works? Or was their rendezvous exactly what it seemed to be: two healthy people enjoying the pleasures of the mating ritual.

Heat pooled in his lap as he dwelt on the possibility she'd welcomed him because she'd been as caught up as he had in their physical compatibility.

A twinge of conscience followed, but he had long ago rationalized that his heart and his body were separate when it came to sex. He had the same basic needs as any living thing, requiring nutrition, a sheltered environment and a regular release of his seed. If a peculiar mix of chemistry intensified his reaction when that last happened, well, he couldn't be held responsible. It was hormones, not emotion.

It was not infidelity against Luiza.

And Tiffany would have no reason to pursue him for sex

to gain his business. It would only complicate what might otherwise be a wise and lucrative association.

Something he should take under consideration, he supposed, scraping the side of his thumb against the stubble coming in on his jaw. It didn't matter how he cast their tryst. It shouldn't happen again.

Except there was one other fact from this report that kept teasing him.

Mr. Holbrook, Tiffany's father. An architect by education, he'd quickly become a career politician who'd worked his way up the ranks of local councils into a senator's mansion. He was now running for the presidency.

Suppose last night had been pure coincidence. Why then had the Holbrooks requested he meet them here, under the discreet curtain of *Q Virtus?* If they feared making a play for his business would hurt the senator's chances, they wouldn't have met him at all. No, it must mean they knew the United States was leaning toward recognition.

A flush of excitement threatened to overtake him, but Ryzard reminded himself to be patient. Backing from the United States would influence many other countries to vote in his favor, but nothing was confirmed.

Still, one thing was clear: he needed another meeting with Tiffany Davis.

Tiffany woke foggy-headed to a noise in the main room like dishes rattling on a cart. Leaping from the bed, she staggered to the door into the lounge and found Ryzard Vrbancic directing one of the *petite q's* to set a table on the balcony.

"What are you doing?" She turned the lapel of her robe up against her cheek.

"I thought you were showering, but apparently you went back to sleep."

"What?" Tiffany scowled at him. "How do you know

what I've been doing? I thought these rooms were completely secure," she charged the woman in the red gown.

"I used my override to bring in the meal you ordered… didn't you?" The young woman looked suspiciously at Ryzard, but he was quick.

"We did, thank you. I'll manage from here. You can go." To Tiffany, he said, "Don't confuse the staff just because we've had a tiff." A mild snort and, "You're aptly named, aren't you?"

"Get out of here," she cried.

The *petite q,* already hurrying, ran to the door and out.

Goggling at Ryzard, whose mouth twitched, Tiffany said, "Seriously?"

"You're overreacting."

"I want you to leave."

"I'm about to make you an offer you can't refuse. Quit hiding and accept."

She narrowed her eyes on his back as he moved onto the balcony, not interested in anything from him except assurances her family would never find out what had happened between them. Not that she was willing to say so.

It took everything in her to stand tall and say, "What kind of offer?" She was writhing inside at everything that had happened, yet had wound up dreaming about him. It had been erotic until it had turned humiliating.

"I can't hear you," he called from the balcony.

Clenching her teeth, she wavered in the doorway, hanging back while telling herself not to let him get away with this manipulation. At the very least, she ought to cover up. She didn't so much as go for milk in the middle of the night without concealer for fear of frightening the staff at home. The only reason she'd forgone it this morning was because she'd expected to keep her mask on.

Ryzard Vrbancic had seen her, however, and she was

still flopping like a fish out of water, gasping for air, waiting for the boot that would send her careening off the boat.

Everything in her cringed with a need to hide, but maybe seeing her again like this would repel him into moving along.

Yanking tight the tie on her robe, she marched to the open French doors and said, "I'm not interested in any offers from you. Please leave."

"I thought you were dressing," he remarked, squeezing fresh lemon across raw oysters in their half shell. They were arranged on a silver tray of ice. Next to them sat a tapas platter of fritters, flatbread, shredded meat, guacamole, salsa and something that looked like burritos but they were wrapped in a type of leaf.

Her stomach growled. She tried to cover the sound with her hand, but he'd heard.

"You're hungry. Eat," he urged magnanimously. As if he wasn't trespassing in her room.

"I prefer to eat alone." She indicated the door, not subtle at all.

He picked up an oyster and eyed her as he slurped it into his mouth, chewed briefly, then swallowed. Raw oysters were supposed to be an aphrodisiac. She'd always thought they were disgusting, but what he'd just done had been the sexiest thing she'd ever seen. She followed the lick of his tongue across his lips, and a wobbly sensation accosted her insides.

Reacting to him made staring him down even more difficult than it already was, but she held his gaze, inner confidence trembling as she waited for another flinch to overtake him like the one this morning. His expression never wavered, though. He let his gaze slide to her scarred cheek, but then it went south into her cleavage, where the swells of her breasts peeped from between her lapels. His perusal continued over her hips, lingered on the dangling ends of her belt and ended at her shins, one white, one mottled.

Involuntarily, her toes curled as she reacted to his masculine assessment. She couldn't tell if she was passing muster or being found wanting. She told herself it didn't matter, that she didn't want his approval or any man's, but in her heart she yearned for a hint of admiration.

He pulled out a chair. "Sit down."

Swallowing, telling herself to keep a straight head, she deliberately provoked a reaction to her flaws by saying, "I'm not supposed to go in the sun."

He shrugged off the protest. "It will set in twenty minutes."

"Look, I'm running out of ways to tell you to get lost without pulling out the big one. I don't want anything to do with you. I was against giving you that letter in the first place, and I'm sorry I came here at all. We won't work for you."

He finished another oyster, but she had his full attention. She could feel it. When his tongue cleaned his lips, she imagined he was licking her all over.

Ignore it, she chided herself.

"Why?" he asked.

Why what? Her brain had lost the plot, but she quickly picked it up, reminding herself of *his* flaws.

"Because I don't like your methods. You're no better than the criminal you replaced."

"I'm a lot better than the criminal I replaced. Check my human-rights record," he growled while a flush of insult rose to his cheeks.

It was enough antagonism to give her pause and make her reconsider deliberately riling him, but despite how much she hated herself for having sex with him, she was still aware of a pull. She desperately needed to cut him down and out.

"You're living pretty large while your countrymen starve. How many people died so you could eat raw oysters and watch the sun set?"

"You know nothing about what I've lost so my people can eat," he said in a lethal tone.

As he spoke, he turned aside to toss his empty shell on the cart, but she glimpsed such incredible pain she caught her breath against an answering stab of anguish. She quickly muffled it, but something in her wavered. Was she misjudging him?

She shook off the thought, scoffing, "Did I strike a nerve? Do you not like having your repulsive side exposed?"

He shot her a fierce look and she thought, *Shut up, Tiffany.*

"You're acting out of bitterness, and it's not with me. We promised not to be cruel."

That gave her a niggle of guilt, which she didn't like at all. She looked at her perfectly manicured nails.

"You might have promised," she said haughtily. "I didn't."

"You like to deliberately hurt people? You do have an ugly side."

That lifted her gaze, and his expression made her heart tremor where it clogged the base of her throat. He had very patrician features. Very proud and strong. Right now they were filled with contempt.

Shame lunged in her. She might have been spoiled and self-involved, but she never used to be mean. But she was angry. So angry. And there was no one to take it out on. She had to look away from the expression that demanded she apologize.

She wavered, uncertain of her footing, but she had enough unscrambled brain cells to remember he was a dictator, not some do-good pastor.

"What do you expect, a welcome mat?" she hazarded, tucking her fists behind her upper arms, affecting a bravado she didn't feel. "You've invaded my territory—"

"You're not angry I'm here. You're angry you had to face the man you made love to last night. That I saw your secret. You're not repulsive, Tiffany."

"As I said, you're stepping into places you haven't been invited."

"I was invited." He picked up an oyster, and his tongue curled to chase and catch the slippery flesh before he pulled the morsel into his mouth.

Inner muscles that were still vaguely tender from their lovemaking clenched involuntarily, sending a shimmer of pleasure upward to her navel and down the insides of her thighs.

When he took a step toward her, she took a hasty one back, bumping into the rail of the balcony.

He raised his brows as he pulled out her chair another inch, reading way too clearly what kind of nervousness she'd just revealed.

"I want you to leave," she insisted.

"We'll clear the air first."

She almost mumbled an adolescent, *I don't want to clear the air.* Because she didn't. She wanted to hit and bite and push away.

She wanted to be left alone to die of loneliness.

Oh, don't be such a baby, Tiffany.

It was true, though. She was like a wounded animal that snarled at anyone who tried to help it. It was the source of the horrible tension with her family. They didn't know what to do with this new Tiffany who hated her life and everything in it.

She glared at Ryzard, loathing him for being the man to show her how twisted she'd become. He'd caught her in a moment of terrible weakness last night, playing pretend that she was normal. He'd sliced past the emotional scar tissue she'd grown, and he seemed to still be doing it. That made him dangerous.

"The sun is about to set. It won't hurt you to be out here," he said.

She whipped around to see how close it was to the horizon. She hadn't been in the sun for more than a handful of steps between a house and car in two years. As she stepped into its rays, the heat on her face felt good. The fading red ball filled her with rapture as it lowered toward the sea.

Holding her breath, she strained her ears.

The band started below, making her slap a hand on the rail in disappointment. "I wanted to hear it!"

"Hear what?" he asked, standing next to her.

"When the sun touches the water."

He gave her a skeptical look that said, *Aren't you a bit old for that?*

She turned away, hiding that yes, she clung to certain childish fantasies that reminded her of easier, simpler times. Being lighthearted and silly didn't come naturally to her anymore, and she desperately longed to find that part of herself again. Tiny moments of happiness were like bread crumbs, hopefully leading her back to a place of acceptance. Maybe even contentment.

"You're really quite sensitive, aren't you?" he mused.

"No."

"And contrary." He waved at the chair he'd pulled out for her. "I have some questions for you. They're important. Sit."

"I'm not a dog."

"No, you're as aloof and touchy as a wet cat. The purring version is worth all the scratching and hissing, though."

"I don't want to talk about that," she rushed to state, unnerved by the suggestiveness in his remark.

"We won't. Not yet," he agreed, and his touch on her shoulder nudged her to sit.

She did, mainly to avoid the way the light contact of his hand made her stomach dip in excitement, and partly because her mother was lecturing her in her head. The members of their family, in all their greatness, were ambassadors, obligated to set an example of good manners and rising above the unpleasant. Such an annoying legacy.

She was also starving. Taking care of herself had become a habit through her recovery. Good food was one of her few real pleasures these days, and this stuff looked awesome.

He watched her build a flatbread into a soft taco, not being shy with the high-calorie avocado paste, either.

"What?" she asked defensively.

"I'm not used to seeing a woman eat like that."

She bit back a spiteful, *Too busy watching them starve?* She really didn't want to be that person, but she didn't know how else to handle him.

"Why are you here?" she asked instead.

He paused in preparing his own flatbread. "Why are *you* here, Tiffany? Why did your family send you to meet me?"

The weight of his gaze turned her shrug into a shiver. "Apparently I'm the only one who is a member."

His brows went up in surprise.

"I inherited my husband's fortune. My father isn't exactly struggling, but he doesn't qualify."

"I read about your accident. I'm sorry for your loss."

She prickled, waiting to see if he would make more of it, dig deeper, question how a married woman could have been a virgin.

"I'm also a member and was one long before our civil war. The money you accuse me of stealing is Bregnovia's. It's earmarked to fund our recovery."

She eyed him, seeing a contrary mix of Euro-sophistication and obdurate leader. When he caught her looking at him, her heart skipped. She looked away.

"I'll have to request a report on you from the powers that be. Find out how you made your fortune," she said.

"I'll tell you. It's a spigot system I developed for the oil industry, inspired by what I learned working in vineyards after finishing my engineering degree."

Despite her inner warnings to hold him off, she was intrigued. "That seems an odd choice. What was an engineer doing in a winery?"

"Rebelling," he said flatly, not inviting more questions as he reached to the wine bucket and drew out a dripping green bottle. "This is from my country. You'll enjoy it."

Of course she would. Who would dare not?

His arrogance was growing on her if she was finding it more amusing than annoying.

"What do you mean, you were rebelling?"

He drew a subtle breath, as though gathering himself for something difficult. "If you were to order a report on me, you would learn my parents sent me to live in Germany when I was six. For my safety and to give me a better life. Our country has been annexed by one neighbor or another since before the First World War. There were constant outbreaks of independence-seeking followed by terrible repression. My parents couldn't leave, but they smuggled me out to friends. I can't complain. My foster parents were good people. The husband was an automotive engineer who pressed me to follow in his footsteps. As a vocation I didn't mind it, but when I graduated I felt as most young people do. That this was my life and I could do as I liked." He shrugged, mouth twisting in self-deprecation. "I'm not proud of abandoning my potential to pick grapes, but it allowed me to bring a fresh perspective when I went to Russia, planning to make my fortune drilling for oil."

"Where you fashioned this doodad that is so popular it made you into a bazillionaire?"

"Da," he confirmed with a nod.

"Humph." She reached for her wine. "Does the rest of the world know this?"

He lifted a shoulder dismissively. "The press prefers to sensationalize what I did with my money."

"Which was to fund a war."

"I freed my country."

"And now you own it."

"I lead it. What do you think of the wine?"

She was no sommelier and didn't bother with sniffing and swirling, but she thought the light color was appealing and she enjoyed the way the initial tang, almost fruity, eased into something more earthy. Not oaky. Vanilla?

She tried again, wanting to determine what it was. But as much as she loved wine, alcohol had been off-limits as her body had needed every advantage to recover. That made her a lightweight. She had to be careful about losing her head around him.

As the memory of their dirty dancing and everything that followed bathed her in heat, the proximity of a bedroom and sitting here in her robe suddenly seemed incredibly dangerous and intimate.

Ryzard watched a glow of awareness brighten Tiffany's skin, filling her compelling blue eyes even as she looked into the crisp white wine she set aside. Her reaction might be in response to the alcohol, but his male instincts read her differently.

He shifted in his chair, widening his knees to make room for the growing reaction tugging insistently between his legs.

Tricking the waitstaff into granting him entry to her room had been the oldest one in the book, but as he'd suspected, she wouldn't have seen him otherwise and he wanted answers. At this precise second, however, he found himself with only one thing on his mind: her. She was more complex than he'd given her credit for, both when he'd lost himself in the mecca of her flesh and when he'd assumed she was attempting to manipulate him.

She was far more beautiful than he'd taken the time to notice this morning, too. Then his attention had been drawn to the scarring, his focus on the pain it indicated. Now he could see what had existed before discoloration and a raised jagged line had bisected her cheek. Blonde, blue eyed, with skin like a baby and the bone structure of an aristocrat, she was Helen of Troy.

Not that he was prepared to go to war ever again, but he could imagine men who would. Her young husband must have been intimidated, knowing how coveted she was.

"It's rude to stare," she said, growing redder in one cheek.

"I'm not staring. I'm admiring."

Her mouth shrank in rejection, and so did his brain. He forced himself to look away from thick lashes that swept down to hide her eyes. This meeting wasn't about kindling an affair that had barely started, no matter how much the thought appealed.

It appealed far too much. He could barely concentrate as memories of her pushing her ass into his groin as she writhed with pleasure under his slippery touch filled his head. The heady power of fondling her to orgasm had made him drunk and was overshadowed only by how good she had felt squeezing him in her hot, perfect depths.

But his country came first. He couldn't forget that. Couldn't forget anything.

He shook himself out of his fascination and spoke briskly.

"Your father seems exceptionally well connected in Washington. By sending you to speak to me, he is signaling that your country is likely to support my petition for recognition at the UN, is he not? Has he told you this is forthcoming?"

"He's under that impression, but who knows what the attitude will be tomorrow? Welcome to politics. You know how these things work."

He did, and the hardest lesson he had learned after being in a war was when to back off and use diplomacy instead of force to get what he wanted. It was also standard practice to weigh a person's impact on an agenda before developing a relationship.

Maybe he hadn't properly examined how their affair could affect his goal before he made love to her, but Tiffany's knowledge and connections suggested she could have a very positive influence.

A wild rush of excitement flew through him as he found a rationale to continue their affair, but he forced himself to hold on to a cool head and gather information first. "Does your father have any sway over your country's decision makers?"

"He has followers. Believers in his vision. Isn't that how you got elected, by cultivating the same?" The remark was somewhere between haughty and ironic.

"You don't seem to be one of them. His followers, I mean. It's quite obvious you're not one of mine. Yet."

"Ha," she choked, but she lowered her lashes as if to prevent him reading something different in her eyes. "Never yours and while I'll always cheer for Dad, I'm tired of living my life by his career," she said with dour humor and popped a cherry tomato into her mouth, pursing her lips in a pout as she chewed.

"When is the election?" he asked, trying not to watch her plump lips too closely.

"Not for a year, but the campaigning is well under way. He was leaving for Washington as we were coming here."

"We?" he asked sharply, territorial instincts riled.

"My brother and I."

"Ah. That's fine then." He frowned. Whatever relief he felt in knowing there wasn't another man in her life was buried under the discomfort of revealing he saw himself in the role. What was it about her that not only affected him but also lowered his ability to hide how much?

She lifted her brows. "Jealous?" Her smile was taunting, but her voice thinned across the word, suggesting a vulnerability that further undermined his resistance to her.

He shouldn't want her this badly, but he did. Last night had been exceptional, and she was a practical connection to cultivate. Where was the sense in fighting it?

"Possessive," he corrected. "You have a lover, *draga*."

Her shocked expression masked into something complex. Her lips tightened in dismay while her brow flinched in pain. A stark yearning drew her features taut while her swallow indicated a type of fear. Then it all smoothed away, leaving him unsettled, wondering if an affair with her could become more complicated than it needed to be.

"Had," she said in a husky voice. "Past tense."

"I'm not talking about your husband," he growled, stirred to jealousy after all.

The blank look she sent him disappeared in a raspy laugh. "Neither am I."

His sharp brain caught a hidden meaning, but she kept talking, distracting him.

"Last night was a departure from my real life, not something I'll ever do again. Why would you even want to—" Dawning comprehension waxed her features before her face gradually tightened in rejection and something more disturbing. Anguish. "Wow. Nice to know some things haven't changed," she said bitterly.

"What do you mean?" Clammy palms seemed an overreaction to being rejected as a one-nighter. He'd done it himself in the past, but he didn't like it. Not from her.

"I'm still capable of being used," she answered. "You think that if you keep me close, you'll keep my father's cronies closer."

A pinch of compunction gave him pause, but that's not all that was going on here. And now she'd piqued his curiosity.

"Who used you in the past? How?" It was a tender point for him. Only a blind fool would fail to see the advantage to him in associating with her, but there were lines, especially with women. When Luiza was taken, it was to use her as leverage against him. She'd ended her life to prevent it. He never took manipulation of the unwilling lightly.

"Who *hasn't* used me?" she demanded. "I thought if there was one silver lining to this—" she drew a circle around her face "—it was that I was no longer a pawn. Thanks for dinner." She stood up, tossing him a pithy look. "A girl in my position is lucky when a man shows her a bit of attention. You're a helluva guy, Ryzard."

Her contempt burned like acid as it dripped over him. It might not have seared so deeply if he hadn't grasped at the advantages of an affair to justify exactly how badly he wanted to continue theirs.

He didn't want to admit how fierce his hunger for her was, but the hurt beneath her words told him she didn't see any at all. Wounding her, especially when she was so sensitive about her desirability, had a disturbing effect on him. Guilt assailed him and provoked something deeper. A compulsion to draw her close and make up with her.

He didn't want to be so enthralled. It went against everything he'd promised himself and Luiza's memory. Nevertheless, he reacted to the way she rejected him with a pivot of her body. It incited him to strike fast to keep from being shut out. Fear that had nothing to do with the best interests of his country goaded him to act.

"Don't underestimate what's between us, Tiffany." He

inwardly cringed at revealing so much, but he was even more averse to her thinking he was capable of low motives. "The attraction between us is real and very strong."

"Oh, give it up! You don't want me. You—"

"Shall I prove it?" He rose and easily stalked her across the tiny space of the balcony, using her outstretched hand to tug her close and pulling her resistant body into to his own.

"What do you think you're doing?" she demanded, wriggling for freedom then stilling when she felt his arousal. "You—" Confusion stilled her and she searched his expression.

"As I said." He lowered his head, setting a determined kiss over her protesting mouth.

Tiffany continued to press for distance, but he wasn't being mean, just insistent. Still, she was awfully confused. The way he'd given her that moment of hope that she could be attractive to someone before she realized it was all a ruse had been devastating. Now he was coming on strong, making her want to melt into him. Really, seriously, turn to mush in his arms. It was so frightening to be this affected. She did the only thing she could think to do. She tried to bite him.

He jerked his head back. "Are we playing rough, *draga?*" He shot his hand beneath her robe, grasping her breast in a firm hand, dislodging the slippery tie of her robe so it started to fall open.

"Don't!" she cried, hunching and scrambling to keep as much cloth in place as possible. "Please, Ryzard, don't do this. Not out here where anyone could see."

He froze, then slowly withdrew his hand. The tips of his fingers grazed a distended nipple, sending a pulse of pleasure-pain through her. She was too humiliated to respond and too shaken by the fear of exposure to appreciate his obeying her plea.

"Tiffany," he scolded as he held her in loose arms. "I'm not trying to hurt you."

Pushing back until he reluctantly let his hold on her drop away, she ensured she was completely covered, but couldn't lift her head.

"I've seen battle scars, you know." The hand he used to smooth her hair back from her bad cheek was surprisingly compassionate.

Rather than turn into his caress, she averted from it.

"I'm your first lover since the accident? That's why you're so shy?" Ryzard was still trying to catch up to the way her shield of toughness had fallen away so quickly into such tremendous vulnerability. One second she'd been a worthy adversary, the next a broken fawn in need of swift protection.

"Yeah." Her snorted word held a hysterical note. She tried to step over the chair he'd upended, trying to move away from him. Tears sheened her eyes, her emotions so close to the surface he knew she was near a tipping point.

He bent to right the chair, allowing her to move away into privacy because pieces were falling into place in his mind in a way he couldn't quite believe. Her back seemed incredibly narrow and bowed under a weight as she entered the suite. He could hardly countenance what he was thinking, but her gasp of pain last night rang in his ears. He had thought she just wasn't quite ready, but…

Cautiously he followed, one hand going to the door frame to steady himself as he asked, "Tiffany. Am I your *only* lover?"

She didn't turn around, but her shoulders seemed to flinch before she lifted her head to say cockily, "So far, but with my looks and connections, I'm encouraged to believe there's more in my future."

He bit back a curse while his free hand clenched into a

fist at his side. He wanted to shake her out of sheer frustration with her cavalier attitude, but at the same time he had a deep compulsion to cradle her against him. The erotic memory of their coming together grew sweeter even as he struggled with the ramifications of being a woman's first. He'd done it once before. He knew the emotional ties it pulled from both parties.

A splintering sensation accosted him as he once again compared her with Luiza. His first instinct was to walk away. Confusing emotions tumbled through him like a rockslide, tainted with the intense grief he'd managed to avoid as the aftermath of war had consumed him. He once again hated himself as a traitor for having more than a passing interest in Tiffany, but learning he was her first changed things. He wasn't so archaic he thought virginity was a seal of quality, but losing it was an important marker in a woman's life. He couldn't be dismissive of her or what she'd offered him, even if she was trying to be.

"Can you explain to me how this is possible, *Mrs*. Davis?"

Tiffany looked to the ceiling, battling back stupid tears and a deeper sense of vulnerability than she'd ever felt. There had been a time when her confidence, her belief in her own superiority, had been unflagging. In an instant she had become weak and broken and dependent. Finding her way back from that seemed impossible, and she hated that Ryzard saw her at this low point. He was so strong and sure of himself. Where had he been when she'd had all her defenses in place and could have handled his forceful, dynamic personality?

A dozen sarcastic responses to his question came to her tongue, but the nearest she could get to flippant was to say, "I was afraid I'd fall in love with someone else if I didn't save myself for Paulie."

She tightened her belt and turned, surprised to catch him in an unguarded moment.

The faraway look in his eye suggested he had dark thoughts of his own. Seeing he might not be as completely put together as he seemed gave her the courage to continue with more outspokenness than she'd ever allowed herself.

"Our marriage was written in stone. Our fathers were friends, and his mother was my mom's maid of honor. Paulie and my brother, Christian, were inseparable through childhood. The architect and engineer designed the bridge between our families when Paulie and I were still in diapers. By the time I was in high school, no other boy had the guts to ask me out. They knew I was already taken."

"You didn't date? Didn't sleep with him?"

"*Paulie* dated. He sowed enough wild oats for the both of us. He took me to the Friday night dances, and on Monday I would hear what had happened at the parties he went to after he dropped me at home. He came *here* and had affairs."

"And you put up with that?"

She sighed, hugging herself. "I believed him when he told me he was getting it out of his system. He swore that once we were married, he would never stray. I still believe he meant it. He encouraged me to do the same," she offered with a shrug, "but like I say, no one offered and I told myself it would be romantic to wait."

"Did you love him?"

She sighed, chest aching as she admitted what she'd never told anyone. "I adored him like a best friend. That's a good foundation for a marriage, right?" She had needed to believe it, but hearing it now only made her hug herself tighter.

She tried to stem the emotions swelling in her, but the rest of her feelings, the churning doubts and anger and grief, gathered and poured out. "I miss him like crazy. He's the one person who would have been right beside me through all of this, keeping my spirits up, saying all the right things. But I don't know if I'd even be speaking to him because I'm so angry. I hate him for dying, really truly hate hi—"

A sob arrived like a commuter train with a whoosh and a suck of air. She held herself steady as grief rose and peaked. She blinked and trembled until she could assimilate it. After a long minute, she found control again and managed to continue.

"I hate him for getting behind the wheel that night. I hate Christian for giving him the car. I hate myself for thinking one spin up the drive when we were all so drunk would be okay."

Something tickled her jaw, and she realized a tear had bled down her numb cheek to burn her chin. She swiped it away and sniffed back the rest.

Through blurred eyes, she saw Ryzard looked gray, but she was coming back from a dark place. The whole world looked dull and bleak.

"I've never admitted that to anyone," she confessed. "I think it needed to come out. Thank you." She rubbed her arms, becoming aware she was frozen and achy.

Ryzard's long legs and wide chest appeared unexpectedly before her. He drew her into his arms even as she drew a surprised breath. His expression was stark and filled with deep anguish.

"Don't say anything," he said heavily, overcoming her automatic stiffening and pressing her into the solid strength of his body. "Just be quiet a minute."

He smoothed hands along her back to mold her into him, warming her. It wasn't a pass. It was comfort. After a hesitant moment, she let her head settle into the hollow of his shoulder and closed her eyes. He stroked her hair and she let her arms wrap around him, hugging him so the bruise that was her heart still ached, but felt covered and protected by the shield of his solid presence.

"Sometimes anger and hatred are the only things that get you through the injustice," he said so quietly she wasn't sure she really heard him, but the tickle across her hair told her his voice was real. "I envy people of strong faith. They never seem tortured by the why of it."

She swallowed, floored to realize they were sharing a moment, something so deep and personal it didn't need a name of a lost one for her to know he understood her utterly and completely. He suffered as she did.

Her hand moved on his back, soothing the tension in the muscles alongside his spine. She relaxed into him and they held each other for a long minute.

Gradually she realized he was becoming aroused. He wasn't overt about it, but she knew and an answering thread of response began subtly changing her own body. Her internal organs felt quivery and her breasts grew sensitive. Awareness of their stark physical differences expanded in her mind along with how intimately they'd fit themselves together last night.

As heat suffused in her, she tried to pull away and keep her head ducked so he wouldn't see how she was reacting.

He kept her close and tilted her face up. His mouth twitched ruefully, but his eyes remained somber. "You see?" he murmured. A sensation of pressure made her think he might have stroked his thumb over the scar tissue on her cheek. "We're a good fit. You should let me give you the after-party you deserved before your wedding."

"Tempting," she said, backing out of his hold because a resurgence of warmth that had its feet in embarrassed longing tingled through her. "But I'm not a charity case you need to offer a pity lay. Give me your email and I'll let you know if my father learns anything."

"My desire for you has nothing to do with my political

agenda," he dismissed with a heavy dollop of annoyance. "I want you."

She snorted. "Why?"

"Because, Tiffany, if you had any experience with men, you would know that last night was remarkable. There are people who have been together years and not been so attuned to each other." He flinched a little as he said that, but she was too busy reacting to his outrageous claim.

"That's not what you said this morning." She tried to sound unaffected, but she was still feeling unfairly spanked. It reflected in the raspy edge on her tone and filled her with debasement long after the insult had landed. She couldn't even look at him.

"I was under a wrong impression and behaved unpleasantly. I apologize."

She eyed him, skeptical.

"I don't apologize often. I suggest you accept it."

"No doubt," she allowed with a twitch of her lips. His arrogance ought to turn her off, but he seemed to have a right to it. His inner strength was as compelling as his obvious physical virility. When it wasn't turned against her, that combination was lethally attractive.

"Come here," he cajoled in a smoky invitation, even though he stood within touching distance and only had to reach out if he really wanted to.

"Why?" She stayed where she was, but everything in her gravitated to him.

"I want to kiss you. Show you how good we are together."

"Seduce me?"

He offered a masculine smile so tomcattish and predatory, it made her stomach dip in giddy excitement. "I would very much like to make love to you again," he said.

An image of her naked body, the one she avoided in the

mirror every day, flashed in her mind. She drew the lapels of her robe together and shook her head.

"Find someone else. I'm not playing hard to get. I just don't see the point."

Rather than argue, he pursed his mouth in regret. "I've damaged your trust in me."

"There wasn't much to begin with," she assured him with a tight smile.

"And the claws are revealed once again." He seemed more amused than irritated. "You trusted me enough to share your—what does your American singer call it? The wonderland that is your body."

"Yes, well, I was pretending to be someone else," she dismissed with false breeziness, inner foundations unsteady as she recalled how completely she'd deluded herself into believing what she'd done was okay.

"Do it again," he commanded.

"Ha!" She couldn't help it. The man was so lofty and single-minded.

"I'm serious," he insisted. "Put on your mask. We'll go downstairs and find that woman capable of such delightful spontaneity."

"It's—no. I can't."

But she couldn't think why. At least, not fast enough to have an answer ready when he demanded, "Why not?"

"Because..." She searched for a reason.

"We could dance again. We both enjoyed that. Of course, we could do that here." He glanced to where the balcony doors stood open. The music from the band below drifted in with the sea-scented air and the swish of waves on the shore.

The mood and music came across as a lazy, exotic throb.

"No," she said firmly, smart enough to be wary of his power once he got his hands on her. The way he'd felt her up on the dance floor last night had obviously been a spell of some kind.

"Downstairs it is. Shall we say one hour? I can shave and change in fifteen minutes, but you women need twenty just to find a pair of shoes."

"He said," she mocked, "demonstrating his vast experience with the opposite sex."

"I won't apologize. We're adults. We can enjoy each other if we want to." He moved forward to set a brief but profound kiss on her startled mouth. "Sure you don't want to stay in?" he asked in a private tone that made her blood flutter in her arteries.

Oh, she was tempted, but she shook her head. "I'm not sure I even want to see you again."

"Meet me downstairs, Tiffany, or I'll come looking for you. But I don't want to waste time searching. Set your watch."

She shook her head. "I don't like people thinking they can talk to me. I'd rather leave it on Do Not Disturb."

"Set it so *I* can find you." At her blank look, he gave her a head shake of exasperation. "Where is it? I'll show you."

A few minutes later she stood in her empty suite wondering how she'd gone from crying in the shower to having a date, one that made her feel more awake and alive than—this was dangerous—any other time in her life.

Oh, Tiffany, be careful. You could still fall for the wrong man.

No, she wasn't that pathetic and vulnerable, she assured herself. Nor was she strong enough to stay in her room and risk his coming for her. Besides, she had enjoyed feeling normal. There was no crime in that, was there?

She liked even more the idea of making him see her as beautiful. Turning, she went to see what treasures the designers might have left her.

CHAPTER FIVE

RYZARD MOVED THROUGH the three-dimensional images of a *carnivale* parade. He had to be careful. There were real people, *Q Virtus* members and *petite q's,* dressed as colorfully as the fake partiers, but for the most part he walked right through projections of extravagant floats and scantily clad women wearing beaded bikinis and feather headdresses. He stopped for a troupe of men in checkered pants and neon elephant masks when they began a tumbling routine in front of him, nearly convinced they were real.

His watch hummed, indicating Tiffany was close by, but *where?*

His need to see her again, to know she'd come down here for him, was out of proportion to any normal sort of anticipation. He brushed it aside, thinking if he could have her just once more, he'd be able to forget about her. It didn't matter that she'd revealed more about herself than he'd ever heard from all other *Q Virtus* members combined. Like most of the happenings here, their private conversation would stay locked in his own personal vault, not even to be revisited by him.

He especially refused to dwell on their comforting embrace when her mixture of grief and anger and self-blame had struck a chord in him. Even though, for the better part of a minute while he held her, he'd been at peace for the first time in a long time.

He stepped on a man's hands and looked through the feet that would have struck him in the nose if the vision was real. Music blared, voices cheered, and the holographic players were so dense he might as well have been in a crowd on the street.

There. All the hairs stood up on his body as he took her in.

She had her head bent to study her watch and pivoted as though trying to orient herself with a compass. The movement allowed him to take her in from all sides.

She really was strikingly beautiful. Tall and slender, but generously curved in the right places. He swallowed. She wore some kind of jumpsuit that clung from knees to elbows, then flared into ruffles down her forearms and over her shins. It had a subtle sparkle in its midnight blue color and clung to her ass so lovingly, his knees weakened.

He mentally recited the populations of Bregnovia's cities, trying to keep hold of his control as he approached her. Sidling up behind her, almost touching, he inhaled where she'd left the right side of her neck bare, gathering her hair to the left so it covered the scars.

"What the hell are you wearing?"

Her head came up. "You don't like it?" She jiggled the watch in her hand. "This thing was buzzing at me, but I couldn't figure out if you were over there or over there."

"I'm here," he growled, wanting so badly to palm the firm globe near his crotch his hand burned.

"So you are." She turned to study his mask from behind her own. "Hello again, Mystery Man. Buy me a drink? I've had a terrible day with the most arrogant, self-aggrandizing jerk you can imagine."

Few people could get away with insulting him so openly, but he found her brashness refreshing. Maybe even reassuring. She wasn't as vulnerable as she'd seemed in her suite. Good.

Testing the waters, he said, "I'm looking forward to one myself. I was stuck all evening with the most infuriating female, smart as a whip, but *blonde*. No offense." He tugged one of her ringlets.

For a moment her mouth stayed flat and humorless, just long enough for doubt to creep over his conscience. Then her lips twitched and a pretty, feminine chuckle erupted, sounding a shade rusty, as if she hadn't laughed unreservedly in a long time, but it engaged him in a way he hadn't expected. He instantly wanted to hear it again.

"None taken," she assured him breezily, turning to grasp his arm above his elbow, demonstrating how much self-assurance she possessed when she wasn't paralyzed by self-consciousness. "Can you believe this parade? I thought it was real."

Despite wanting to remark on the sudden change in her, he decided to go with it.

"The first time I saw this technology, it was a rain forest. It wasn't as robust as this, but the rain effect was quite something."

"You've been coming to these shindigs for a while?"

"This is my twenty-fifth. I earned a pin." He lifted his lapel to draw her eye to the small gold button.

"Nice. What does it do? Beam you up? Shoot lasers?"

"It tells people I belong."

Ryzard's mouth tightened after he spoke, as if he hadn't meant to reveal that, which piqued her curiosity all the more. "What do you mean?"

He shook his head, trying to dismiss her curiosity. "They have a live performance on the beach tonight. Shall we check it out?"

"Are you sensitive to not belonging because of the UN thing? You must know how slowly the wheels of political progress can turn. If the old boys' network is refusing to pick you for their team, tell them to stuff it."

His mask annoyed her. He was already pretty stoic, and now she had to try reading his emotions from the way the corner of his supersexy mouth flattened with disgust.

"I've learned to do exactly that, Tiffany. And it really doesn't matter to me if I'm rejected or found wanting, but I can't bear for my country to be discriminated against."

Discriminated. There was a big word. As a woman she'd been on the short end of that nastiness even in her own home in favor of her brother, but she couldn't imagine it happening to a man who showed so few weaknesses. He wasn't a typical representative of the people she understood to suffer the worst end of biases.

"When were you picked on? Why?" she asked, allowing him to steer her through the shower of candies that should have landed with a sting or crunched under her platform shoes.

He shrugged as if the details were inconsequential. "Different times. When I was a child and didn't yet speak German. I was late to sprout and quick to fight, angry that I couldn't see my parents. My temper was a problem. Getting a legitimate passport was a nightmare, so I was forever in a country illegally. That's one of the reasons I picked grapes. Things like visas can be overlooked when the fruit is ripe and a transient offers to help. But when I tried to go to America, they wanted nothing to do with me."

"So you went to Russia."

"There are parts as wild as your early frontier. Misfits are the rule."

"Which country's passport do you travel on now?"

"Bregnovian," he asserted, as if that should be obvious.

"But it's not recognized? That still keeps you from entering America?"

"I wouldn't be allowed into Venezuela."

"But you're welcome here." She pointed at the floor of the club.

He nodded once, still seeming bristly.

She considered how that might feel, always being separated and left out. Being who she was had always ensured her entrée into virtually any situation. For all her father's faults and detractors, he was still welcome everywhere. Even with her scars, she wasn't locked out. It was her choice to stay home.

She looked up at Ryzard, wanting to ask how he'd come to finally go home and fund a war, but they had arrived on the beach. Bending, she removed her shoes and allowed him to take them so she could walk barefoot in the cool, powdery sand.

"That's an excellent cover band," she said as they moved toward the music.

"It's the real band," he told her, making her chuckle.

He looked at her and the corners of his mouth curled again, but his mask and the strobing lights made it hard to tell if he was smiling because he was in a good mood, or if he was laughing at her.

"I can't get used to this," she excused. "It's a lot to pay just for an exclusive concert, isn't it? The membership fee, I mean."

"If you hadn't been sulking in your room, you could have attended some of the lectures. There was an excellent one on the situation in Africa. Last quarter, I brokered a free trade agreement that will ease a lot of strain on our wheat and dairy production."

She weighed that, seeing new value in these meetings and wondering if she would come to another. Maybe see him again.

Or see him with someone else.

The chasm that thought opened in her chest was so great,

she quickly distracted herself by declaring with false crossness, "I wasn't sulking."

"You're still pouting," he claimed and took her jaw in a firm hand, nipping her bottom lip with the firm but tender bite of his.

A zing of excitement shot straight down her breastbone into her abdomen, then washed tingles into her limbs. Her hands instinctively lifted to his waist, but she held him off by proclaiming, "I've heard that all my life. I can't help it if my bottom lip is fat."

He drew back enough to sweep a gaze of masculine appraisal across her masked features, then bent to take a slower, more detailed tour of her mouth, allowing them both the luxury of a small feast. Absently she shuffled toward him, knees and thighs shifting so he could fit their frames together. His erection pressed into her stomach and her breasts ached as she flattened them to his chest. The music seeped through her and he began to rock them in a slow dance.

More like making love to her in public again, but who cared? No one even knew who they were. God, he felt good under her roaming hands.

"Come to my room," he intoned against her good ear.

She had her hands fisted in his shirt beneath the jacket of his tuxedo. Everything in her wanted to hang on to him forever. It was such a dangerous precipice to stand on, so threatening of a bad fall. But she couldn't escape how good it felt to feel wanted and beautiful and capable of giving him pleasure.

Without even doing much soul-searching—just like last night—she offered a shaky nod and let him guide her back into the club then into an elevator where they kissed with barely schooled passion. A minute later, he thumbed the sensor that opened his door and pivoted her into the foyer of his suite. It was grander than her own, but he *was* a twenty-five-visit member. Still, she barely saw it. One second later, she was in his arms.

Knocking off his mask, he dipped his head and kissed her again, discipline abandoned as he let her know with the thrust of his tongue exactly what he wanted to do to her. His hands roamed over her restlessly and he finally jerked back to say, "What the hell is this thing? I can't find a zipper."

Which was why she'd chosen it, she recalled dimly. Even the neckline was a difficult entry point. She didn't have the courage to be naked with him, but she wanted to make love to him.

Smiling secretively, she fingered open the buttons of his shirt and gazed appreciatively at the sleek bronze chest plate she revealed. A narrow line of hair delineated the center of his chest and outlined his squared pecs, which were flat, firm statements of strength.

Above his left nipple, a scrolled phrase in blue ink gave her pause. Some of the letters were oddly accented, but she thought she read the word *Bregnovia*. Framing it with the finger and thumb of her splayed hand, she asked, "What does it say?"

Tension stole through him. He seemed to expend a lot of effort drawing in a pained breath. "Luiza, Martyr of Bregnovia."

"Like our Lady Liberty?"

She drew a circle around his nipple and he jerked, making her smile.

"Yes," he rasped. "She's revered—damn. By all."

Other questions crowded into her mind, but she was too distracted by his gorgeous physique. Her hands couldn't resist smoothing over the hot satin of his skin. "You're so perfect, Ryzard. It's intimidating."

"Take off your clothes," he urged, plumping her breasts through her spandex suit.

Cruising her hand from his waist to his belt and lower,

she explored the shape of him. He grunted with pleasure and was so hard against her palm, her internal muscles clenched in anticipation. She swallowed and used her other hand to fumble his pants open.

He tried to remove her mask, but she pulled away and shook her head. "Not yet." She was too intent on being the anonymous Tiffany, the one who followed impulse and seduced a man if she wanted to. Lowering his fly, she managed to expose him, and *oh*. She went to her knees because he made her so deliciously weak.

"Tiffany," he groaned raggedly.

She was barely touching him, too new at this to do more than brush light fingertips over him. His breaths were audible hisses of anticipation, his erection jumping in reaction to her caresses. When she smoothed her lips against silky skin over steel, the weight of his hand came to rest on her head. The other stroked her exposed cheek, fingers trembling.

An experimental lick imprinted her with the taste of him. This was new territory for her, something she'd always been curious about, but it was so much more enthralling than she'd expected. She could sense how much power she had as she learned his shape with her tongue and open-mouthed kisses

When she took the tip into her wet mouth, he growled a string of foreign words, guttural and tortured, but sexy and thick with pleasure. If she could have smiled, she would have. Instead, she focused on finding his sensitive points, wanting this to be something he would never forget.

She never would.

Ryzard managed to hitch his pants back into place, but wasn't capable of much else. His head was swimming, his muscles trembling, and he was too wrung out to properly close his fly. He needed the wall to keep himself upright.

Water ran in the powder room, but he was barely aware of anything else. What Tiffany had just done to him had blown his mind. Her inexperience had been obvious in her tentative touch and first nervous licks, but after that she'd been so generous and given over to what she was doing, he'd lost it completely.

The door latch clicked and he turned his head. She walked out of the powder room with her clothes and mask in place, but there was an adorable self-conscious flush on her exposed cheek and an even more exquisite glow of arousal coming off her like an aura. Her nipples were pencil tips beneath her second-skin jumpsuit, and the way she walked held the hip sway of the sexually aroused.

Unbelievably, he twitched back to life below his unbuckled belt. He instantly wanted to strip her and have her under him.

"I'm going to eat you alive," he warned her.

She shook her head. "I have to go."

"The hell you do." He'd tie her up if he had to.

"No, I do," she insisted.

"What happened?" He looked to the powder room, wondering what had changed between seconds ago and now.

"Nothing. I just... This was really nice, but I want to leave it like this. As a nice memory for both of us."

"We can keep the lights off," he blurted in a burst of panic.

"Ryzard, please." There were tears in her eyes. "Just this, okay?"

He swiped his hand down his face, unable to think where he'd gone wrong. *Why the hell was she shutting him out?*

"I won't force you to make love with me. You don't have to go." Hell, the last thing he was capable of right now was *talk,* but it would be better than her leaving.

"I know you wouldn't, but I want to. Thank you again."

She skittered a wide circle around him and slid through the cracked door.

She'd got him off and thanked him twice. *What the hell?*

Tiffany was still trembling when she slid between her sheets, both angry with herself and relieved. Maybe she should have stayed with him. Maybe this was her chance to get over her scars so she could pursue a relationship with another man in the future.

But she didn't want anyone else, and she didn't have the courage to expose herself to Ryzard.

With a moan of despair, she rolled onto her stomach and groaned into a pillow.

A muted bell sounded. She lifted her head and noticed a light flashing on the bedside phone. Picking it up, she said a wary, "Yes?"

"It's me. Where are you?"

His voice sent a race of erotic excitement through her veins and into her loins. "In my room, obviously," she said, unable to control the husky edge on her voice.

"In bed?"

"Sleeping, yes," she lied.

"Liar."

She rolled her eyes. *So* arrogant.

"What are you wearing?" he asked.

"Flannel jammies and a nightcap."

"Well, take them off, *draga*. I'm about to tell you what you missed by running out of here."

"You're going to force me to have phone sex?"

"Hang up any time."

"I might have enough without adding more," she murmured in a considering tone.

"Hmm? Oh. Clever," he said with dry amusement. "I never know what to expect from you, Tiffany. Although

I'm quite sure you're still aroused. Have you been thinking of how you nearly killed me tonight?"

"Did I?" She couldn't help smiling.

"So smug. Yes, you did. I didn't thank you, and I should have. You're a delightful lover."

She curled on her side so the phone was tucked under her ear. "Thank you for saying that."

"Are you naked yet? Because if my hands will not be stroking your gorgeous body, then I will listen as you do it."

"You wish." But she tingled at the thought. He was right about sexual excitement hovering under the surface. Her skin prickled to sharp life, making her feel sensual and deeply aware of all her erogenous zones.

"Satisfy my curiosity," he said in a low voice. "Are your nipples still hard?"

"It's dark, I can't see."

"Feel them."

She closed her eyes, tempted, but, "Ryzard, I meant it when I said we should leave it at tonight."

Silence.

Had he hung up on her?

"Are you still there?" she asked, hearing a forlorn note in her voice.

"At least tell me why you're cutting me off." Underlying the brisk frustration in his tone was an edge of something she'd heard this evening when he'd said, *It shows I belong.* She'd hurt him.

Through an aching throat, she managed to blurt out the worst cliché around. "It's not you, it's me. I'm the biggest head case going."

"You're concerned that I will be repulsed by these scars of yours."

"Yes," she admitted, breathing a little easier at his understanding.

"Why would that bother you if I was?"

"I— What?" Her whole body tensed. *Did* she disgust him?

"Why would you care about my opinion? Who am I to you? Just some stranger you slept with on a wild night, right?"

So many protests choked her, she couldn't speak. He wasn't just anyone, not after some of the conversations they'd had and the physical intimacies they'd shared, but she couldn't admit that to him. He was already way too close to sensing he meant more to her than their brief association should warrant. His opinion mattered a lot.

"You're expecting me to get naked, be as exposed as I possibly could be, and risk being rejected," she said in a strained voice. "Wouldn't that bother you?"

"It bothered the hell out of me when you walked out tonight. I was as naked as a man needs to be the first night." His anger blistered off the receiver, making her squinch her face in a cringe. "You've done it to me twice."

"I'm sorry." The words burned from all the way in the pit of her sick stomach. "I didn't look at it from your perspective. I wasn't rejecting you."

"You need to start looking beyond yourself, Tiffany."

"I just apologized. That doesn't happen often. I suggest you accept it."

He sighed with frustration, then said with austerity, "You have been dealt a cruel blow from life. I won't dismiss that. But it didn't kill you, so start learning to live with it."

Wow. He didn't pull any punches, did he?

"How?" she demanded in a burst of angry despair. "You're not telling me anything I don't know, but how do I just get over it?"

"You want to be with a man, Tiffany. You like it when I touch you. Be with me."

He did make her feel more confident, but it would take

about a hundred of these heart-to-hearts before she'd be able to face being naked in front of him.

"We could meet for breakfast," she offered. The inside of her cheek stung and she realized she was biting it, feeling very insecure at putting herself out even this much.

"Where?" he asked.

"I assume they have a buffet or a restaurant downstairs."

"I meant your place or mine, but I see. Yes, they have a breakfast room. Nine?"

He wasn't making any effort to hide his disappointment, but she only confirmed, "Downstairs at nine. It's a date."

Ending the call, she rolled onto her back and stared at the dark ceiling. What was she doing? There was even less point in seeing him at breakfast on their last morning. They'd never see each other again after that.

Still, just thinking about seeing him made her body feel ripe and wanton. Running her hands over the hard swells of her breasts with their taut tips poking sharply against her rippling fingertips, she tried to erase the sensations nagging at her. The hunger deepened, provoking memories of Ryzard leaning on the wall, disheveled pants barely containing flesh she had memorized with her mouth, his eyes heavy lidded and voracious.

Rolling a frustrated moan into her pillow, she wished she'd said yes to the phone sex.

When she arrived in the dining room, Ryzard was standing in the entrance talking to another woman.

It was a low blow and nearly made her turn in retreat, but he lifted his hawkish mask and held out a hand to her even before he locked his gaze on her.

Stupid watches. Hers was shivering at its nearness to his, just like her to him. As she walked across, she experienced a little thrill at how good he looked in simple black pants and a white shirt open at the throat. His hair, clipped so short you could barely tell it curled, was still damp.

A dip of insecurity accosted her at the same time. The woman gesturing so passionately in front of him wore a light cover-up over a bikini that barely contained her flawless figure. Her mask was equally spare, just a sleek line from temple to temple.

Tiffany felt overdressed in her pants suit and elaborate mask as well as intrusive as she arrived, causing the woman to break midsentence.

Ryzard grasped her hand in a firm, warm grip, drawing her a step closer while continuing to give his attention to the other woman. "Please continue."

"I—" She was obviously disconcerted by Tiffany's arrival. Her body language changed from enticing to standoffish. "I just wonder if the sudden rumors being spread about this weekend, talk of dirty deals and Greek Mafia connections, could be true. Zeus's reputation is important for all of us, and if he's no better than a crook we should talk about it. Figure out what to do."

Tiffany was a little lost, coming in late and distracted by the strength and heat of her *lover*. He smelled freshly showered, and his flimsy white shirt was hardly any barrier, allowing her to nearly taste the texture of his skin.

Still, being excluded niggled at her. She'd been The Family Behind Him too many times for her father, a required face in a photo, but heaven forbid she open her mouth. Being relegated to arm candy here, where she was supposed to be an equal, was the final straw.

"Who *is* Zeus?" Tiffany asked.

"No one knows," the woman said, dismissing her with a patronizing jerk of her shoulder, adding, "Which is part of the problem. He should identify himself so we can decide if we want to continue associating with him."

Tiffany followed the entreating glance the woman sent

to Ryzard. She was obviously trying to pull him over to her side for reasons other than any real concern about the club.

"That seems hypocritical, doesn't it?" Ryzard said calmly. "When we keep our own identities secret?"

"I have to agree. It's quite possible to have a wrong impression about someone until you know them better," Tiffany said with a significant look upward to Ryzard.

"Well, we don't keep any secrets from Zeus, do we?" the woman insisted. She wavered with indecision a moment as her gaze touched on his hand holding Tiffany's so possessively. Then she made a noise of impatience and muttered, "I'm just saying," before she walked away.

Tiffany raised her brows, not that Ryzard could see them and appreciate her pique at coming upon a woman hitting on him so blatantly.

"Good morning," he said before swooping to kiss her.

She stiffened, but he took his time, working swirls of reawakened passion down through her torso and into her belly until she softened into his loose embrace. When he lifted his head, he said, "I'm starving. You?"

Food was the last thing on her mind, but she followed him through the indoor/outdoor dining room to a table near the lagoon-shaped pool. They accepted coffee and placed their orders before she lost her ability to stay silent and asked, "Do you pick up women at all these things?"

Setting down his coffee, he regarded her with a hard look. "Your pretty blue eyes have gone quite emerald, *draga*."

"Who is she?"

"That's a question I can't answer. Members do not out other members. That's why I didn't introduce you."

She narrowed her eyes. "If I had looked at my watch, would I have seen her nickname?"

He shrugged. "Possibly. Mine is turned off except for

you. She only spoke to me because we happened to meet at the door and have spoken before."

"About?" she prompted.

"It's confidential."

"Have you seen her away from these things?"

"Also confidential."

"So you won't tell me anything."

"This is how the club works. That's why it works. But I will tell you that I have never had a sexual relationship with her."

"And she would never admit to one if you had because members don't out other members. I'm just supposed to trust that you're telling me the truth."

"Yes," he said firmly. "I do expect you to trust me."

Her gaze dropped to the button he'd only half pushed through its hole in the middle of his chest.

"If you had let me make love to you last night, you would not be feeling so insecure this morning," he added.

Her heart skipped at that, but she only said, "I'm not insecure. I don't *know* you."

"Exactly."

Oh, he was infuriating. And sexy. Her eyes were eating up the way his shirt was perfectly tailored across the line of his shoulders and hugged the strength in his arms. Her fingers itched to unbutton the whole shirt and expose his very promising chest again.

It's just hormones, she tried to insist to herself, not wanting to succumb to feelings that were a lot more complex than mere lust.

"I'm jealous of her for being pretty," she admitted in an undertone, ashamed that she was this shallow, but, "I used to be and it gave me confidence. Don't deny that being physically attractive is powerful," she warned with a point of her finger. "My mother still turns heads and uses it every day. And she places so much importance on looks."

The weight of that knowledge slumped her into her chair.

"Sometimes I wonder if that's why she chose Dad and not Paul Sr. He wasn't ugly by any stretch, but Dad's got that Mr. President, all-American look. Mom wanted the best-looking kids in the state and she got them. Now, when she looks at me…"

Time to shut up. Her throat was closing and it was impossible to fix.

"Your mother sounds very superficial." His tone of quiet observation told her he'd heard and weighed every word she'd said. Being such a tight focus of his concentration made her feel oddly vulnerable and safe at the same time. It made her think he genuinely cared about what she was revealing.

"She's the wife of a politician. Her world revolves around how things look. You're judged on everything in that position. Looks matter."

"I suppose," he allowed with a negligent tilt of his head. "Did she push your father into politics?"

"No, it was something he wanted, but maybe that's the real reason she married him." Tiffany considered her parents' marriage a moment. "Dad is a good father, a super husband, a really good man, but he aspires to be a Great Man and Mom aspires to be the wife of one. She set me up to…" want? demand? "expect the same thing."

"Was your husband planning to go into politics?"

"If our parents had anything to do with it, yes." She curled her mouth in mild distaste.

"You didn't want him to."

Once again she was able to speak a truth to him that she couldn't say aloud to anyone else.

"I honestly didn't think I had a choice. But I've seen how that life has affected my mother over the years. Every word she says is guarded. Half the time she's Dad's mistress. His work is his wife. Our family day at the fair was always a photo op with Dad glad-handing everyone except us. He couldn't buy me the candy floss I wanted. A taffy apple was a better message." She sighed, still more bewildered than bitter. "My life was staged to look like the life I wanted, but we weren't allowed to actually live it that way."

"Another reason why I will never marry. Too much sacrifice on a family's part."

"Another' reason? You don't intend to marry? Don't you want children? That's the one thing I looked forward to when I agreed to marry. I wanted to give my kids the childhood I hadn't had."

As the words left her mouth, she realized how leading they sounded. As if this was a conflict they'd have to resolve before proceeding with their relationship. She never talked this openly, except maybe to her therapist, but who else did she talk to these days? She was out of practice with hiding her real thoughts and feelings.

"You can still have a family," he said with a calm blink of his eyes within the holes of his mask. "Why couldn't you?"

Behind her own mask, she burned with self-consciousness, her gaze fixed to his. Her finding that kind of happiness wasn't as easy as he made it sound, and he knew it. With her teeth bared in a nonsmile, she said, "Why don't you want to marry?"

"I'm married to my country," he stated. "As you said, my work is my wife. Everything I do, I do for my people."

She tried to ignore the dull pain that lodged in her chest. That was good, wasn't it? She admired patriotism, and that certainly kept things simple between them. No false expectations.

"How did you become, um, president?" she asked, faltering because it was an impulsive question that sounded a lot more loaded than she'd meant it to.

"I was elected," he said coolly.

She waited while their meals were delivered, then said, "I meant, how did people come to know who you are and want to vote for you? I'm sure it was covered in the news, but as you've said, that's usually slanted, and quite frankly I've had other things on my mind for the last few years. I missed how it all happened. I'm really asking what drew you back to your country and into representing it."

"My mother was killed in a random attack. I went back for the funeral and my father was determined to fight. I couldn't leave him to it. I was angry with myself for not returning sooner, for thinking someone else would sort out the trouble and I could return when there was peace."

"You're either part of the solution, or part of the problem," Tiffany murmured. "I'm sorry about your mom." Was that whom he'd been talking about yesterday, she wondered, when he'd held her in shared grief? "At least your father is safe."

"He died, as well. Fighting."

"Oh. I'm so sorry."

He waved that away with a lift of two fingers. "I believe he wanted it that way. To be with my mother."

"Still…" She swallowed, ready to cry for him because he seemed so withdrawn and contained. Tears would never dare to seep from his bleak eyes. "I'm sure he would be very proud of you for what you've achieved."

"Once you've paid the price of a loved one, you don't stop until the job is done. I managed to bring enough of our various factions together to throw over our corrupt government and campaigned on a promise of peace. There is still a very long road. The biggest challenge is keeping the country from falling back into fighting, but we had some corruption charges work through the courts recently that gave people confidence. Small things like that matter."

She nodded, tipping a little further into the primordial

world of deeper feelings for him. Genuine admiration. Awe. Empathy.

Careful, Tiffany.

"Shall we take the art walk?" he asked when they finished eating.

"I didn't know they had one." She looked around, expecting artists with pads and a jumble of still lifes and caricatures had arrived to line the stones near the pool.

"They set it up inside to avoid sun and humidity damage."

"Really? What are we talking about? Priceless artifacts? Da Vinci?"

"If something like that is on the market, absolutely. Most of it is contemporary, but they're all good investments."

Moments later, they entered a gallery of comic book art competing with old-world landscapes and elegantly carved wooden giraffes. She fell in love with a stained glass umbrella, mostly because it was so ridiculously useless.

"How much is it?" she demanded, searching for a tag.

"The auction is in a few hours."

"We'll come back?"

"If you like."

"I want to use it as a parasol against the sun." It had to weigh fifty pounds. It was the most impractical object ever created and she *had* to own it.

"You have a beautiful laugh," he remarked, tugging her into a space behind a giant sculpture of ladies' shoes. "I'd like to see you smiling under this umbrella of yours, your face painted by the colored glass. I'd like to see you sunbathe naked under it," he added in a deeper tone that seemed to stroke beneath her skin and leave a tingle.

At the same time his words put a pang in her heart. She wished…

He bent to kiss her, pulling her into his aroused body as if they were the only two people in the room. A second later, as his tongue invaded her mouth, she forgot everything except the feel of him, shoulders to thighs, branding her.

"I want you in my bed," he told her huskily, as he found her bare earlobe and drew it between his lips.

Her body felt as if it swelled to fill his arms, breasts aching, all her skin thin and sensitized. Willpower and self-protection fell away as she confided in a whisper, "I want that, too."

He lifted his head. His possessive hands stilled and firmed on her. "Yes?"

Her heart stalled. He wouldn't accept any more waffling. She swallowed, still terrified by the idea of being naked in front of him, but she would hate herself forever if she refused him out of sheer cowardice. With breath held, she gave an abbreviated nod.

His smile should have alarmed her. It bordered on grim, but a light of excitement behind his eyes made her tremble with anticipation. He really did want her.

Blood rushed in her ears so she barely heard him speak to a *petite q* as they made their way back to the main floor.

"Early checkout?" she repeated as he led her through the door the *petite q* released with a thumbprint and security override card.

"Gold membership has its privileges," he said drily. "But they'll only let me leave early. They won't allow us back in."

"Oh, but what about my things—?" She paused on the ramp down to the marina, where several eye-popping luxury yachts bobbed like toys in a bathtub.

"Our luggage would be packed for us regardless. That's the level of service we pay for, Tiffany." He waved and called something in Bregnovian to a young man as they approached a catamaran. It was called the *Luiza* and had an orange sail wrapped around its single mast. The body was such a brilliant white she had to squint.

"We'll remain docked a few hours yet," Ryzard said in

answer to a question from his crewman. "Unless we have to move to let someone out." He nodded at the boat they'd traversed to reach this one. "Tell the captain we're aboard and will order lunch when we're ready, but we don't wish to be disturbed."

Tiffany blushed behind her mask, thinking Ryzard was making it incredibly obvious what they were about to do. He didn't seem concerned, however, as he led her through the interior salon of sleek curved lines, the colors a soothing mix of bone and earth tones. Panoramic windows slanted over the lounge and bar, bringing splashes of turquoise water and cerulean sky into the room. Bypassing a short staircase that led to an elevated pilothouse of some kind, he brought her down a half flight of steps into the master stateroom.

"This is amazing," she couldn't help blurt. No stranger to the finer things in life, she was awestruck by the simple elegance and understated masculinity in the surprisingly spacious room. Drawers and cupboards in blond teak lined the space below the windows that provided a one-eighty view. A door led to an exterior deck on this side and into a well-organized head on the other. One curved radius corner of the room was a scrupulously efficient work space, the other a rounded sofa that looked to a flat-screen television set into the wall offset from the bed.

The bed itself was a king-size statement of power, tall and stalwart, its linens almond colored with a bold chocolate stripe across the foot. She dragged her eyes away from it as she heard a whispery sound and the light changed.

Ryzard moved with deliberation to draw woven shades down into a clip, allowing filtered sunlight to penetrate, but giving them privacy.

Her stomach swooped and she put out her hand, not sure where to find purchase when the floor was dipping at the same time.

"I thought we'd go to a room in the club," she said, linking her hands before her to hide that she was trembling with nerves. And excitement.

He turned from the last window and brushed away his mask, tossing it aside. "As I said, I don't want to be interrupted."

By staff wanting to pack their belongings, she imagined he meant, but couldn't speak because he came close enough to remove her mask.

She stopped him.

"I've seen your face, Tiffany."

"I don't want you to see how scared I am."

He frowned. "Of me?"

"Your reaction."

He shook his head, dismissing her fear as he trailed light fingertips over her clothing, grazing the sides of her breasts and settling warm hands on her waist. "I'm afraid I'll hurt you again. I wish you'd warned me the other night. I wasn't nearly as gentle as I could have been."

"I know pain, Ryzard. That was nothing."

"It was something," he told her, pulling her close enough to brush his mouth against hers, not properly kissing her. Teasing. "I'll never forget it."

An odd expression spasmed across his face before he controlled it, as if he hadn't meant to admit that to her, but she drew in his confession like air, deeply affected, wanting to hold on to this special feeling he provoked in her. Everything in her yearned so badly to please him, and she was so sure she wouldn't.

Get it over with, she told herself. She had to let him see and judge and reject before she climbed too high in optimism and desire. A long fall from excitement to disgust would be more than she could bear. If she did it now, before they'd gone too far, she'd still be able to dress and trudge into the nearest town to phone her brother—the one she kept forgetting about.

For now, she had to gather her courage.

Gently removing Ryzard's hands from her waist, she took a step back. The mask seemed like a tiny bit of necessary protection so she kept it, reaching first for the single button that held her linen jacket closed.

Removing it exposed her arm, marbled in streaks of red and pink, some parts geometric patterns from the grafts, other edges random and white. Not looking at him, she opened her pants and stepped out of them. Her left leg was as bad as her arm, and the top of her good right thigh was peppered with rectangles where they'd taken skin to patch the bad. Her stomach had the same types of scars. She threw off her sleeveless silk top and stood there in her cherry red bra and underpants and gold gladiator sandals.

For the life of her, she couldn't lift her chin. Her eyes were glued to the floor, her mind full of the rugged road map her body had become. No ivory virgin here.

"You do know pain, Tiffany," he said quietly.

That brought her eyes up. He studied her gravely, all the way to her toes, and gradually climbed his gaze back to her face. Stepping closer, he touched her chin to bring her face up and looked into her eyes. His were somber, but glowing with something fierce.

"You humble me. I don't know if I could have fought through such a thing."

She had to bite her lips to keep them from trembling.

Gently he removed her mask and let it fall. She felt incredibly vulnerable, standing before him nearly naked when he was clothed.

"Do not be ashamed of your courage to survive."

She had wanted to be told she was pretty despite her scars, but what he said was better, filling her with an emotion she couldn't describe. Tipping into him, she hugged him tight.

And realized he was aroused. His hand swept her bare back down to where her thong exposed her naked cheek. With a purposeful clench of his fingers into the firm flesh, he tilted her hips into pressing where he grew harder by the second.

"You're turned on," she breathed in wonder.

"I've got you naked next to a bed. How the hell else would I react?"

That made her laugh, then she squealed as he picked her up and lightly tossed her onto the mattress. Coming up on her elbows, she accused, "Caveman."

"Believe it," he confirmed, yanking off his shirt and dropping it away. His pants came off with similar haste. "Off with the rest," he ordered, jerking his chin at her lingerie. "This time we're both naked."

He was, in record time, and pulled off her shoes without ceremony.

"Don't wreck them. I like those," she protested, pausing in finding the clip between her breasts to reach for the strap of her shoe.

"What about these?" he asked, hooking two fingers in her panties at her hip. "Special favorite? Because I'm out of patience." He snapped them.

"Oh!" Why his primitive act turned her on, she couldn't imagine, but the way he loomed over her, practically overwhelming her with his strength, gave her a thrill. Probably because she felt totally safe despite his resolute expression and proprietary touch. He was impatient, but not without discipline. He threw away her bra, but then he simply held her, his weight on one elbow as he studied her breasts.

"Does this hurt?" he asked, tracing where her scar licked like a flame up the side of her breast.

"I can barely feel anything. Just a bit of pressure. Nerve

damage. You know how your face feels after the dentist and the freezing is just starting to come out?"

"Good to know. I'll focus where you can feel it." He cupped her breast and flicked her nipple with his thumb.

The sensation was sharper than she anticipated, and she flinched.

"No?" he prompted.

"I— No, it's good, just really…" She blushed. This was surreal, lying in full light with a gorgeous man naked against her. Twin desires to curl into him and to stop and give herself time to take it in accosted her.

He lowered his head to lick, and her inner muscles clenched like a fist, tearing a sound of reaction out of her.

Almost experimentally, he switched to her other breast, teasing and making her shift restlessly. It felt incredible, but wasn't quite as intense as the other.

He moved to her left one again and another shot of extreme sensation went through her, flooding her loins with a heated rush of pleasure. She didn't know if her nerve endings were compensating for others nearby that had ceased to work, but the way his tongue toyed so delicately made her pinch her thighs together.

"That one is really sensitive," she panted, smoothing her hand over his short, thick hair and clutching at his shoulders, not sure if she wanted him to stop or take her over the edge.

"I can tell," he said with smoldering approval. Opening his mouth on her, he sucked delicately, nearly levitating her off the bed.

"Ryzard," she cried, knee bending and thighs opening as she tried to grasp more of him. With a growl, he slid down and bit softly at her inner thigh. "Do you know how many things I want to do to you?"

Moaning, she threw her arm over her eyes and surrendered. "Do anything. I love everything you do to me."

For a second he did nothing. She wondered if she'd done something wrong and started to drop her arm away. Then she felt his touch delicately parting her. His mouth. Pressing the back of her wrist against her open mouth, she muffled her throaty groan of abject joy. To be wanted like this, so deliciously ravished, brought tears of happiness to the seams of her closed eyes.

And *oh* that was nice. Pleasure coiled and built on itself through her middle, winding her into the sweetest tension. She wanted release and she wanted this to go on and on. Then he slid a testing finger in her, and she knew exactly what she wanted.

And told him.

"I can't wait, either," he said in a raw voice, as if the truth stunned him. In a sliding lunge across her, he nearly yanked the bedside drawer from its table and seconds later smoothed latex down his length.

When he pressed into her, she welcomed him with a gasp, nails tightening into his skin as he possessed her with ruthless care, slow and inexorable. Through her lashes, she watched him watching her and bit her lip, feeling deeply exposed, but moved by the intimacy at the same time.

"I can't believe I'm the only man who knows how amazing you are," he said gutturally, hands holding her head as he rocked side to side, settling deep inside her, sealing their connection.

Her body didn't feel like her own. She trembled in arousal, limbs both weak and strong, clinging to him. Her mouth offered itself, parting and begging for his.

With a tortured growl, Ryzard kissed her, thrusting his tongue into her, wanting more and more of her. All of her. Indelibly.

But that intense, deep possession couldn't be sustained forever. Eventually, he drew back enough for ecstasy to strum through him as her sheath stroked and clenched around him. She smelled incredible, felt even better, tasted like forbidden substances. He became animalistic, purely in his physical state, senses captured and held by this creature who entranced him. Nothing entered his vision except the expression of exquisite torture against the unique pattern on her face.

In a rare moment of unguarded openness, he removed his internal shields so he could fully absorb the pure, sweet light of her. His only thought was to fill her with the same all-encompassing rapture that held him in its grip.

She sobbed his name and he increased his tempo, reacting to her need and compelled to fulfill it. She met him thrust for thrust, their bodies so attuned they scaled the cliff together and soared into the abyss with perfect affinity. Clutching her tight under him, buried deep in her shivering depths, he let out a ragged cry of triumph as he gave in to pulse-pounding release.

CHAPTER SIX

RYZARD ROLLED AWAY, then settled on his back, his body brushing hers, but only incidentally. He wasn't embracing or meaning to touch her that Tiffany could tell.

She turned her head to see his profile was unreadable. Not displeased, but not...

Oh, she didn't know what she was looking for. A spear of inadequacy impaled her. While she had been caught up in their lovemaking, she'd been fine, but now she was back to being scared and self-conscious of her scars. She sat up.

"Don't go anywhere," he said, hand loosely cuffing her wrist.

Ha. Where could she go? They weren't allowed back into the club. *Hello, big brother, can you pick me up at the docks?*

Glancing over her shoulder, she tried to read his mood behind his heavy eyelids, but his spiky lashes made it impossible.

"You seem..." She didn't want to reveal how sensitive she was to disapproval right now. They might have been intimate in other ways before, but this was different. It wasn't just the physicality or revealing of her scars. She'd been incredibly uninhibited, exposing the very heart of herself.

"It's probably best if I go," she managed in a husky voice.

"I don't know what I seem, but I'm only trying to assimilate something that—" He breathed a word in his own language. She suspected it was a curse, but his tone was kind of awed and self-deprecating at the same time.

Facing forward, she closed her lids against a sudden sting, biting back an urge to beg him to continue what he'd almost said. It sounded as if he was as moved by their love-making as she was, which was balm to her tattered soul.

He released her wrist to stroke her lower back, making her lift her head from where she'd let it droop to rest on her knees.

"Are you okay?" he asked.

"Just trying not to act like a first-timer."

"This is unique for both of us."

She tried not to drink too deeply of that heady assessment. She was already falling for him in little ways and couldn't afford to become too enamored. This was merely an extension of their one-night stand.

"You keep condoms in the drawer by the bed," she pointed out. "I'm not that unique."

A beat of dark silence, then, "*I* never claimed to be a virgin."

She wanted to glare at him, but couldn't risk him seeing how hard it was for her to acknowledge his experience. Why? What right did she have to possessive feelings? She was lucky to be included in his special club at all.

"And this won't be the only bed I'll ever be in, so—hey!"

He had her on her back and under him before she realized he could move that fast.

"Here's a tip for someone new to this," he growled. "We don't discuss past and future lovers, particularly when we're still making love to each other."

She blinked in shock, heart hammering.

His aggression fell away to a baffled, tender caress that he smoothed along her good cheek. "Don't make me feel guilty for my life before I met you. How could I have known that what I thought was pleasure…" His expression clouded with a look of such angst, it made her heart hurt.

"It's just chemistry," she assured him, teetering inwardly against her own words even as she attempted to comfort him with them. The remark went directly against her girlish desire to hear that she was actually very special to him.

She held her breath, hoping against logic that he'd offer such a pledge.

"Exceptional chemistry," he agreed. His hungry gaze followed his hand as he caressed from her lips to her collarbone, across the damp underside of her breast and down to her hip where his thumb aligned to the crease at the top of her leg. "But you do understand this is simply an affair? It can't lead to anything permanent. I'm not the sort of life partner you're looking for."

His blunt statement fell between them like a metal wall, softened only by the expression of regret on his face.

"Glad you said it first," she said with a poignant smile, hoping it hid the way she tensed internally. She was as wary of certain fantasies as he was, but not nearly as adept at cutting her emotions out of her heart. "I told you what I think of being the woman behind the man. You're merely a guilty indulgence, like cheating on a diet."

His brow winged, indignant but amused. "Let's fatten you up then."

Ryzard gave up trying to work. They'd been sailing three hours already, so he had another word with his captain, then remained at the helm while his instructions were carried out. As the wind whipped his shirt through the open windows of the pilothouse, he once again congratulated himself on having the wisdom to switch from a single-hulled sailboat to the double construction of a cat. The three-sixty views and flexibility with anchorage were worth the ribbing he received from traditionalists.

Hell, if he had allowed his concentration to wander like this on his old schooner, they'd all be dead, but here he could indulge himself with recollecting every delicious minute of his day. He'd devoted several hours to learning each and every one of Tiffany's pleasure triggers, stimulating both of them as he expanded both of their educations in physical delight. Sweetest of all had been her generous straddling of him, broken voice asking for direction as she tugged him along her path to bliss.

They'd been like drunkards at that point, sheened in perspiration. Her eyes had been glassy, her pouted lips reddened by a thousand kisses. Her breasts had swayed with their undulations, her hips an instrument of torture he wielded on himself as he guided her with hands clamped tight in ownership.

He'd been sure he would die, it had been that good.

Rubbing his face, he dragged himself back to reality, yanking open his collar in search of a cool breeze to take his libido down a notch. They were flying over the waves, skipping at a light angle, demanding he pay attention, but all he could think was, how could he be this aroused again? She'd drained him dry. They'd collapsed into unconsciousness, utterly exhausted from making love.

He'd woken soon after, sweaty and thick with recovery, wanting her again.

When he'd shifted, she'd grumbled without opening her eyes, "Don't move. My hip hurts. I need to keep my leg propped."

He didn't doubt it. His joints had protested his rising from the bed, and he'd never crashed and burned in a roadster. He'd substituted a pillow under her thigh and watched her settle back into sleep before taking his insatiable libido for a cold shower in a spare cabin.

Then he'd made a decision he was still second-guessing, but it was done. She was his.

I love everything you do to me. The power of that statement unexpectedly exploded in his mind again, but that first bit, *I love...*

He scratched his chest where a sensation gathered like sweat trickling. The tickle was behind his breastbone, uncomfortable and impossible to erase. *It's just chemistry,* she'd said as he'd been reeling from a depth of pleasure he'd never experienced before.

He'd agreed with her, clinging to that simple explanation, but it was harder to blame chemistry when he'd found himself unable to wake her and send her on her way.

Why not? Why was his response to her, on every level, so much more intense than it had been with the woman he'd loved, the one he'd pledged to marry? He hated himself for it, but he couldn't deny it.

He and Luiza hadn't had the luxury of time and privacy to soak themselves in sexual intimacy, though. Their bond had been forged by shared secrets and ideals. She had loved him when he'd had no one else. Her vision had become his.

She'd died before her dream could become reality, but he was still striving to make it come true. There was no reason to suffer pangs of infidelity just because he wanted to play out an affair with a particular woman for a little longer than a weekend.

He clenched his hands on the wheel, telling himself that the fact Tiffany had been a virgin weighed into his decision to extend their association. No man wanted to be a woman's first and her worst. He owed her more time and consideration than the average jaded socialite.

And she happened to have a sexual appetite to match his own. He kept mistresses when it suited him for that very reason. This was still a temporary arrangement, and Tiffany understood that's all he ever intended to have with any woman. His heart belonged to Luiza. If he couldn't marry her, he wouldn't marry anyone.

Having relegated Tiffany to her rightful place in his mind, he was ready to see her again. He nodded at the first mate, and the young man swung the sail to catch more gust.

Tiffany was falling out of bed.

She woke with a cry and a start, arms splayed to orient herself on the mattress. The room glowed a brassy yellow, the bed was a wreck and her body felt as if she'd been thrown down a flight of stairs. She held very still, trying to come to grips with the odd feeling the boat was not just bobbing in its slip, but moving.

It was. They were at sail!

She'd been on sailboats, but unlike the sharp angle that resulted in stumbling around to grip her way across a deck, this catamaran was only a hair off level, allowing her to rush the window and snap up the blind. Yep. Not another boat in sight. Just a speck of land on the horizon and glittering waves in every other direction.

"What the hell, Ryzard?" she said aloud.

Glancing around for her clothes, she caught sight of herself and cringed. Her hair was naturally straight, and all that sweaty sex had weighed it down into a droopy haystack. The side of her breast felt raw where it had been abraded by stubble and when she turned her nose to her shoulder, she could swear she smelled Ryzard's unique scent on her skin.

An odd, sexy feeling overcame her, making her want to loll in bed and call him to her, but she gave herself a firm shake. Where the hell was he taking her?

A very quick shower later, she dressed in her pants and sleeveless top to go in search of him. She forced herself not to be so cowardly as to wear the mask, but she still peered around corners, avoiding his staff.

She found him lounging in the shade of the aft deck,

taking up all the cushions of the built-in sofa as he read his tablet and sipped a drink made with tomato juice. A stalk of celery rested against its salted rim. He set it down when she appeared.

"I thought a few sharp turns might shake you out of bed," he said.

"Are you familiar with the term *kidnapping?*"

"I have business in Cuba."

"You're taking me to Cuba?" She gave a wild look around. Nope, not one hint of assistance in sight.

"Much as I'd love to anchor somewhere private and shirk my responsibilities, I can't. My weekend was booked for *Q Virtus,* but now we'll have to carve out our time around other commitments."

"Commitments like the one I made to get on a plane with my brother two hours ago? He'll be frantic." Dumbfounded, she braced a hand on her forehead trying to gather her scattered wits enough to formulate a plan.

"My staff spoke to him when they collected your things."

"Your staff collected my things. And brought them here?" She pointed to the deck, so astounded she could barely form words. "After they informed my brother that I was carrying on with you?"

"They're discreet enough to simply say you're my guest. Naturally he needed to be told why you weren't meeting him as arranged. Why are you upset? Relax. I realize you avoid the sun, but you can enjoy the view from the shade. I have a masseuse aboard, if you need."

"Ryzard," she said with a ring of near hysteria in her tone. "You said we'd stay in dock."

"For a few hours. We did. You overslept."

"You should have woken me! Not said things to my brother. He doesn't need to know about this. No one does. It's nobody's business but mine!" She splayed a hand on the place in her chest where he was taking up way more room than he should. Where he was lodged very close to places no one was allowed to go.

"When you called me your dirty little secret, I didn't realize you meant it," he replied stiffly.

Oh, she would *not* feel guilty. Maybe she was overreacting, but he didn't realize what kind of firestorm he would have set off with her family. This was bad.

"You should have asked me," she insisted. "And let *me* talk to my brother. Is there some way I can contact him?" Panic gripped her.

"If your mobile doesn't work, ask the captain for the ship to shore." He still sounded stung, but dealing with Ryzard came second to smoothing things over with Christian. What would he think of her?

She'd left her mobile in her room at the club and found it in her purse in the cabin where her things had been unpacked. Not Ryzard's cabin, she noted, but a separate one—and why did that bother her? She was upset with him, not supposed to be mooning about what it meant if he set her up to sleep apart from him.

Keying her code into her phone, she saw that her brother had left her a dozen messages.

"What the *hell,* Tiff," were his first words when she reached him.

"I know." She closed her eyes. She really should have thought this through before dialing. She was just so frantic to undo what had been done. But how?

"How does something like this even happen?" he demanded.

His askance reaction crystallized the confused self-consciousness inside her, so she felt very fragile and very brittle all of a sudden. Ryzard, despite his assumptions and autocratic ways, was not the villain. The problem with her family knowing about their affair, she realized, was the impossible vision she was supposed to live up to.

"You're the expert on picking up women. You know how it works," she retorted. "He came on to me with a great line. I fell for it."

The door clicked and Ryzard entered in time to hear most of what she said.

She averted her gaze from his darkening expression, prickling as her brother said, "You're too smart for that."

"Am I? Maybe I'm weak and desperate. Maybe I'm grateful for attention from *any* man."

In her periphery, Ryzard's arms folded and he said in an ominous undertone, "Is that true?"

"I knew it. He's taking advantage of you."

She sucked in a jagged breath, more hurt than words could express, but it was the ugly truth they'd all been dancing around since her accident. She wasn't worth a man's attention.

She flashed a look of resentment at Ryzard, angry that he was witnessing her humiliation. At the same time, she wished he didn't look so thunderous. She was desperately in need of backup. Instead, he'd probably leave her on a sandbar somewhere, but that was almost better than sending her back to the bosom of her kin.

"Thanks, Chris," she choked. "Thanks for letting me know there's no way he could possibly be attracted to me. I'm some broken, awful thing that ceased to be valuable when I ceased to be perfect. Shame rains upon us and it's my fault. Has Mom taken to her room?"

A weighted pause. She didn't dare look at Ryzard.

"I didn't say that," Christian said quietly.

"But it's true! Tell me something. How many times have you stolen a weekend with someone? Hundreds," she quickly provided. "How many times have you had to answer for it? *None.* And I never worked up the nerve to even kiss another man because I had a reputation to uphold. Not just mine, but the entire family's. Paulie's even."

He swore. "Okay, I get it. You're entitled to a private life, but this isn't exactly the time, is it?" he seethed. "Or the man."

"You haven't told Mom and Dad, have you?"

"I didn't know what to think, Tiff! This isn't like you."

"When have I ever had a chance to be who I am?" she cried. "I've been Dad's daughter, Paulie's intended. The bride who wore bandages. For God's sake, I'm an adult. A married, *widowed* woman. I shouldn't have to defend myself like I've committed a federal crime."

"No, you're right, I'm sorry. Truly."

"How bad is it?" she asked, hanging her head, weighted by guilt despite all she'd just said. "Do I have to talk to them or better to wait?"

"They don't know what to think, either. But they don't want to see you get hurt in any way, ever again. Is this thing serious with Vrbancic?"

She glanced at Ryzard. He didn't look quite so much as if he wanted to wring her neck, but he had an air of imperative surrounding him. As if he didn't intend to wait much longer for her to give her attention back to him.

"Not, um, really," she murmured.

Christian's sharp sigh grated in her ear.

"Oh, I'm sorry, did I miss where you married everyone you ever slept with?" she railed.

"So it's gone that far."

He didn't have to take a tone like the septic was backed up!

"Goodbye, Chris. Tell Mom and Dad whatever you want." She stabbed the end button and threw her phone onto the bed. Then dropped a pillow on top of it for good measure. And added a punch that left a deep indent.

"I'd like to say I'm above caring what people think of me, but when my family judges me, it hurts." Her baleful gaze met one that didn't so much judge as measure.

"You knew they would disapprove. That's why you were upset."

"Not because it's you. They would have been scandalized no matter who I slept with. Although, I'm sure there's some shock value that they sent me to talk to you and here I am. As God is my witness, I'll never, ever tell my mother I didn't even see your face the first time, let alone know your name." She buried her hot face in her clammy hands, reacting to all that had happened since she'd woken so abruptly. "This isn't the way I usually behave, Ryzard. I can't blame them for being shocked."

"Be careful how much you hate your parents, *draga*. They're the only ones you have."

"You're going to judge me now?" She lifted her face in challenge.

"I'm only offering the benefit of my experience."

"You hated your parents?" She didn't believe it.

"I was angry with them for sending me away. Keeping me away from my home. It felt like a rejection."

He hadn't explained that part before. A pang struck at how lonely and discarded he must have felt.

Beneath the pillow, her phone burbled. Tiffany made a noise and started from the room, then said, "Actually, I want to change. It's too hot for long pants."

Ryzard closed the door, but remained in the room. Apparently he intended to watch. Hell. The man gave her goose bumps without making any effort at all.

Skimming past the one-shoulder and long-sleeved shirts and dresses, she pulled out a skimpy sundress she would have worn only in the privacy of her suite yesterday. It was patterned busily in neon pink and green and yellow, hopefully bright enough to draw attention from her equally busy skin patterns.

The scared mouse in her wanted to hide under layers, but a spunky, more daring part of her wanted to test whether she still held his interest.

Stripping unceremoniously, even dropping her bra, she shrugged her arms under the spaghetti straps and tugged it into place, then picked up the flared skirt in a little curtsy, spinning under the direction of his twirled finger.

"Adorable. Now come here."

"And risk making love on that telephone? Possibly landing on buttons that could have serious consequences? No. You promised me a meal and we skipped lunch."

"Yet I recall being very satisfied with everything I tasted," he mused, one hand on the door latch. The other caressed her bottom as she exited in front of him.

Her blood skipped in her arteries, and she was blushing hard as she led him outside to where a table was set and chilled wine was ready to be uncorked. The sun sat low on the horizon, ducking beneath the shade to strike off the silver and crystal.

Ryzard held a chair in a corner for her and asked for a filtered shade to be drawn.

"I'm sorry I was such a pill," she said contritely. "You took me by surprise with this." She indicated the extravagance of the cat. "I thought we'd part ways this afternoon and maybe I'd see you with someone else at a future *Q Virtus* event. This is better," she allowed, but met his gaze with a level one. "But I do have to work."

"Apology accepted. And I've already instructed my crew to set up a work space in the cabin where your things were unpacked. It should be completed by morning."

"They're going to work while I'm sleeping in there?" she asked, already anticipating his reply.

"You won't be in there, *draga*. And you won't be sleeping."

* * *

Ryzard flipped through his emails on his tablet while he waited for Tiffany to finish her call. They'd had a surprisingly productive morning, despite lazing in bed first thing. An easy, affectionate companionship had fallen between them after her rather explosive reaction to waking at sea yesterday.

He still chafed a little, recalling it, even though he now understood it to be her own baggage with her family that had caused her to push him away like that. His reaction, however, continued to niggle at him no matter how much he wanted to ignore it. Her claim that she was with him out of desperation had slapped him with a surprisingly sharp hand.

She was volatile. A woman as sexually passionate as she was would have strong feelings in every aspect of her life, he supposed. He could only imagine what kind of mama bear she'd be about her children.

Sucking in a breath at having taken such a bizarre turn in his mind, he lifted his head to see her set aside her phone.

"Done. Really sorry," she said.

"Don't apologize. We both have to work. I made you wait this morning."

She gave him a look that said, *Seriously?* and slid her eyes to the crewman setting out their air tanks.

He grinned, amused by her blushing over his referring to the way they'd been driving each other into a frenzy, fresh out of the shower, when he'd had to take a call that couldn't be put off. Afterward, they'd nearly ripped each other apart, and breakfast had been a quietly stunned affair when her bare foot atop his had pleased him well beyond what was reasonable.

They'd parted ways after, each moving to their separate work spaces, but he'd been distracted by her proximity. With most women, that would signal the end for him. Not with Tiffany. His brain couldn't even contemplate an end to this. It had barely started. She was too extraordinary.

Her phone rang and she turned from removing her wrap, clad only in her bikini as she stepped toward the table where she'd left the phone. "I don't have to get that. We'll pretend we're already in the water and— Oh shoot, it's my brother. I should answer. Why are you staring?" She followed his gaze to her torso, then sent an anxious look to the crewman who had lifted her tank, ready to strap it onto her.

"I'm staring because you're hot as hell," Ryzard prevaricated. "Take your call or you'll be wondering what he wanted."

Somewhat flustered, she stabbed the phone, then held the screen before her for the video call. "Hey," she said as she picked up her wrap and shrugged her arm into it.

Ryzard sighed inwardly. He hadn't meant to make her feel sensitive. He'd been looking at her scars, yes, but only thinking that a woman with less zeal for life would have succumbed to such injuries. Tiffany's ferocious spirit was the reason she'd survived, and he was very glad she had.

"You're naked?" Her brother frowned. "It's the middle of the day. I thought it would be safe to call."

"Excuse me, darling," Tiffany said to Ryzard. "My brother has called to ask if the sun is over the yardarm. Could you lift the sheet and see?"

Christian sputtered, Ryzard looked to the sky for patience and his crewman buried a snort of laughter into his shirt collar. Although Ryzard had to admit it was nice to know she gave others a hard time, not just him.

"We're about to go swimming, you idiot," she said to her brother. "See? Bathing suit." She ran her phone down her body as if she was scanning for radioactivity, showing him the strapless band and itsy slash of blue. Then she turned the phone to show him the equipment on the deck. "There are the breathing tanks and scuba flippers. There's

the mask that's going to give me an anxiety attack so Ryzard will have to buddy-breathe me to the surface. Is my
virtue restored? Want to tell me now why you called?"

"Dad hasn't come across anything useful yet, but said
he'd ask around."

"Motivated, is he?" The way Tiffany's blond lashes lifted
to send a resolute look toward Ryzard made his blood kick
into higher gear. "Tell him I appreciate anything he's able
to pass along."

"As do I," Ryzard told her as she hung up. "If you're
talking about what I think you are."

"I asked Christian to put a bug in his ear. Dad's not
speaking to me directly right now, but I don't know if that's
because he's in Washington and doesn't have time for the
kind of conversation he thinks we need to have or if he's
genuinely angry. I hope you don't mind, but I was worried
Dad might—" She shrugged apologetically. "I'm his little
princess. I didn't want any grumpiness he felt toward you
to come out with anyone in a position to affect your situation. If he knows I have an interest in the outcome, he'll
take care to support your petition. Or at least not damage it."

His ears rang with the impact of what she was saying.
"He has that kind of influence?" It wasn't like him to underestimate people, but his sexual enthrallment had temporarily shortened his sight of the bigger picture.

"He's very well connected. And I'm being overcau-
tious," she assured him, moving to put a hand on his arm.
"Don't worry. He wouldn't do anything rash. Something
like throwing support behind a leader who hasn't been recognized… It's too big a gamble going into an election. If
anything he'll be even more circumspect, couching his reaction while trying to find out everything he can. He's not
going to stir up a lynch mob or anything."

"No shotgun wedding?" he prompted, throat dry. How
far would her father go for his daughter's groom?

"Absolutely not," she assured him.

He should be relieved. He couldn't betray Luiza's memory by contemplating marriage to another woman, but in the back of his mind a voice whispered, *If it was for your country...*

He brushed the thought aside, trying to remind himself this was a simple fling. Two people enjoying sexual compatibility and the luxury of Caribbean waters. If he took a moment to reassess Tiffany, not just because she was lissome and golden, not simply because she had a quick, intelligent mind and a clear understanding of politics, but because she could soon be first daughter of the United States of America, that didn't mean he was being disloyal to his one true love. Luiza had had a dream for their country, and he was obligated to consider any avenue to achieve it. That's all he was doing.

He watched her frown at her diving mask, lips white where she pinched them together. She'd told him about her aversion to wearing things tight against her face, but he watched her draw in courage with a deep breath and wrestle the mask onto her face.

"I'm really worried I'll freak out down there," she said in a tone made nasal by the mask covering the upper half of her face. Her eyes behind the glass were anxious.

"You're tough," he told her, pride and regard moving in him. "You'll handle it."

"You don't know that." She set a hand on her bare chest. "My heart's going a mile a minute."

"But you're trying anyway, despite your anxiety. That's why I know you'll be fine," he assured her.

He quickly slipped into his own gear, not wanting to make her wait for the distraction of reef and shipwreck to take her mind off her fears. Holiday fun, he insisted to himself. Nothing so complex as wanting to coax her past bad memories because he felt compelled to share the wonder below the surface with her.

Why it mattered to him that she go with him was a puzzle he didn't study too closely. He could just as easily dive with one of his crew and had in the past, but he was aware of a preference for staying aboard with her over diving without her.

That wasn't like him. He was not a dependent person. Tiffany had been surprised the other day when he'd told her he didn't want a wife or children. He understood the reaction. Everyone in the world wanted a lifetime companion and offspring, but after Luiza, he'd closed himself off to the idea.

He *didn't* want emotional addiction to another being. It made a person vulnerable, and he couldn't afford such weaknesses.

But the thought of marrying Tiffany kept detonating in his mind, trailing thoughts of sleeping with her every night for the rest of his life.

It was because of the advantages she offered him. It would be a practical move, not something he did out of a need to connect himself irrevocably to her. He didn't want or need *family*.

He needed to stabilize his country and make good on his promise of peace.

"You look like a frog," she said as they readied to jump.

"So kiss me, Daddy's Little Princess. See what I turn into."

She did, quick and flirty, then bit her smile onto her mouthpiece and fell back into the water.

He leaped after her.

CHAPTER SEVEN

"THAT WAS FANTASTIC!" Tiffany panted, still breathless from their ascent from a shipwreck covered in coral and barnacles, populated with colorful fish darting in and out of fronds. Ryzard had carried a spotlight so the wash of blue-green from the filtered sunlight had disappeared, revealing the true brilliance below.

He handed off his tank to his crewman, then heaved himself to sit on the platform at the stern of the boat, legs dangling beside her. "Up?" He offered a hand.

"Still recovering. Give me a sec," she said breathlessly.

He relayed their gear as they both stripped, lifting her tank off her back, muscles flexing under the glistening latte of his tan. His black bathing suit was ridiculously miniscule, making American men such as her brother seem like absolute prudes with their baggy trunks. She'd heard people refer to those teensy tight suits as banana hammocks and budgie smugglers, but on the right man, they were sexy as hell.

A crooked finger came under her chin, and he lifted her face to look him in the eye. Beneath the water, his foot snaked out to catch her at the waist and guide her into the space between his knees.

"What?" she challenged, hands splaying on the steely muscles of his flexing thighs.

"Are we staying in the water a little longer?" he asked suggestively. "You can't look at me like that and not provoke a response."

She flicked her gaze downward and saw he'd filled out the tight black fabric to near bursting.

"Don't ever let anyone tell you you're not beautiful, *draga*. When you smile, you light up the room, and when you're aroused, I can't take my eyes off you."

The water should have bubbled and fizzed around her, she grew so hot and flushed with joy.

"Will you come to Bregnovia with me?"

Oh. It was an out-of-the-blue question with huge implications, the most important being, *he wanted to keep her with him.*

Surging upward, she straightened her arms and let her chest plaster into his, meeting his hot kiss with open-mouthed, passionate joy.

"Yes," she agreed.

One big hand came up to cradle the back of her head and the other dug into her waist, holding her steady while his calves pinched her thighs, bracing her in the awkward position. Their kiss went on for a long time, sumptuous and thorough.

With a tight sound of frustration, he jerked back. "No condom," he muttered.

"What? There's plenty of room in that suit for one."

"Not much room at all, actually," he growled. "You'll take the lead into the cabin."

Laughing unreservedly, she let him pull her the rest of the way out of the water and onto his lap. "At least we know what you turned into down there."

He raised his brows in query.

She whispered, "Horny toad."

He pinched her bottom as he urged her inside.

* * *

The landscape from the airport was one of a country in recovery. When her brother had said Bregnovia could use their firm's expertise, he hadn't been kidding. They left the partially bombed-out tarmac, wound past a scorched vineyard and turned away from one end of a shattered bridge that spanned a canyon to zigzag into the riverbed, where they four-wheeled over a makeshift crossing before climbing the hairpin curves on the far side to enter a city that looked like a child had kicked over his blocks.

But what a city it had been. Bregnovia's capital, Gizela, was a medieval fairy tale on a river that, until dammed for electricity and irrigation, had been a trading arm in and out of the Black Sea. Low canals still lapped at the stone walls in its village square. Beyond that quaint center, stark communist housing stood next to even more modern shopping malls, but nothing escaped the wounds of recent war. Rubble punctuated in a small landslide off a facade here, crooked fencing kept children out of a teetering building there.

Fascinated by the contrast of beauty and battle, Tiffany barely spoke until they drove through gates that were twelve feet high and thirty-six feet wide. Their ornate wrought-iron grillwork with gold filigree appeared startlingly new and grand.

"This is your home? It looks like Buckingham Palace."

"It is a palace," Ryzard confirmed casually. "Built as the dacha for a Russian prince during tsarist times. The communists spared it—a KGB general appropriated it—but it was the last stand for my predecessor. We're still repairing it from the siege. It's only mine while I'm president, but I'm paying for the refurbishment, as my legacy."

Despite the bullet holes and the pile of broken stones that might have once been a carriage house, the palace made the White House look like a neglected summer cottage, especially with its expansive flower bed that formed a carpet beneath a bronze statue of a woman with an arm across her breast, the other outstretched in supplication—

Tiffany read the nameplate as the limo circled it. Inexplicably, her heart invaded her throat, pulsing there like a hammered thumb. *Luiza.*

Ryzard had said she was his country's martyr, revered like their Lady Liberty, but this statue wasn't staid. It didn't project a state of peace and optimism with a torch to light the way forward. It was anguished and emotional and raised all the hairs on her body. This statue wasn't a symbol or an ideal. She was a real person.

Whose name was tattooed on Ryzard's chest.

Not wanting to believe the suspicion flirting around the periphery of her consciousness, Tiffany left the car and walked inside to confront an oil portrait of the same woman in the spacious drawing room. Here, Luiza's serene smile was as exquisite as Mona Lisa's, only eclipsed by her flawless beauty.

Again it didn't seem like a commemorative pose that a country hung in the National Gallery. There was a wistful quality to the painting. It was the kind of thing someone lovingly commissioned to enshrine a memory.

Luiza's eyes seemed to follow Tiffany as she accepted introductions to Ryzard's staff. Thankfully they quickly left her behind as Ryzard and his porters took her up the stairs and along the colonnaded walk that circled the grand entrance below and brought her to a place he called the Garden Suite.

"It's the only one in the guest wing that's habitable," he said with a minor twist of apology across his lips. "But your work space is here." He left the bedroom and crossed the hall to push through a pair of double doors into a sitting room that had been tricked out with office equipment and a replica desk that Marie Antoinette would have used if she had run a modern international construction firm. "You won't have any problem working outside your country? With the different time zone?"

"We're global and I've been working from the family mansion. The advantage to living like a recluse is that no one will expect me to show up in pers— My umbrella!" The stained glass piece hung at a cocked angle in front of the window, just high enough for her to stand under it. "You said we slept through the auction," she accused.

"I placed a reserve bid before we left."

Moving in a slow twirl, she closed her eyes and imagined she could feel the colors as they caressed her face. "You're spoiling me."

"I want you to be happy. You will be?"

She opened her eyes to the window and the back of Luiza's bronzed head beyond the glass. Her floating spirits fell like a block of lead. She couldn't shake the feeling that Ryzard had a statue of his old girlfriend on the lawn.

"Tiffany?" he queried, voice coming closer.

"Where will you be?" she asked, leaving the window and leading him back across the hall to the bedroom. Here, at least, the windows faced the river.

"Too damned far away," he replied.

"Why? Security? No outsiders in the president's bedroom?" she guessed.

"Certain customs remain quaintly adhered to."

"Mmm." She pushed her mouth to the side, hiding that she was actually quite devastated. "I don't suppose our president could get away with bringing women home, either." The porter had gone so she jerked her chin at the door, saying, "See if that door locks."

"Subtle," he said drily, "but I can't."

"I don't know what you think I'm suggesting," she challenged, tossing her head to cover up that she rather desperately needed to reconnect physically. The emotional hit of what looked quite literally like a monumental devotion to Luiza shook her tenuous confidence. Badly. Now he was rejecting her, inciting a quiet panic. "I only meant that if I'll be sleeping alone, I need to feel safe."

"You won't be alone."

"I can have a guard with me?"

"That would be detrimental to the state of peace I'm trying to maintain," he stated with one of his untamed smiles. "No, I will sleep with you, but right now I have to go outside and salute my flag. It's a custom I observe when I return after being away. People gather to see it. It reassures them of my commitment. Would you do me the favor of putting on something suitable and joining me? They'll be curious."

Here we go again, she thought with an unexpected face-plant into dread.

I bet Luiza would do it, a taunting voice sang in follow-up.

"Problem?" he asked, obviously reading something of her reluctance.

"Just disappointed we can't test the bed," she prevaricated.

"They stand at the gate, if you're worried they'll see you close up."

"It's fine," she assured him.

It was. When she stood outside thirty minutes later, face shaded by a hat from the surprisingly hot sun, her entire being swelled with admiration as she watched Ryzard in his presidential garb stand tall and make a pledge to his flag. He wasn't a man going through the motions. His motives were pure, his heart one hundred percent dedicated.

With tears brimming her eyes, she watched him step away from the flag with a bow, taking his respectful leave. Then he turned and saluted the statue of Luiza, first pressing the flats of his fingertips to his mouth then offering the kiss to her in an earnest lift of his palm.

Tiffany stood very still, fighting not to gasp at the slice of pain that went through her. It wasn't the gesture that struck her so much as the anguish on Ryzard's face.

Her suspicions were confirmed. He loved Luiza, really loved her as a strong man loves his soul mate. His pain was so tangible, she could taste its metallic flavor on her tongue.

She reached out instinctively, longing to comfort him, but he stiffened under her touch, catching her hand and gently but firmly removing it from his sleeve.

"When I asked about your tattoo, you never said—"

"I know," he cut in, releasing her and taking one step away. "It's difficult to talk about."

"Of course," she managed, curling her fingers into a fist even though the blood was draining from her head, making her feel faint. Would she have come here if she'd known? The starkness of his rejection felt so final she could barely stand it. "I'm so sorry."

She meant she was sorry for overstepping, but he heard it as a lame platitude and dismissed it with an agitated jerk of his shoulder.

"I never want to go through anything like it again. To love like that and lose— Never again," he choked, flashing her a look that was both adamant and apprehensive.

He quickly looked away, but that glimpse of his resolve struck like a blow. She knew what it meant: he would never *allow* himself to love again. It would make him too vulnerable.

Making another quarter turn, he bowed his head toward the gates.

That's when Tiffany noticed the crowd of fifty or sixty people with faces pressed through the uprights of the gate, witnessing his rebuff and her humiliation. They didn't applaud, didn't wave, just stared at them for a few moments before slowly beginning to disperse.

Even they seemed to know she had no place here.

As she followed Ryzard back into the palace, she couldn't tell if Luiza's portrait met her with a smug smile, or a pitying eye. Thankfully, they both had work to catch up on. She needed space, even one situated with a prime view of Luiza's last haircut.

Oh, don't be bitter, Tiffany.

Ha, she laughed at herself. Bitterness had been her stock in trade after the pain of her recovery had receded from blinding to merely unrelenting. She really had believed her life was over, but Ryzard had shown her she could have a measure of happiness.

She considered the boundaries of her happiness later, as she soaked in a tub of bubbles. Ryzard had had to take a call, leaving her to dine alone, and she felt very much as her mother must have for much of her marriage. Not so much slighted as resigned. This was the reality of living with someone in his position. If he had loved her, the sacrifice might be worth it, but he didn't.

His heart belonged to Luiza. Indelibly.

A tiny draft flickered the candles in the corner of the tub and sudden awareness made her glance toward the door, then sit up in a startled rush of water and crackling bubbles.

Ryzard slouched his shoulder against the frame, arms folded, hip cocked. The most decadently wicked glint of admiration gave his shadowed expression a sexy cast.

She'd set a stage for him if he chose to come looking for her. A delicate lily-of-the-valley scent hovered in the humid air and a low-volume saxophone hummed sensuously from the music player. That hadn't prepared her for the impact of his tousled hair, wrinkled collar under a pullover sweater, or the way her heart leaped when he reached to tug his sweater over his head.

"I came to sneak you down to my room, but you've made me an offer I can't refuse. Before I forget, though…" He leaned over her, one broad hand cradling her chin while he crushed her mouth in a hard, thorough kiss that made her murmur in surprised delight.

"You were in danger of forgetting to do that, were you?" she asked breathlessly as he straightened to take off his shirt and kick away his pants.

"An undersecretary from your State Department called. It's not a promise to vote in favor, but it's a promising sign they're leaning that way."

"Oh!" The impulsive clap of her hands sent bubbles exploding like flakes off a snowball. "That's wonderful."

"That's thanks to you." He eased into place behind her, his muscular body buoying hers as he pressed her to relax back into him.

"I didn't do anything."

"I'm sure it was your father's influence at play."

"Mmm." She let her head loll against his shoulder, absently playing with his fingers where he roped his forearm across her collarbone. Her brow pleated. She wanted him to be happy, wanted peace for his country—who wouldn't wish peace for everyone in the world? But a pang sat in her chest. She wished something more personal had brought him to her this evening.

"It's a very big step," he said, drifting his hand down the slippery slope of her breast. "Do you know how many countries hesitate to make a move because they fear instigating something with yours? If America supports us, the other two-thirds of the votes I need would fall into place fairly quickly. I know I said I wouldn't force any dress-up on you, but there may be a few state dinners in our future."

She bit back a huffing laugh. *So* not surprised.

Just say no, Tiffany.

But refusing to play her part meant refusing this relationship. Despite it's misty future, she wasn't ready for it to end.

Especially when Ryzard lightly toyed with her nipple, making her murmur approval and slide against him. Was he manipulating her with her own responses, she wondered distantly? He was hardening against her, so he *did* want her.

Still, she hated herself a little for being so weak and easily managed. If she couldn't have the same effect on him, she at least wanted to break through his control. Rolling over, she grasped him in a firm hold, the way she'd learned he liked, and nipped his bottom lip.

He jerked his head back. The gold flecks in his green eyes glinted like sparks off a sword. "It's like that, is it?" he growled.

She grinned and sent a small tsunami across the ledge as she dragged herself onto her knees and straddled his thighs. As she kissed him with all the passion releasing inside her, she used her whole body to caress him, wiggling her hips to encourage the palms that shaped her backside.

Licking into his mouth, she reached to caress his thick erection again and started to take him into her.

"*Draga,* wait," he rasped against her open mouth. "Protection." He leaned away to reach for his pants.

Inhaling anguish along with a small dose of shame, she wondered what she had been thinking, offering unprotected sex. Was she that desperate for something permanent with him?

"Actually, let's go to the bed," he said, pulling away to leave the tub and let water sluice off him onto the floor. "It'll be more comfortable." He reached to draw her onto her feet, then lifted her out, carrying her wet and dripping into her bedroom, where he followed her onto the bed.

She bit him again as he tried to kiss her.

"What has got into you?" he asked, pulling her scratching nails off him and pinning them above her head in one hand.

"Not you," she taunted, inciting him with the arch of her body into his. "What's taking so long?"

With a bite of the packet and a stroke of a finger and

thumb, he was covered and pushing into her, not rough, but not gentle. Inexorable. She was ready, but not entirely. The friction caused her to draw in a breath of both surprise and anticipation.

"Better?" he asked, holding himself so deep inside her, she released a little sob. He eased back. "Tiffany, what's wrong?"

She shook her head. "Just make love to me."

Ryzard did, because he couldn't be with her like this and not thrust and withdraw and savor and bask. But he held out, making it last a long time for both of them, sensing a wall that needed prolonged lovemaking to erode. He blamed himself for the distance. He was struggling with having her here. It had been an impulse to ask her and he didn't regret it, but he was still having a hard time adjusting.

For the moment, however, he closed his mind to his inner conflicts and opened himself to Tiffany.

She writhed beneath him, so beautiful in her struggle to resist the little death of orgasm, clinging to him as she hung on to their connection. It couldn't last forever, though. Nothing could. His heart stopped. The whole world did. Ecstasy overtook them and nothing existed for him except her.

He stayed in that trance for hours, trying to sate their appetite for each other with repeated joinings. The wall between them receded and he didn't worry about it again until the next morning, when she woke in his bed.

She glanced around with the perplexed befuddlement of the bubbleheaded blonde he sometimes teasingly called her. "Where am I?"

"The Presidential Bedroom," he answered, shrugging into his suit jacket while he enjoyed the show.

The sheet slipped as she sat up. Her blue eyes blinked and she smoothed a hand over her tangled hair. "Why?"

"Your bed was wet," he reasoned, distantly aware that wasn't the whole truth. He had wanted her in here before he'd ever gone looking for her, but he was distracted by the shadow that passed behind her clear-sky irises as she looked around.

"Problem?"

She only lifted the sheet and glanced at her naked body. "Please tell me you put clothes on me when you carried me here."

"You were awfully heavy. I couldn't manage another ounce."

Her baleful gaze held a dire warning that made him grin. He picked up her robe from the chair and tossed it to the foot of the bed in answer.

She stood to pull it on, not returning his smile. The niggling sense of being held off returned full force.

"Are you all right, *draga?*" he asked, moving forward to cup her cheek and force her to look up at him.

She didn't quite meet his eyes, only saying with an ironic twist to her mouth, "Let's just say it's a good thing I had a warm bath to loosen my muscles before we played for gold in that triathlon last night."

"Shall I rub you down?" he offered, stroking a hand down her back in concern. He was ready to insist, wanting the physical connection to her even if it wasn't a sexual one. The way she stayed resistant to his touch bothered him.

"I thought it was verboten for me to be in here? I'll be fine. I'll have a hot shower and do my stretches." She kissed him, but it was a minimal brush of her lips against the corner of his mouth before she disappeared.

He frowned as he crossed to pick up his phone from the nightstand. Absently he straightened the snapshot of him and Luiza on horseback, wondering if he was imagining the wedge between him and Tiffany.

It was probably for the best if there was one, he reasoned. This was an affair. They couldn't afford to develop deeper feelings.

Still, he left his room with a pain cleaved into his chest.

CHAPTER EIGHT

TIFFANY TRIED TO ignore the fact that Ryzard was in love with a dead woman and soak up what he offered her: generous lovemaking and a boost to her confidence.

On his catamaran, she'd quit trying to hide herself from his crew. Three days in Bregnovia and she was even more comfortable in her own skin. He kept threatening to take her along on his public appearances and she always managed to talk him out of it, but part of her longed to go on a date the way they had at *Q Virtus*.

Pressing a strapless dress in sunset colors to her front, she decided to have a pretend date with him tonight. She imagined that like all men he had a thing for short skirts and low necklines. She'd knock his socks off.

An hour later, she'd run the straightening iron over her hair to give it a sheen and applied a final layer of glossy pink to her lips, making them look pouty and ripe. The dress offered her breasts in half cups, hugged her waist and clung so tightly across her hips she could barely walk. The gladiator sandals didn't help, but man did she look hot. The fact her scars were fully revealed by the itty-bitty dress didn't faze her.

She paused to consider that. A light coat of concealer downplayed the mottled scar on her face, but she wasn't about to smear her whole body with the stuff. Ryzard wouldn't notice or care either way. He thought she was gorgeous exactly as she was. It was such a painfully sweet knowledge, she had to stop and cradle it and blink hard or ruin her carefully applied makeup.

Digging her nails into her palms, she focused on the sting to clear her head, aware she was dangerously close to tumbling into love with him. It was because he was her first, she reasoned. He was gorgeous and smart and *so* patient with her moodiness and baggage. He commanded everything around him with calm ease, and that would make anyone feel safe and protected and cherished.

The real tell would be when they separated. She couldn't hide from her parents forever. The one stilted conversation with her mother had centered on exactly how long she intended to be away.

Tiffany hadn't wanted to admit she was afraid to leave. Would Ryzard miss her if she went home for a week? Or would it be the end of their associations?

She shook her head, having learned to be present in a moment, especially if it lacked pain. No one had a crystal ball telling what would come next. For now, she and Ryzard were together and happy.

With a calming breath, she searched him out in his office. He was watching his favorite newscaster and remained behind his desktop screen as she entered, head bent in concentration as he listened, expression grim and contained.

"What's happening in the world to make you look so severe?" she teased as she sidled up to him. "A beautiful woman just walked in. Whatever you're watching, forget it and notice *me*."

His arm came around her waist, grasping her close and tight, but his other hand caught hers before she could press his head down for the kiss she wanted. The look in his eyes was not easily interpreted, and the voice beside her startled her out of trying.

"Should we continue this later?" the newscaster asked.

"No," Ryzard answered.

Tiffany cried out in surprise and jerked against Ryzard's arm, but he held on to her without laughing.

"I thought you were watching a broadcast," she gasped, covering her heart.

The familiar face on the screen gave a tight smile of acknowledgment.

"I didn't realize I was walking into a video call. I apologize. Oh, gosh," she realized with a belated hand going to the bad side of her face. "I can't imagine what you think of me, making an entrance like that."

"I was already aware you two were close," the talking head said. He was a globally known face, one who'd elevated from foreign-correspondence stories to hard-hitting investigative stories and in-depth analyses of world politics.

At the moment she didn't have much choice with regard to how close she was to Ryzard. His arm was like a belt of iron, pinning her to his side, his tension starting to penetrate as she read zero amusement in his expression over her mistake.

"What's wrong?" she asked, instinctively bracing herself.

"We had company after our dive," he replied.

"Paparazzi?" She tried to step back, but he kept a tight grip on her.

"It doesn't matter, Tiffany."

"Of course it matters! Otherwise your friend here wouldn't be calling to warn you. Is it photos or video?"

"Photos." Ryzard fairly spat the word.

"The photographer knew I would never touch something purely to incite sensation," the newscaster said. "So they didn't offer them to me or I would have kept them off the market completely. Instead I heard about it secondhand and I've suggested a countermeasure to draw attention from their release."

"What kind of countermeasure? What are they saying?" She looked between the screen and Ryzard, panic creeping into her bloodstream.

"They don't sell clicks by being kind," Ryzard said brutally. "We'll meet in Rome," he told his friend on the screen. "You're right that a face-to-face broadcast interview will have more impact than something thrown together remotely."

"I'm not going on camera!" Tiffany cried.

"No," Ryzard agreed with the full impact of his dictatorial personality. "But you'll accompany me to the interview—"

She shook her head, growing manic. Part of her wanted to explode in rebellion, the other desperately needed to crawl away and hide.

"I need to go home." Had her father heard yet? She struggled against Ryzard's steely grip, then froze, thinking of her mother's reaction. "My family will be livid. They're already barely speaking to me—"

"Calm down." He thanked his friend and promised to be in touch with his travel arrangements, then turned off the screen. "The sun will still rise tomorrow, Tiffany. No one has died."

"It would be better if I had. That's what they'll be thinking."

"Don't talk like that. Ever." He gripped her arms and gave her a little shake.

She quit struggling, but kept a firm hand of resistance against his chest. "We're not one of these families who has a disgrace every minute, Ryzard. My accident was the worst thing Dad has ever had to field with the press. Given it was more tragedy than scandal, it didn't do him any harm in the polls, but it was still a monumental circus. He won't appreciate this."

The look of wild outrage Ryzard savaged over her made

her shrink in his hold. "Your father enjoyed some kind of political *benefit* from your near death?"

"He didn't mean to! I'm just saying that's how it works. Chris and I know that. We don't go off and sleep with people who are shaking up the maps of an atlas, putting the UN on notice, then get ourselves photographed for the gossip rags so Dad has to make explanations for our behavior. This, what you and I are doing, has to stop. I have to go home." She tried again to push away.

"So you can be shunned and cloistered? No," he gritted through his teeth, holding her in place. "The photographer is the villain here, not you. Not us."

"I'm still about to be vilified, aren't I? And I don't want…" Her voice wavered. Her muscles ached where she still held him off. "Home is my safe place, Ryzard. I'd rather be there when— How bad are they? The photographs, I mean."

"Don't think about them," he commanded. "You'll never see them if I have anything to do with it." His voice sent a wash of ice from her heart to her toes, it was so grim. "But I can't allow you to be away from me when they're released. They'll say I've rejected you, and that's not true. Besides, it doesn't sound as if your family will support you, so no, you stay with me."

She drooped her head. "They would support me," she insisted heavily. "The wagons get circled at times like this. And after it blows over, they would still be there for me. They do love me. It's just complicated."

"I will *ensure* it blows over," he said, forcing her chin up and looking down his nose from an arrogant angle, but his touch on her gentled even if his voice didn't. "You're coming to Rome with me, Tiffany."

She held back from pointing out she was perfectly capable of booking a charter flight and getting herself anywhere she darned well wanted to go. If he was only being authoritarian, she probably would have, but he sounded concerned. He sounded as if her feelings mattered, not just his image. That softened all the spikes of umbrage holding her stiff, making her shudder in surrender.

"Okay," she acquiesced.

"Good girl."

"Don't push it," she warned, but turned her face toward the caress of his fingertips as he smoothed her hair back behind her ear. Her eyes drifted closed.

"I'd like your father's contact number."

"Oh, no, I'll call Dad." She straightened, but found herself still in the prison of his hold.

"No, Tiffany. This is my fault. I should have taken more care to shield you. He's already uncomfortable with our relationship. I should have introduced myself before something like this made our first conversation an unpleasant one."

"I really think—"

"We're not negotiating, *draga*. We'll stand here until you've given me his number, but I'd like to get to Rome sooner than later, so make this easier on both of us."

"You're unbelievable," she choked.

"His people will have questions about the arrangements I've made. Quit being stubborn," he pressed.

Her? Stubborn? Kettle. *Black*.

With a sigh of defeat, because she really didn't want to face down her father *and his people,* she offered up his private mobile number.

How could he kiss something so hideous?

She didn't know why she looked it up. She should have known better, but she'd been compelled to know what they were saying. It was horrid. Beyond cruel.

Ryzard had been furious when he had emerged from

his shower and found her with his tablet in her lap, fingers white, throat dry, eyes unable to meet his.

"Why would you take a dose of poison? It's self-destructive, completely against everything you are," he'd growled, nipping the tablet away from her and tossing it across the room onto the bed.

Somewhere in his words she supposed a compliment lurked, but all she heard was disapproval. It made her cringe all the more.

The flight to Rome was exhausting and silent, his mood foul, but she hadn't wanted to speak, either. She didn't want him to notice her. She seemed like a burden, something he was carrying with him because he had to, not because he wanted her. How could he want anything to do with her when she was bringing shame on him like this?

Like sleeping with snakeskin. She shuddered at the head-lines and comments from trolls that would stay in her mind forever. *Her husband was lucky he died and didn't have to stay married to that.*

Ryzard's interview was staged in a hotel room, the pris-tine white decor too bright for her gritty, bloodshot eyes. Neither of them had slept despite lying next to each other for a few hours. He'd stroked her for a time, but she hadn't been able to respond, too frozen inside. Feeling betrayed. Her parents hadn't called, not even replying to her text that she was available if they wanted to talk. The only friend she had right now was Ryzard, and he was so remote he might as well have stayed in Bregnovia and sent a wax double in his place.

She'd been too afraid to ask what he intended to say and wound up standing at the side of the room, staring dumbly from the shadows into the light as he took his seat. The in-terview began.

Her father had done a million of these things, so she wasn't surprised to hear them tiptoe through a variety of political tulips on the way to the meat of the interview. Ryzard's devotion to his country was on full display, and she imagined the whole world was reevaluating him as he spoke passionately about Bregnovia's desire for peace and plans for prosperity. She hoped so. He deserved to be taken seriously.

She grew more and more tense as the interview dragged on, however. Didn't they realize the audience was waiting for the mention of her name?

Twenty-five minutes in, the question finally came.

"Photos have circulated showing you with American heiress Tiffany Davis. Is it serious?"

"I take very seriously that your bottom-feeder colleagues are making their fortune on photos that for all we know have been manipulated for a higher profit."

Nice of him to defend her with such an implication, but the photos had not been airbrushed. She genuinely looked that bad.

The interviewer smiled tightly. "I meant is the relationship serious?"

"That's between us. We're private people," Ryzard stated implacably.

Tiffany caught back a harsh laugh. Did he really think he'd get away with as little as that?

"My sources tell me you met at the notoriously secret *Q Virtus*," the newscaster continued.

See? she wanted to cry. The press never rested until they drew as much blood as possible, even when they called themselves a friend.

"That's true," Ryzard allowed.

"*Q Virtus* is a rather exclusive club, isn't it? What can you tell me about it?" the journalist pressed.

"I'm sure contacting them would get you more information than you'd ever get out of me," Ryzard said smoothly.

Oh. Ha. That was smart. She relaxed under a ripple of

humor. The public's insatiable curiosity would now turn to the club. Papers could trot out as many before-and-after photos of Tiffany Davis as they wanted, but viewers and readers would be more interested in learning the names of other people in the secret club. They'd hungrily eat up the scant yet salacious details of what went on there. She and Ryzard would be old news before the credits rolled on this broadcast.

In fact, when she watched later that evening, she noted that while the names rolled, her own image came forward to Ryzard's reaching hand. She shook hands with the newscaster and thanked him, all of them standing in friendly banter. Her good side was angled to the camera. Her hair was done and her makeup was decent. Wearing a simple alabaster suit, she looked...normal. Pretty even.

Ryzard clicked it off as it went to commercial. She collapsed on the foot of the hotel bed, emotionally exhausted. Could it really be over as easily as that?

Ryzard watched Tiffany as he unknotted his tie and released first the cuffs, then the front buttons of his shirt. As tough as she was, he'd seen what a toll this attack had had on her. She'd been shutting him out as a result, and that infuriated him. Her talk of running away where he couldn't reach her had nearly put him out of his mind.

He was still beside himself that this incident had happened at all. His captain had warned him that an unidentified boat kept turning up in their radar, but he'd shrugged it off. None of his mistresses in the past had warranted much attention, but he supposed his own profile was elevated to the international stage these days. Tiffany's family was certainly of a level to feed the appetite of her country's gossip columns.

And she's not just a mistress, is she? The question beat in warning like a jungle drum in his chest, ominous and dark.

His plans for his relationship with Tiffany were changing, but he hadn't wanted to allude to anything more in his interview. The last time his link to a woman had been public and indelible, she'd been used as a pawn in his country's civil war and the outcome was fatal.

Seeing Tiffany beaten and wounded by words shook loose his nightmare of losing Luiza. He'd grasped at anger to counter his resurgence of helplessness, hating that he couldn't stem the damage being done to her, but agony and guilt were constant. He should have protected her better. If he could have stopped Tiffany from searching out what they were saying about her, he would have. Humanity's capacity for ugliness astounded him. His job, the one he'd taken on for his country, for his own sanity, was to push brutality and attacks to the furthest fringes of existence that he could.

And keep himself apart so the pain of life couldn't reach inside him and wring him into anguish.

It wasn't easy when Tiffany sat with her spine slouched and her golden hair trailing loose from its neat bun, seeming incredibly delicate, like a dragonfly that had its wings crushed. When she was like this, she stirred things in him that needed to stay in firmer places. The chin-up, spoiled and cheeky Tiffany he could easily compartmentalize as a friendly partner in a game of sexual sport. Like a tennis opponent who gave him a run for his money, athletic and quick.

The vulnerable Tiffany frightened him. She made him feel so ferociously protective he would do violence if he ever found the photographer who'd reduced her image to a commodity in filthy commerce.

Shaken by the depth of his feelings, he tried to pull them both out of the tailspin with a blunt, "Dinner out or in?"

She sighed and looked up at him. Her heartrending expression was both anguished and amused. His heart began to pound in visceral reaction, and he swayed as though struck with vertigo, not sure why.

"My first thought is, *Duh, Ryzard.* Of course I'd never dine in public, but how could I be such a coward when you've just defended me so fiercely? No one else has. I can't tell you how much that means to me."

A sensation of wind rushing around him lifted all the hairs on his naked chest, as if he was free-falling into space. Her gaze was so defenseless, he couldn't look away. She reached inside him with that look, catching at things he couldn't even acknowledge.

"You already know I would only wish away your scars because I hate that you were hurt at all. But I see them as a badge of your ability to overcome," he heard himself admit. "Your sort of willpower, your deep survival instinct, is rare, Tiffany. You probably don't realize it because it's such an integral part of your nature to fight, but not everyone accepts such a life blow and makes herself live through it."

Luiza hadn't, he acknowledged with a crash of his heart into his toes. Thinking about her when he was with Tiffany, contrasting them, was wrong. Setting aside Luiza in his mind was like ripping an essential part of him away and abandoning it, but he had to do it. They couldn't occupy the same place inside him, and right now Tiffany needed him.

"All my life I heard, 'You're so pretty.' Like that was the most important thing to be. You're the first person to compliment me on having substance. I really thought I'd lost everything by losing my looks."

Where Luiza had built him into the man he was with vision and belief in him, Tiffany slayed him with honesty and vulnerability. His heart felt as though it beat outside his chest. When she rose and came to him, and went on tiptoe to brush soft lips against his jaw, he closed his eyes in paralyzed ecstasy. Deep down, at a base level, it felt wrong to be this gripped by her, but he couldn't help it. In this moment, she was all he knew.

"Thank you for wanting me exactly as I am."

He did. God help him, he wanted her in ways he couldn't even describe.

They shouldn't come together like this, with hearts agape and defenses on the floor, but he couldn't *not* touch her. Pulling her in, he settled his mouth on hers, tender and sweet. The animal in him wanted to ravish, but the man in him needed to cherish.

She drew an emotive breath and kissed him back in a way that flooded him with aching tenderness. The sexual need was there, strong as ever, but it sprang from a deeper place inside him. Hell, he thought. Hell and hell. Lingering feelings of infidelity fell away. This woman was the one he had to be faithful to. *This one.*

The rending sensation inside him hurt so much he had to squeeze her into him to stop what broke open, fearing his lifeblood would leak away if he didn't have her pressed to the wound. Her arms went around his neck, light palms cradling the back of his skull as she fingered through his hair, soothing and treasuring and filling the cavernous spaces in him with something new and golden and as unique as she was.

When they stripped and eased onto the bed and came together, it was with a shaken breath from him and a gasp of awe from her. She gloried in his possession, and he bent his head to her breast in veneration, golden lamplight burning the vision of her into his memory with the eternity of a primordial being caught in amber.

Twin fingers traced on each side of her scar, the sensation dull on one side, sweet on the other. She stretched in supreme pleasure and reached for him without opening her

eyes, finding only cool, empty sheets where he was supposed to be.

"I'm already showered and dressed, *draga*," he said on
her other side. "You said to let you sleep and I did as long
as I could, but we have to leave soon. We have a dinner
engagement in Zurich."

"Are you serious?" She rolled onto her back so she could
see him where he stood over her, his knife-sharp suit of
charcoal over a dove gray shirt set off with a subdued navy
tie. He looked way too buttoned-down, hair still damp, chin
shiny and probably tasting spicy and lickable. She skimmed
the sheet away and invited, "Come back to bed."

"Your parents are expecting us. I already agreed to see
them, but if you'd like to send our regrets…"

"They're in Zurich?" She sat up, bringing the sheet to
her collarbone as if her father had just walked in the room.
"How? Why?"

"I left it to our collective staff to work out the how. I
simply extended the invitation when I informed him about
the photos. He wanted you to come back to America. I said
you were accompanying me to Rome and that I had a commitment in Switzerland, but that we'd be pleased if they
could meet us there."

"How delightfully neutral. I guess that explains why they
haven't been in touch. They've been traveling." She threw
off the sheet and walked naked to find her phone, pleased
at the way he pivoted to watch her.

Sending him a saucy smile over her shoulder, she clicked
her screen and tapped in her code, reading aloud the message she found. "'Staying with the deHavillands in Berne.'
That's the American ambassador. Mom went to school with
her. Longtime friends of the family. 'Where will you be
staying?'" She looked to him.

"At the hotel where the banquet will be held. My people
should have sent the details already. I'll ask them to extend

the invitation to include your parents' friends." He reached inside his jacket pocket for his mobile.

Tiffany heard only one word and lowered her phone, barely hanging on to it with limp fingers as she repeated, "Banquet?"

He gave her a long, steady look. "Something I arranged months ago. I've been trying to ease you into the public eye, *draga*. Don't look so shocked. It's not something I can miss since it's a charity I personally fund. We remove land mines and petition to stop their use completely. They're an appalling weapon."

She felt as though she stood on one, but he didn't coddle her over what attending would mean. Given everything that had happened, she supposed it was time to set aside her fear of being in public. As long as she had him by her side, she'd be okay, wouldn't she?

CHAPTER NINE

A FEW HOURS LATER, she wasn't so sure. She'd taken an *in for a penny, in for a pound* approach and forgone the one-shouldered gowns that would have disguised a lot of her scarring, deciding instead to let her freak flag fly. Her halter-style gown set off her breasts and hips beautifully and was the most gorgeous shade of Persian blue that glistened and slithered over her skin as she walked.

...snakeskin...

Stop it. She pretended she was her old self, the somewhat infamous fashionista who had graced more than her share of best-dressed lists. With her trained yoga posture reaching her crown to the ceiling, shoulders pinned back with pride, she entered the lounge and took the druglike hit that was Ryzard in a tuxedo.

"I knew you wouldn't disappoint me," he said. His smile was sexy and smug, but held a warmth of underlying approval.

Winded, she dissembled by checking her pocketbook, trying to grasp hold of herself as she reacted to him and the effect he had on her. Did he know how defenseless she was around him? She suspected he did. He was coming to know her very well, maybe too well. There was an imbalance there because he could see right past her defenses, but he remained unpredictable to her.

As if to prove it, he came forward and threaded a bracelet up her marred arm until it wrapped in delicate scrolls against her biceps. It was a stunning piece of extravagant ivy tendrils fashioned from platinum. Diamonds were inset as random pops of sparkling dew, fixating the eye.

"It's beautiful."

"When people stare, you can say, 'Ryzard gave it to me. He thinks I'm a spoiled brat, but wouldn't change a thing about me.'"

She wanted to grin and be dismissive, but she was too moved. Her voice husked when she admitted, "You do spoil me. I have no idea why."

"You inspire me," he confided, then swooped to set a kiss against the corner of her mouth. "Lipstick, I know," he muttered before she could pull away in protest. "In the future, don't put it on until I've finished kissing you."

"Then we'd never leave the room, would we?"

"And how is this a problem?" He held the door as he spoke, the light in his eye making her laugh, reassuring her the evening would turn out fine.

They stopped by another suite on their way downstairs. He'd arranged it for her parents and the ambassador. Her father greeted her with a long hug before he set her back. Then he looked between her and Ryzard, not seeming to know where to start.

She quickly introduced them and included the ambassador's husband, Dr. deHavilland, using Ryzard's title as the president of Bregnovia, and heard the crack in her voice as she queried, "Mom didn't come?"

"The ladies are fussing down the hall," the doctor said after kissing her cheeks. Taking her chin, he turned her face to eye her scar. "The specialist did wonders, didn't he? It's good to see you out, Tiffany. Ryzard, what's your poison? We're having whiskey sours."

He accepted one and she squeezed his arm. "Do you mind if I...?"

"Of course, go say hello, but we need to be in the ballroom to greet the guests in fifteen minutes."

"Five," she promised with a splayed hand and hurried in search of her mother, nervous of the confrontation, but experiencing the homesick need to reconnect.

Following voices through a bedroom to the open door of a bathroom, she approached and set her hand on the inner door only to hear a makeup compact click over her mother's voice. "Are we supposed to believe he's in love with her? Any fool can see he's using her for our connections."

"Any fool except me?" Tiffany blurted, pushing the door farther in while outrage washed over her. It was followed by a stab of hurt so deep she could barely see.

Nevertheless, her vision filled with the flawless image of her mother turning from the mirror. Shock paled her mother's elegantly powdered cheeks. An automatic defense rose to part her painted lips, but first she had to draw a breath of shock as her gaze traveled her daughter's appearance and measured the amount of exposure. A trembling little head shake told Tiffany what her mother thought of this gown.

"You won't be comfortable in that."

"You mean *you* won't," Tiffany volleyed back and turned to leave. A type of daughterly need for her mother's bosom had driven her in here, and now she wished Barbara Holbrook had stayed home.

"Tiffany Ann." The strident voice didn't need volume to stop Tiffany in her tracks. "He told your father he wanted to marry you. You met him last *week*. What are we supposed to think?"

Tiffany spun back, thrown by the statement. "He did not."

Her mother held her lady-of-the-manor pose, the one that had too much dignity to descend into a did-so, did-not quibbling match. Instead, she gave Tiffany another once-over and asked primly, "How on earth did you come to be his guest? I mean, if he had brought a party aboard, I'd understand you being swept along, but obviously he wants us to believe he has a romantic interest in you. What sort of promises has he made you?"

Tiffany heard the strange lilt in her mother's voice. Concern, but something else. Something shaken and protective…

She felt her eyes go wider and sting with dryness as understanding penetrated. Her mother genuinely believed she was being used—and was too blind to see it.

If her high school diary had been passed around the football locker room, she couldn't have felt more as though her deepest feelings were being abused. If only she could have defended Ryzard. If only she believed he had deeper feelings for her beyond the physical and amusement with her "great personality."

God, maybe he didn't even feel that much for her. Maybe it *was* all about who her father was. Insecurity nearly drove her to her knees, but she made herself stand proud and state what she'd let herself believe.

"He hasn't made any promises. He wants me for my body. It's mutual."

Dumbly she turned and walked out, floored by what her mother had said about Ryzard wanting to marry her. Was it true? Because if it was, her mother was right. It wouldn't be love driving his interest in her. They *had* met only ten days ago.

She tried to swallow away the painful lump of confusion that lodged itself high behind her breastbone.

Ryzard set down his drink as she appeared and held out his crooked arm. "Ready? We'll see you downstairs," he said to the men.

"Tiffany," the ambassador scolded, following her with a

swish of skirts. "You can't speak to your mother like that. She's been telling me how worried she's been for you, not just because you dropped out of sight with a stranger—I apologize if that sounds rude," she added in an aside to Ryzard. "But since—"

"I *know*. The accident. I've been a great burden on them, but can you understand how sick I am of having that define me? I'm better now. It's time for both her and Dad to butt out of my life."

She yearned for everyone to leave her alone so she could lick her wounds in private. It pained her horribly that everyone could see how weakly she'd fallen for this incredibly handsome, indulgent charlatan who had soothed her broken ego and wormed his way toward her heart. All in the name of advancing his own agenda.

"Where is this rebellion coming from?" her father clipped in his sternest tone. "You were never like this before. Your mother and I can't fathom what's got into you. Letting you go to work has obviously put too much stress on you."

"*Letting* me." She jerked up her chastised head, filling with outrage.

Beside her, Ryzard took her good arm in a warm, calming grip. "If you'll pardon an outsider's observation? Every child has to leave the nest at some point, even one who was blown back in and needed you very badly for a time. Your daughter is an adult. She can make her own decisions."

Despite that statement of her independence, she found herself letting him make the decision for both of them to leave. A crazy part of her even rationalized that even if he *was* using her, he was also helping her find the state of autonomy she longed for.

As they waited for the elevator, a jagged sigh escaped her. "I can't do this, Ryzard."

She meant the banquet, the evening, but he misunderstood.

"Don't let this upset you. Listen, I visited Bregnovia after finishing university. I could have stayed. My mother wanted me to, but I chose to drift across Europe like pollen in the wind. I was making a statement. They had forced me to leave as a child, but they couldn't make me stay as an adult."

"And now you hate yourself for not spending time with them. You think I should go back and apologize?" She looked back down the hall, hating the discord with her family even as she dreaded facing them again.

The elevator car arrived and Ryzard guided her into it.

"I don't hate myself as much as I should. Everyone does need to leave the nest at some point, *draga*. But be assured that your parents are operating from a place of love. Your father had some very pointed questions for me. He is the quintessential father who feels a strong need to protect his baby girl."

With bloodless fingers clinging to her pocketbook, she lifted her gaze to meet his. "Did you tell him you want to marry me?" Her voice sounded flayed and dead, even more listless than the tone she had used to discuss her prospective marriage to Paulie.

Surprise flashed across his expression before he shuttered it into a neutral poker face. "He asked me about my intentions when I called. I said they were honorable. What else could I say?"

"You told me this relationship wouldn't lead to anything permanent. When did you decide it could?"

He turned his head away, profile hard with undisguised impatience, then looked back, fairly knocking her over with the impact. "What are you really asking, *draga?*"

The car stopped and she swayed, stomach dipping and clawing for a settled state. "You weren't ever going to marry, but then you realized exactly how useful my father could be. Is that right?"

"Yes." No apology, just hardened, chiseled features that were so remote and handsome she wanted to cry.

"We talked about how much I enjoy being used, Ryzard."

The doors of the elevator opened. His handlers were waiting, one reaching to hold the door for them.

"We need a moment," he clipped.

"No, we don't." Her voice was strangled, but she stepped from the elevator into the bubble that was its own bizarrely familiar shield against reality. Her skin burned under the stares of his people, but she allowed only Ryzard to see how much that tortured her as she turned to glare up at him. "If this is what I'm here for, then let's do it. I'm probably better on stage than you are. Smile. Nothing matters except how this looks."

"Tiffany," he growled.

Arranging the sort of warm, gracious smile her mother had patented, she sidled beyond his reach and asked a handler, "Where would you like me to stand in relation to the president?"

Talk about land mines. Ryzard felt as though he stood in a field of them as he welcomed his guests and waited for the misstep that would cause Tiffany to discharge. She was the epitome of class though, greeting people warmly as he introduced her, maintaining a level of poise that made his heart swell with pride even as his blood ran like acid in his veins.

We talked about how much I enjoy being used.

He struggled to hide how much his conscience twisted under that. Did she think he couldn't see what this evening was costing her? He was so deeply attuned to her that he felt her tension like a high-pitched noise humming inside his consciousness, keeping him on high alert. It was fear, he realized with a *thunk* of dread-filled self-assessment. She would run given an opportunity, and that kept him so fixated on her he could hardly breathe, braced as he was to catch her before her first step.

He ought to let her go if that's what she really wanted, but he couldn't bear it when she hadn't even given him a chance to explain. The way she'd thrown her accusation at him in the elevator had been a shock. He'd answered honestly out of instinct, because any sort of subterfuge between them was abhorrent to him.

But distance was equally repugnant to him, and she was keeping an emotional one that didn't bode well for sifting through things he'd barely made sense of himself.

As for her pithy suggestion that all he cared about was his image, she was dead wrong there. He cared about her. Thinking about how much he cared made him feel as though the elevator's cable had been cut and he was still plummeting into the unknown.

They didn't have a chance to speak freely again until they were dancing after dinner. He kept his gaze off her, dangerously close to becoming aroused from holding her. Every primordial instinct in him wanted to drag her into the nearest alcove and stamp her as his own. The way they moved perfectly together no matter what they did seduced him unfailingly.

"Another one bites the dust," she murmured.

"What does that mean?" he asked with a flash of his glance into furious eyes that scored him with disdain.

"You can't keep your eyes off my mother. I told you she was beautiful."

He realized he'd been staring at the distraction of white hair swept in a graceful frame around aristocratic bone structure. Mrs. Holbrook's blue eyes stood out like glittering sapphires on the sateen of flawless skin as she watched them. Where Tiffany had a seductively full bottom lip, her mother's was narrow and prim, but that hint of severity lent her countenance keen intelligence. She was the height of elegance when she smiled and scrupulously well-mannered. She had thanked him warmly for inviting them even as her gaze consigned him to hell.

"She's not the one giving me a hard-on, *draga*. She's keeping it from becoming obvious. I'm in danger of catching pneumonia from her glare. I take it she doesn't approve of our affair?"

"I thought we were engaged." Limpid eyes, as capable of beaming frost as her mother's, glared up at him.

He involuntarily tightened his hands on her. "Not here, Tiffany. Not now."

She snorted, lashes quivering in a flinch, but it was her only betrayal of how much his deferral stung. He silently cursed, realizing he was forcing the taffy apple upon her.

"We'll talk upstairs as soon as I can get away," he promised.

"Mom and Dad are going back to Berne with the deHavillands first thing in the morning. They want me to come, so it would probably be better if I stayed with them—"

"Like hell," he said through his teeth. She was so stiff in his arms, he thought she'd shatter if he held her too tightly, but the idea she'd leave him made everything in him clench with possessiveness.

She showed him her good cheek, the skin stretched taut across it. Her voice wavered. "You were so appalled at the idea that Dad would use my accident for his own gain, but the minute you saw an advantage to your own precious country, you—"

"Enough," he seared quietly through gritted teeth. "Marriage is not something I take lightly. Even thinking of marrying you is the breaking of a vow I made to myself and a dead woman. You have no idea what it costs me."

With a little gasp, she stopped moving, forcing him to

halt his own feet. He looked down at her, as appalled by what he'd revealed as she seemed to be.

"Luiza," she stated under her breath, lips white.

He flinched. Hearing her say his beloved's name was a shock.

"Da," he agreed, nudging her back into dancing, feeling cold.

The air of thick tension surrounding them threatened to suffocate Tiffany, but she was a trained pony. The dance continued and her company smile stayed in place while all she could think about was the snippets of information he'd revealed about his tattoo, his lady liberty, his marriage to his *country*.

The rest of their waltz passed in a blur of tuxedos and jewel-colored gowns, glittering chandeliers and tinkling laughter. When he returned her to their table, her parents rose with their friends, ready to take their leave.

"Goodbye, Ryz—" she began.

"Don't even think it," he overrode her tightly.

"I have a headache," she lied flatly. "I'd like to leave."

"Then we will," he said with equal shortness. "Let me inform my team while you say good-night to your parents."

Seconds later he cut her from the herd and whisked her up to their suite.

"You're not making friends behaving like this, you know," she whirled to state as he closed the door behind them. "My father won't have your back in any arena if you continue to kidnap his daughter."

"I know your father hates my guts, but you will not let him separate us. If you're angry with me, then you stand here and tell me so," he railed with surprising vehemence, yanking off his tuxedo jacket to throw it aside. "Do not put yourself out of my reach. That is the one thing I will not tolerate."

Deep emotion swirled from his words at hurricane force, buffeting her. She unconsciously braced her footing, absorbing his statement with a wobble of her heart in her chest that left all the hair standing up on her body. It wasn't fear exactly. More of a visceral response to his revelation of intense feeling. Her body was warning her not to take his outburst lightly. He was startlingly raw right now, and anything but taking great care with how she reacted would be stupid and possibly hurtful to both of them.

She could hurt him.

A reflexive shake of her head tried to deny the thought. His face was lined with grief, emotions he felt for someone else, but a glint of something else in the stark, defensive gaze stilled her. A strange calm settled in her mind despite the racking pain of being used still gripping her.

The suspicion he feared being wounded by her was so stunning, she could only stand there hugging herself, not knowing what to say.

She had to say or do something. His hurting destroyed her. It was particularly intolerable because it had its roots in his love for another woman, but as much as she wanted to sublimate that knowledge, a masochistic part of her had to know the details. It was like assessing an injury so she'd know how to treat it.

"Was…" She cleared her throat. "Will you tell me about her?"

He turned away to the wet bar. Glass clinked as he poured a drink, drained it, then refilled his glass and poured one for her. When he brought hers across to her, his face was schooled into something remote while his eyes blazed with suppressed, but explosive emotion.

"Were you married?" she asked in a strained whisper. *Did you love her?* She couldn't bring herself to ask it.

"Engaged. She wanted to focus on winning the war, not planning a wedding. She was a protestor, an idealist, but very passionate and smart. I met her when I came back for my mother's funeral. I was beside myself, ready to seek retribution, but Luiza helped me develop a vision that people would rally behind. She was the velvet glove to my iron fist."

"You said she was your country's icon. That everyone revered her. What happened?"

He brought his glass to his lips, took a generous swallow then hissed, "She was captured and would have been used against me. She took herself out of the equation."

Appalled horror had her sucking in a pained breath, one she held inside her with a slap of her hand across her mouth. *Once you have paid the price of a loved one, you do not stop until the job is done.*

She stared at Ryzard over her hand, brutally aware there were no words to compensate for what he'd just told her. She didn't need the details. The horrifying end was enough. The truly shocking part was that he wasn't twisted into bitterness and revenge by loss.

He was stricken with guilt and anguish, however. It showed in the lines that appeared on his face before he turned away again.

"I'm so sorry," she breathed, reaching toward him.

He shrugged off her touch. "There's nothing that can be done. We both know that death is final. Nothing in the past can be reversed."

"No," she agreed, staring at her mottled arm folded across her good one. "You can only learn to live with the consequences. And preserve their memory," she added, feeling as though her chest was scraped hollow like a jack-o'-lantern. "That's what you want to do, isn't it? Achieve what she sacrificed herself for? That's why you'll do anything to bring peace to Bregnovia. You're doing it for her."

"I'm not the only one who lost people, Tiffany. I want it for all of us."

She swallowed, understanding, empathizing, yet feeling very isolated. Her heart ached for him, but for herself, too, because she instinctively wanted to help him. Maybe he was using her, but as he kept demonstrating, his goal was noble. And she loved him too much to refuse him outright when his need and grief were very real.

She loved him.

Staring at the red flecks in the carpet between their feet, she absorbed the bittersweet ache that pulsed through her arteries and settled in her soul. Part of her stood back and mocked herself for having such strong feelings after a mere week and a half of knowing this man. Surely her mother was right and this was a type of Pygmalion infatuation. God knows it was a sexual one.

But when she compared it with what she'd felt for Paulie—exasperated affection and the security of friendship—she knew this was the deeper, more dangerous shade of love. The mature kind that was as threatening as it was fulfilling because it made her needs less important than his. It gave him the power to cripple her with nothing more than his eternal love for another woman.

"I told myself if I couldn't marry Luiza, I wouldn't marry at all." He drained his drink and set it aside, turning to push his hands in his pockets. "Then I met you."

And realized how useful she could be.

"I understand." She fought to keep her brow from pulling.

"Do you? Because I don't. It wasn't a vow of celibacy. I'm not dead. I gave myself permission to have affairs. That ought to be enough. With every other woman it has been."

A strand of something poignant thrummed near her heart. She tried to quell it for the sake of her sanity, trying not to read anything into what he was saying. In a lot of ways what he'd offered her was more than she'd imagined she'd ever find, so she shouldn't be yearning so badly for more.

"I realize you have to look out for your country's best interest, Ryzard. You've been very kind and supportive of me—"

"Oh, shut *up,* Tiffany. Looking out for my country's best interest is how I've been rationalizing your presence in the presidential bed, but even that doesn't work. Do you think I can use you in good conscience after Luiza *died* as a pawn? *Hell, no.* But allowing you to push her out of my heart would be an even greater betrayal."

She could see the tortured struggle in him. He might never love her, not when to do so would mean accepting the debilitating guilt that accompanied it. Who could accept such a deep schism to their soul?

As she absorbed that reality, her breath burned in her lungs like dry smoke.

"But each time you talk of leaving for America, I start thinking about a length of chain about this long." He showed her a space between his hands of two or three feet. "With a cuff here and here." He pointed from his smartwatch to her wrist.

She couldn't help a small smile.

"For such a sophisticated, educated man, you're incredibly uncivilized. You know that, right?" She rubbed the goose bumps off her arms, trying to hide how primitive she was at her core, responding to his caveman talk like some kind of kinky submissive.

"Your parents have every right to be suspicious of me," he allowed drily. "But it's important to me that you know my intentions toward you are not dishonorable."

That's exactly what she had feared after overhearing her mother. It had gutted her. Meeting his gaze was really hard with that specter still haunting her.

"I don't expect you to love me, Ryzard." The words fractured her soul. "But I have to insist on honesty. If you're really just with me because of my father, please say so and I'll—"

"I can't believe I'm going to say this," he cut in impatiently, "but sometimes I wish to hell you'd had other lovers so you would appreciate what we have. *I* do."

"Oh, well, let me just accommodate that right now."

He grabbed her before she'd taken two steps toward the door.

"Gorilla! Brute! You're hurting me," she accused as she found herself bouncing over his shoulder toward the bedroom.

"Honesty, Tiffany," he reminded in a scolding tone. "You just demanded it, and so do I. Lie to me and so help me, I'll spank you. That is not a bluff." He flopped her onto the bed and retreated to slam the bedroom door.

"You scare me," she cried, sitting up. "Not like scared you'll hurt me," she protested with an outstretched hand, trying to forestall the outrage climbing in his expression. "The way you make me feel. I'm terrified you'll stop wanting me. You saw what I was like before you came along. I don't want to be that person again. I don't know how to handle how important you are to me, or how horrible I'll feel when this ends."

The tense line of his shoulders eased. "I can't imagine that happening."

"But I don't know how honorable *my* intentions are. I told you how I feel about living in the public eye. If it's just an affair…"

She trailed off, distracted as he joined her, his big body crowding and overwhelming, sending her onto her back under him with the force of his personality, barely even touching her. She melted in supplication, slave to his authority and the tenderness in his eyes.

"This is more than an affair," he insisted.

That didn't allay any of her misgivings, but she wasn't sure what she wanted him to say. She rather wished she had more experience with relationships herself, but from everything she'd observed, she doubted anyone was truly confident with whatever sorts of relationships they had. It came down to trust, and as much as she wanted to believe in Ryzard, she didn't have much faith in herself.

She touched the pad of her fingertip to his lips, tracing the masculine shape that so entranced her.

"Where do we go from here?" she asked, meaning emotionally, but he took her literally.

"I have quite a few appearances. I would like you to accompany me. Will you?"

Her heart stalled, but refusing meant bringing The End forward to now, and she could already see it would be horribly painful. She wasn't ready for that, so she said the only thing she could.

"Of course."

CHAPTER TEN

DESPITE TIFFANY'S AGREEMENT, despite the unflagging passion between them, she grew less like the cheeky woman he'd come to know and more like the chilly mother he'd met in Zurich.

Of course he was pressing her inexorably into her mother's role. He couldn't help it. The opportunity was too ripe, the timing at hand, and she was damned good at it. She stepped forward with a gracious remark when needed and backed off the rest of the time. No matter what came up or when, she accepted the pull of his attention with equanimity. If she didn't like it, no one could tell, not even him. When he asked, she assured him everything was "Fine."

A sure sign that it wasn't.

But neither of their schedules had room for the type of downtime that had brought them together in the first place. She'd been up for several hours two nights in a row trying to resolve a problem with her firm. Now he'd dragged her to Budapest for an Eastern European conference. A black-tie reception opened the event, and her best makeup couldn't hide the exhaustion around her eyes.

Still she smiled, always ignoring startled reactions to her scars or simply moving past an awkward moment with a calm "Car crash." Then she would distract with a compliment or question, her warm manner disguising the fact she maintained a discreet bubble of distance.

So why was she currently clasping two hands over a stranger's? Her expression was uncharacteristically revealing, not the cool mask she usually wore at these events. The man was older than Ryzard, somewhere in his fifties, but not someone he recognized. Tiffany was sharing deep eye contact with him, and her profile was somber.

He excused himself and crossed over to them, possessive male hackles rising to attention, especially when they both stiffened at his approach and lowered their gazes.

"Ryzard, this is Stanley Griffin, minister of international trade in Canada and my late husband's cousin. Well, cousin to my mother-in-law, Maude."

Despite the legitimate reason for familiarity, he used the introduction to extricate Stanley's hand from Tiffany's grasp.

They briefly chatted about his country's mission to, "Do what we did with the EU here in Eastern Europe." Ryzard expressed his desire to participate, but first he needed recognition so if that message could be conveyed to Canada's prime minister…?

Stanley left with a promise to do so, but made a point to ask Tiffany, "Please stay in touch." Once again, Tiffany had proved her worth to him politically, but her coziness with the man rankled Ryzard for the rest of the evening.

"You seemed very familiar with that Canadian," he said later when they were undressing in the hotel suite. He was tired of being away and wished they were home.

Home. Did she regard his country the way he did? She wasn't happy here in Hungary, despite her expressed desire to see the country and her interest in this city's history. He couldn't be sure she'd been happy in any of the places they'd been recently.

"He was at my wedding. I didn't remember him, to be honest, but he certainly remembered me. He started to tell me how much he loved it when Paulie had spent summers with their family, when the boys were young, and I thought we were both going to—" She clamped her lips together, then pressed a knuckle to her mouth, turning away.

Stricken by her edging toward breakdown, he moved to grasp her shoulders in bracing hands. "Shh. Don't talk about him."

She reacted with a violent twist away from his grip and glared up at him with eyes full of tears and betrayal. "Oh, that's rich. Why can't I talk about my husband? Luiza is right *there* every time we're naked." She poked two fingers into his chest.

Her hostility took him aback, as did the underlying challenge. He bristled, but managed to keep himself from pointing out her scars were an equally indelible reminder that she had had a life before he entered it.

"I didn't say you couldn't talk about him, but it's obviously upsetting you so you should stop," he managed, barely hanging on to a civil tone.

Her jagged laugh abraded his nerves, plucking his aggression responses to even higher alert. "Yeah, well, if that's the criteria, there's a lot of things I should stop doing."

Don't ask, he told himself, but the elephant in the room had grown large enough to put pressure on both of them. A few weeks ago she hadn't had the courage to go to the grocery store in her hometown. Today she was being shoved into a supporting role on the world stage. If she didn't want to do it, she ought to have said so by now, but apparently that was up to him.

"You're not happy in the spotlight. I understand that." He removed his belt and flung it away, angry with himself for turning a blind eye to what was obviously damaging their relationship, but he couldn't undo who he was any more than he was willing to have Luiza's name erased from his chest.

"Stanley said Paulie's mother was always jealous of my

mom because she looked like she had it all, but at least
Maude had privacy. All I could think is, *What am I doing?
Why am I here?*" She lifted helpless hands.

"Tiffany, you're good at this," he began.

"I'm good at sex. Should I do that with every man who
asks?" she snarled back.

He recoiled, shocked by her vehemence and scored by a
remark that made it sound as if she only tolerated sleeping
with him. "As I said—" The words ground from between
his clenched teeth. "You shouldn't do anything that fails
to give you some level of enjoyment."

Her fierce expression flickered toward remorse, before
she collapsed in a chair, elbows on her knees, head in hands,
shoulders heavy with defeat. "I'm sorry. I know better than
to have this fight. It accomplishes nothing because at the
end of the day, you still need me beside you."

"I *want* you beside me, Tiffany. I don't need you. If
you're feeling used then you know my feelings on that. I'll
achieve my two-thirds votes with or without you."

She lifted her head out of her hands to stare at him, face
like a mask, half of it tortoiseshell reds, the other side white.
Slowly her flat gaze moved to the floor while her hands
twisted together. She forced herself to sit upright, but her
shoulders remained bowed.

"That certainly tells me where I stand."

The ice maiden was back, causing cold fire to lick behind his heart, leaving streaks of dead, black tissue.

"I'm saying you don't have to participate if you don't
want to. We can still be together. It doesn't have to change
anything," he said rather desperately, sensing things slipping away without any chance to control it.

"It changes everything, Ryzard! What am I going to
do? Sit in your presidential castle waiting for you to come
home? *There's* a departure from turning into my mother,"
she said with a caustic laugh. "What else could I do? Fol-

low you around but never be seen? That would be living as a recluse again. If you—" She bent her head to stare at her pale knuckles, but he saw the pull in her brow of deep struggle. "If we loved each other, it would be different."

He couldn't help his stark inhale of aversion. Marriage he might rationalize. Pulling his heart from the grave where he'd buried it next to Luiza was impossible. There, at least, it was safe from another blow of great loss.

Silence coated the room in a thick fog for a long minute. Tiffany was the first to move, swiping at her cheek before speaking haltingly.

"I thought my life was over, that I'd never be able to have a husband and family. I even reconciled myself to it and figured out how to fill my life with other things. I could live unmarried and childless with you, Ryzard. But you're the one who made me believe I shouldn't sell myself short. If someone could love me, if I have a soul mate out there, I shouldn't settle for anything less than finding him."

He clenched his hands into fists, trying to withstand a pain so great it threatened to rend him apart. She *did* deserve to be loved. He couldn't keep her here to serve his passion while he withheld parts of himself. It would wear on her self-esteem. If he wasn't capable of giving her all of himself, he had to let her go.

But the agony was so great he wanted to scream.

The weariness and misery in her eyes when she lifted them to meet his gaze was more than he could bear though.

"It's time for me to go home," she said gently.

He nodded once, jerkily, incapable of any other response. His throat was blocked by a thick knot of anguish, the rest of him caved in on itself so his skin felt like a thin shell, ready to crack and turn to powder.

"I'll go make the arrangements," her voice thinned over the last word as she stood and rushed from the room.

She didn't return.

When he couldn't stand it any longer, he went looking for her and came up against a locked door. He could hear her sobbing inside the bedroom, but he didn't knock. He silently railed at her for shutting him out, but the truth was, he was close to tears himself. Drowning himself in a bottle of vodka looked like a really good idea.

Taking one to his room, he sat on the bed then left it untouched on the nightstand as he stayed awake through the long, dark night, willing Tiffany to come to him.

CHAPTER ELEVEN

BARBARA HOLBROOK WANTED to know exactly what had happened.

"Mom," Tiffany protested, feeling cornered in her room, jet-lagged and wondering how she still had a doll propped on the pillows of her made bed. It was an antique, granted, but seriously. "I'm about ten years too late for having my heart broken by my first crush. That's all it was."

That's what she kept telling herself anyway. She sure as heck didn't want to deconstruct everything that had happened with Ryzard. It was too painful.

But she missed him. Sleeping alone sucked and stalking him on the web only made her heart ache. Or laugh aloud.

Mrs. Davis and I remain on excellent terms. Print something negative about her at your own peril, she read over breakfast one Saturday morning and got herself goggled at by her entire family for her outburst.

"What," she hedged, amusement fading. "It's funny," she insisted after reading it to them. She wanted to kiss his austere image, feeling as though he was flirting with her from far, far away. He'd been so contained that last night, so willing to let her go without a fight. That had made her feel insignificant, but reading that they remained "on excellent terms" bolstered her.

"You'll be seeing him again, then?" her father asked, sipping his coffee.

"Why? Does sleeping with him help your approval rating?"

"Tiffany," her mother gasped.

Christian sent her a hard look. "Come on, Tiff."

Setting her cup into its saucer like a gavel announcing a judge's decision, Tiffany said, "That was out of line. I apologize. But I'm tired of being a bug under a microscope. It's time I went into the office."

"You've been in there every day since you came home," her mother said with confusion.

"Not my office here, Mom. The real office. In the city."

"What? When?" Chris asked swiftly. "I can't drive you for a week at least. I told you I'm working from here until I get that design done, so I'm not interrupted."

"And I have to be in Washington," her father said with apology.

"I have an appointment in New York at the end of the month, darling," her mother offered. "You can come in for the day with me, but are you sure you're ready?"

She wished she'd had her tablet set to record. Ryzard would shake his head at this display and probably claim this coddling was the reason she was such a spoiled brat. She suspected he'd also remind her how lucky she was to be so loved.

Misty emotion washed over her in a flood of gratitude for the family she had and an ache of longing for the man she didn't.

"You guys are awesome. I love you," she said, meeting each pair of eyes in turn to let her sincerity sink in. She silently thanked Ryzard as she did it, finally able to see herself as a whole, independent adult because he had treated her as one. "But it's time for me to be a grown-up. I'll drive myself to New York and stay in the company flat until I find my own place."

Her mother's gasp and near-Victorian collapse didn't

sway her. On Monday she walked through the glass doors of Davis and Holbrook, palms clammy and half her face hidden behind giant sunglasses. By Thursday the worst of the buzzing and staring was behind her. Friday morning she was interrupted by a delivery of flowers.

"Wow," she couldn't help saying, stunned by the bouquet arranged to look like a culmination of fireworks. Her heart began to gallop in her chest. "Who is that from?"

"I couldn't say, ma'am." The uniformed man tapped the subtle *Q Virtus* crest on his shirt pocket. "I work for their concierge service. All I get is a pickup and delivery address."

"Oh, um, would it be from *Q Virtus* itself, then?" That was disappointing. And made the significance of portraying fireworks a little creepy.

"There's usually a 'compliments of Zeus' card if it is. Without one, I'd guess it's from one of their members, but I really couldn't say. I'm not privy to much that goes on there. *You* could be a member for all I know," he added with a shrug.

"I imagine there are members who don't know they belong," she murmured ironically, thanking him with a generous tip, then burying her face in the perfume of the bouquet. She wanted to gather the fragrant leaves and butter-soft petals into herself, trying to feel closer to Ryzard.

How could he be this sweet, this pleased by her stepping out of her comfort zone and taking control of her life, and not love her a little?

Luiza, she thought with a pang. She could never compete with a woman who had shown such a level of bravery.

Taking a page from Ryzard's book, she had *Q Virtus* arrange a nice lunch when her mother came to visit at the end of the month. Being scrupulously efficient, they located it in a penthouse that fit exactly what Tiffany was looking for as a new home. The decor was a bit too colorless for her taste. It needed a stained glass umbrella to jazz it up, but the floor plan and views were astonishing.

Her mother pronounced it excellent for entertaining, which only made Tiffany think of holding court with Ryzard and miss him all over again.

She sat across from her mother in tall wingbacks at a circle of white marble facing a floor-to-ceiling view of Central Park, sipping from crystal water goblets with brushed gold trim, thinking she'd rather be staring at that heart-wrenching statue if it put her back in his proximity.

"This isn't at all how I imagined things turning out for you," her mother murmured.

She seemed surprised that the words had escaped her and glanced toward the kitchen, where the noise and staff were well contained beyond a small service pantry.

Tiffany set down her glass and linked her fingers together, subtly bracing for reaction as she admitted, "I think it might have come to this eventually. I didn't love Paulie. Not in a way that would have kept us together forever."

"I know," Barbara sighed.

"You did?"

Her mother's perfectly coiffed head tilted in acknowledgement. "Not until you started up with that Bregnovian fellow, but once I saw the lengths you were willing to go for him, I realized you and Paulie never stood a chance. I should have seen it from the outset, but it would have been so convenient, Tiffany."

She sputtered a laugh at that. "Yeah, well, the situation with Ryzard was more convenience on his part. You were right about that much." Deep angst threatened to rise up and squeeze her in its clawed grip.

"Is that true? He seemed so protective of you. Still does."

"I think that's his nature," Tiffany said shakily, finding it really hard to hold on to her control. "He was so supportive, made me feel so good about myself, but when it came down to it he said he didn't need me or my connections. He—" Her voice broke, but she had to say it aloud so she could get over it and move on. "He doesn't love me."

"But you love him."

Through blurred eyes, Tiffany saw her mother's hand cover her own. The gesture was bittersweet and made her think of all the times her mother had held her hand through her recovery. Through her whole life. She was the wrong person to be mad at.

"I shouldn't have pushed you away so much lately," she husked.

"Shush. Your brother did it when he was eleven. I've been lucky enough to keep you close this long. I'm just glad I can be here for you when you need me."

"Are you going to tell me there's plenty more fish in the sea?"

"I'd like to, but there are so few worth reeling in," her mother bemoaned, making Tiffany chortle past her tears. "It's so good to see you smiling again," her mother added with her own misty smile.

She didn't know how often Tiffany cried. How she combed for news and photos of Ryzard, how she quietly kept tally of the countries recognizing him. She was doing exactly that one afternoon before going into a meeting, getting her fix to get her through one more day without him, when she came across a horrifying update.

Coal Mine Explosion in Northern Bregnovia, Dozens Unaccounted For, one hour ago.

Leaping to her feet, she shouted for her assistant.

Even though sabotage was not suspected, it was war conditions all over again. Ryzard could hardly bear it, but quick response on the recovery effort was critical. There was no time to ask the fates why his country should suffer this way. No way to reassure his people that they could live without fear. There were only feet on the ground, hands digging into the rubble, people trying to save people into the night.

Dark was receding, exhaustion setting in and spirits low when a throaty drone began climbing on the air. The latest batch of survivors, many badly burned, had just left on what aircraft he'd been able to muster on short notice. They hadn't had time to drop and be back so soon. That didn't bode well.

Squinting into the silver horizon, he saw what looked like an invasion, and his heart stopped. Then the hospital crosses on the underbellies of three of the helicopters became visible and he relaxed. Someone asked if the Red Cross was finally here. He had no idea. His phone was charging in the one small shack that had a power generator for electricity.

Jerking his chin at someone to greet and direct them, he threw himself back into the work at hand.

Sixteen hours later, he was knee-deep in rubble, numb and almost asleep on his feet, losing the light, when his eye—and half-dead libido—was caught unexpectedly by a pair of skintight jeans tucked into knee-high black boots. A blond ponytail swung against the back of a black leather jacket as the woman nodded at whomever she was speaking to.

He was seeing things. He clambered across to her, swaying on his feet as he pulled her around by a rather despondent grip on her arm, distantly surprised to catch at a solid person and still not believing his eyes, even when he saw the familiar patch of color on the side of her face.

"You're real," he said dumbly.

She smiled tenderly and set a hand against his cheek. Her touch was surprisingly warm, making him aware how cold he was. How utterly empty and frozen he'd been for weeks.

"All I could think was that no country would be equipped for this many burn injuries. We have a triage set up. I hope you don't mind, but I'm sending the victims with their families to whoever can take them."

He couldn't speak, could only string clumsy arms around her and drag her into him. Closing his eyes, he drank in the sweet, familiar scent of her hair.

Tiffany ran soothing hands over him, feeling the chill on his skin beneath his shirt, trying to ease the shudders rippling through his muscles. He was heavy, leaning into her, beyond exhausted.

"Come with me," she urged, dragging him stumbling across the trampled yard to the tent where cots and coffee were on hand for the rescuers.

His arm was deadweight across her shoulders. When he sat, he pulled her into his lap.

"You need to sleep," she insisted as she tried to extricate herself.

He said something in Bregnovian, voice jagged and broken. He snugged her closer, his hold unbreakable.

Not that she really wanted to get away. It felt so good to be near him. He was grimy and sweaty, but he was Ryzard. She blinked damp eyes where he was keeping her face trapped against his chest, surrounded in his personal scent.

"You need to lie down, Ryzard. You're not even speaking English."

He brought her with him so the cot groaned beneath them. When she tried to rise, he threw a pinning leg across her and tangled his fingers in her hair. "Don't leave," he murmured and the lights went out. He became a lead blanket upon her.

Since she was jet-lagged and had been on her feet for hours, she relaxed and dozed until activity around them woke her. Then she managed to climb free of his tentacle-like hold and carry on with the rescue effort. The trapped miners had been reached and the final victims would need transport.

* * *

Ryzard woke thinking he'd dreamed her, but the jacket draped across his chest told him he wasn't crazy. She was here, somewhere.

Coffee in one hand, jacket in his other, he went in search and found her trying to comfort an anxious wife as an injured miner was packaged into a helicopter. The woman clutched a baby and had a redheaded boy by the hand, and Tiffany held a matching toddler on her hip.

"Oh, Ryzard," she said when he draped her jacket over her shoulders, "Please tell her I'm sure her husband will live. The burns are bad, but they didn't find internal injuries. I've lost my translator and she's so upset."

Together they reassured the woman and made arrangements for her to catch up with her husband at the burn unit in Paris.

Calm settled as everyone was accounted for. There was a longer journey ahead to bring the mine back into operation, but the immediate crisis was over. Tiffany stifled a yawn as she thanked people and gave them final directions for breaking down the field hospital they'd erected.

"I can't thank you enough for this," Ryzard said.

"When you're part of a club, you pitch in to help your fellow members when they need it, right?"

She was being her cheeky self, but he wasn't in a frame of mind to take this gesture so lightheartedly.

"I'm being sincere, Tiffany. I hope your motives were not that superficial."

She sobered. "I told you last night that this struck close to home for me. But I don't suppose you remember, being pretty much sleepwalking at the time."

Was it only empathy for fellow burn victims that had brought her here? He flinched, wondering where he got off imagining she could have deeper feelings for him when he'd pushed her from his life the way he had.

"Hey, Tiff," some flyboy called across. "You catching a lift in my bird or...?"

"Oh, um—"

Ryzard cut her off before she could answer. "You'll come to Gizela with me."

"Will I," she said in the tone she used when she thought he was being arrogant, but he only cared that she acquiesced. He did *not* care for the way she hugged the pilot and kissed his cheek, thanking him for his help.

Ryzard lifted his brows in query when she turned from her goodbye.

"He grew up with Paulie and my brother. I've known him forever," she defended. "We needed pilots so I called him."

It was petty and ungrateful to think, we didn't need them *that* badly, but he was still short on sleep and deeply deprived of her. His willingness to share her, especially when he was so uncertain how long he'd have her, was nil.

His own transport arrived. They fell asleep against each other in the back of the 4x4 for the jostling four-hour drive back to Gizela.

The palace looked better than ever, Tiffany noted when she woke in front of it. Its exterior was no longer pockmarked by bullet holes and the broken stones were gone, giving the grounds a sense of openness and welcome. Inside, she went straight up the stairs next to Ryzard, both anxious for a shower. They parted at the top and she went to her room, where, he had assured her, everything she'd left was still there.

She wasn't sure what it meant. A dozen times she'd thought about asking for the items to be shipped, but she'd been afraid that contacting him would be the first step toward falling back down the rabbit hole into his world. Or it would have been final closure, something she hadn't been ready for. Had he felt the same? Because he could have had the things shipped to her at any time.

The not knowing hung like a veil over the situation, making her wonder if she was being silly and desperate when she dressed for his flag salutation, or respectful and supportive. He wouldn't have brought her here if he didn't want her here, she told herself, but she faltered when they met at the top of the stairs.

He wore his white shirt, black suit and presidential sash. His jaw was freshly shaved and sharply defined by tension as he took in her houndstooth skirt and matching wool jacket. "You don't have to," he said for the second time.

She almost took him at his word, almost let herself believe that he only wanted her, didn't need her, but his eyes gave him away. They weren't flat green. They burned gold. As if he was taking in treasure. As if she said she wasn't ready, he would wait until she was.

"I want to," she assured him, wondering if she was being an imaginative fool. Why would she want to do this? Pride of place, she guessed. It made her feel good to be with him no matter what he was doing. She admired him as a man and took great joy in watching him rise to his position.

Outside, it was blustery and tasting of an early-fall storm with spits of rain in the gusting wind. Leaves chased across grass and their clothes rippled as they walked to the pole. The flag snapped its green and blue stripes as he made his pledge and saluted it.

A burst of applause made them both turn to the crowd gathered at the gate. It was a deeper gathering than Tiffany had seen any other time. Hundreds maybe. A fresh rush of pride welled in her.

"Your predecessor wouldn't have cut up his hands freeing trapped miners," she said, picking up his scabbed hand. It was so roughened and abused, she instinctively lifted it to her lips.

The cheering swelled, making her pull back from touching him. "Sorry. That was dumb."

"No, they liked it. They're here for you as much as me. They know what you did for us." He faced the crowd and indicated her with a sweep of his hand and a bow of his head.

.His people reacted with incendiary passion, waving flags and holding up children.

"They're thanking you, Tiffany." He lifted her hand to his own lips, and another roar went up.

They stood there a long time, hands linked, waving at the crowd. No one walked away. They waited for her and Ryzard to go in first.

"Are you crying?" he asked as they entered the big drawing room. It was such a stunning room with its gorgeous nineteenth-century furniture and view overlooking the sea, but she still wasn't comfortable in it.

Averting her gaze from Luiza's portrait, she swiped at her cheeks. "That was very moving. I didn't expect it. I had the impression they thought of me as an interloper." Now she couldn't help straying a glance at Luiza, as if the woman might be eavesdropping.

For a long moment he didn't say anything, only looked at the portrait with the same tortured expression she'd seen on him before, when his feelings for Luiza were too close to the surface.

She looked away, respecting his need for time to pull himself together, but taking a hit of despair over it, too.

"It's my fault you felt that way," he said in a low, grave voice. "But please try to understand what she meant to me. Luiza made me see that Bregnovia is my home. That if I fought for it and made it ours, *mine*—" he set his fist over the place where her name was inked forever "—I would always belong here. That was deeply meaningful after so many years of being rootless and displaced."

She nodded, unable to speak because she did understand and felt for him.

"I needed her love after losing my parents. I would have shut down otherwise. Become an instrument of war."

Instead of a leader who had retained his humanity. It was one of the qualities she admired most in him, so she could hardly begrudge the woman who'd kept his heart intact through the horrors of battle and loss.

"When I lost her, I couldn't let myself become embittered and filled with hatred. It would have gone against everything she helped me become, but I couldn't face another loss like it. The vulnerability of loving again, knowing the emotional pain of grief if something were to happen... It terrifies me, Tiffany."

He said it so plainly, never faltering even when he was exposing his deepest fear.

She wanted to look to the ceiling to contain the tears gathering to sting her eyes. It killed her to hear that he couldn't give up his heart, but she couldn't look away from him.

"It's okay. I admire her, too," she managed. Her voice scraped her throat with emotion, but she was being sincere. "I wish I'd met her. She had amazing willpower. I wouldn't have had the guts to do what she did."

"Guts." The harsh sound he made was halfway between a laugh and a choke of deep anguish. "Luiza had ideals. Now she is our martyr and a symbol of our sacrifice and loss. I would do her a disservice to forget or dismiss that, but it doesn't make you an interloper for living where she died, Tiffany. She had a vision. When I look at you, I see reality. Our reality. Scarred by tragedy, but so beautiful. So strong and determined to carry on."

His tender look of regard had its usual effect of striking like an unexpected punch into her solar plexus, making her breath rush out. She had to cover her lips to still them from trembling.

"I don't like comparing you. It's disrespectful to both of you, but you're right. You and Luiza are very different. You wouldn't have killed yourself. Given the same situation, you would fight with everything in you to stay alive until I came for you, no matter what happened. That's who you are. Your courage astounds me."

He ran his hand down his face only to reveal an expression of profound regret.

"When I sent you away, all I could think was that I didn't want to risk the pain of loss again. And did you crawl back in your cave even though I'd hurt you? No. You went on with your life without me, and I was so hurt and so proud at the same time."

She lowered her head, touched beyond measure, and saw a teardrop land on the hardwood. She swiped at her numb cheek, finding it wet. "Thank you for the flowers."

"The flowers were an apology. You made me feel like a coward, refusing to embrace love when it's as precious as life. I wanted to come to you and to hell with your Customs and Immigration, but I had to finish my obligation to Luiza first. I've done that. Official announcements will be made later in the week. I have the votes I need."

"Oh, Ryzard, that's wonderful!" She was elated for him, but still reeling from his mention of embracing love. Did that mean…? She searched his inscrutable expression.

"After the last few days, this country needs good news." He sighed and rocked back on his heels, regarding her. "It also means the worst is over for a time when it comes to state functions. I won't run in the next election. Could you live with two more years of being in the public eye, knowing it would be temporary?"

"What?" Her nails cut into her palms as she tried to stay grounded, not leaping too high on what he was saying. Not reading too deep. Definitely not wanting to hold him back in any way. "Ryzard, you *are* Bregnovia. It's barely on its feet. You can't hand it over to someone else so soon. I couldn't live with myself if all this stability you've fought for crumbled."

"I don't want to wait that long to marry you, *draga*. I ache every night and barely get through my days. I need you."

"You do?" Her voice hitched and stayed awfully small, but the world around her seemed to expand in one pulse beat, stealing the oxygen and filling the air with sparks. "You really want to marry me? *Me?*"

"*You*. Not the daughter of the next American president, not Davis and Holbrook, not the woman who charms heads of state without even trying. You."

"Because you love me?" she hazarded, curling her toes and pulling her elbows in, bracing for the worst.

"Because we love each other."

His tender gaze held hers, gently demanding she give up her heart to him. She did, easily.

"If I hadn't been trained from birth to pretend everything was fine no matter how miserable I was, I couldn't have got through these last weeks. I love you so much, Ryzard, and I hated myself for not letting my love be enough to keep us together."

"I shouldn't have made you feel like it was all up to you," he said, coming across to draw her into him. With his lips pressed to her forehead, he added, "I will never hold back from you again. I thought I was being noble, letting you find the man who would love you like no other could, but that man is me. I love you with every breath in me, Tiffany. A different man loved Luiza. This one is yours."

She relaxed her forehead against his nuzzling lips, touched to her soul. Fulfilled. Hopeful. *Happy*.

He traced a soft kiss along the raised line of her scar,

following it down to the corner of her eye and across her cheek until he was almost at her mouth.

"We should take this upstairs," she said against his lips. "I have a feeling it won't stay PG rated for long."

He quirked a rueful grin and led her upstairs. In his bedroom, he took a moment to lift the snapshot from his bedside table and walk it into his sitting room.

When he returned he found her seated on the bed, hands tucked in her lap.

"We have to talk about one more thing before we go any further," she said.

"What's that?" he queried.

"Children."

"At least two. I want them to have each other if something happens to us," he affirmed.

"I was going to say six, but okay. Coward."

"Ambitious," he remarked in a drawl. "I can keep up if you can." His smile was a slow dawn of masculine heat that twitched with amusement. "I've missed you, Tiffany. You make me laugh."

She threw herself into his arms.

EPILOGUE

THE MILKY WAY stretched from one edge of the horizon to the other, diffusing into more stars against Zanzibar's indigo sky than Tiffany had ever seen in her life. If Ryzard hadn't kept her pressed firmly against his side as he steered them down the jetty toward the island bar, she likely would have stumbled into the lagoon.

"What the hell are you up to?"

"I know, I'm sorry, but I've never seen anything like— wait, what?" She realized Ryzard had been talking to a man in a mask who'd just passed them on the jetty. She glanced back the way they'd come to see the member break off his lip-lock with a *petite q* and hurry her toward the interior of the club.

"Who was that?"

"A friend. One who knows better than to play with Zeus's toys." He dragged his puzzled gaze to her expectant one. With a low sigh, he bent to whisper, "His name is Nic." Straightening, he added, "Don't ask me to say more than that. Even though you're my wife, I still have an obligation to respect other members' privacy."

She grinned, pleased more by her title of "wife" than anything else.

The DJ's electronica pulsed louder as they finished their walk into the open-air bar. *Q Virtus* members and *petite q's* danced and jumped to the beat, making the wooden floor bounce.

Tiffany refused a drink offered by a passing *petite q,* but Ryzard drew her to a side bar. "Iced coconut. Nonalcoholic," he said.

Her condition wasn't official, especially since they'd been married only a day, but they'd stopped using protection weeks ago. She was pretty sure, and they were both so quietly, ferociously happy it was criminal.

The server tilted his array of cones for her to peruse. They were stunning, not merely shaved and frozen coconut with a splash of color, but intricately decorated works of art in more shades, flavors and hues than the stars above them.

Tiffany almost picked the one that looked like a bouquet of sweet peas, but maybe the mandala was prettier. The paisley?

"It just hit me," Ryzard said in a tone of discovery. "It was never about the taffy apple being better optics. You couldn't decide what color candy floss you wanted."

Grinning, she admitted, "You caught me."

"I'm convinced it's the other way around, *draga,*" he retorted.

She laughed in delight, but contradicted, "I distinctly remember a kidnapping on the high seas."

"I remember fireworks," he said with a smoky look from behind his mask. "Choose something or we'll miss these ones."

Face warm with pleasure behind her own mask, she took two cones and gave him one, leaning her weight into him as he hooked his arm across her shoulders and steered her toward the rail overlooking the Indian Ocean.

"I see them every night, you know. Fireworks. 'Cause I'm spoiled."

"You are," he agreed, leaning down to bite at her cone before he offered his. "So am I."

"Mmm. We're in the right place for the privileged, aren't we?" she mused, licking clove-and-orange-flavored coconut from her lips.

He stopped and turned her so they held each other in a way that felt perfect and familiar and right. "As long as I'm with you, I'm exactly where I belong."

* * * * *

If you enjoyed this book,
look out for the next instalment of
THE 21ˢᵀ CENTURY GENTLEMAN'S CLUB:
THE ULTIMATE REVENGE
by Victoria Parker

THE ULTIMATE REVENGE

BY
VICTORIA PARKER

Victoria Parker's first love was a dashing heroic fox named Robin Hood. Then came the powerful, suave Mr Darcy, Lady Chatterley's rugged Lover—the list goes on. Thinking she must be an unfaithful sort of girl, but ever the optimist, she relentlessly pursued her Mr Literary Right, eventually found him lying between the cool crisp sheets of a Mills & Boon and her obsession was born.

If only real life was just as easy. . .

Alas, against the advice of her beloved English teacher to cultivate her writer's muse, she chased the corporate dream and acquired various uninspiring job-titles *and* a flesh-and-blood hero before she surrendered to that persistent voice and penned her first Mills & Boon romance. Turns out creating havoc for feisty heroines and devilish heroes truly *is* the best job in the world.

Victoria now lives out her own happy-ever-after in the north-east of England, with her alpha exec and their two children—a masterly charmer in the making and, apparently, the next Disney Princess. Believing sleep is highly overrated, she often writes until three a.m., ignores the housework (much to her husband's dismay) and still loves nothing more than getting cosy with a romance novel. In her spare time she enjoys dabbling with interior design, discovering far-flung destinations and getting into mischief with her rather wonderful extended family.

To my *Q Virtus* compatriots,
Maya Blake and Dani Collins.
Thank you for the laughs and chats as we concocted
and conceived our brave new world.
It's been an honour and an absolute pleasure.

And for the fabulous Jennifer Hayward,
my CP and best bud. Like Olympia Merisi, you rock!
So this one is for you. . .

CHAPTER ONE

THEY SAY YOU can't plan a hurricane.

Nicandro Carvalho could. He could wreak havoc with a smile. And after ten years of planning and months of whipping up a storm he was finally ready to unleash chaos.

Zeus. I am coming for you and I will annihilate your world. As you destroyed mine.

The Barattza in Zanzibar, this weekend's ostentatious venue for the quarterly meeting of Q Virtus, was warm, and so muggy his flimsy white shirt clung to his body like a second skin and moisture thrived beneath his mask. Still, he strode ruthlessly through the crush of elite billionaires, intent on his pretty 'Petit Q'—his backstage pass into Zeus's lair, in the form of a five-foot-three brunette in a haute couture red gown designed to attract and blend in equal measure.

Look but don't touch was the cardinal rule.

As if Nicandro had *ever* followed the rules. *'Rules are for boring fools,'* as his mother would say, although her voice was now a distant echo from the past.

Numerous greetings vied for his attention and he offered a succinct nod or a quick 'good evening' and volunteered nothing more. Conversations were like fires—they tended to sputter out if he deprived them of enough air.

His purposeful stride didn't break—hadn't since he'd been Nicandro Santos, a terrified seventeen-year-old boy who'd boarded a cargo ship in Rio to hide in a filthy container bound for New York. It hadn't faltered when he'd concocted a new identity to ensure anonymity from his past life, emerging as one Nicandro Carvalho, who'd sold his pride on the streets of Brooklyn and then wrenched it back by working his fingers raw on construction sites to put some semblance of a roof over his head.

Nor had it swayed when he'd bought his first property, then another, over endless harrowing years, to earn enough money to bring his grandfather from Brazil to be by his side.

An unrelenting purpose and a cut-throat determination that had rewarded him with obscene power and wealth—until he'd been graciously accepted into the covert ranks of Q Virtus, where his sole purpose was to infiltrate and take it down from the inside.

So here he was. And this was only the beginning.

A plan over ten years in the making. Rewriting history to make the Santos Empire—his legacy of a life that had been stolen from him, along with his parents—whole once more.

Nic shut down his thoughts as mercilessly as he did everything else. Otherwise the burning ball of rage that festered and ate away at his insides like a living, breathing entity would surely explode and incinerate everything and everyone in its path.

'Hey, Nic, what's the hurry?'

Narciso's voice shattered his ferocious intent and this time he did turn, to see his friend looking dapper in a tailored tuxedo, *sans* jacket, leaning against the main bar, Scotch glass in hand, the top half of his face shrouded in a gold leaf mask that reminded him of a laurel wreath.

Nic felt the constricting steel band around his chest slacken as a smile played at his mouth. 'All hail, Emperor Narciso. *Dios*, where do they come up with these things?'

'I have no idea, but I'm certainly feeling on top of the world.'

He resisted the urge to roll his eyes. 'Of course you are. How is the ball and chain?'

Narciso grinned at the blatant cynicism, his smile reaching the scalloped edge of gold.

Hideous masks. Requisite to afford them some anonymity, but they only served to aggravate Nic to the extreme—just as everything about Q Virtus did.

A gentlemen's club for the elite. Prestigious. Illustrious. The most sought-after membership in the world. Run by a deceitful, murdering crook.

Ironic, he thought, that grown men, multi-billionaires, would sell their soul to be a member of Q Virtus, virtually handing their business confidences, their reputation, their respect and trust to a common criminal.

Not for much longer. Not after Nic had finished exposing the cold, hard truth and crushed Zeus beneath his almighty foot.

'She's as beautiful as ever. Come, take a spin of the wheel with me. I'd like a quiet word.'

Impatience clawed at him with steel-tipped talons, slashing his insides, but Nic resisted the compulsion to decline outright. It had been too long since he'd seen his friend and he wanted a quiet word of his own.

'Let's grab a private table,' Nic said, not wasting a moment, simply ushering Narciso towards the lavish roulette room and a private table at the back.

Within ten minutes they had drinks in hand and the full attention of a male croupier dressed in red footman's livery. 'Gentlemen, please take your bets.'

Nic tossed a five-thousand-dollar chip haphazardly at the marked numbers adorning the roulette layout and waited for Narciso to make his choice.

'Twenty thousand dollars on black seventeen,' the croupier confirmed impassively.

Nic whistled a huff of air. 'Feeling reckless without your lady present?'

'Feeling lucky. That ball and chain does that to me.'

Yep, his partner in crime was still drugged on a potent cocktail of regular sex and emotion. He just hoped the hangover was a long way off. Nic didn't relish seeing the lights go out in his eyes. Sad, but inevitable.

The wheel spun in a kaleidoscopic blur and he eased back in his seat to afford them a modicum of privacy. With time at a premium and his patience dwindling he jumped right in. If he waited for Narciso to start the conversation he might be there all night.

'Tell me something. Don't you think it's odd that we've never seen a glimpse of QV's Mr Mysterious? Not once.'

Narciso didn't waste time pretending not to know exactly who they were discussing. He simply arched one dark brow and spoke in that rich, affluent tone that had used to fell women faster than a forest fire. 'So the man likes his privacy? Don't we all?'

'There's got to be more to it than that.'

'So suspicious, Carvalho.'

The white ball plopped into black seventeen and a satisfied grunt filled the air. Typical. Served Nic right for not even caring where his chip landed, but right now he had more important thoughts swirling around the vast whirlpool of his mind in ever-narrowing circles. Always leading back to the same thing. *Zeus.*

'Maybe he's not fit for polite society,' Narciso suggested. 'Ever thought of that? Rumour has it the man is associated with the Greek mafia. Maybe he's scarred with a dozen bullet holes. Maybe he's mute. Maybe he's shy. Over the last few months—since the last meeting, in fact—the rumour mill has churned up all kinds of ludicrous tales.'

Oh, he'd heard the rumours. Of course he had. He'd started most of them.

'Doesn't it bother you that Q Virtus could be dirty?' he asked, his voice all innocence with the required edge of concern. 'It obviously bothers some. There are a few members missing this weekend.'

Amazing what a few 'have you heard?' whispers in the right ears could achieve. Doubt was a powerful thing—destructive, flammable—and Nic had lit the torch with a flourish, sat back and watched it spread like wildfire.

Narciso shrugged, as if the thought of being a member of a club that was morally corrupt was water sluicing off a duck's back.

'The club might've had shady beginnings, but even my father and his cronies say the place is clean as a whistle now. You and I personally know several members, and all of them have made billions from mutually beneficial business deals, so I doubt any of it is true. Rumours are generally fairy stories born from petty jealousy or spoken from the mouths of people who have an ulterior motive.'

Very true, that. But the fact that Nic had numerous ulterior motives was something he kept to himself.

'Still, I want to meet him.' What he wanted, he realised, was back-up if something went wrong tonight. If he conveniently disappeared he wanted Narciso to know where he was headed.

'Why? What could you possibly want with Zeus?'

To bring his world crumbling down around his ears. To make him suffer as his parents had—as he had and as his grandfather had.

That old man, whom he loved so dearly, was the only family he had left. The man who'd harangued and railed at him to stand tall, who had propped him up as he'd learned how to walk again when Nic would rather have died in the same bloodbath as his parents.

'Is there something you want to tell me, Nic?'

Yes. The shock of it made him recoil, push back in his seat until he could feel the knotted gold silk poke through his shirt and agitate his skin. Problem being he didn't want

Narciso dragged into the epicentre of a storm of which he was the creator.

'Not particularly.'

Mouth pursed, his friend nodded grudgingly. 'And how do you intend to meet the mysterious, *reclusive,* notorious Zeus?'

Nic tossed back another mouthful of vodka as his gaze flickered to the Petit Q he'd been wooing since he'd arrived the night before. There she was, standing near the doors, unobtrusive as always, yet only a hand-motion away. All it had taken was one look into her heavy-lashed slumberous gaze and he'd thought, *Piece of cake.*

One romantic midnight stroll along the beach and he'd had a thumbprint lifted from her champagne flute. One lingering caress of his hand round her waist and he'd slipped the high-security access card from the folds of her red sheath. What remained was one promise of seduction in her suite that he'd fail to keep and would ensure she was gone from his side.

Narciso followed his line of sight and huffed out a breath. 'Should've known a woman would be involved. I like your style, Carvalho, even if I *do* think that vodka you drink has pickled your brain.'

Nic laughed, riding high on the narcotic mix of anticipation and exhilaration lacing his veins. That was until he looked into his friend's eyes and the mirth died in his throat.

What would Narciso and their buddy Ryzard think of him when Nic whipped the Q Virtus rug from beneath their feet? When he lost them the chance of schmoozing with the world's most powerful men, creating contacts and thriving on the deals that cultivated their already vast wealth. They would understand, wouldn't they? Narciso was the closest thing to a best friend he'd ever had and Ryzard was a good man. Surely he was doing them a favour of sorts—he knew what Zeus was capable of; they hadn't a clue.

'Speaking of rumours,' Narciso murmured, in a tone that made Nic's guts twist into an apprehensive knot. 'I hear Goldsmith made you an offer.'

He practically choked on his vodka. 'How do you know that?'

Narciso looked at him as if he'd sprouted a second head. 'Do you honestly think Goldsmith could keep the possibility of the mighty Nicandro Carvalho, an unequalled dominant force in real estate, becoming his son-in-law a secret for one second? He told my father. Who told me. And I told *him* that Goldsmith is delusional.'

Nic checked an impatient sigh. This was the last thing he wanted to discuss. Except his silence pulled the air taut, pinching Narciso's brow and turning his smart mouth into a scowl.

'Do *not* tell me you are seriously considering marrying Eloisa Goldsmith.'

No. Maybe. 'I am considering it, yes.'

'You've got to be joking, Nic!'

'Keep your voice down! Just because you've been blinded by good sex and emotion—ah, sorry—I mean to say just because you've found *everlasting bliss*,' he muttered, with no small amount of sarcasm, 'it doesn't mean I want to sign my own death warrant. A business marriage is perfect for me.'

'You're as jaded as I was. Heaven help you if you meet a woman strong enough to smash your kneecaps and drop you at her feet.'

'If that ever happens, my friend, I'll buy you a gold pig.'

Narciso shook his head. 'Eloisa Goldsmith. You're insane.'

'What I am is late for a rendezvous.' He downed the last of his drink as he bolted upright, the lock of his knees thrusting his chair backwards with an emphatic scrape.

'Why would you even consider it? She's a country mouse—you'll be bored within a week.'

Exactly. He could never fall in love with her and he'd have a sweet, gentle, caring woman to be the mother of his children. As to the why—there was only one reason Nic would walk down the aisle at twenty-nine years old. The final goal in his grand slam.

Santos Diamonds.

The business phenomenon that had taken generations to build: his great-grandfather's love affair, his *avô*'s pride and joy, the legacy Goldsmith would only gift to Nic along with his daughter's hand.

He wasn't enamoured of the idea, but he'd promised himself he'd consider it while he whisked up a vengeful hurricane for Zeus to flounder within. So consider it he would. If only for Avô to see Santos Diamonds back where it belonged. It was the least he could do for the old man.

'I will be content. Now, if you'll excuse me, I have an appointment with pleasure.'

The pleasure of the ultimate revenge.

PRIVATE. NO ENTRY.

Blood humming with a lethal combination of exhilaration and eagerness, Nic swiped his nifty keypad over the high-access security panel. While he'd loathed those early days in New York when he'd been lured to the streets of Brooklyn, he'd met some interesting if a smidgeon *degenerate* characters walking on the more dangerous side of life, who had always been willing to teach him a trick or two.

Still, his heart slammed about in his chest like a pinball machine until the fingerprint recognition flashed green and he was standing in Zeus's inner sanctum.

Moroccan-style ironwork lanterns cast eerie shadows down the long corridor and painted the white stucco walls with a brassy wash. The floor was a continuation of the small intricate mosaic that ran through the hotel but here, in Zeus's lair, the colours were richer—deep amber, bronze and heavy gold, as if gilded by Midas's touch. And that

touch had embellished every scrolled door handle, finger-
plate and urn.

Arched double doors, elaborately carved, encompassed
the entire wall at one end of the floor, and as he drew
closer faint murmurs slithered beneath the gap like wisps
of smoke unfurling to reach his ears. Someone having unpleasant dreams, if he guessed right. Definitely female.

Mistress? Wife? The man was reclusive and malevolent
enough to hoard a harem as far as he knew.

Gingerly Nic curled his hand around the gold handle
and smirked when the lever gave way under the pressure
of his palm. This was just too easy.

Door closed behind him, he stifled a whistle at the vast
expanse of opulence.

Ochre walls were punctuated with arched lattice screens,
allowing the shimmering light of the ornate candelabra to
spin from one room to another and dance over every gilt-
edged surface almost provocatively. But it was the heady
scent of incense that gave the atmosphere a distinctly sultry feel, heating his blood another few degrees and coaxing his eyes towards the bed.

Mosaic steps led up to a raised dais, at least eight feet
square. The entire structure was shrouded by a tented can-
opy made with the finest gold silk—the weighty drapes
closed on all four sides, with only a small gap at the bottom edge. Clearly an invitation to take a peek as far as he
was concerned.

Nic slipped off his shoes by the door and stepped closer
on sock-clad feet, his pulse thrumming with the devilry of
being somewhere he shouldn't and half hoping, half anxious that he'd be caught.

The sudden bolt of lightning that flashed through the
room, followed by a sonorous crack of thunder didn't help.
His heart leapt to his throat.

Sumptuous cushions and layers upon layers of superfine silk in white and gold embraced the still mound of a woman veiled by the caliginous shadows.

He watched, waiting to ensure she slept on, frowning at the odd sizzle of electricity that ran beneath his skin. If he were the suspicious sort who believed in Brazilian clap-trap he'd think his ancestors were trying to tell him to get the hell out of here. *As if.*

Nic shook himself from the bizarre trance and skulked round the rest of the palatial suite, prowling between over-stuffed sofas in a rich shade of cocoa, towering fern trees that plumed from barrel-wide bronze urns and the ritzy copper-toned spa tub raised on another dais in the bath-ing room.

The entire effect was stunning, but it had a homely feel—as if the guest was in fact the owner and he'd decided to give the sheikhs of the Middle East a run for their money.

Finally, in the farthest room, was the answer to his prayers. A wide leather-topped desk strewn with business files and paperwork.

Hope unfurled and he sniffed at the air tentatively, while anxiety curled its wicked tail around his ribcage. Not fear of being caught—more fear of never finding the truth. Never finding what he was looking for. Never coming eye to eye with Zeus himself. Or should he say *Antonio Merisi.*

Ah, yes, Antonio Merisi—aka Zeus. A name that had evaded him for years—as if trying to connect the god-like sacrosanct prominence of Zeus with a flesh and blood human capable of being destroyed was impossible. But Nic had friends in places both high and low, and anything was procurable for a price.

It had been a torturous exercise in patience to discover any other Merisi business interests apart from Q Virtus. Not an easy feat, considering they'd been buried in aliases, but he'd struck gold within weeks and found one or two to set the wheels in motion. Make dents in the man's bank balance. Contaminate his reputation. See how he liked his empire destroyed. As long as Nic got to watch it crumble. To see the very man responsible for his parents' death languish in hell.

Standing behind the desk, he hauled himself up from his pit of rage and resentment and fingered the portfolio at the top of towering pile.

Merpia Inc.

Merpia? The largest commodities trading house in the world.

Eros International.

That one he'd guessed, from the abundance of Greek mythological connotations surrounding the club and a brief mention of the Merisi name in the company portfolio. Consequently he'd plagued the stockmarket with rumours two weeks earlier.

Score one Carvalho.

Ophion—Greek shipping.

Rockman Oil.

Dios…

Multi-billion-pound ventures. Every single one of them. This man wasn't wealthy— he was likely one of the richest men in the world, with millions scattered across a vast financial plain.

The dents Nic had made would be a drop in the ocean.

He battled with an insurgence of disheartenment until another file snagged his eye.

Carvalho?

His hand shot out…then froze when a sharp voice splintered his rage.

'I wouldn't do that, if I were you. Hands up, back away from the table, then do not move a muscle or I'll blow your brains out.'

Busted. Just when things were getting interesting. Still, his lips twisted ruefully at the sound of a husky, sultry feminine voice.

Nic flicked his hands in the air with a high school level

of flippancy to lighten the mood and twisted his torso to spin around.

'Now, now, *querida*, let's not fight—'

The practised snick of the safety catch on a revolver made him rethink. *Fast.* It was a sound that resonated through his brain and threw him back thirteen years. Even his back stiffened, as if he were waiting for the echo of a bullet to penetrate his spine. Rob him of the dreams of his youth. End life as he knew it.

'Stay right where you are. I did *not* give you permission to move.'

A shiver glanced over his flesh at the cool, dominant tone, as if he'd been physically frisked not just verbally spanked.

'As you wish,' he said, taking his voice down an octave or three and coating it in sin. 'Though I'd much rather conduct this meeting face to face. More so if you are as beautiful as your voice.'

Maybe it was her barely audible huff or maybe it was the impatient tap of a stiletto heel on wood but Nic would swear she'd just rolled her eyes.

'Who are you and how did you get into my suite?'

Suddenly the ridiculousness of the situation hit him. Was he actually being controlled by a *woman*?

Shifting on his feet, he made to swivel. 'I'm turning around so we can have this conversation like two adul—'

A sharp sound like a whip cracking rent the air and Nic's jaw dropped as he married the sound of a silenced bullet with the precise hole in the oil painting of a wolf about three feet from his head.

How ironic. *Lobisomem.* Portuguese for werewolf. His Q Virtus moniker.

Omen? He damned well hoped not.

The smell of the gunpowder residue curled through his sinuses and the past seemed to collide with the present, making his stomach clench on a nauseating pang. Sweat trickled down his spine and he had to surreptitiously clear the thickness from his throat just to speak.

'Crack shot, *querida*.' Question was, why wouldn't she let him turn, look at her?

'The best, I assure you. Now, tell me I have your undivided attention and that you will behave.'

Nic had the distinct feeling he wasn't going to win this argument. And that voice... *Dios*, she could read him passages from the most profoundly boring literature in the world and he'd still get sweaty and hard at the sound of her licking those consonants and vowels past her lips.

'I will be on my best behaviour. Scout's honour.'

Not that he'd ever been one. At the suggestion his mother had arched one perfectly plucked, disgusted brow, told him the idea was simply not to be endured and that she'd rather take him to the country club to play poker.

How he'd loved that woman.

Ignoring the misery dragging at his heart, he strived for joviality. 'Though if it's co-operation you're looking for, I'll be far more amenable without a gun trained on my head by an expert marksman.'

'Trouble must follow you if you're familiar with the sounds of a loaded gun. Why does that not surprise me?'

'Guess I'm just that kind of guy.'

'A thief? A criminal? Insane?'

Dios! Why was everyone calling him insane today?

'*Misjudged* was more the word I was thinking of. Or maybe I'm simply enigmatic, like your lover. Or is he your boss?'

'My...*boss*?' she replied, with a haughty edge that said no man would ever lord it over *her*.

He almost rolled *his* eyes then. 'Okay, then, your lover.'

That earned him a disgruntled snicker.

'Think again. And while you're at it who are you talking about? Who is my boss supposed to be? Who are you looking for?'

'Zeus, of course—who else?'

The room hushed into a cacophony of silence; the lack of sound so loud his ears rang. No doubt a pin dropping would have detonated in an explosion of sound.

Nic pounced on the lull—he'd always liked creating a big bang. 'I have a meeting with him here. Tonight. So if you'd like to run along and get him I'd be greatly appreciative.'

A stunned pause gave way to a burst of incredulous laughter. The kind that was infectious. It was rusty—as if she didn't get much practice—but it was out there, all smoky and sultry, and it filled him with a scorching hot kind of pleasure.

Who the devil *was* she?

'A meeting, you say? I think not. And I believe you are toying with the wrong woman, stranger. So forgive me if I just *run along* and leave you with some friends of mine.'

From nowhere three hulks had three guns trained on various parts of his anatomy and he fought the violent urge to cup his crotch. Because 1) despite evidence to the contrary he was of high intellect, and 2) despite their tailored Savile Row attire their eyes were dull from a hard life and the inevitable slide into madness.

Splendid.

For pity's sake, why guns? Why not knives? He hated guns!

'Ah, come now, *querida*, this is hardly fair. Three against one?'

'I wish you the best of luck. If you survive we will meet again.'

He'd always been a lover, not a fighter. Still, living on the streets had taught him more than how to break a lock—which was just as well because he was nowhere near done with this night or this woman.

CHAPTER TWO

SHE SHOULDN'T HAVE LEFT. Walked out. Left them to rid her of the criminal in their midst. Here she'd been expecting news of his disposal to the authorities, or his being shoved onto a plane to Timbuktu, and instead she was standing in the security room faced with three decidedly sheepish guards and a fifty-two-inch plasma screen filled with the image of a prominent, high-profile billionaire tied up in her cellar!

'I don't believe this,' Pia breathed.

Exquisitely tall.

Beautifully dark.

Devastatingly handsome.

And infamous for satisfying his limitless wants and desires. *Not*—as far as she was aware, and she generally knew more than most—renowned for being a felon.

'Nicandro Carvalho. I almost shot Nicandro Carvalho!'

Pia's insides shook like a shaken soda can ready to spray. He'd been in her bedroom. Maybe watched her sleep. She'd been half naked when he'd swaggered into her rooms and for a split second she'd thought her past was catching up with her.

But what really ratcheted up her 'creeped-out' meter was the fact she'd shot her favourite painting. Of a werewolf. *Lobisomem*. How freaky was that? Considering she'd code-named him herself.

'It would have been his own fault! What was he doing, snooping around in there?'

All three testosterone-dripping men in the room flinched at Jovan's holler but Pia was used to his bark—especially where she was concerned. Protectiveness didn't come close to the way he went on. Ridiculous. You would think she was eight, not twenty-eight.

'More to the point, how did he even *get* in here?' she said, glaring at her supposed security staff, who flushed beneath her scrutiny. 'Find the breach and deal with it. Someone betrayed me today and I want them found.'

Skin visibly paled at her tone. 'Yes, *madame*.'

Purposefully avoiding the image on screen—because every time she looked at Carvalho the lamb she'd eaten for dinner threatened to reappear—she speared Jovan with her displeasure. 'Did you realise who he was before you roughed him up? Tell me you went easy on him.'

'*Easy?*' Jovan said, with a hefty amount of incredulity, and she only had to glance across the room to see why.

One of his men sported a black eye and a broken nose, the other winced with every turn and the third had a pro-nounced limp.

'The guy should be a cage fighter! I recognised that pretty-boy face within minutes and I *still* wanted to pul-verise him, regardless. He could have hurt you, Pia! So what if the man has money? Only last year they discov-ered that billionaire who had buried thirty-two bodies in his back yard!'

Heaven help her.

'All right—calm down.' If he worked himself up any more he'd either have a seizure or charge back in there to finish Carvalho off. Which would now be a manageable feat, considering he'd tied the stunner to a chair so tightly the ropes were likely cutting off his circulation. 'Like every member, he's been checked out thoroughly.'

Born in Brazil to a lower class family, he'd sailed to New York to make his fortune. The fact he'd come from nothing, was a self-made man, had gained her deepest respect from the start. Pia had first-hand experience of being hungry, feeling worthless, powerless, and she never wanted to re-visit *that* hellhole ever again. The amount of determination it would have taken Carvalho to rise from the ashes with no help had fascinated and charmed her in equal measure.

'If there was something amiss about him I would know.' Yet suddenly she wasn't so sure. Her instincts screamed that this man was far more than he'd initially appeared.

'People don't tend to put "serial killer" and "rapist" on their résumé, Pia.'

Valid point.

She tapped at the pounding spot between her brows, feeling as if she'd been given a complex puzzle with half the pieces left out.

'I'm missing something vital. I must be. First he breaks in, then he has a snoop at the files on my desk. Eros longer than most—I'd know that red file anywhere—and then...' She ran her tongue over her top front teeth. 'Now, isn't *that* a coincidence? That Eros International should catch his eye.'

The company had taken a suspiciously abrupt beating on the stockmarket of late. Though in all honesty Eros's share decline had been the least of her concerns. Ugly rumours were abounding, hitting her where it hurt. Her reputation.

Could he be the thorn in her side? The man who'd been making discreet enquiries about Zeus, about the club, about her businesses—the very man who'd been spreading filth and lies?

Maybe. After all, in her world anything was possible. But why?

Stuff it. She had no intention of waiting around while some property magnate ruined her life. *If* he was to blame.

'Turn off the screens. I'm going in there.'

She wanted answers and there was only one way to get them. She just hoped she was wrong and there was some perfectly good explanation for his breaking and entering.

Yeah, right. Call her foolish, but she didn't want Nicandro Carvalho to be at the centre of her current storm.

'*What?*'

'You heard me.'

While Jovan dismissed his men with a quiet word her gaze sought out Nicandro Carvalho once again. Obscenely grateful that her dinner stayed put and she remained apathetic and unflappable. As if the sight of a six-foot-plus Brazilian hunk with a bloodied lip was an everyday occurrence. She was good at that. Projecting absolute calm composure while her stomach revolted at the sight of her *Lobisomem* in a snare.

She rubbed her own upper arms, sore with the faint echoes of pain. She wanted to scream and rail at Jovan for trussing him so tightly. Perhaps she'd tie *him* up until control was lost, handed to another. See how *he* liked it.

'Did you *have* to cut off his blood supply?' she asked, cringeing inwardly at her snippy tone. Not for Jovan's sake. He was more like the bothersome older brother she'd never had, so she didn't bother to pull her punches with him. But the last thing she needed was to come over unhinged to her staff. '*Women are emotional liabilities,*' her father would say. Not her. Not since he'd made her into a living, breathing machine.

'Who cares if I did?' Jovan asked.

Pia cared—for some bizarre reason. But she wasn't about to tell him that. Just as she wasn't about to admit that at times she'd secretly watched Nicandro Carvalho over the past year. There was something darkly arresting about him. One look at his brooding beauty, at that dark skin that looked as if exotic blood ran through his veins, and she felt giddy with it all.

Pia was tall for a woman, and yet his towering height, wide shoulders and the thick biceps bulging from where his arms strained made her feel like a porcelain doll. Though he was snared, anyone could see his bearing was straight, confident, almost regal—like titan warriors and powerful gods. Not an image she would expect from a boy born in the Rio slums. The fact that he took pride in that fact, felt no shame for his poor origins and preferred to acknowledge the truth and stand tall with dignity, had lent him a kind of reverence in her eyes. *She'd* never been able to shake the stigma of it all.

Hung loosely about his face, his hair was the deepest shade of brown. She suspected it would curl when wet, drying into untamed flicks that twisted to his shoulders and fell wantonly about his face. Sharp brooding eyes almost black in their depths were framed lavishly with thick dark lashes: luscious, evocative and dominating.

And there was that word again—*regal*—rolling through her mind as she frantically tried to piece together the *how* and *why* he had broken into her suite and was now trussed to a chair. None of it made sense.

Jovan's hard voice ripped her attention from the seriously ripped Carvalho and she spun to see him leaning his six-foot-five frame against a bank of security screens.

'He did this to himself, Pia. Let me deal with him—please?' His chiselled features twisted, playing out a complex series of emotional shifts.

'No. He wants something.' Right then she flashed back to their brief conversation. 'And I suspect it is something only Zeus can give—otherwise why lie about having a meeting prearranged? So before he destroys my club with his ugly rumours, or costs me another twenty-five million on the stockmarket, I want to know why.'

Jovan grumbled in the way Pia had learned to ignore. 'So what do you intend to do with him?'

Stress and worry lined his brow, reminding her of the day they'd met. When he'd swept her into his arms as she'd lain knocking on death's door outside her father's palatial entryway. Sixteen years old and before then she hadn't even known her father existed. Without Jovan, Pia doubted she would have survived in her father's frigid Siberian world.

'I can't believe I'm saying this, but I have no idea.'

Commodities? A cinch. Juggling multi-million-dollar investments every day? A breeze. Dealing with people? Excruciating torture.

'I'll just have to play it by ear. Question him. Find out what he wants and why.'

Jovan snorted. 'Good luck with that one. He is arrogant. Overly cocky and dangerously determined.'

'Then we are equally matched. I don't believe in coincidences, Jovan. My gut tells me he's responsible for the rumours and the mayhem at Eros, and if so he wants something and won't disappear until he gets it. It would be foolish of me to take my eyes off him for one second.'

'So we put him on watch. Twenty-four-seven.'

'Or I go in there. Deal with him. Quickly. Quietly.'

'Pia, please. It is too risky.'

'Since when have I been afraid of a little risk?' *Never.* Fear would never touch her heart again. 'He's sure to tell me far more than he would ever tell you, and I'll hazard a guess he'll remain obstinate until he meets the man behind Q Virtus anyway.'

'He'll be waiting a long time.'

'Quite. So I'll put him off. Persuade him to deal with me and figure out what he's looking for. Why he'd chance his membership, his reputation, his business and fortune, by toying with the club. With me personally. He must know Zeus could bring him down.'

'But you'll place yourself in jeopardy. Under the spotlight. What if he realises you and Zeus are one and the same person? That your father is dead?'

Without thought Pia let her fingers creep up to her throat, where her pulse beat against her palm in a wild tattoo. Such an outcome wasn't even worth contemplating.

'He won't. He's a man. He's predictable and he won't

look beyond my breasts. Women are designed for whoring or childbearing in his world—the truth wouldn't occur to him in a million years. Granted, very few people know Antonio Merisi had a daughter, but my existence is no secret. If he looked in the right places he'd know I exist. When I tell him he'll think I am merely ornamental—a pampered child—so I doubt he'll crow to his friends that he was wrestled to the ground by a mere female.'

The man had a superb business mind and a vast IQ, but he was arrogant and conceited and as dominant as they came. Any battle between them would likely stay behind doors.

'This is my life we're talking about and the future of a club I swore would stand the test of time.' Damn the old rules. '*Damn* the dinosaurs that litter the ranks of my club.'

They'd never accept leadership from someone with a sullied past such as hers. Not only that, but the gentlemen's club was bound by rules—archaic, chauvinistic rules created by troglodytes—that declared only a Merisi man could lead. Only a man could own and control the largest business interests in the world.

Yet here she was. Groomed. Her path decided the moment her father had seen her, semi-conscious in Jovan's arms. She'd become the son Antonio Merisi had never had. His heir. His corporate assassin. The girl he'd called worthless, tainted, illiterate trash at first glance, making her feel dirtier than the clothes on her back. The same girl who'd then taken his fortune and quadrupled it within the first two years of living under his excessively opulent roof.

She was master of the most exclusive club in the world. Perpetually in hiding. Habitually alone. And that was the way it must stay.

'If my instincts are right he's declared war and I'm fighting blind—ignorant of the cause. If I'm to have any chance of surviving I need the right weapon to wield. Turn off the screens, Jovan.' Her tone brooked no argument. 'I'm going in.'

The monitors flickered to black and a moment later a faint tap on the door preceded Clarissa Knight, one of the Petit Qs, shifting on her feet as she was nudged through the space, a telling flush driving high on her cheekbones.

The pennies dropped more quickly than a Las Vegas slot machine flashing 'Winner' in neon lights.

Oh, wonderful. A lovesick puppy.

Pia checked a disgusted growl. 'Oh, Clarissa, tell me he promised you the world—or at least a permanent position in his bed?'

Simultaneously Clarissa's eyes fell to the floor and Jovan raised a small, flat high-tech sensor pad in the air, his expression warning her not to underestimate their intrepid foe.

Fingerprint recognition.

Her anger dissipated as fast as it came. She wasn't going to ask Clarissa how it felt to be used. She remembered humiliation and worthlessness all too well.

Somewhere in that dark abyss between unconsciousness and lucidity a razor-sharp rapping registered and Nic tried for a gentle head-shake. His temples loathed that idea, twisting his stomach into a tight knot, pleading with him not to even attempt it a second time.

Prising his bruised eye open wasn't much of a picnic either, but his heuristic brain—not to mention his sense of self-preservation—was keen to know exactly how much trouble he was in.

And he *was* in trouble. The ropes cutting into the skin of his wrists was a dead giveaway.

Well, he'd been in worse situations. *Look on the bright side, Nic. You're in. Zeus is here. Somewhere. They haven't thrown you out. Yet.*

Neck aching from being slumped forward, he cautiously raised his head to take in his surroundings.

His mind registered the darkness, the shadows prancing around the bare room, before he focused on a single stream of moonlight shining through the only small window, illuminating one stiletto-heeled foot tap-tap-tapping on the floor.

Ah. He suspected that was the culprit responsible for the lethargic woodpecker hammering at his head. Yet, oddly enough, all was forgotten as his appreciative eyes glissaded upwards.

Vintage towering black patent heels with an inch-thick sole. Sculpted ankles and toned calves. Sheer stockings draping long, long luscious legs and disappearing beneath a short, black figure-hugging pencil skirt.

His mind took another detour, wondering when he'd last had sex. Full-on, hedonistic, mind-blowing, erotic carnality usually kept his body taut, but now he thought about it he hadn't felt the need in months. Little wonder he was famished.

'Good evening, Mr Carvalho.'

A rush of heat shimmered over his skin like a phantom fire. 'Well, well, well—if it isn't my little gunslinger.'

'We meet again. How are you feeling?'

Mouth as dry and hot as the desert sands, he licked his lips. His voice *still* came out gravelly with repressed need. 'Much better for seeing you, *querida*. Or at least the half that I can see. I do wish you'd come a little closer. You can trust me.'

'Said the wolf to the lamb,' she quipped. 'Was it that charming reprobate tongue you used to gain access to my private suite, Mr Carvalho?'

'Call me Nicandro, please. I'd like to think my submissive aspect puts us on first-name terms at least. Right now you could do anything you desired to me.'

Straddling his lap would his first choice. Pressing her

breasts into his chest and licking into his mouth and down the column of his throat would be the second. The agony of feeling her all over his body but being unable to touch… Exquisite torture.

'Very well…*Nicandro*.'

His name rolled deliciously from her mouth with a hint of European inflection. Italian, or maybe Greek. He didn't miss the fact that she still hadn't given him her name, but he was too busy imagining thick, dark curling locks and hazel eyes to match that smoky, sultry voice.

'Let us discuss the misdemeanour of breaking and entering. It stands to reason—our being on first-name terms, after all—that you should tell me exactly what you were doing in my private rooms this evening.'

'Tell me your name and I will.'

That she didn't want to was clear. But two could play this game, and he hadn't needed to hear the safety click of her revolver or the commands she'd issued to the staff to tell him this woman held power. Exactly how much he had yet to figure out.

'My name is Olympia Merisi.'

Now, *that* was unexpected. He barely managed to swallow the sharp hitch in his breath.

'Ah. The little wife, then?' A healthy dose of disappointment made him frown. What did he care *who* she was chained to?

'Little? Now, *there* is something I've never been called. As for me being a wife—angels will dance in hell before I submit to any man.'

Nic could soon change that. In fact he was tempted to make it his mission. Which was incongruous, considering he hadn't even seen her face yet.

'A more accurate description for me would be…*daughter*.'

Everything stopped, as if someone had pressed 'pause' on the drama that was his life.

Zeus had a daughter. Well, now, every cloud had a silver lining and it seemed the fates were looking down on him tonight.

How utterly opportune. How devilishly delicious.

This new information gave him extra verve to break loose and he regained his attempts at loosening the knots binding his wrists as he found his tongue.

'In that case I do hope I didn't cause too much damage to your father's security staff. I was hoping to meet the man himself to apologise.' If he were Pinocchio his nose would have poked her eye out by now.

'That is very decent of you,' she said, skating the lines of sarcasm.

'I thought so too. I'm a very decent man.'

'That remains to be seen. You see, I have the very old-fashioned view that seducing a member of my staff and breaking into private quarters does not decent make.'

He flashed her a mock-aggrieved look. 'Now you are just nitpicking, *querida*. I was curious, that is all.'

A small flat black box spun through the air and landed at his feet with a clatter.

Ah. Busted.

'I would expect to find such high-tech equipment in the hands of a CIA operative, not a man who is merely curious to meet another. I very much doubt you'd find such a thing in the electronics section at the local store.'

Nic shrugged. Forgot he was slightly incapacitated and wrenched his shoulder. *Dios*, it hurt like hell. He was going to get her back for this and he'd enjoy every single second.

What had she said? The local store? He wished. It would have been a damn sight cheaper. 'Let us say I have friends in high places.'

'MI5? The White House?'

'The Bronx.'

She huffed out a genuine laugh and, just as it had earlier, a hot kind of thrilling pleasure infused his blood with a sullen pulse of want. *Come on, Olympia, show me your face. You're beautiful—I know it.*

'Any normal person would've asked for an appointment. Ever heard of a phone?'

'Believe it or not, I much prefer the personal touch—'

'Oh, I believe you,' she interrupted snarkily.

'Maybe curious was too bland a word,' he went on regardless. 'Tenacious?'

'Foolhardy? Reckless?'

He settled on, 'Intrepid.' It sounded better to him.

'Why? What exactly is it you want?'

'An audience with the all-powerful mystery man himself. One hour with your father.'

'Impossible,' she declared, without missing a beat.

There was something no-nonsense about her. She was overtly frank. And, call him a fool, but he believed her. Thinking about it, she didn't seem the type to waste time messing around. As if her time was at a premium.

He pondered that while he doubled-checked. 'He isn't here?'

'No, I'm afraid not. On this occasion the journey was too far for him to travel.'

She had an odd tone to her voice he couldn't fathom, but he still trusted her word. Dangerous? Probably. Considering who her father was. Her father who *wasn't* here.

'Pity.' Or was it? Eventually this woman would lead him directly to Zeus himself, and in the meantime...? The game was afoot and his to master.

A few days or weeks in the company of this woman would be no hardship. He could burrow into her life, find potential weak spots, and seduce her into his bed. Imagine Zeus's horror when he discovered Nic had tasted his precious daughter. It was too delicious an idea to reject outright. It needed serious consideration.

'Is it a private matter, or business?' she enquired.

'Both.'

'Then I'm happy to talk to him on your behalf, or deliver any message you wish. You have my word it will be delivered with the utmost secrecy.'

She began to lean towards him and Nic watched, mesmerised, breath held, pulse thumping frenetically, as she came into view inch by delectable inch. It occurred to him then that she was trying to gain his trust by coming out of the shadows, making eye contact, and figured it was entirely too possible that he was underestimating her.

Nic's eyes strained to focus as she leaned further still, bending that tiny waist, bringing the low, severe slash of her black V-neck shirt into the light, showcasing a deep cleavage of pearly white skin that made his blood hum.

Every blink of his eyes felt lethargic, every punch of his pulse profound, as she came closer…closer—

Dios…

Legs crossed, she sat with her elbow on her bent knee, chin resting on her lightly curled fist; she was the picture of seductive power.

His jaw dropped so fast it almost dented the floor. He felt his IQ dip fifty points. 'You are…' *Stupefyingly beautiful.* 'Blonde.'

Eyes sparkling with amusement, she tipped her head to one side, as if he'd given her a complex mathematical equation and no calculator.

'Ten out of ten, Mr Carvalho. What exactly did you expect?'

'Greek.' It was the only word he could muster. Pathetic, really, considering his reputation. But holy hell and smoke and fire, the woman looked as if she'd just stepped off a film noir set, playing the leading role of *femme fatale.* Visually dominant and unrepentant.

Thick flaxen hair the colour of champagne had been swept back from her face and perfectly pinned in a chic 1950s Grace Kelly look. Then again, the image of Grace Kelly aroused words like *innocent, serene.* Whereas Olympia Merisi exuded danger and sin. A woman who would refuse to be defined by any man or to submit to her sexuality. All mysterious and seductive. The type whose charm ensnared a man in the bonds of irresistible desire.

There was no other word for it—her beauty was otherworldly, almost supernatural. Pale flawless skin that shimmered like a pearl, high slashing cheekbones that any supermodel would weep for, huge, ever so slightly slanted violet-blue eyes thickly rimmed with black kohl, and full pouty lips painted in the deepest shade of unvirtuous red.

She should have been called Aphrodite, as undeniably goddess-like as she was. An enchantress able to weave her magical powers, leaving her morally ambiguous. She was danger personified—and didn't *that* just ratchet up his 'want meter' into the stratosphere?

This wasn't a woman you married—hell, no: the very idea was ludicrous. This was a woman you bedded. Found ecstasy in her body over and over, until neither of you could walk, talk or summon the energy to breathe.

Hauling in damp air, he silently prayed for his arousal to subside, wishing he'd felt one zillionth of this visceral attraction for the Petit Q he'd earlier declined.

'Your mother…? Norwegian? Swedish?' With that natural colouring she had to be.

If Nic had blinked he would have missed it. That pained pinch of her mouth, that subtle flinch of her flesh. It didn't take a genius to work out that her mother was a touchy subject.

'French,' she said, in a tone so cold it was a welcome blast of air-con sizzling over his hot, damp skin and leaving goosebumps in its wake.

Nic shrugged. What was a couple of thousand miles? 'European. Close enough.'

Her displeased pout told him to drop it, and even he knew some battles weren't worth fighting. So he did. Well, sort of…

'Please allow me to apologise for waking you earlier, *querida*. Or maybe you should thank me. Your dreams seemed too dark to be pleasant.'

Right there. Ah, yes. She might ooze power and control, but beneath all those chilly layers she was still a woman, swayed by emotions, capable of vulnerability. This was going to be child's play.

'What haunts your sleep, Olympia?' And since when had he ever been interested enough in a woman to care?

'A mere headache.'

Poised and graceful as a ballerina, she stood and pirouetted on her heels, turning her back on him. No doubt to soothe the raw nerve he'd struck. But what really bothered him was the weird, not to mention scary idea that he wanted to take it back, soothe her pain himself.

Instead his eyes followed her like a heat-seeking missile, and he detonated at the sight of the tight curves forming her lush heart-shaped bottom and the perfectly straight black seams splicing down her sheer stockings.

Every thought in his head exploded with the extra blast of heat to his groin.

Holy smoke. She was the sexiest thing he'd ever laid eyes on. He couldn't wait to taste her. To get up close and personal with that stunning hourglass figure. To mould his hands to her flesh, sip at her skin for days. And he would. There was no woman in the world he couldn't beguile and lure into his bed.

After she'd taken a turn around the chair she came to stand in front of him. Up close and personal.

Nic ground his back teeth, scrambling for a reprieve from the sexual tension that choked the air around them and took his hard-on from uncomfortable to agonising.

Turned out the fates had had their eye on the ball the entire time—because if there was one sure-fire way to rid him of lust they'd found it.

Olympia bent slightly at the waist—to look into his eyes

or to endeavour to intimidate him, he wasn't sure and didn't particularly care—and he reckoned he was so far gone he would have begged for her mouth right there and then. *If* a large black diamond teardrop, spectacular and rare, edged with twenty-four brilliant-cut white diamonds totalling fifty-two carats, with a net worth of approximately forty-six point two million dollars, hadn't chosen that precise moment to tumble from the sumptuous lace confection encasing her breasts.

Nic jerked as if that bruiser bodyguard was back with a fist in his guts. One punch and a tsunami of anger and hate and pain threatened to pull him under, drag him into the depths of hell. His chest felt crushed and toxic adrenaline rushed through his body, hardening his wide shoulders, searing down his arms, until he was able to contort his wrists and almost pull free of the ropes. *Just a few seconds more.*

He wanted to rip that platinum chain from around her neck, tear those jewels from the warm cavern of her skin. Just as Zeus's henchman had ripped it from his mother's lifeless body.

O Coracao da Tempestade. The heart of the storm. The Santos diamonds.

He couldn't tear his eyes away. So many memories. So much heartache. So much pain.

Nic had always surmised that Goldsmith owned the jewels, along with the rest of the company. The thought that they'd been separated thoughtlessly, like meaningless pieces of chattel, had broken his heart. He could only presume that when Zeus had sold off Santos he must have kept the diamonds to gift to his pampered daughter like some kind of obscene trophy.

Did she know how her father had come to own them?

A shudder racked his entire body and he broke out in a cold sweat.

Dios, did she know they were smothered in blood?

If she did he would make her life a living hell.

The fist gripping his heart threatened to squeeze the life out of him. It took everything he had to remain calm, not to jump to conclusions or lose the hold on his temper.

Gracefully she straightened before him, and the vigilance narrowing those striking violet eyes told him she was well aware that the *Lobisomem* now sat before her, struggling to stay leashed.

Not any more.

The rope finally fell away from his wrists and it took all his remaining strength to keep hold of the bonds, control his face into an impassive blank slate so she would be none the wiser. Timing was everything, and he hadn't bided his for years only to trip over his anger and fall at the first hurdle.

Nic discreetly cleared his throat and turned his voice to a rich, evocative volume that would diffuse her doubt.

'Apologies, *querida*, my mind wandered. While I appreciate your offer to relay my business to your father, I stand firm. Let us say the topic is of a delicate nature.'

Olympia took another step back and he dug his nails into his palms to stop himself reaching out, gripping her waist, hauling her into his lap, punishing that seductive temptation of a mouth, taking his revenge on her glorious body.

Instead he carried on—as if his heart *wasn't* tearing apart. 'I don't know you well enough to discuss it with you. I'm sure you understand.'

Stalemate. He knew it. She knew it.

Agitation leached from her. 'No' was clearly not a word she was used to hearing.

'Then I can't help you any further, Mr Carvalho. As for this evening—I'm sure *you* understand there has been a breach of trust, and as you're unwilling to explain yourself your membership will be placed under review. I can—'

'However,' he continued, as if she'd never spoken, knowing it would rile her, determined to gain the upper hand, 'if

I had the opportunity to get to know you I might change my mind. Spend a few days with me, *bonita*. I'd love the chance to put things right between us. To prove I'm not so bad after all.'

She crossed her arms over her ample chest and arched one flaxen eyebrow. 'You think me a fool, Mr Carvalho. The way to my father is not via my bed.'

Brainy and beautiful.

'Maybe not, but I guarantee you would enjoy the ride. You're tempted—admit it.'

'As much as I am tempted to skydive from thirty-thousand feet without a parachute.'

He grinned—he couldn't help it. Despite her unfortunate parentage and the bauble now nestled back in her deep cleavage he kind of liked her. Such a shame she wore a harbinger of tragedy around her delicate throat. He wondered then if she truly knew of its origins, because surely no woman in their right mind would wear it if they were well-versed in the omen it carried. The wrath of his ancestors. Strange, he'd never really believed in any of it. Until now. Because clearly Nicandro had been led to it—to her—to wreak his revenge.

He wanted it back. And he would have it. *After* he'd taken her. *After* he'd slid the diamonds from her throat in a slow, erotic seduction she would never forget.

Nic ignored the remnants of his Catholic morality—the stuff that still percolated inside whatever passed for his soul these days—which were suggesting he wasn't being strictly fair, involving her. Odds were she was as crooked as her father.

'I could have you in a heartbeat,' he declared. Exaggeration on his part—she would be hard work. She was feisty and wilful and brimming with self-determination—which would make her final moments of surrender all the more delicious, precious.

'You will never have *me*, Nicandro.'

By the time he'd figured out those were her parting words he was wrestling with a bout of what was surely affront—because the little vixen was halfway to the door.

Nic lurched from the chair and reached the door before she did, slamming his palm flat on the dense block of wood. If she was shocked he'd torn from his hold she covered her surprise quickly enough—simply froze to the spot like an ice sculpture and peered at him the way someone would a cockroach.

'Want to bet?' he said, making his voice smooth, richer than cognac and twice as heady.

A cold front swept over him, pricking his skin through the superfine material of his shirt.

'Anyone ever tell you that you're supremely arrogant?'

'Often. I'm not averse to hearing compliments, Olympia. And nor do I imagine are you. You really are stunning, *querida*.'

Up close she was even more exquisite. He couldn't take his eyes off her.

'Save it, Romeo. You may be infamous for your limitless wants and desires, but I'm afraid you've reached your limit with me.'

He might have believed her if he hadn't trailed the back of his index finger down her bare arm excruciatingly slowly and relished the shimmy rustling over her body. Impossible as it was, her infinitesimal gasp and the ghostly pinch of her brow gave him the notion that she hadn't known a simple touch could affect her in such a tremendous way.

'You're scared. Maybe even petrified. Afraid I will prove you wrong? Or fearful you'll enjoy every minute of it?' He was baiting her, but there was one advantage to toying with an intelligent woman: he knew exactly what buttons to push.

'I fear no one. Least of all you.'

That haughty retort hung in the air, coaxing another smile from him. She was sewn up tighter than a drum.

'Prove it. Spend two weeks in my company. If you win and evade my bed I will desist in my attempts to meet with your father and resign my membership from Q Virtus with no fanfare. You have my word.'

Because her evasion would never, *ever* happen.

Those big violet eyes narrowed on his. 'Together with a full explanation? Because I know there's more to you than meets the eye and far more to this meeting you desire with Zeus. I want to know why.'

It occurred to him then that she must work for her father in some way. Must have come in his place this weekend. She might have already put two and two together and suspect he was at the root of the dissent at the club. Not that she could prove it.

'Of course I'll tell you everything you want to know. However, if you lose, and I take your body as mine, have you at my mercy, you'll arrange a meeting with Zeus and take me to him.'

Two days and she'd succumb. Three at the most.

For long moments she simply stared at him, and it was shocking to admit but he'd have given half of Manhattan to know what she was thinking. He'd never given much credence to the term 'closed book', but this intriguing package was still wrapped in Cellophane.

Finally she gave a heavy sigh, as if she really didn't have much of an alternative. As if he'd pushed her into a corner with his refusal to tell her anything and she had nowhere else to go but to follow him.

What had he said? Child's play.

'All right. Here's the deal. Zeus will be in Paris in eight days. *If* you win, I guarantee you'll meet at a specified time and place. You have my word.'

A smile—so small yet inordinately confident—curved her luscious lips. He wished she'd do it more often—it made his heart trampoline into his throat.

So bold she was, so sanguine, so sure he would fail and she would be the victor. He almost felt sorry for her.

'But when you lose I will have you on your knees, *Nicandro*.'

'*If* I lose I'll go down with pleasure, *Olympia*.'

Eyes locked, they stared at one another. Neither giving an inch. And he'd swear the air sparked with electricity, tiny arrows of fire that bounced from one point of contact to another. One strike of a match and they'd blow sky-high.

'Then you have a deal…*Nic*…'

Welcome to three days of torture.

Even the way she purred his name like that, drawing out the N, made him hard.

'Splendid. And every deal should be sealed, don't you agree?'

Without giving her time to bat an eyelash he slowly lowered his mouth to hers. There was no better place to start the war, and his body begged for just one kiss, one taste.

Gossamer-light, Nic brushed his lips across hers and lavished the corner of her mouth with a lush velvet kiss. Electricity hissed over his skin, his blood seared through his veins on a scream of satisfaction, and before he knew it he stepped closer. Her breasts crushed against his chest and he fingered her sweet waist while he swept his tongue across the seam of her lips, demanding entry, commanding more.

Dizzy, as if she'd put him under some kind of spell, his mind stripped itself clean and he nipped at the plump flesh and sucked gently, desperate to be inside her warm heaven. She tasted of sweet, hot coffee liqueur, and if she'd just let him in…

After a few more seconds he drew back. Frowned.

Passive, emotionless—she hadn't moved one muscle and her skin was like ice, her blood-red lips equally devoid of warmth. Even her violet-blue stare was cold and vacant.

The shock of it made his tone incongruous. 'Olympia,

you are frozen, *querida*.' A coil of serpents in the pit of his stomach couldn't have unsettled him more.

Lifting her chin she gifted him a small smile. Except it wasn't cold—it was sad.

'I *am* frozen…*querido*. Inside and out. Ah, Nicandro, you really have no idea who you are playing with, do you?'

Her hand to the handle now, she hauled the door wide and he floundered for a beat, stepping backwards, his foot crushing the small black sensor pad she'd tossed at him earlier.

The inevitable crack snapped him back to his wits. 'Hold up there, ice queen. The Petit Q. She was innocent in all this. Promise me the girl will—'

'Be removed from the premises. Good evening, Nicandro.'

Next thing he knew she was gone—the razor-sharp tap-tap of her towering heels vibrating in the void around him.

'You really have no idea who you are playing with, do you?'

Wasn't that the truth?

CHAPTER THREE

PIA PULLED THE double doors to her suite closed behind her
and fought the urge to slump against the carved wood. Bad
enough that she raised her fingertips to the corner of her
mouth to chase the faint echoes of his kiss, shimmering
over her lips like an iridescent butterfly.

Old habits truly did die hard, because for the first time
in years she was second-guessing herself—and that really
didn't bode well. Suddenly spending time with Nicandro
Carvalho seemed like a bad, bad idea. But what alternative did she have? Wait it out until he struck again? God
only knew what havoc he'd wreak next, and she could not
let that happen. Not in *her* world.

'Pia?'

She jumped clean off the floor, then flushed guiltily
like an idiotic schoolgirl who'd just had her first kiss from
a long-time crush and her big brother had been spying on
her. She didn't want to think how close to the truth that was.

'Where did you come from? I thought you were escorting our nefarious burglar to his suite?'

Jovan watched her warily from where he sat looking
incongruous—his large frame stiff and upright—perched
on the edge of her delicate gold silk daybed.

'Mission accomplished.'

Oh.

Pia's eyes shuttered at the concern marring his face. He
wanted to ask if she was okay but he wouldn't. He didn't

like making her feel weak. Emotional. Not when she was supposed to be a machine. But therein lay the problem. Machines didn't tremble with the touch of man's hand, at his finger breezing down her arm. Machines didn't suffer a glitch after a soft evocative kiss from his warm lips. And machines certainly didn't stare into his eyes and feel something close to longing, wishing for the impossible.

For one heart-stopping moment she would have done anything to kiss him back. Anything to feel his scorching heat melt some of the ice inside of her—ice that was so terribly, terribly cold. But Pia knew that surrendering to meaningless brief moments could shower you in a lifetime of regret, and he'd chosen the one route to her bed with a guaranteed outcome of failure and causing her maximum levels of pain.

He was using her. To get to Zeus. To Q Virtus. Ignorant of the fact he'd already been in Zeus's company for most of the evening. If it wasn't so humiliating and didn't exhume such loathsome feelings of worthlessness she would laugh. *Sorry, Nic, I've already learned my lessons in love.* Pia could spot a seduction routine a mile off and erect her barricades with ease.

Being used for the Merisi fame and fortune years ago had thrown her hard-earned self-respect to the wolves— with a little help from her father's constant stream of berating anger during the miserable aftershocks of her affair.

'*Women are weak fools with vulnerable hearts, Olympia. You think he wanted your body? Your mind?*' he'd hollered, as if the idea that any man could desire her for simply being Pia was unfathomable. '*True lust is greed for money and power. Surrender to a man and he will strip you of your fortune and glory and leave you as nothing more than a whore in his bed. Trust no man. Not even me.*'

That her hollow, cold flesh should now answer to the practised tongue of a Don Juan with criminal tendencies who was quite possibly trying to take her down could only be the cruel joke of a universe that despised her.

Now she had to drag him across Europe for the next few days, on a schedule that was impossible to change, trying to delve into the intricacies of his mind while he tried to delve into her knickers.

Not in a million years.

She'd just have to keep her head on straight and her eyes on him. The man could hardly kick up a storm if she was watching over his shoulder, and it would give her plenty of time to unearth what game he was playing and why.

The anxiety of it all—the possibility that she was in danger of having everything she'd worked so hard for taken away—made her feel sick to the stomach. *And that's not the only thing that has you rattled*, a little voice said. She told that voice to hush up.

'You look tired, Pia,' Jovan said.

She was. Bone-deep tired. But machines weren't supposed to get tired. So instead of crawling into bed she tried to pretend that she didn't ache all over, lifted her chin, strode towards her office and got back to business.

'I'm fine. You worry too much.'

That wasn't fair. He cared about her and she would be for ever grateful for that small mercy in her life. It would have all been so easy if there'd been flames of attraction between them, but there wasn't so much as a flicker—never mind the high-voltage current that was still racing through her body from—

No, no, *no*. She was *not* going there.

'Get Laurent from Paris on the phone and tell him I've found him a new concierge. Then ask Clarissa Knight to pack her bags and come to my office. She's wanted to be based near her mother for months and this is the perfect opportunity. With a bit of luck she'll find some fresh eye-candy in days, and Mr Carvalho will be reduced to a distant memory. Just make sure Mr I'm-Sex-Incarnate-and-I-Know-It doesn't see her leave.'

It was far too dangerous to keep her here, bewitched under Carvalho's spell. No doubt he'd promise her the world for more secrets, and if the girl thought Pia was casting her out of a job *and* had convinced herself in love with the Brazilian bad-boy anything was possible.

Even Pia—who'd been vaccinated against the Nicandros of the world—had sensed him drizzling charm all over her as if she were a hot waffle. Clarissa wouldn't have stood a chance. Had he slept with her? Devoured her over and over again? And why *that* imagery made her feel queasy was anyone's guess.

'You are going soft in your old age, Pia,' Jovan said.

The only thing going soft was her breasts.

'I'm not so vain that I can't admit to fault. The girl is far too sheltered to be surrounded by Q Virtus players, some of who are no better than vultures preying on female flesh, but she needed the extra money to send home and I caved.'

While those were the facts it wasn't the entire truth, and she knew it. The truth was Nicandro had used the girl, and it left a bitterly sour taste in Pia's mouth. She was utterly disappointed in him—and that was highly idiotic, because it meant she'd placed him on a pedestal just from what she'd read of him, meant her emotions had been engaged. *Fool.*

'Of course you caved. The girl genuinely needed you. I know you hate to admit it, but you *like* being needed.'

'No, I don't.' Did she?

'Okay, you don't. So, do I have the pleasure of escorting *him* to the airport?' Jovan asked, with no small amount of enthusiastic glee, as he walked towards her desk, where she was standing shuffling papers from one towering pile to another.

The fact she was making a mess to avoid this subject didn't go unnoticed.

Oh, hell, this was not going to go down well.

'No.' And since she didn't have the energy to tell Jovan he'd be escorting them both—together—and then deal with the inevitable fall-out—which was so unlike her it was frightening—she said, 'I'll explain later. Get going or you'll miss Laurent.'

Jovan did a quick U-turn and headed towards the door—and the action popped a memory like some maniacal jack-in-the-box. Nicandro's swift *volte-face*. One minute the consummate charmer, the next a predator. The *lobisomem* she'd seen from the start.

Strange, that all it had taken was one scan of his membership request, one perlustration of his past, one glance at the nebulous depths of his eyes and his moniker had bitten into her brain. *Lobisomem*: werewolf. A survivor despite or perhaps in spite of his origins. A lord of the night. His darkness a phantom entreaty to her soul.

But for several heartbeats in that room there'd been such violent anger in his eyes. A change so swift, so absolute, she'd felt the sharp edges of panic for the first time in years.

Where had it come from, that vitriol mutating his gorgeous whisky-coloured eyes to black pools of hate? Indifference she might have understood—but hate? Such a strong emotion. Made him appear dangerous. Deadly.

At first she'd thought his abrupt one-eighty had something to do with her diamonds—the only gift her father had ever given her, the only time he'd ever shown her he cared. It was the only possession she'd ever truly adored. Yet Nicandro had stared at them with a look of abject horror. It was the *why* that was bugging her. Yes, large black diamonds were extraordinarily rare—hers was one of a kind—but the way he'd gone on you would think it was an evil eye, some kind of black art mumbo-jumbo.

Rubbing at the aching spot between her eyes, she decided it was nigh on impossible to figure him out.

'Jovan, before you go, what's the name of that private investigator we occasionally use?'

He stilled beneath the archway leading back to the main suite and looked over his shoulder at her keenly. 'We have several. Though it's usually Mason, who tows the legal line—or McKay, who has no compulsion about being morally corrupt if given the right incentive.'

Another crook. Wonderful. Bad enough she was hearing rumours of Q Virtus being associated with the Greek mafia. Did she have Mr Carvalho to thank for that one too? She'd thank him, all right. With a swift knee-jerk in his crown jewels.

When she had the proof. *If* it was him.

So foolish, Pia. You're still hoping there's a perfectly reasonable explanation for all this—an explanation that has nothing to do with Nicandro Carvalho, aren't you? She couldn't answer that question and not hate herself.

'That's him—he'll do. McKay. Ask him to look into the history of Santos Diamonds. I don't suppose you remember how and when my father took control of the company, do you?'

Jovan paused. Stared at her with an indecipherable look. He *never* paused.

'Jovan? Did you hear me?' Pia hadn't seen him like this in ages. Almost haunted.

He gave his head a quick shake. 'Yes—sorry…distracted. No, haven't a clue.'

He also never lied to her.

'It's probably nothing, but let's have the information anyway.'

'Not a problem,' he murmured, in a low, hesitant tone that said trouble was coming. The kind of trouble that could rock the very foundations of her life.

She just hoped he was wrong.

As soon as the door closed behind him she dumped the papers on her desk and without thinking of posture, or performing for an audience, she collapsed into the chair and sprawled all over it.

She couldn't remember the last time she'd done this, she realised, head tipped back, staring at the ceiling. It reminded her of being no one—a forgotten girl in a basement room that shook with the heavy metal pounding from above, the acrid scent of drugged hopelessness drifting through the floorboards. The girl with a tainted past and only prospects of a no-good future.

In the next second, as if a ghostly fist had thumped the table, she bolted upright, pin-straight, and opened her laptop, pushing that girl—the girl who no longer existed—from her mind once more.

Nic woke to a warm, richly scented African morning, with a foul disposition from the unfathomable unrequited desire he'd suffered throughout the night and a note pushed beneath his door.

I am leaving at twelve noon and flying to Northern Europe on business. If you still wish to join me be ready at eleven.
Olympia Merisi

Join her? 'I do not think so, *querida*.' Did he look like a lapdog? Next she'd want him to bark.

Dios, he felt vile.

He dismissed the flash of self-honesty that his lack of sleep—when he should have slept like a babe after his major victory at the end of an eight-day quest—was making him too grumpy to think straight, and lurched out of bed with a hot head, ready to yank her into line.

His disgusting mood ruined a perfectly good morning as he showered and said goodbye to Narciso and Ryzard—taking one hell of a ribbing about the slight swelling around his lip, which they presumed was thanks to a ravenous Petit Q—and was led to Pia's private suite.

One of the brutish security guards from the night before

reluctantly let him in, and the fact that he looked a damn sight worse than Nic did, sporting a huge black eye, made him feel remarkably better.

'You're early,' was her greeting when he strode through the door, ready to play hell and inform her that *she* would be travelling with *him*.

He didn't notice her sleek, sophisticated up-do, or her flawless skin, or her kohl-rimmed eyes, or that pouty, provocative red mouth. Nor did he take any interest in the sharp-as-a-blade black business suit hugging her sinuous figure and nipping her waist. Absolutely not.

Her beefcake security guard plonked a case near his feet, no doubt wishing it were his head.

'When did you arrive in Zanzibar?' Nic asked, eyeing the cluttered floor.

'Friday—same as you.'

'You have a lot of luggage for a three-day stay, *bonita*. Did you bring the kitchen sink?' Clearly her father paid her well for being…what? A glorified PA on a power trip? She could, of course, be his only heir. He'd have to kiss that out of her too.

'Not this time. That one is Jovan's,' she said, pointing to the smallest of the designer six-piece set.

'And Jovan is…?' For a terrible moment he suspected he was experiencing a flicker of jealousy.

Dios, he was all over the place. What had she done to him?

'My bodyguard.'

Yeah, right.

'And a friend.'

Sure.

His mother had had lots of so-called 'friends'. He'd actually liked a couple of them. Especially the one who took him to a Brazil game, where he'd met the players, but for the life of him he couldn't remember the guy's name. Which was odd, because he always remembered names—

was good with them. It had used to come in handy when his father would innocently name-drop to catch him out. Anything to avoid the screaming matches that had inevitably followed.

Then he realised it was because he was still staring at Jovan—her *friend*.

It took him a while—what with Othello's green-eyed monster riding his back—but he got there eventually.

'*Que?* No. No way. He is not coming with us. That was *not* the deal.'

'Oh, I'm sorry,' she said, all innocent and light, in cunning contradiction of the devilry in her eyes. 'Zeus insists. You don't want to get on his bad side, do you?'

Nic's temper gauge ratcheted up.

'Fine. But not him. I don't think he likes me.' *And he likes you far too much.*

'How observant you are, Nicandro.'

She lowered her voice to a conspiratorial whisper and leaned forward until he tasted her sweet breath.

'In truth, he'd kick you as soon as look at you. So I suggest you stay on your best behaviour.'

From nowhere he had the impulse to grin, and he let it fly in the most wicked, debauched way imaginable. Naturally he earned himself a nice, slow stunned blink from her gorgeous violet-blues.

Unrequited, my foot.

'Now I get it. He's the modern-day equivalent of a chastity belt.'

She must be worried. Downright petrified of being alone with him.

As if a third wheel would dissuade him. He'd once outrun several of New York's finest after he'd stolen a bagel for breakfast to appease his crippling hunger pangs, so he was damn sure he could lose *this* guy.

The edginess he'd felt the previous night evaporated

at the warmth in her million-dollar satisfied smile as she shrugged one cashmere shoulder. So beautiful. So *his*.

Olympia Merisi wasn't frozen. She only needed the higher heat from a slow burn to melt her resistance. He'd moved too fast, his impatience calling the shots, when he should have known better. He had to stop thinking of her as any other woman and use his brains instead of what was between his legs. Not that he'd ever had the need to switch or polish his technique, but people didn't call him a dynamic powerhouse for nothing.

The reason he'd stormed up here now seemed unimportant. Like a tug of war that wasn't worth landing on his ass for. And he was coming to realise he'd have to pick and choose his battles where this woman was concerned or they'd be at loggerheads for ever and he'd alienate her before he'd even begun. So he'd play along, for now, and slowly but surely gain her trust. When the time was right and he held her in the palm of his hand—*then* he'd take control. She wouldn't know what had hit her.

'Did you want something? You're much too early.'

'No, I simply wanted to see you sooner.' And the hell of it was that was the God's honest truth. Not that he intended to panic about it. His desire was to reach his end game and Miss Merisi was going to take him the scenic route. 'Let's do breakfast. I'm starving.' *For more than food.*

'Pia?' the guy *Jovan* said, in an overly familiar way that said he would move Nic bodily if she gave the word.

Go on, buddy, try it. See how far you get.

'Pia…' Nic repeated, staring into those huge seductive eyes and watching them flare as he rolled the shortened name around his mouth as if he liked the taste of it on his tongue. 'Very pretty.'

He watched her delicate throat convulse. 'You may call me Olympia.'

She sounded so haughty and uptight he wanted to ruffle her feathers.

'I think not. If he can call you Pia why can't I? Unless, of course, Olympia is reserved especially for me. For those fortunate enough to have shared body fluids with you.' He licked his lips to emphasise his point—to remind her that despite her deep freeze he *had* kissed her, and he would kiss her again, and next time she would melt.

Her gasp was so faint only he could hear, but any spectator would have to be blind not to see the pink flush enhancing the perfect sweep of her cheeks.

Oh, yeah, she wanted him, all right.

One look at the way her hands fisted by her sides and he also knew she wanted to thump him.

Score one, Carvalho. Ball in the back of the net.

Though it didn't take long before his smile faltered and a dart of panic sped like an arrow into his gut. Had he seriously just stamped his possessive mark on her? No, impossible. He'd merely been staking his claim for the next eight days. After that she could do whatever she liked and he'd feel neither care nor concern because he'd have exactly what he wanted: Zeus.

She was still glaring at him, her glorious eyes flashing with unconcealed irritation. At second glance he revised that to absolute fury.

'I'm going to have to say no to breakfast, Nicandro,' she hissed hotly. 'With that *none too subtle* reminder I seem to have lost my appetite.'

All this frisky repartee was a serious turn-on. Between her posture and his arousal both of them were as stiff as a board. She seriously needed to loosen up.

Right then it struck him. The key to Pia Merisi. He had to coax the woman to liberation. Unpin that hair, unstrap that dress, unhook that bra, unchain all that control. Unleash all that fire.

Undo her one button at a time.

Reaching up, he stroked the side of his finger down her smooth cheek and felt her vibrate like a tuning fork.

'Ah, *querida*. I think I've just given you a different kind of hunger—that is all.' Then he brushed his thumb over her bottom lip and pressed against it in the guise of a kiss. 'Until later, *tchau*.'

Then—in a satisfying juxtaposition to the night before—he sauntered from the room and left *her* standing there, likely foaming at the mouth, watching his retreating back.

CHAPTER FOUR

PIA KEPT HER head high as she slid gracefully into the leather interior of the luxurious Mercedes waiting outside the private back entrance of the Barattza, still holding on to her temper by the skin of her teeth, frankly amazed that she hadn't followed Nic to his suite and ripped him to shreds.

As she'd watched his retreating back, with an oppressive silence thickening the air around her, she hadn't been able to chance a look at their little audience. She only had to think of how that pow-wow must have looked to her people. Hoping beyond hope that she hadn't just plummeted in their estimation.

Sharing body fluids?

Had he deliberately been trying to belittle her? Undermine her?

Didn't he know how hard she'd had to work to be taken seriously just because she was a woman? Of course he didn't. In his eyes she was probably some stylish Jezebel, playing secretary just to feed out of the troughs of her father's cash, sullied with her own craven self-importance!

She could just imagine what her father would have said if he'd witnessed that overtly sensual display of Nicandro stroking her cheek and thumb-kissing her. Her stomach churned at the mere thought.

'You're a woman—you have to work twice as hard to gain respect. Whoring yourself out will do you no favours, Olympia.'

So at the risk of making the situation look even worse, or blowing her true identity and a plethora of secrets sky-high, she hadn't blown a fuse in front of her staff. No, she'd kept her cool. And it had almost strangled the life out of her. Still was.

When she'd made this deal with him she hadn't expected to face these kinds of problems. How it would look to other people. How she would feel about his opinion of her that her value was only high enough to grace his bed.

It stung.

It was a poisonous battle between her hard-won pride and the need to protect Q Virtus.

Dammit, she wanted him to take her seriously. To know she was a successful woman in her own right. Then maybe he wouldn't treat her like some two-bit tramp.

Tough. She was just going to have to swallow it and suffer.

It would have been so much easier if she could have cancelled this business trip to Northern Europe but the time of year was imperative. Winter was setting in and the window for her hotel rebuild was so small she had no wriggle room.

Fact was he was bound to discover some of her interests over the next few days. It was inevitable.

Well, she'd just have to play the pretty little heiress, helping Daddy to uphold the ranks as she judiciously scrutinised her every discerning word.

Or, better yet, not talk to him at all. *If* he ever got his gorgeous taut backside inside this car. Clearly his time-keeping was as abysmal as his integrity.

Briefcase to the floor, table down in front of her, she flipped up the lid on her laptop and scanned the trading page to check the stockmarkets. Her every action pre-programmed into her psyche. Her body on autopilot, going through the motions like the machine she was.

Until from the corner of her eye she saw the man himself stroll from the hotel as if they had all the time in the world.

It was that insolent swagger that revved her temper—the very temper that had been idling for hours—into first gear.

As if there were a glitch in her system Pia's fingers mashed the keys, and no matter how hard she tried to re-boot, despite every firewall in her arsenal, she felt as if she was being infected with a virus. The Carvalho Virus. It even sounded deadly.

Case in point: she was now staring out of the window, watching that hateful, sublime, ripped body saunter towards the car beneath the bright flood of the African sun, dressed in suit trousers and a fine tailored black shirt that clung to his wide sculpted chest as the breeze licked over him, his jacket hanging from the finger curled like a hook over his shoulder.

Her stomach did a languorous, wanton roll that utterly appalled her.

There he was—a study in contrasts. With that imposing regal bearing and yet the dissipated air of a roguish bad-boy, with unkempt hair, huge designer sunglasses and voguish shoes. The heady mix collided to make some kind of prince of darkness.

Pia could count her past lovers with very few digits and little enthusiasm, but she instinctively knew what sex with Nicandro would be like—carnal, dark, and completely hedonistic—not her kind of thing at all. Which likely made her dead or a liar.

The door swung open and he slipped onto the leather bench, all smooth elegance as he made himself comfortable beside her. He smelled fresh from the shower and splashed with a hint of expensive cologne that prodded her hormones to sit up and take notice. She ignored them—and him—while her temper shifted into third gear. Lord, she had to calm down before she exploded.

Thinking about it, she always strove to remain on an even keel—her temper having been verbally beaten out of her years ago, when her father's patience had fizzled out and Pia had recognised her snippy tongue for what it was: fear that he wouldn't keep her. But even before that she'd never felt like this. So mad she was flushed with red-hot heat as if she were burning up. Even her clothes felt too tight, compressing her chest like a steel band that suffocated her from the inside.

So by the time the car rolled out of the hotel grounds she was raring to go, her body slamming her temper into fifth gear.

Breathe—for pity's sake, breathe.

'*Boa tarde*, Pia. Where are we headed on this beautiful afternoon?'

One roll of her name around his mouth, one perfectly innocuous question in that deep luscious voice that seemed to brush dark velvet across her nerve-endings, and just like that she lost it.

Pia whipped around to face him. 'How...how *dare* you?'

His dark brows came together in a deep frown but he said nothing, just glanced around the leather interior as if the answer to her fury lay in the cup-holders or the magazine pouch.

'Have I missed something?'

'Only your integrity, your decency and your brain—and that's just the beginning!'

After a pensive scratch of his jaw, he settled his sharp gaze on her laptop and she could just imagine what he was thinking. That she'd found some proof of his villainy to stick on him. Oh, she wished she had!

'I think this conversation would go much better if you told me the precise problem, *querida*.'

'The problem, *Nicandro*, is you belittling me in front of my staff! The problem is you making me feel three inches tall. How dare you bring up last night—a kiss that I didn't want or reciprocate in any way—in front of the very people I have worked hard to gain respect from? You know fine well that *sharing body fluids* could imply far more than a kiss and, considering you'd just broken into my private suite, how did that look? It made me look like a worthless whore with no self-respect, that's what!'

His eyebrows shot skyward. Then the mouth that had invaded her dreams curved in devilish amusement and he flicked those whisky-coloured eyes sparkling with striations of gold her way.

'You are not serious?'

He thought she was *joking*?

After she'd glared at him for a few seconds he finally got the message. 'You are perfectly serious. A *whore*?'

That was what her father would have said, wouldn't he? 'Yes, a whore. Why? Why would you do that to me?'

Glancing away, he flushed hotly, distinctly uncomfortable, and she wished to God she knew why.

'Did I dent your ego so badly it was payback?' she jeered.

'No. Absolutely not,' he said with the force of a gale.

His sincerity almost blew her away.

'I didn't think it would affect you in that way. I was…'

'What?'

He wouldn't say, but his embarrassment was acute and… well, those carved, tanned cheekbones slashed with red made her insides go a bit gooey. Whatever it was, it obviously bothered him.

In the awkward silence that followed she shifted around in her seat, not sure of her next move. Because from his point of view he didn't know who she really was.

This was why her temper was the enemy.

So in the end she let it go. The reason being, she assured herself, to get back on her even keel and wrestle back some control. Because honestly she was starting to act a little crazy. Unravelling like a tatty jumper wasn't like her at all.

'Just don't do that to me again. All right? The deal between you and I is private. I've worked too hard for my respect and it's important to me, okay?'

Shrewd—that was surely the only word to describe his expression.

'So you *do* work for your father, then?'

No, I damn well don't!

'Yes. Women *are* capable of such things, Nic. What are you? Primordial? Anti-feminist? Or just plain chauvinist? I dress well, I live well, and so you assume I freeload off my father by shuffling his papers?'

He had the good grace to look abashed. 'I think I've found one of your hot buttons.'

'How astute you are.'

'And not the one I was looking for.'

Pia threw up her arms with exasperated flair. 'And there you go again! *Must* you look at me and think sex?'

'I think I must. But come on! Give me a break. *Look* at you!' He gestured at her with his hands, as if that helped his argument. 'And, to be fair, I seem to remember thinking you radiated power. It was clear you held some. So there—see? You really must stop thinking the worst of me.'

She coughed out an incredulous laugh. 'Like *that* is ever going to happen.'

Now he threw *his* arms in the air, but his were longer, and far stronger, and the loud smack of his hand bashing off the window reverberated through the car.

'I can't win!' he growled, and followed it up with a blue streak of unintelligible curses as he flung himself back against the seat.

'As soon as you realise that, the better!' she sneered.

As for Pia—she actually felt much better. Sort of cleansed. Who knew that having an argument and not keeping everything bottled up inside her could feel so good? It was a revelation.

When Romeo seemed to find his calming centre again—which didn't take long, so she figured he shared her quick hot temper—he twisted to face her, and ended up doing a double-take at her small smile.

'I suppose you could say I've known many "pampered princesses" very well, but you are right, I'm sorry. I was stereotyping and didn't think it through and that was very bad of me. Forgiven?'

He sounded like a little boy right then. Pia would bet he'd been loved beyond reason, despite his family's lack of fortune, and the remnants of her ugly mood dissolved, morphing into a puddle of envy.

'Forgiven.'

'Good,' he said, looking back out of the window at the tropical white sandy beach as opposed to the lush plantations on her side of the car.

He seemed miles away, pensive, so when he reached over and lightly brushed Pia's knee with the very tips of his fingers she wondered if he realised he was doing it. Back and forth he went, the tickling sensation on her sheer stocking making her tremble.

'Please move your hand. Are you always so liberal with your touch?'

Just as she'd thought, he glanced at his hand quizzically as he slipped it from her leg. Heaven help her—she wanted it back.

He shrugged, flexing his wide shoulders. 'Brazilians are very affectionate people, *querida*. We think nothing of gushing about what is beautiful, or *lindo maravilhoso*, or expressing fondness with a hug or a kiss. Aren't you Greeks used to lavish displays of affection? Or did you grow up in France with your mother?'

Pia kept quiet. There were always exceptions to the rule, and the very idea of thinking about her mother made horror swarm through her veins.

Seconds later she found herself tapping away at her laptop.

'What is so fascinating that you'd rather do that than talk to me?'

She shook her head at him. 'My, my—you have an exceedingly high opinion of yourself.'

He gave her an insolent shrug that said his ego was well founded and she was telling him nothing he hadn't heard before.

'I'm working. Don't *you* have work to do? A real estate empire to run?'

'Not right now. I'm one of those people who can't read as a passenger—the headaches and sickness linger for hours.'

Her fingers paused on the keypad at that statement—the first honest words to pass his mouth and a tiny insight into the real Nicandro Carvalho that gave her a ridiculous little thrill. How pathetic was that? Then again, she'd always been intrigued by him. Much to her dismay.

'You can get pills for things like that. Anti-sickness. I'm exactly the same.'

He murmured in agreement, sounding distracted, and Pia glanced up, hopelessly drawn to the tanned column of his throat, the pulse she could see flickering as he undid the top buttons of his shirt. He must be hot, she thought, because she could feel the heat rolling off him. Hot and ripped enough to make her stomach flip-flop and her lower abdomen clench.

He was just so horridly handsome. So many angles made up his beautiful face, from the prominent bones of his cheeks to the slash of his jaw. Even his mouth was chiselled, almost carved, with that exaggerated cupid's bow punctuating his frown as he read.

'Is that Merpia?' he asked, tilting his head farther to one side for a better look at her screen.

Pia snapped out of her drooling stasis, thoroughly disgusted in herself, and threw him a baleful look. 'You have a filthy habit of snooping, Nicandro.'

He cocked one dark brow. 'Right now, I promise you I'm not being nosy—I am genuinely interested. You have an obsessive compulsion to get back to that...whatever you are doing and I'm itching to know why.'

'God, you're insufferable.'

Truly, she didn't like talking about work, and it had nothing to do with secrecy or her need for privacy. It was the turmoil she felt. Like living on a knife-edge. Sometimes she woke in a cold sweat, thinking that her father had been wrong and she really couldn't do it all—would somehow fail to juggle the million balls that were thrown at her what seemed like every minute of every day. That one of these days she'd be exposed as the illiterate nobody she was—not the mathematical prodigy and business whiz her father had excitably claimed her to be not eight months after she'd landed at his door.

I devote my entire life to a thousand jobs I never really wanted...would never have chosen if I'd been free.

The sudden vehemence of her thoughts shocked her to the core and made her feel ashamed. Every time she thought that way she felt hideously selfish. She'd been given a new life—a second chance—something many people would sell their soul for. She should be more grateful. She *was* insanely grateful. Yet sometimes she just wished the merry-go-round would stop, so she could breathe if only for a little while.

Nicandro was watching her with a quiet intensity that made her uneasy—as well as grateful that he couldn't read minds. Still, thinking about it, he'd already seen the Merpia files on her desk. It was unrealistic to think he wouldn't see things, hear things and discover things about the Merisi business during their time together. She should draft some kind of non-disclosure agreement asap.

With a drawn-out sigh she spun the laptop around so he could see the full screen.

'Merpia. *Pia. Dios, com certeza!* Of course. He named it after you. You run it for him?'

She gritted her teeth together and prayed for poise and some semblance of self-control. Merpia was her baby. Her pride and joy. Her first true personal accomplishment, started when she'd been twenty-six years old. The one thing she was truly proud of.

'You could say that,' she bit out.

Those gorgeous eyes grew wide as he whistled in awe. And, though it wasn't directed at her *per se*, pleasure flooded through her in a warm rush. It had been four years since Antonio Merisi had been lowered into the ground, and she still hadn't managed to outgrow her need for approval. That she was basking in it now from the wolf sniffing around her life was disturbing to say the least.

'Rumour has it—'

She snatched at the opening like a life-preserver. 'You shouldn't believe or partake in rumours, Nicandro,' she said irritably. 'Very dangerous business. Are you a propaganda man?'

The look he gave her held a hefty amount of lethal softness and it was a timely reminder of what he was capable of.

'There is an element of truth behind every rumour, *querida*. Of that I am certain.'

There they were once again, dancing around the subject of Zeus and Q Virtus and rumours and lies. Neither of them giving anything away; they just stared at one another, locked in some kind of battle of wills, the stifling air between them as high-octane as always.

What was he saying? That every rumour that had been spread was partly true? That Merisi was Greek mafia? That Zeus was a dirty dealer? A crook not to be trusted? If Nicandro was the source he couldn't possibly have proof of any of that.

'Case in point,' he continued, his voice still sharp as a blade. 'Merpia. Rumour has it the *man* currently behind the commodity mask is a genius, with the work ethic of a machine.'

'Really?' she said, as if that particular flash was news to her. 'I would argue it was more a combination of hard work, a dash of good luck and superb instincts. My instincts rarely let me down, Nic. May I call you Nic?'

For some reason the familiarity of him calling her Pia had left her feeling strangely unbalanced in the power stakes, and it wouldn't do any harm to unleash *her* charm and knock *him* off his stilts a time or two.

His ruthless dominance instantly mellowed. 'Of course, *bonita*,' he said as he reached up and brushed a lock of hair from her brow. The gesture was so tender it made her ache.

Careful, Pia, he's playing you.

'So what do your instincts tell you about me, Pia?'

'That you're an extremely dangerous man and I would do well to barricade my bedroom door at night.'

While he leaned closer she edged farther back, until she found herself plastered to the leather seat, his weight crushing against her side, making it hard to take a breath.

'One day you'll leave it open and unlocked, just for me. One day you'll beg for my mouth on yours. One day you'll melt…only for me.'

Considering the heat pouring off him, she wouldn't be surprised. *Please don't kiss me again. I have nowhere to run this time and I'm not sure I'll be able to resist.*

He sank one hand into her hair and the graze of his fingertips against her scalp made her tremble.

Pia scrambled around her fuzzy brain for something curt to say. 'You're going to mess up my hair, Nic.' *What?* That was the best she could do?

A little closer and he nuzzled up to her jawline until her eyes felt heavy and fluttery and her heart leapt to her throat.

With one tiny kiss at the sensitive skin beneath her ear, he whispered, 'One day. Very soon.'

Then he was gone. Taking away his heat and that delicious scent she could practically taste. Lounging back in his seat with all the debauched lethargy of a satisfied wolf.

'So where are we headed? You mentioned Northern Europe? England?'

Considering she was in the same spot he'd left her in, mentally and physically, the abrupt change in topic threw her sideways.

'Headed?'

He grinned evilly, flashing his teeth as if he knew *exactly* what he was doing to her. '*Sim, querida.* Where are we going, this fine and beautiful day? Where are you taking me? Where will I have the pleasure of spending time with you?'

Oh, he was good. She'd thought Ethan was supremely adroit, with the most artful tongue on the planet, but he had nothing on this guy.

Worse still, for a minuscule moment some secret place inside her longed for every seductive murmur to be the truth. Hopelessly wished he wanted to spend time with her for no other reason than that she was a woman he genuinely admired and liked—wanted to get to know. *Foolish, foolish Pia.*

She'd do well to remember that every word he spoke, every move he made, had a dubious agenda. That she was protecting not only Q Virtus but her entire life.

'Not England, no,' she said, pulling herself together, mentally re-erecting her shields. 'Finnmark. Norway. The northernmost part of continental Europe.'

'*What?*' His head jerked upright, eyes wide, horrified. 'Why the devil would anyone choose to go that far north this time of year?'

She didn't tell him it was the most beautiful place on earth, where the air was so crisp and clean it cleansed the filth of a multitude of cities and a dirty past. Nor did she tell him that she hoped it would numb the sensations he wrought in her, turn down the heat that continually flared between them.

All she said was, 'You'll see.'

CHAPTER FIVE

'WELCOME TO THE Ice Castle.'

Nic opened his bleary eyes at the first words Pia had spoken since they'd left Zanzibar and focused on a staggering feat of architecture, auroral beneath the bluish twilight. A hotel made of ice.

He shivered just looking at it.

'Why would anyone in their right mind wish to vacation in extreme Norway?' he said, his tone one of utter disbelief.

Truth be told, there was a part of him still amazed that he'd followed her here and not whisked her away to some tropical desert island where privacy was gratis and he had a cornucopia of heat at his disposal.

Now look where they were. Ice, snow, ice and more ice. As far as the eye could see. Then again, didn't they have sensual thick furs and warm cabins with blazing, crackling fires in these places? Perfect for seduction.

'Why *not* vacation here?'

'Isn't the persecution of minus fifteen degrees enough?'

Dios, he loathed the cold. It reminded him of being close to dead. Those long, endless minutes when he'd watched the life drain out of his parents. Waiting, praying for the pain to stop.

'It's Finnmark, not Antarctica. It's slightly warmer—even more so inside.'

Nic noticed she said this while pulling a thick cream wool hat over her head and shoving her fingers into mitts.

By rights she should look like a twenty-year-old snow bunny, off to the Alps for a jaunt—but, oh, no, with a deft grip she kept a tight hold on the leash of her stylish sophistication.

The doors of the rough-terrain four-by-four opened and she swung her legs around gracefully and flowed from the car. Nic followed seconds later, the chill pervading his bones and numbing his blood. A violent shudder made his breath puff in front of his face in a voluminous white cloud.

'Warmer, you say? For polar bears maybe.'

'I think you'll find polar bears prefer the Arctic Circle.'

The way she said it reminded him of his buttoned-up high school teacher. The one who'd finally lost her patience with him in the art cupboard.

'I was being facetious,' he said.

'Ah, yes. Another one of your less admirable traits.'

He grinned at her over the car bonnet. 'I really shouldn't like you so much. It's asking for trouble.'

Wasn't that the truth? In the end he'd been grateful for the cold shoulder since Africa. It had given him a chance to regroup and remind himself what he was doing in the company of Zeus's daughter and why. When he took her to his bed he had to stay detached, and by God he would. So that meant no drowning in those big violet-blue eyes and no inhaling the scent of her neck as if it was nectar of the gods.

'Trouble seems to be something you are exceptionally good at.'

Nic swaggered round the front of the car, leaned in and murmured. 'Oh I'm good at lots of things. Especially heat, ice queen. Speaking of which—is this your natural habitat? Is a lion going to prowl from my wardrobe tonight?'

She nudged him away from her. 'Only if you get high enough. There's a bar on the north side that only sells vodka. Your kind of place.'

Obviously she knew more about him than he did about her. Or at least she thought she did.

'Do you watch me, Pia? When you help with Q Virtus?'
Clearly she'd been sent to Zanzibar in her father's stead,
and he wondered how many other meetings she'd attended.
Exactly how hands-on she was.

Pia flushed a little and turned to stare determinedly at
the forest of towering pine and Siberian spruce that he'd
only just noticed. The silvery twilight enhanced the sweep
of her cheek, the flawless pearl shimmer of her skin. He
couldn't take his eyes from her—was conscious of every
breath she drew, the way her full breasts rose and fell, the
tiny sigh of exhalation.

'At times I have to watch everyone; don't take it personally.'

'*Have* to?' he asked, and the question made her flinch—
as if she'd said something she shouldn't have. 'So you help
to run Q Virtus as well as Merpia?'

Not forgetting this hotel and whatever other companies
besides. He wasn't sure why he was coming over so incredulous. It wasn't as if a man couldn't manage—why not
her? *Because deep down, despite the signs of power, you
thought she was salad dressing. The pampered daughter
of a powerful man, with a healthy ego to boot, who helps
out around the office looking pretty.*

That he was comparing her to his mother bothered him.
An heiress who did the bare minimum in the boardroom
to reach the country club by noon. But Pia seemed to take
it far more seriously than that. She hadn't stopped working for five seconds since they'd left Zanzibar; her phone
continually bonged with mail, or texts, or calls from some
nameless face she spoke proficiently to with that icy cool
composure that simultaneously made him shiver and want
to divulge her of her clothing to warm her up.

He'd underestimated her, and for a second he wondered
what else he was missing. Wondered if his certainty that
she would quickly tumble into his bed wasn't a product of
arrogant folly.

Pia smiled wryly, as if she knew exactly what he was thinking. He didn't like being transparent. It boded ill. The only way he'd get through the next few days was to be as mysterious as her father and say nothing that would jeopardise their meeting in Paris.

'Q Virtus takes up some of my time, yes,' she said, as if choosing her words carefully.

And with the past swimming round his head like sharks intent on their prey it was on the tip of his tongue to say, *It won't when I'm finished, so I hope you have a career-change*, but she'd switched gear so quickly he reckoned he'd have whiplash by morning. Which was just as well. Because it occurred to him that the voice of his conscience was getting louder, demanding to be heard. Soon he'd be forced to listen to the repercussions of crushing Pia's world, along with her father. And he didn't want to hear it—didn't want to know.

'You have two choices of sleeping arrangements.'

'I thought you'd never ask, *querida*. Show me the way.'

She shook her head, as if despairing of an incorrigible boy. 'Either one of the cabins, or inside the hotel on an ice bed. Whichever you choose it will be hiking distance from my room, I assure you.'

Ice bed? Like hell. 'But who will keep me warm?' he asked, lending his voice a seductive lilt that promised sinful debauchery.

Nic told himself the tremor that rustled over her was thanks to him and not to the abysmal temperatures in this godforsaken place. He had to snatch encouragement where he could.

'I'll send a member of staff with extra blankets—and before the thought even enters your head, Carvalho, the staff are strictly off-limits here. Please spare me the headache of getting rid of another girl.'

That was another thing. He didn't like the reminder that he was responsible for getting a Petit Q fired. He'd been on the phone all morning, trying to find her, all to no avail. It was as if she'd disappeared like a spectre into the night. It made him distinctly uneasy.

'What's the matter, Nic?' she asked sweetly—a striking contradiction to the inscrutable fire in her kohl-rimmed eyes. 'Worried about your little friend?'

Dios, he was becoming as transparent as glass. But he lavished himself with the theory that she was jealous and used the opening for what it was. *Perfect*.

'Maybe all the rumours of you Merisis being Greek mafia make people suspicious?'

She let loose a humourless laugh. 'What colourful imaginations people have. I promise you, the Merisis have never had any association with the mafia, and when I find out who started that uproar he'll have to answer to me.'

'Not to Zeus?'

'Oh, absolutely. Zeus too. And if you think *I'm* scary you've seen nothing yet.'

'Scary? You are a pussycat, *bonita*.'

'Keep pushing and you'll feel my claws,' she grated out.

Nic grinned. 'Promises, promises…'

The main doors opened before them and Pia's countenance shifted, lighting up like a child on Christmas morning. Such elation, such a beautiful sight. It made something unfurl in the space behind his ribs and flap like the wings of a bird. *Weird*.

Arched tunnels were held aloft by ice columns currently being sculpted by artists with chisels and picks. In the next room ice chairs were being carved into throne-like works of art. In fact the actual artwork was so stunningly intricate the time it must have taken to create the place had to be astounding.

Pia was talking away with a luminous light in her eyes that was just as breath-stealing. 'The walls, fixtures, fittings, even the drinking glasses are made entirely of ice or compacted snow and held together with snice. Which I suppose would be your equivalent of mortar.'

'You love this place, don't you?' he asked.

Splaying her fingers, she glossed over a smooth ice table. 'I like art, and this place is a year-round art project. I like to see it planned and built, the ice chiselled and shaped. I love the fresh crisp air. I can finally breathe in purity rather than the fumes of a car or a jet. This place is magical to me. When it melts in spring I always feel sad, but when it's rebuilt, given another chance to come to life and give joy, I feel...' Her smooth, delicate throat convulsed. '*It* feels reborn.'

Nic almost lost his footing on the discarded shards of ice block scattered over the ground.

Mesmerising was the only word he could think of when she talked that way. Candidly, yet almost dazed. As if she was miles away. He'd hazard a guess she'd forgotten who she was talking to. But Nic hadn't missed the way she'd hitched on her words and spoken as if she'd seen so much darkness and ugliness in her life that the idea of being reborn appealed to her.

When she caught him staring she frowned. 'Do I have icicles running off my nose?'

Nic had no idea what possessed him, but he curled his arm about her waist, pulled her up against him and pressed his warm lips against her frozen little nose.

Just as before, she remained motionless. Not resisting, not exactly passive, but it was as if he held a vat of explosive energy that was too compressed and thought better of daring to move.

After a while he became concerned that she would pass out from lack of oxygen so he eased back. 'Better?'

A gorgeous flush pinkened her cheeks, but the pensive pleat in her brow said she didn't trust him as far as she could throw him. Which even he could admit wasn't very far.

Gingerly, she stepped backwards. 'Yes, thank you.'

'You're very welcome,' he said huskily, wanting her back in his arms, crushed tighter against him. 'So, are we the only guests here?'

'Afraid so. Other guests won't arrive for another week or two.'

She backed up another step, creating a gulf as vast and bleak as the Grand Canyon. If she wasn't the main player in his game of revenge he would be worried that the distance made him feel…empty.

'I think we should turn in for the night.'

'Let's not. The night is still young. I say we ditch our bags and hit the bar. Join me?' When she gave her head a little shake he unleashed the big guns and smiled with every ounce of sinful charm in his arsenal. 'Please, *bonita*?'

Hot loganberry juice warming her hands, Pia tipped her head back to gaze at a sky full of darkness and began to count the stars within a mind grid. When they didn't make an even number her clavicle started to itch so she started again. Anything to distract her from the man lounging obscenely close beside her—those dark bedroom eyes lingering on her throat as he threw out pheromones in great hulking waves.

There really shouldn't be anything sexy about a man padded out in warm gear, knocking back vodka as if it was mineral water.

Pia had coaxed him outdoors before he either drove her insane or destroyed the bar. His mere presence had cranked the temperature in the room so high she'd imagined the ice melting, pouring down the walls in silvery droplets until there was nothing left but the midnight stars.

Right then she felt the shift in the air. 'Wait for it… watch.'

'I am watching.'

'No, you're not, you're watching me.' And it was starting to annoy her. The contrived deceit of it. Why would Nic truly be interested in bedding a cold, uptight, neurotic mess like her? He wouldn't. This was a bet, a deal, and she'd do well not to go all jelly-legged next time he kissed her frozen nose. '*Now*. Look up.'

A whirlwind of pale green light appeared and swirled above, the streaks tossed about with abandon. Then dark red clouds of fire pulsated in waves and arcs, undulating against the midnight sky and darting towards the heavens.

It was a collision of energetic charged particles that never failed to make her heart float in her chest and her blood sing a chorus of joy that she was still alive.

'*Dios*. I take back everything I said. This is amazing, Pia. I've heard of the Northern Lights but this…'

'Aurora Borealis—named after Aurora, the Roman goddess of dawn, and Boreas, the Greek name for the north wind.'

Nic tutted good-naturedly. 'Should've known the Greeks would have something to do with it.'

Pia pursed her lips to contain a smile. Okay, so she had this fluttery feeling going on in her chest. It was bizarre. Not at all like the soft and gentle flapping of butterflies' wings people spoke of—no, no, no. More like pterodactyls swooping and clipping her heart with every pass. Actually, maybe bizarre was the wrong word. Terrifying was more like it.

She snuck a peek at him from the corner of her eye, then cursed herself for the urge.

Languid and sprawled out on the bench seat beside her, head tipped back, thick glossy hair curling in waves over his collar, he was simply too gorgeous for words. He was gazing upward, his whisky eyes full of awe and Pia shuddered with the need to taste the liquor glistening on his full mouth.

Why did looking at him make her want so much? Long for him to pull her into his arms.

The ache in her chest bloomed into self-disgust when he caught her staring and conjured up one of those glorious smiles that did odd things to her internal organs. Like jiggle them around a bit.

'What's the plan for tomorrow?' he asked.

'I'm touring some land where we're considering building more warm lodges. I'll be gone all morning.'

'*We* will be gone all morning,' he shot back, in that honed Carvalho dominating tone.

The very one she ignored.

'I can't see the huskies liking you, *Lobisomem*. They know a threat when they see it. Astute creatures.'

'I've never understood that moniker,' he said.

She didn't miss the way he'd brought the topic right back round to Zeus. She chalked up the ability to his incredibly shrewd mind. The *why* of it was what escaped her.

'Maybe Zeus saw a predator in you.'

'What's with the Greek mythological connotations anyway?'

'My great-grandfather started the club and he was obsessed with the stories. He was also a successful businessman in his own right, and if you ask me I'd say the control went to his head. In the years before he died he apparently believed himself a god. Sounds like a whacko to me.'

'Does your father believe himself a god, Pia?'

His voice was hard enough to shatter the bench they sat upon.

Had her father believed himself a god? 'I have no idea.' Sometimes she'd had no clue what had gone through his head.

'None? Are you saying you aren't close?'

She resisted the compulsion to shuffle in her seat. 'If you're speaking in terms of general proximity then no, we're rarely close.' She knew fine well he wasn't, but this was the last thing she wanted to discuss. Just prayed he'd drop it.

'I'm talking about emotions, *querida*, and you know it. A trip to the zoo when you were in pigtails. A loving face in the crowd at your school recitals. A celebratory meal when you passed your exams. Now sharing a bottle of wine and laughing over dinner, reminiscing over the good times. *Close*. As a father and daughter should be.'

A mass of stark yearning hit her shockingly hard in the solar plexus and she bowed forward, pretending to adjust the ties on her boots to ease the pain. She was unsure why she should feel that strongly, since her father had given her the important things in life—a roof over her head, food on the table and some measure of calm.

She sat upright and drank the last mouthful of logan-berry, the sweet tartness exploding on her tongue. 'Not in the least,' she said. Only to wish the words back a second later. How pitiful they sounded. The empathy in his eyes didn't help. Whisky eyes, warm enough to melt her heart. *Impossible*.

'Any brothers or sisters?' he asked.

Translation: *Are you his only heir?*

Pia held an exasperated sigh in check. She wasn't sure how much longer she could take this. Every word, every touch had an ulterior motive. Most likely even his warmth and sincerity. And *still* there she was, cradling that soft, secret place inside her, hopelessly wishing he spoke the truth and wanted nothing more than to genuinely know her. Such a fool. She knew better.

'No brothers or sisters. You?'

'Only child too. One of those impossible dreams, but my mother... Well, let's say she wasn't particularly maternal.'

Join the club.

It wasn't until he said, 'Not close to her, then?' that she realised she'd said it out loud. Good God, she *had* to get away from him!

Digging her feet into the ground for a firm hold, she stood tall. 'I need some sleep. There's no need for you to come along tomorrow, so do yourself a favour and stay warm in your chalet bed.' *Give me some peace—leave me be, please.*

'You couldn't *pay* me to sleep on ice. I suppose to you it's like coffins for vampires.'

He said it with a wicked smile, as if he was trying to lighten the mood, but it went down like a lead balloon.

She gave him a withering glare. 'Aren't you hilarious? You should've been a comedian.' Though in a way he was right. She wanted the cold to numb the sensation of him, banish the heat he injected into her veins.

'I still don't understand what would possess you to sleep in the main hotel on packed ice. Believe me, if you knew what it was like to sleep on the streets—'

'It's an experience,' she said quietly, glancing at the doors to the Ice Castle with a painful kind of desperation.

'Ah,' he said derisively, and the change in him drew her eyes back to his. 'Like those celebrities who go to developing nations and starve just to know what it feels like. Except they can't *possibly* know what real, true, gripping hunger feels like. So if you're trying to prove something...'

On and on he went, and his tone got harder and more cynical. Right then he reminded her so much of her father that she started to shake and she...she... *Don't say it, Pia. Don't do it.*

Throat raw and swollen, every word hurt as they tore from her mouth. 'Maybe I do it not only for the experience but because I've been there, and I need to remember where I've come from so I can see what I've achieved. Maybe I like to feel the cold biting into my back in order to feel grateful that I'm one of the lucky ones and I now have a warm bed every night. And *that,* Mr Carvalho, is something I'll never take for granted. *Ever. Again.*'

Pia squeezed her eyes shut, hating both of them in that moment. She couldn't believe she'd just told him that.

Oh, come on, Pia, deep down you wanted him to know

you've shared some of his darker days, that you have some-thing in common. That you're more than the sum total of your parts.

Nic blinked up at her, jaw slack. 'When? I don't under-stand…'

'For the first seventeen years of my life. So don't you *dare* judge me!'

'Where was your father?'

'I wouldn't know, okay? I didn't meet him until I was seventeen. Now, if you'll excuse me, I need some sleep.' Her voice sounded quivery and she hated it—*hated* it. And—*oh, my God!*—the backs of her eyes were stinging.

'Hey, hey…' he said, launching from the bench and reaching for her, strong arms wide open.

Pia backed away. 'Don't.' *Or I'll beg you to hold me and I refuse to crumble, especially in front of you.*

He clenched his hands into fists and then raked his fin-gers through his hair. 'Okay, but let me come along in the morning. I'd love to see the land. I promise no more talk of your father—the past is out of bounds. I just want to spend some time with you. Okay?'

She said nothing.

'Okay?' he repeated, this time adding a touch of con-cern and a dash of despair to his act. And that was the final nail in *his* coffin.

CHAPTER SIX

SHE'D GONE WITHOUT him. The beautiful, obstinate, control freak that she was.

Nic let go of a sigh, heavy with annoyance and frustration.

One step forward, two steps back. For every tiny piece of information he squeezed from her she retreated farther away from him and he only had himself to blame. Pushing, pushing, *pushing* her to talk about her father, her past. Clearly that cool, calm composure had cracked under the strain.

The virtue of patience had been a blessing to him in the past few years. He'd had little choice but to bide his time. Until now. Now he wanted her surrender. *Needed* it to get to Zeus and destroy Q Virtus, he told himself for the millionth time. And yet…he *did* want to spend time with her.

The hell of it was, she intrigued him. He wanted to know how her mind ticked. How she juggled so many balls. What drove her. Why she hadn't known her father for the first seventeen years of her life.

So many questions that had nothing to do with taking Zeus to Hades and everything to do with the invisible rope that pulled him towards her when she was near. Like the *femme fatale* she was. Spell-binding him, luring him in, toying with him like a cat would a mouse.

His mouth twisted at the ridiculous notion. Nic knew

what he was doing, had a firm grip on the reins of his control, and no woman had the power to beguile him in deceit.

The log burner crackled, popped and hissed as he peered out of the window at the heavy grey skies, wondering how long she'd been gone and if she'd make it back in time before those laden clouds wept snow over the packed ice. An idyllic picture that struck him as nature's trick to disguise peril.

Nic smiled wryly and shook his head. Granted, he didn't feel like himself this morning, but now even the weather was duplicitous? What was more, the slosh and churn of worry inside him was a surprise he hadn't foreseen. Nor was the thought of her cosying up to her *friend* Jovan on a wooden slatted bench, covered in heavy fur rugs, being hauled by huskies across the snowy plains. A scene from some dreary romantic chick flick that likely flicked her switch. And why did that idea drive him to drink like a crazy *pessoa*?

Ah, careful, Nic. Jealousy will take you into the realms of obsession and beyond.

Like hell it would.

The irony of the situation knocked him sideways with the heft of a midfield striker. To anyone looking in there he was, waiting for the little wife to come home, and just like that he was staring at his father pacing the floors, fists clenched, waiting for Nic's mother to return from some shopping trip with friends, or lunch with her clique, or— worse—a night dancing about town. Always obsessing. Possessive. Angry when she wasn't home. Furious when she ignored him. Unstable. Erratic. Unnatural in Nic's eyes.

Narciso had asked him why he was considering marrying Eloisa Goldsmith. Truth was, while he'd loved his parents, after years of witnessing their volatile marriage he refused to sign up for the same fate.

Such love. Such passion. Such a hideous disaster.

His mood now a mire of filth, sucking him into the dangerous quicksand of the past, he slammed his feet into his boots and shoved his arms into the puffy warmth of his ski jacket. The thought of standing here waiting around for Olympia Merisi to grace him with her presence was taking him from vile to hostile.

Nic pulled the cabin door closed behind him and negotiated the packed ice, his feet crushing the thin dusting of new-fallen snow as he tramped down the path towards the main lodge. Huge white puffs of his breath formed in front of his face as he cursed the lack of Wi-Fi in his room. 'Going back to nature' translated to revisiting the Dark Ages as far as he was concerned.

The lodge greeted him with a warm blast of air and the sharp tang of espresso, but that, amazingly, wasn't the source of his overwhelming surge of relief. In the far corner of the main room sat Pia's sidekick, talking animatedly with another man, and he *hated* how the sight mollified him beyond measure. For pity's sake! He was not jealous. Or obsessed. He wasn't anything of the sort.

By the time he'd settled in front of his laptop and fired off a few e-mails to encourage the ruckus and fan the flames at Q Virtus he craved a long drink and his sanity. So he did what any sensible person would do in this situation. Rang his grandfather. To remind himself exactly why he'd chased a woman across Europe.

'Nicandro!' Instantly that gruff voice eased the tension that threatened to spiral out of control.

'Avô, how are you, old man?'

'Fine, fine, my boy. Just whooping Oscar here at Gin Rummy. Man doesn't know how to lose gracefully. Spat his teeth out twice in the last five minutes.'

Nic laughed out loud. 'You're a shark, Avô.'

'How was Zanzibar?'

'Hot.' In every way imaginable. Shocking. Satisfying. Frustrating. Nic condensed twenty-four hours of breaking and entering, gun-wielding, being tied to a chair and meeting the most stunning woman in the world to, 'Nothing to write home about.' Else the man would have heart failure and it was Nic's turn to look after *him*.

'Are you on your way back? I have a date with Lily tonight but I can put her on the back burner.'

Nic pictured that old Cary Grant style movie star face and silver hair. 'No, old man. No need. Go see Lily—enjoy yourself. I've stopped off in Finnmark, Norway. Minus fifteen if we're lucky.'

'*What?* Who the devil wants to go to Norway?'

Nic grinned, thinking they'd been almost his exact words.

'Forgot your origins, boy? Brazil—land of soccer and samba. A Santos needs heat. What's in Norway? A woman?'

Nic could hear the usual cacophony of chortles and chatter in the background and his heart ached. *Dios*, he missed this man. '*Sim*, Avô. A woman.'

'A special woman if Nicandro Carvalho traipses after her.'

Special? Yeah, she probably was. Not that it mattered.

'A necessary woman.' *If I'm to restore your glory. Place Santos Diamonds back in your hands before I lose you.*

The mere thought made Nic press his lips together and fight the sting at the back of his eyes. The fact that his grandfather had only a few good years left had kicked him into high gear, and he wouldn't downshift or stamp on the brakes until he'd reached the end of the road. A gift for the man who'd cradled him as a baby when his mother could not. Or maybe would not. What did it matter? Nic had still loved her like crazy. Her stunning face and her million-dollar sassy smile. She'd been zest and spirit and fiery heart and, yes, a big ol' handful of trouble—but there'd been something endearing about that. At least to him.

The one time she'd attended a football match she'd stood in seven-inch stilettos, a long cigarette in her hand, huge sunglasses covering half her face, yelling at the referee to 'Get that dirty brute off my son's back!' After that Nic had appealed to her well-deserved vanity, told her she distracted the players—no lie: her figure had stopped traffic—and asked her to stay away, else his reputation would have gone to the dogs.

His reflection in the window gazed back at him, wistful and nostalgic, and like a freight train another image rolled over him, just as vivid.

Himself at fourteen, when she'd picked him up from school—two hours late—raised a perfectly plucked brow and asked if he'd lost his virginity yet. He'd blushed and stammered and told her to shut up.

Hopeless in the maternal stakes, truly the farthest thing from a tree-hugging, celery-crunching supermom, but what she *had* been was a glorious, fun-loving woman who hadn't deserved to die. Certainly not with a cry lodged in her throat and a bullet in her head. Triggered by the man who—

Pain so acute it set his heart on fire made him gasp sharply, and he tried to cover the choking noise with a cough.

'Nic, my boy? What's wrong? Is there something you're not telling me?'

The concern in his grandfather's voice yanked him back to the here and now, just as it had done thirteen years ago and then continued for endless harrowing months as he'd harangued him to stand, then to walk—one small step, then two, then four. While Nic had bathed in a vile pit of despair and rage, wishing he'd just died in the same red river as his parents and the dreams of his youth.

There he'd been, dubbed the next Brazilian football sensation, destined to play with the best team in the world, lying with a bullet in his back. *Game over.*

Nic squeezed his eyes shut and cleared his throat. '*Non,* Avô. Everything is well. Everything is going to be just fine. As it should have always been.'

The sound of aged breathing, heavy from Cuban cigars and cognac told Nic he hadn't quite managed to disguise his turmoil.

'What have I always told you, Nicandro? Stand up, walk forward. Do not turn and look back or you will fall.'

Impossible. He was so at rock-bottom there was no void beneath him in which to plunge. *You also told me there were answers to be found, people to repay, legends to restore. So I stood and I walked forward to do just that.*

'Worry not, Avô. We'll talk again soon.'

'No, Nicandro, my boy, *wait*. Promise me you will return safe.'

'Always. *Tchau*, Avô.'

Nic's thumb pressed the 'end call' button and he gripped the handset as he stared beyond the glass. Beyond the cobwebs of frost glistening on the panes. Beyond the thick pelts of snow driving from the east. To the dark clouds laden with the promise of a continuous storm. Nature at its most dangerous.

By the time he'd sobered up he was frowning at the darkness. *Where are you,* querida? *Don't disappear on me now. I need you.* To quench this lust. To incinerate this incongruous need. To get him to Paris for the next step in his end game.

Sensing Jovan shift at his side, Nic shoved his fists inside his jacket pockets. 'She should've been back hours ago.'

Black eyes glared at him. 'Like you care. Or maybe you just care for the wrong reasons. I am on to you, Carvalho. You are not what you seem and I am watching you.'

The poor attempt to intimidate Nicandro Carvalho made him smile coldly. 'How does it feel to want a woman who doesn't want you back?'

'You tell me,' Jovan sneered, before walking away.

Nic's fists clenched with murderous intent as fire raged behind his ribs. Had she told her *friend* their chemistry was one-sided? Told him not to fret because she felt nothing but ice inside? Yet what really bothered him, he realised, was that the man might be right, and Nic felt his heart sink with the thought that she didn't desire him at all. That those seductively coy glances and the burning heat in her violet-blue eyes was all an act.

But what was seriously disturbing was that right now he couldn't care less. Either way, he wanted her back here. With him.

The striking solitary landscape was tinged with blue from the cold and deep orange from the sun's struggle towards the horizon and Pia breathed deeply, trying to ease the anxiety knotting her insides. Or was it guilt that she'd left without Nic?

'I'd love to see the land...spend time with you...'

He'd seemed so sincere, but every time she wanted to think the best of him she napalmed the idea.

'The storm is coming in, Miss Merisi. I vote we take a shortcut back to the Castle early. Either through the forest or across the lake.'

'One moment,' Pia told her guide, Danel, as she snapped another shot of the clearing. 'This land is perfect—especially with the salmon river close by for cold sea fishing.'

She'd taken enough photos. He knew it. She knew it. Problem was, she didn't want to go back. Not yet. She only wanted to ignore Nic's magnetic pull a while longer, to enjoy the beauty and tranquillity before he dragged her into another whirlwind of unwanted memories, unfathomable need and sleep deprivation.

'Miss Merisi, please. We must head back.'

Pia closed her eyes, inhaled a lungful of cleansing air and trudged back towards the sled. 'I don't mind which way—your call.'

'We'll cut across the lake. Much quicker.'

Once she'd settled in her seat the silence was broken by

the panting of the huskies and the soft whoosh of the sled gliding over crisp white snow. As they skirted the dense woodland of towering spruce the scent of pine infused her mind and the rhythmic rocking lulled her tired, sore eyes to close. As long as she didn't dream of her mother again—anything but that…

She must have dozed, because the next thing she knew the sled had jolted sharply to the left and the sound of spooked huskies filled her ears with piercing whimpers.

Pia bolted upright. 'What's wrong?' Then she shivered violently as streaks of icy water ran down her face, soaked her hair. God, she must have been out of it.

Danel struggled with the reins as snow thrashed against his face. 'Storm came out of nowhere. Hold on—we'll take cover in the forest.'

Fear lodged in her chest and she gripped the edge of the bench until her knuckles screamed. *Don't panic. You've been through worse, far worse than this.*

The sled veered right, the movement holding her on a knife-edge. Visibility was virtually non-existent, and then it all happened so fast her head spun.

The sled tipped. The sound of grinding wood tore through her ears. As did the distinct crack of ice.

Danel yelled over the furious howl of the wind, his words muffled. Obscured. Then she was tossed up into the air like a ragdoll, only to plunge to the hard-packed surface, the agonising crash sending pain shooting through her body.

A cry ripped from her throat, then her head smacked off the unforgiving lake and her last thought—that she'd done the right thing, was glad she'd left without Nic and he was safe back in his cabin—was obliterated as the lights went out.

He'd had enough. Nic couldn't take it any more.

The thundering, purposeful stride that had brought him

to this place, this woman, took him to the manager's suite on the other side of the lodge via the snow that swirled in eddies and whorls, whipping at his skin and biting through his clothes.

Nic burst through the door, sending papers flying off the desk. 'I want a search party out there for the last hour of light. She's been gone too long.'

'We don't have anyone to send—'

'I'll go myself. Give me a map of their route and get me a four-by-four. I can ice-drive with the best of them.'

'I am sure all is well, sir. I—'

'Do it. *Now*.' His lethal voice caromed around the room and he watched the ruddy complexion of the man pale and bead with sweat. And all the while Nic's guts roiled with worry and dread and an outcome that didn't bear thinking about.

Nor did the reasons why.

CHAPTER SEVEN

PIA'S TEMPLES THROBBED, pain swirled around her head, but worst of all she was cold. So cold. And she was so tired of being cold.

This couldn't be real, but it felt so much like reality it was frightening. She kept having brief flickers of *déjà-vu* as hands grabbed her arm, manacling her at the shoulder and wrist, bruising as they pinned it to the bed.

'No, no, *please*—get off me!'

White light flickered in front of her closed eyelids, the black beats in between like snapshots of time replaying in her mind...

Voices. Her mother's shrill. And Pia knew Mama was on the ledge again, fighting with an opium haze of madness, because her panic slithered through the cracks in Pia's basement door like curling wisps of smoke, threatening to choke her.

Karl yelled, 'We've gotta run—they're coming after us.'

Pia's legs buckled as drawers opened and slammed shut. Drug money. The dealers. Coming after them. *Oh, God.*

'It's her damn fault, that useless kid of yours. No good for nothing. She didn't take the money.'

No, no! When she'd gone to deliver the money they'd wanted far more than cash from her and she'd run. *It wasn't her fault—it wasn't. It really wasn't.*

'So we'll take her to Merisi and he can pay seventeen years of child support so we can disappear.'

Pia froze, ear pressed against the hollow door as the bottom fell out of her world. Child support? She had a daddy?

'To Zeus? No, Karl, he'll kill me.'

Her mother's voice shook. She was terrified.

'He doesn't know.'

Kill her? He sounded worse than *this* nightmare. She'd be trading one hell for another.

Nails black, deeply encrusted with dirt, Pia clawed at the door. Heart thumping frantically. *Don't leave me here, Mama. Take me with you. Please. I'll be better. I'll be good—do whatever you want. Just please take me with you.*

Then they were in Pia's room and holding her down, and she was thrashing and twisting and trying to sink her teeth into the arm that was pinning her hard.

'No, no, *no*—get off me!'

A big hand slapped across her cheek, setting her skin on fire, but she just got back up and clawed and hissed and screamed for her life.

Until that cold metal pricked her arm and freezing liquid seeped into her veins and peace finally stole her pain.

Memories, always ready with daggers—as Nic knew—were stabbing her subconscious, making her voice a wavering chord of desperation as she lay half-naked and ghastly pale beneath a blanket on his bed.

He couldn't keep still—just paced back and forth alongside while her slow, shallow breathing and mumbles and cries gripped him by the throat. He should have searched for her sooner. Another hour lying on the cracked ice of the lake, soaked through to the skin, and she would have been dead. Another hour from now and she *would* die if they couldn't warm her up. Hypothermia had set in, and unless she calmed down and allowed the drips...

Dios, she looked so vulnerable. *Was* so vulnerable. It was a fist in his heart as he remembered what it felt like to feel paralysed.

Another shriek ricocheted off his taut nerves.

'Do something, for heaven's sake!'

The man who *claimed* to be the senior of the two medics hovering tried to hold her arm still once more, but her every contorted muscle and frozen vein screamed genuine fear.

Pia brushed down her arms, her movements frantic yet uncoordinated as she shivered and slurred. 'Please...*please*, no! Don't do this.'

On and on she went, crying out for her mama, then talking of Merisi, Zeus—private, personal nightmares—and he *hated* it. Hated that she was baring her soul in such an anguished, agonising way in front of complete strangers. He wanted them gone. Would have banished them from the room if he could.

Instead he said, in a voice that brooked no argument and warned of dire consequences, 'She's delirious—has no idea what she's saying or doing.'

Nic watched silvery tears trickle down her temples as her energy depleted and she turned to look him right in the eye. '*Please*...don't...do this to me.'

That was it. That heart-wrenching plea coming from a woman like Pia was the final straw.

'Stop. Just *stop*! Her heart must already be at risk from the strain, and if she gets any more worked up—'

'She needs to get warm quickly. Intravenous fluids are the way to go. Unless we bypass her blood, warm it through, but that's still going through a vein.'

'That's it? Those are our options? *Dios!*' His voice sounded as if he'd swallowed a razorblade. He couldn't stand seeing her like this. It made him want to crawl out of his own skin.

'My only other suggestion would be for you to get in there. Skin to skin. It'll probably take longer, but it should still work.'

Right—*right*. Why hadn't he thought of that? *Because she obliterates your brain cells, that's why.*

'This would have been useful ten minutes ago,' he gritted out. With a deft roll of his shoulders his heavy coat slipped down his back and he tossed it over the nearest chair.

'We didn't think there would be a problem, and...' This from the second medic. A tall redhead who was staring at his hands as he uncuffed his shirt.

'You may leave.' He punctuated the words by grabbing his shirt at the tails and tearing it open.

The redhead's lips parted and colour flushed her white skin as buttons bounced off walls and pinged off the floors. He toed off his shoes and went to work on his trousers and her eyes trailed down his flexing biceps, across his wide chest, then paused as he hooked his thumbs into the waistband of his briefs.

Fighting the shivers that could only have come from being outside half the night in minus fifteen freaking degrees, Nic stared down at Pia, lying on the bed, eyes closed, trembling.

Commando or not?

She was out of it, but he didn't want her waking up in his bare arms being frightened. Didn't want her to think he'd taken advantage of her for a second. *Innocent* wasn't a word he would associate with her, but where sex was concerned, or being comfortable naked, in your own skin...? He wasn't so sure about that.

'I can leave her bra and panties on, yes?'

'They look insubstantial enough, so I doubt they'd make much difference.'

'From this moment it is not your place to look,' he growled, throwing in a lethal glare for good measure. Ridiculous as it was, his protective instincts had kicked in with a ferociousness that astounded him. 'I repeat. You may leave.'

He ushered them out through the door, agitated by the way the redhead was devouring him with her eyes. Why couldn't Pia look at him like that? Then maybe she wouldn't have swanned off without him this morning and he would have been there all along to keep her safe.

Once he'd locked his door behind them he was back to the bed, fingers flexing on the corner of the blanket. Nervous? Eager? He didn't know. His concern was so overwhelming it drowned every other emotion out.

Gingerly, he pulled the covers back, just enough to allow him to slip beneath. Nic tried to shut off every thought in his head, loath to admit to the arousing anticipation of feeling those lush curves against him. Then he sent up a prayer of thanks that he'd kept her in her underwear as— *Fala serio*, could someone cut him some slack, *please*?— frivolously skimpy as it was.

Under the covers, he didn't pause to take a breath, not wasting a second of time when his heat could be seeping into her body, protecting her life.

It hit him then. What he was doing. Saving the daughter of the man who'd destroyed his parents and almost taken Nic's life. He could hurt Zeus in the same way—make him feel the same pain Nic had felt for so long. An eye for an eye. But the fact was it wasn't in him. Not even if Pia had pulled the trigger herself. He simply wasn't made that way. Life was too precious to take.

No pause, no hesitation, he tucked one arm under her shoulders and eased her against him, front to front, skin to skin, cheek to cheek. All her softness against his hard strength. Cold flesh against heat. He'd expected a struggle, at least a murmur of protest. What he got was a contented purr when, like a kitten, she burrowed and nuzzled closer, as if trying to climb into his body, where it was warm, so she could go to sleep, protected and safe.

Nic cupped her head, tucked her into the warm space where his neck met his shoulder and gently wrapped his leg around hers until they were one, until the only thing that could be missing was his hardness sliding inside her.

Oddly enough, this felt closer—an affection he'd never experienced before. Far more intimate than sex could ever be.

Nic lay there, holding her, gently stroking her hair, burying his nose in the damp waves, inhaling the cold scent that lingered on her body and there…right *there*…was the faintest hint of that velvety black scent she wore like a sultry signature: jasmine and gardenia and something elusive that sang to his body in a siren's song. And, *Dios*, it turned him to stone. He shifted and cursed under his breath, trying his damnedest to ignore the lush satiny dips and curves that fitted perfectly against him.

Tried, too, to quieten every alarm bell shrilling in his head, not to think about what might have been for the first seventeen years of her life. *Too late.*

At the age when Nic was kicking a football around a field and fishing in the river with his Avô, with not a concern or care in the world for anyone or anything, Pia had been living in her own kind of hell. The fact that she'd been subjected to drugs and abuse from her own mother made him want to lash and snarl and bite like the werewolf she claimed him to be. He realised, too, that her father must have taken her in, taken care of her…

It was a conflicting choking agony to want to feel gratitude to the man who'd caused his parents' deaths, if only for a second. It tore at his heart even to think it. Yet he was glad Pia had found a better life and a reason for living.

'Is that why you work so hard for him?' he whispered as he kissed her flaxen hair.

Nic finally allowed himself to think of the high likelihood that he'd take Pia down with her father. It made his ribcage contract but he'd come too far for too long to be swayed by emotions now. *She'll hate you. Yes, she will.*

He flinched as she startled him with a soft reply.

'Keep me,' she breathed.

What was she saying? That she worked so hard so her father would keep her?

Nic squeezed his eyes shut and used every weapon at his disposal, every memory he could find, to banish the tumultuous thoughts storming through his mind.

She whimpered and Nic hushed her. 'Sleep *querida*, I have you.' For now.

CHAPTER EIGHT

PIA TRIED TO rouse herself time and again from the murky waters of sleep but it kept tugging her back into the nebulous depths. First there'd been darkness and moonlight, then the glare of the midday sun, but her bones had ached so badly she'd snuggled back into the hard-packed mattress and let it happen.

Not this time. Now the warm scent of expensive cologne tempted and teased her senses awake. Skin and a light dusting of soft hair against her cheek—warm, so warm, and achingly wonderful. She sighed in contentment.

She felt as if she'd slept for days, and as she coaxed her eyes open to the golden fingers of dusk stroking the windowpane she wondered if that were true.

Had she ever been so lazy and sweet inside? Never—

Pia jerked upright so fast the room spun like a whirly top. What the—?

Her gaze snapped to Nic, lying beside her, and her belly clenched with hot longing at the sight of him—so strong, so masculine, and yet so vulnerable. Face relaxed, as if sleep was his only peace, those long sooty black lashes rested against the tender skin beneath his eyes in decadent arcs.

She was dying to run her hand over his defined chest, that rigid six-pack and his flat, ripped stomach, the hipbones jutting just shy of his boxers…

Then it hit her. He was practically naked. And so was she!

'Nic…?' Grabbing the sheet, she covered her breasts and

bottom-shuffled sideways to the edge of the bed. What had he done to her? What had *they* done? 'You…you…snake!'

Stretching with all the lethargic might of a big sleepy lion basking in the sun, he blinked up at her over and over, as if clearing the fog from his eyes. It took a while, and Pia just sat there watching him, her mind all over the place, trying to figure out how on earth she'd got into his bed. Then suddenly he snapped wide awake, and looked so ridiculously happy to see her that her heart leapt.

'You're awake?'

Pia pinched the back of her hand in self-test mode. 'I'd like to say that's a stupid question, but actually I have no idea.' Maybe she was still asleep and this was a dream. *A dream, Pia? Don't you mean a nightmare?*

He grinned wildly. 'Yep, there's that sharp tongue I like so much. You are definitely awake, *bonita*. You had me worried for a while there.'

When his hot gaze dropped to her lace bra he stared at her so hard she craved a shower. Whether hot or cold she couldn't say. Why did every day with him feel like Russian Roulette?

'Don't think for one minute this constitutes the terms of our bet!' At least she hoped to God it didn't. It rather depended on what had happened. Why couldn't she remember? This was awful. *Awful!*

Mischief sparkled in his whisky eyes, lighting them up with flecks of gold as he rolled onto his side playfully and propped his head on one hand. 'I didn't take you for a shirker, *querida*. You *did* beg.'

'I…I…I did?' She had? *Noooo.*

Nic raised one devilish brow and ran his tongue over that gorgeous mouth suggestively. 'Oh, yeah. I told you no over and over again, but would you listen?' He shook his head and tutted. 'No.'

There he was, the perfect picture of dissolute debauchery, tiptoeing his fingers over the rumpled linen and giving her thigh a sultry little stroke.

Pia shuddered and grappled with the blanket to cover her legs, but he was sprawled over them and he couldn't give a stuff—just smiled that bone-melting, tummy-flipping smile and kept on talking.

"'I'm cold, Nicandro.'"

The way he imitated her voice in a brazen purr and batted his eyelashes made her recoil in horror.

"'Please come to bed with me. I neeeeed you. Please.'"

She gasped in outrage at her own behaviour. Mentally scanned her body parts for sensations of wear and tear. Wear and tear? What was she? *A car?*

Okay, so she couldn't remember what *après sex* felt like, but she was darn sure she would feel something—right?

During her moments of castigation, as her mind flitted like a bird from one branch to another, he'd tugged the blanket away and inched closer, prowling like a feral wolf with hunger in his eyes. Pia looked down and watched his long fingers splay over the slight curve of her stomach, then curl around her waist.

Heat sizzled over her skin and her breath grew so shallow she began to hyperventilate.

'Come here, my beautiful Olympia. Kiss me. Just as you did last night.'

A tight, choking disbelief caught her by the throat. But there was no calculation in his eyes, none of the shrewdness she'd noticed in him before, and this joyful, impish innocence was a sharp deviation when she knew he had the tail of a scorpion.

Worse still, when had she got so lonely that she didn't care? Just wanted him near her.

'What did you do to me?' she asked, voice trembling as her pulse careened out of control.

Oh, God, she felt angry, and helpless, and frustrated that

she couldn't remember. But most of all—most alarmingly of all—she felt cheated!

With that thought, she tumbled backwards off the bed and landed in a sprawled heap. No grace to it whatsoever. Then she scrambled to her feet and edged away.

Predator. That was surely the word to describe him in that moment as he crawled across the mattress on all fours—big and agile and poetry in motion—the wickedness in his eyes making her lick her dry lips.

'Ah, you want me to *chase* you?' He drew the word out and added a naughty lilt to it.

'No!'

He sighed theatrically, as if they'd been through all this before. 'Which means yes.'

'No, it really doesn't! What is *wrong* with you?' He was being so frisky and light-hearted. Worlds apart from the practised charmer she'd come to expect.

And his body... *Wow.* All sex and power. The man might be Brazilian but he was like a Greek god. Broad shoulders and carved pecs, rounded thighs and long, athletic sculpted legs sprinkled with dark hair. Quite simply, he was delicious.

Slam. Her back hit the wall and he pressed up against her and thrust his hands into her hair. 'Shall I remind you, Pia? Remind you of the taste of my mouth?'

Yes. *Yes!* Nooooo—bad idea. Really.

She remained frozen, her blood pumping too fast in some places and too slowly in others. Her brain, for instance—no blood at all in there.

Nic cupped the back of her head, his fingers the perfect amount of tingly pressure on her scalp, and leaned in. He kissed the rim of her ear, nibbled on her lobe and whispered, 'Try to remember this one, would you, *bonita*?'

'I don't think...we've done this before.' Because it felt as if she was on the edge of discovery, at the gates of a bold new world. And it was exhilarating and scary all at once.

Electricity arced between them, the shock so violent that Nic jerked back an inch or two and locked onto her eyes. As they stared at one another, her breasts brushed against the hard wall of his chest with every stuttering breath she took. Heaven help her, she wanted it. *Him*. His kiss. Right now.

'You make me crazy, Pia,' he murmured, his gaze intense and considered. His breath a hot rush over her face. 'You turn me inside out and that is the honest truth.'

Leaning in, he touched his lips to hers and she felt as if she'd been plugged into the national power grid. Closing her eyes, she started to panic. Unsure if she could remember how to respond.

Then he laved his tongue along her lips and she opened up, unfurling to him, giving him her all. And in that moment she didn't think or plan or have an agenda. She simply moved and gave him permission to go deep and wet and erotic. Which was exactly what he did, with a feral growl that made her skin tighten.

One hand on her lower back, another between her shoulderblades; he pressed her sweetly but firmly against him. She'd never felt anything like it. Unbearably wonderful.

Pia squirmed closer. He pulled her tighter. *More.* More of the languorous touch of his tongue against her own. And she moaned at the sharp, masculine taste of him—potent and alluring.

It was the hottest, raunchiest, most sensual kiss she'd ever received in her life. He was practically licking her soul.

Nic tightened his hold and she went pliant, revelling in this place where neither of them was alone, letting her body bend to his will as the terror of yearning and the thrill of feeling overwhelmed her.

He started talking out a scene—what he craved doing to her—the words rolling lyrically from his talented mouth.

'I want to taste you everywhere, learn every dip and curve of your beautiful body, feel every inch of you in my hands.' He punctuated the words with the movement of those clever fingers, trailing down her arms—leaving goosebumps in his wake—then sliding them up her ribcage to cup her lace-covered breasts. Just that slight ease of pressure off her shoulders, the heat emanating from his touch, was the most delicious sensation on earth.

He kissed words along her jaw and ground his hips, pushing his groin against her. Pia moaned long and loud as the hot flesh between her legs beat a wanton tattoo and clenched, desperate for him to be inside her.

'I want to feel your surrender, Pia. Will you give it to me?'

Another kiss. Another hard press. More heat curling through her veins, swirling through her abdomen.

'I want to slide down your body and take your orgasm in my mouth. I would do anything…*anything* to taste you. Just once. Before I thrust into your glorious body and take you to heaven and back.'

She squirmed, gyrating back against him.

'You'd love that, wouldn't you, Pia? Me inside you. Taking you long and hard and deep.'

Yes. *Yes.*

Next thing Pia knew, she had *his* back plastered against the wall and she was kissing *him* ferociously—her hands in his thick glossy hair, up on her toes so his huge thick erection nudged her lace panties—unleashing a torrent of carnal need she'd had no idea she was capable of. The scent of him, the feel of his hard body under her seeking hands, was so heady she couldn't get enough. It sent her hormones, her adrenaline, her desire for him into orbit. And when he fisted her hair with one hand and squeezed her left breast with the other stars burst behind her eyelids.

Nic groaned. She almost climaxed. And the shock of it, of being so out of control, burning from the inside out, was like an arrow of ice spearing into her psyche.

Ice.

Mortification prickled over her skin and she wrenched away from him.

'You are ice and fire, Pia,' he breathed, that wide chest heaving.

Ice. *Ice.* Huskies whimpering. Ice cracking. Freezing water seeping into her skin.

'You…you…' It was worrying that that was all the eloquence she had. But, honestly, she was turning into a vacuous bimbo without a lick of sense. He was playing with her!

'Are a good kisser?' he suggested, still breathless, still too suave and sinful for his own good. '*Sim,* I know. You aren't too bad yourself. Come back here and we'll practise some more.'

The way he was looking at her was scary. As if he had voodoo powers—whether for evil or for good she *still* didn't know. But it was the kind that made her think he would keep her drugged on sex for weeks if she let him.

Never in a month of Sundays!

'You, *Lobisomem,* are the lowest of the low.'

Face flushed, he cocked an arrogant brow. 'You weren't saying that when you had your tongue down my throat, *querida.*'

'That was before I remembered the snowstorm. When was that? Yesterday? What happened? How did I get back here?'

He raked a palm across the high ridges of his abdomen as if his chest ached. 'I found you.'

Nic had come looking for her? 'Did you find Danel, too?'

'Yes. He fared a little better than you and came to visit earlier. And, before you ask, the huskies are also fine. They ran for cover in the forest.'

'Good. That's…good.' It hurt even to think, and when she tentatively rubbed the sore mound on the side of her head she winced at the deep throb of pain.

Okay. So he'd rescued them. But—

'How did I end up in your bed?' And on the verge on surrendering! 'Clearly you would've slept with me, taken advantage, just to win a bet,' she said scathingly. 'You would've let me believe it was too late!'

A dimple popped in his cheek as he clenched his jaw and those eyes grew dark with shadows. 'No. Instead I would've stopped before we'd gone too far. Told you you'd been sick with hypothermia and frightened of the needles, and that if I hadn't climbed into bed with you to warm you up death would've been mere hours away.'

Pia swayed where she stood, clinging to hostile suspicion as if it were a life raft. A raft that bobbed and tipped precariously as she recalled waking time and again, wrapped in a cashmere mist: Nic holding her tight, as if she were something precious.

He'd saved her life. First by searching for her and then holding her throughout the night and well into the day. Never moving from her side. And his touch hadn't been grudging or just necessary, because he wanted something in return. It had felt cherishing, gentle, almost covetous. A touch she'd never felt before but wanted to again. Desperately.

Tears stung the backs of her eyes. Not because she was hurting or upset or distressed but because the torrent of strange contrary sensations was close to overload. She was fighting this thing between them with everything she had, and right now it was breaking her.

It had to be the close call with death making her so emotional. *Had* to be.

Nic's sudden launch off the wall made her flinch, and she panicked in case she'd been staring with no filter on.

'I did what I had to do,' he said, brisk and decisive.

Pia could literally see him gathering up the tattered remnants of his control.

'Had to?' she repeated stupidly, commanding her body to stand tall, chin up, projecting nonchalance.

Bending at the waist, he swiped a T-shirt from the floor. One that looked as if it had been tossed away haphazardly in haste.

Smoothing the crumpled material down his chest, he finally met her eyes—and the sardonic smile he tipped her way wasn't quite right. It was sort of forced into hardness, and it made her stomach dive to the rug.

'Oh, I get it,' she said, imposing upon her tone its usual sass. 'How can you win our bet if I'm six feet under, right?'

He didn't bother denying it, just shoved his limbs into clothes as if he wanted nothing more than to run from the room.

All the happiness and wonder and joy from that life-shattering kiss drained out of her and in the void—as if clearing the toxic mess of emotions had given her the space to think clearly again—she picked over his words.

'Frightened? I was frightened of the needles?' Good God, what had she said?

'Petrified, Pia.'

He was looking at her so oddly she couldn't catch her breath. A humourless laugh was trapped in her throat, fluttering, as if she'd swallowed a moth. A choking, frantic tickle.

'Did I talk much? Say anything…interesting?'

A surge of shame hit her with the stunning force of a tidal wave as her filthy past crashed over her, coating her in anguish and dread. The possibility that Nicandro Carvalho might know where she'd come from, who she'd been. The damage he could cause her with that kind of information at his disposal. *But he doesn't know that you're Zeus. Just keep it together.*

'You made little sense, Pia, and said nothing of interest to anyone, I assure you.' All this talking was while he avoided her gaze, and she was positive he wasn't telling her the entire story.

Was he saying her secrets were safe with him? Could she

trust that? Maybe she could, because otherwise he would
have pushed for more, just as he always did. Poked and
prodded until he uncovered a rotting bed of grime.

'Pia!'

It wasn't until Nic shouted her name from across the
room that she realised she was about to keel over.

'*Dios!* I'm such an idiot. You shouldn't even be out of
bed. You'll be weak for days.'

'Your concern is so touching,' she jeered, covering her
embarrassment with sweet sarcasm.

He swept her up into his arms as if she weighed no
more than a child and walked across the floor, his bare
soles slapping on the hardwood, before gently lowering
her to the bed.

Pulling the blankets over her, he tucked her in. She
shouldn't adore the extraordinary contentment of being
fussed over, and nor should she consider going to the bathroom so he'd do it all over again.

'You are still sick, Pia. No more cold. No more ice. Tonight you sleep in my bed and tomorrow morning, when
the sun rises, I'm taking you somewhere warm.'

Not a chance. 'If I'm sleeping in this bed, *you* are on the
couch—and what's more I'm not going anywhere *warm*. I
have a stay-over in Munich and then—'

'I don't care if you have a meeting with the Queen of
England at Buckingham Palace. We made a deal. I came
here—now it's your turn to go where I wish. I have business in Barcelona, so to Barcelona we shall go.'

She didn't like that look. That arrogance and audacity
and command. It was a powerful combination of traits that
had made him a dominant force in real estate and one of
the most sought-after men in the world.

'And if I say no?'

'You'll be breaking the terms of our deal and I'll take
that as forfeit,' he said, with lethal softness.

'What terms?' She pulled the sheets higher over her

body, practically up to her nose. A bit late, of course, but her pride was on the floor in tatters and she needed all the help she could get.

'To spend time with me.'

Pia filled in what he wasn't saying. *To prove I am not so bad. To let me gain your trust.*

Yeah, right.

Collapsing back onto the pillows, she closed her eyes. He had a point. Fact was, she had little choice but to follow him. She still needed answers, needed to know if Nic was behind the propaganda, and she'd given her word. So she'd just have to play nice with the other children and compromise.

'Fair's fair, I suppose. I'll have to cancel my meeting in Munich.' She'd swear she could feel hives pop from her skin. Skin that begged for the scrape of her nails.

'You say that as if it's the end of the world. You've never cancelled a meeting before? Ever?'

'No.'

He paused with his arm halfway into the sleeve of his jacket and looked up. His hair was a tousled mess from her fingers. So gorgeous. 'Do you ever stop? Even for a moment?'

No. 'Why would I?'

'To live. Have fun. See friends. Be happy.'

'I do live.' She had no idea what fun was. As for friends—she didn't have the time. 'I am happy.' *Liar.* Pia and happiness were barely on speaking terms. And since when was she bothered?

She wished she could hit him right now.

'You keep telling yourself that while I head over to the lodge. I need to make the travel arrangements to Spain.'

Barcelona.

It was a horrible mistake. It had all the hallmarks of a

tragic ending. In fact she was starting to feel like the lead in a Shakespearean comedy.

So why was she sitting here, handing over control, waiting for him to turn the next page?

CHAPTER NINE

NIC SLAMMED THE Bugatti into fifth gear, pushed his foot to the floor and spun down the B-10 coast road heading into the heart of Barcelona town. On his right, the long sun-drenched waterfront skimmed the blue crystalline waters of the Balearic and on his left reclining in her seat, was the woman who was turning him inside out.

With a need for speed that echoed the years that had passed he drove himself harder, farther, faster. Running from his mournful memories or towards his predestined future, he wasn't sure.

This was all getting a bit close to home, he thought wryly, his accusation to Pia still fresh in his mind. *'Do you ever stop? Live. See friends. Be happy.'*

The hypocrisy of his words didn't escape him. Avô was rather fond of telling him he needed to slow down, play harder, be happier.

Happy? He couldn't remember the last time he'd felt the sweet tendrils of joy curl around his heart and lift the cumbersome weight of rage. Before yesterday, that was. His relief at seeing Pia up and about had floored him and he didn't want to over-analyse that. It certainly didn't mean he was developing any sort of…*feelings* for her. That would take the crowning glory for stupid moves on his part.

But, if he was being totally honest with himself, for the first time in years his purposeful stride had faltered. Nic would never forget the look on Pia's face—the fear that he knew of her past, the shame that had eviscerated the beautiful pink flush after his kisses.

Yes, okay, he'd wanted to push—to ask why, to dig, to find something he could use to demolish her father. Instead he'd stood there and looked into those exquisite violet-blue eyes, with the sultry taste of her lingering in his mouth and hadn't been able to do it. Couldn't make her relive it. Only wanted to soothe her, help her forget, make it all disappear. Not cause more pain while he was rocking her world, shaking the foundations she'd built her pride upon.

She'd never forgive him, but there was little likelihood they'd meet again after his meeting with her father. Nic would go back to New York and likely marry Goldsmith's daughter, place Santos Diamonds back in Avô's hand. As for Pia, she was strong. The strongest woman he'd ever met. She would close this chapter in her life, stand up and move on, doubtless ruing the day they'd met.

Hands white on the steering wheel, he breathed through the tightness in his chest.

It wasn't as if Pia would be left with nothing, he assured himself. Merisi seemed like an octopus, with tentacles that reached far and wide, so Nic doubted he'd ever know the full extent of his business interests. But one thing he would never falter on—Q Virtus must fall. The coliseum that had held the gladiatorial battle of Santos versus Merisi and witnessed his family's demise. And Zeus must be exposed for the crook he was.

Then he could crawl beneath a rock, as far as Nic cared. Maybe he'd leave Pia to manage what Nic had left alone. He hoped so, because he didn't want Pia starting again from nothing. Not after what she'd been through.

Nic was more anxious than ever to meet the man. Q Virtus was finally cracking under his strain, and by the time they reached Paris the vast majority of members would have disowned it, never to return. Nic had given them enough doubt to disease their minds and ensure they jumped ship while their reputations and businesses were still intact. He couldn't wait to see the look in the other man's eyes when faced with his nemesis. Couldn't wait to tell him his club and the Merisi legacy were dying.

Dammit, he *needed* that meeting. He just had to bed Pia to get there.

The thought was a mighty hand at his throat that gripped without remorse. Why was he suddenly uncomfortable with the idea? It wasn't as if he was seducing her under duress—she wanted him just as much as he wanted her. Mutual pleasure was theirs for the taking, and if the attraction between them had been strong before, now it was off the charts. As if they'd tasted nirvana and craved another shot.

Barcelona town came into view—all grandiose architecture and Gothic flair—and he sneaked a sideways glance at his temptress.

With the top down in his ferocious little supercar, the wind had whipped at that perfect film noir up-do as if taunting her to cut loose and gave her cheeks a healthy lustrous glow of pink. The hypothermia had taken its toll, and she'd slept for most of the flight, but out in the warm air, with huge sunglasses covering half her face, a small smile teasing her mouth, head tipped back as she looked up at the children waving from the bridge, he thought she'd never looked more beautiful. Or so young.

'You know…take away the laptop and the phones and the bodyguards and you look twenty years old, *querida*.'

Pia rolled her head on the cushioned pad to face him and her eyebrows shot skyward. 'How old do I look *with* them?'

'All serious and scowling? Forty at least.' Hideous exaggeration, but he was all for inflation to make his point and get a rise.

'Oh, charming! I thought you were aiming for my bed—not to get pushed off the roof!'

Nic threw his head back and laughed. He couldn't remember the last time a woman had made him laugh, made him lie in wait for the next outrageous thing to come out of her mouth, made him want to find the nearest bed and touch that sinuous, sultry body again. Ice and fire personified.

'So, unless you want me to think the worst you'll have to tell me how old you are.'

'Didn't anyone ever tell you never to ask a woman her age?'

Blame it on the sunshine. Blame it on the town he'd always loved and the opportunity to show it to Pia since she'd confessed she was a virgin to these parts and he suspected her travels were devised for oppressive boardroom play. Hell, blame it on the laughter in his heart, but the words just tumbled out.

'*Sim*, my mother. She used to pay me to tell my friends she was ten years younger. Said she would rather carry the stigma of teenage pregnancy than be seen as old. Mamãe was a great lamenter that you're only as young as you feel.'

Sabrina Santos would have liked Pia, he decided—very much. Talk about irony.

'You speak of her in the past tense. Did you lose her?'

Nic could feel her scrutiny burning into his cheek and found swallowing past the emotional grenade in his throat was harder than he'd expected. 'Yes. A long time ago. Both of my parents are dead.'

Gripping the gearstick, he downshifted as pedestrian traffic became dense and he could see children lining the streets. Distracted as he was, when he felt the startling yet unbearably sweet stroke of the back of Pia's finger down his ear and jaw he flinched.

'I'm sorry, Nic. Your mother sounds like she was a hoot. You must miss her. Miss them both.'

More than you could ever know—and I have your father to thank for it.

The violent need for vengeance flared back to life and it took everything he had to keep his emotions in check. The air grew taut with an uncomfortable silence and from nowhere he wished she would touch him again, so he could feed off a comfort he really didn't deserve.

Instead she filled the quiet. 'Well, if she was right, some days I feel one hundred.'

'But not today.'

'No,' she said softly. 'Not today. This place is just…so stunning. Amazing.'

She raised her arms in the air and he imagined she could feel the cool breeze kiss her palms, whistle through her fingers.

'If I tell you how old I am, will you answer me a question honestly?'

'I'll try my very best,' he hedged.

'I'm twenty-eight.'

Dios, very young. He hadn't expected that. It wasn't that she looked older; it was the way she carried the weight of the world on her shoulders almost effortlessly at times. Then again, with her past, he imagined she'd had to grow up quickly—much as he had.

'So…' she began, threading her fingers into a prayer-hold, knuckles white.

Her pregnant pause made his stomach pitch.

'Have you ever had any business dealings with Antonio Merisi, my father?'

Personally? 'No.'

'I'll never have sex with you, Nic.'

He didn't miss the hard core of determination or the frayed edges of remorse. She desired him, but with this damn bet between them… He was beginning to see the error of his arrogant ways there. One look and all he'd been able to think of was taking her, having her body beneath him, cocksure she'd tumble into his arms within hours. The woman screamed *sex* and he hadn't seen past that *femme fatale* persona. But beneath the façade was a vulnerability that made him ache.

'Why don't you just tell me why you want to meet him,

tell me what the problem is, and I'll try and fix it. I'll find a way. It's the least I can do after you…'

'Saved your life, Pia? Held you in my arms for hours on end?'

Nic waited until he'd pulled to a stop at a crossing before glancing over at her—she was staring at the Barcelonians cluttering the pavement, the back of her hand pressed against her mouth. He'd give his eye teeth to know what she was thinking.

'You can't help or fix it,' he said, wishing she could with all his heart. 'I don't want to discuss him, Pia. Not today or tomorrow. Not until Paris. This time is for you and I. You almost died two days ago and it makes me want to remind you how to live. Forget the bet, *querida*. For the next two days, here in this town, we'll be the best of friends. *Without* benefits. You want to see this city—I can see it in your eyes. So we'll go out. Eat delicious Catalan food that will make your mouth water. Enjoy the sun. See the sights and have some well-deserved fun.'

He truly wanted that, he realised. Just to feel like a man again—a man out with a beautiful woman and no cares in the world.

'What do you say?'

Violet-blue eyes—narrow with cynicism—peeked over the top of her sunglasses. 'I sense a subplot.'

With a chuckle he shook his head. 'Must you be so suspicious?'

She glared at him with a pensive pout. 'I'm not having sex with you, Nicandro.'

He peeked over *his* sunglasses and gave her a sinful wink. 'You keep telling yourself that, *bonita*.'

Pia *did* tell herself that, until it became a mantra in her mind and a torrid persecution in her body.

Nic was like a child with a new toy, and her suitcases had barely hit the floor of his palatial penthouse before he was dragging her down the frenetic La Rambla, strolling through the medieval alleyways and secluded squares of the old city, lyricising about every madcap Gaudi façade. Copious café's dotted the avenues, and she drank oodles of vanilla latte—espresso was Nic's poison—and paused to listen to the buskers, watch the pavement artists and be amazed at the living statues.

Pia adored every single minute of it. In fact she fell head over heels in love with the utter chaos and complete charm of it all.

Which just about described her new *friend* too.

Nic—or should she say tour guide *extraordinaire*—was amazing, with light-hearted mischief gleaming in his eyes as he spun her off in yet another direction. He was wonderful. Until the sight of her business suit sent him into an agitated state of incredulity.

'Don't you own any casual clothes, Pia? Anything that is not black?'

To which she haughtily responded, 'Black makes me look thinner.' Which, apparently, had been the wrong thing to say.

'That is the most ridiculous thing I've ever heard, Pia! I don't want you to look thinner, I want to see those glorious curves illustrated in colour!'

Pia considered the truth of that while she leaned against a drinking fountain in one of the squares, wincing at the pulsing sting of blisters on her heels and toes.

Meanwhile, Nic seemed to be having another fit—arms slashing in the air, frustration leaching out of him.

'Take them off, *querida*. I mean it. Look at your poor little feet! All squished.'

Down he went onto his knees in front of her with suave elegance and eased both shoes off her feet.

Pia frowned. 'What are you doing?' There was some fairytale about a shoe, she was sure.

'Playing Prince Charming.'

'Didn't he put the shoe *on*?'

He waved his hand in the air. 'Semantics.'

Then he grinned up at her—so utterly gorgeous—and shoved his sunglasses upwards to sit on his head, visor-like. She'd swear in any confession that her world tipped on its axis.

Wavy dark hair ruffled by the fingers of the breeze tumbled over his brow and curled around the upturned collar of his bright pink polo shirt. His white linen trousers were pulled tight over his spread thighs and she could see the thick ridged outline of his masculinity and remember the feel of it against her—

'Ohhh. That is *bliss*.' She drew the word out as if it had ten syllables as he pressed into the arch of her foot, banishing all thought. 'Keep going. More. *Harder*.'

He growled from his position between her legs. 'If you don't stop moaning in that smoky, sultry voice of yours I'll have you up against that wall over there and *harder* will take on a whole new meaning.'

Right now she'd probably let him. Spectacular—that was what he'd be. The thought should have shocked her, because sex didn't rate above 'okay' in her book.

Pia closed her eyes, tipped her head back and lost herself in his ministrations. No one had ever given her a foot-rub before—in fact it was the most selfless thing anyone had ever done for her. Those big hands were gentle yet firm, and the slow rub had her arching like a cat.

'*Dios*, look at you. This is torture. We have to move.'

No! Don't stop. 'Walk in my bare feet?'

'Hop on my back and we'll go to the boutique on the corner. I'm buying you new shoes and some decent casual clothes if it's the last thing I do.'

She wasn't sure which idea appalled her most. 'I can buy my own clothes, thank you very much, and there's no way I'm getting a piggyback into a exclusive designer store. How will *that* look?' The idea was preposterous.

He looked at her as if *she* was preposterous. 'Who cares? You might cut your feet otherwise, and you'll never get *those* back on.' He pointed to the offenders with a disgusted sneer, then spun around and lowered into an elegant crouch. 'Hop on.'

Pia swallowed hard as she eyed his wide shoulders. 'I can't believe I'm doing this,' she muttered, inching her skirt up her thighs and sneaking a peek to see who was watching. 'I weigh a ton. I could break your back.'

'You weigh one forty at the most, Pia. *Do it.*'

That commanding tone made her shiver. 'Fine. You asked for it.'

Hands hooked on his shoulders, she executed a graceless little jump and—thank God!—he caught her effortlessly, curling those big hands around her upper thighs as he stood tall.

'I like this,' he said, his thick, rich tone telling exactly how much.

Embarrassed beyond belief, she buried her face in his neck as he sauntered down the street, easy as you please, as if he did it every day of the week. It was all completely surreal. But the astonishing thing was her acute discomfort soon gave way to an odd bubbly feeling…maybe giddiness?…as people passed by and said things like, *Hola!* or *Bon dia!*, smiling at them as though they were sweet sixteen, madly in love and a delightful sight to behold.

And pretty soon she found herself smiling back and hanging on to Nic, her arms wrapped around his shoulders, wrists crossed on his chest, revelling in the feel of all his hard ridges and hot flesh. He felt glorious. Safe. Nuzzling his neck, she breathed in his earthy masculinity and felt his groan rumble up through his back and vibrate over her breasts.

'Good?' he asked.

Pia wasn't certain if he meant the feel of him, the smell,

or her lack of shoes, and decided the answer would be the same for all three. 'Divine.'

Another growl. Another deep rumble vibrating over her chest. And her heart thumped against the wall of her ribcage. She was loving the effect she had on him. No matter what, that wasn't a lie or a secret, and she clung to that as tightly as she clung to him.

For so long he'd played the starring role in her tawdriest fantasies—was it any wonder her resistance was slowly crumbling, leaving her to consider what would happen if she surrendered? Caved. Gave him his meeting. With Zeus. With *her*. Surrendered not only her body but also her true identity, her life. Not for a relationship—she wasn't *that* naïve, and in truth she wasn't interested in putting her heart on the line again for anyone, not after the humiliation of Ethan—but for one night in his bed.

One night of Nicandro Carvalho in exchange for risking it all. Would it be worth it? Probably not. Not to her. Not for sex. A fleeting pleasure versus losing Q Virtus. The old dinosaurs at the club would have her neck in a noose in no time if they knew a woman ruled their world. Heck, she'd only just managed to induct a number of serious-minded businesswomen into the fold, and that had taken her years. Dragging the place into the twenty-first century would turn her grey, she knew.

Rotten, stinking, filthy old laws.

But maybe he'll keep your secret, Pia. He knows about your past, virtually promised he'd tell no one. Maybe she could reveal herself. Trust him.

The infernal internal argument raged on, fuelling her anxiety and frustration. Too many maybes. Too many risks. Especially considering the rumours and the trouble at Eros.

But maybe she'd jumped to the wrong conclusions and he *had* just been looking for Zeus. She had no proof he was responsible apart from the fact that he'd broken into her office and had been snooping, but the more she knew of him the more she thought it was exactly the kind of risky, troublesome thing he'd do to find someone who, to be fair, was impossible to see. It didn't mean he was to blame for all her problems, did it?

Convincing yourself now, Pia? Maybe so, but if he wanted to cause trouble why save her life by holding her in his arms through the night? Why order her to sleep on the flight with fervent concern in his gaze? Why show her around the city and enjoy every minute? Massage her feet. Give her a piggyback so she didn't cut herself.

No. Just...*no.* It didn't fit. Any of it.

Lost in the tangled web of her thoughts, she didn't notice the glass plate frontage of the boutique until Nic came to a stop.

Pia wriggled to be let down. 'You can let go now.'

'I don't want to,' he said, with no small amount of petulance. 'I love feeling you against me, Pia.'

Whether it was his sincerity, the heat between them, or the gruff repressed need in his voice, she wasn't sure but she dipped her head and kissed him open-mouthed on the soft skin beneath his ear.

'Thank you for the ride, big guy.'

It had been considerate and caring and he needn't have done it. Who could blame her for being confused? This wasn't the man she'd met in Zanzibar—the calculating wolf who doubtless had an agenda. This man felt real. And, God help her, she wanted him. Wanted to trust him with everything she was.

Nic loosened his hold and she dropped to the warm stone pavement. Then he spun around, cupped her face and kissed her back tenderly, affectionately, on the mouth.

'Any time, *bonita.*'

As soon as they stepped over the threshold the store assistants were all over him like chocolate syrup—even the browsers couldn't take their eyes off him. Not that she blamed them. *And I've kissed him!* A startled thrill washed over her—the kind she hadn't had in for ever. *I've kissed him and I want to do it again. And again.*

Within half an hour Nic had packed her off to the changing rooms with a pile of clothes and Pia tore off her fitted jacket and skirt. The only way she could describe how she felt in that moment was free. As if her suit had been made of steel and she'd never known it. Eyeing the pile, overwhelmed and not sure where to even start, she heard a child-like whoop, knew it had something to do with Nic, and pulled the curtain aside to spy.

Standing on one leg, he balanced a dark red and blue Barcelona football on top of his elevated sneakered foot and held it there for long moments for the rapt attention of a young boy. After a while he gave a little kick, and Pia's jaw dropped as he started bouncing that ball over and over again. Never dropping it once. A back-kick and it was balanced on his nape with an expertise that had the entire store mesmerised. A second later he was nudging it a few inches into the air with his head repeatedly—she thought they were called headers but, hey, she'd never been into football…she could be wrong—and the young boy was grinning and clapping and cheering with utter delight.

Pia felt a silly smile on her face and her heart began to float in her chest. Before she knew it, snapshots of impossible dreams flashed in her mind.

He would be a wonderful father.

After a childhood of no authority, no order, no harmony, Antonio Merisi's controlled world had appealed to her so much she would have done anything to stay with him. And she had. But, looking back, it had been much like going from anarchy and chaos to despotism. A kind of tyranny.

Nic, on the other hand, was a glorious fusion of chaos and control. He could be commanding and dominant one minute, mischievous and wickedly sexy the next. As a daddy he'd be firm when he had to be, but probably the first to climb the nearest tree or jump in a nearby lake. And in that moment she envied the woman who would share that life with him.

An almighty shattering—like the sound of a hideously expensive vase being knocked off a shelf by a wayward football—splintered throughout the store.

Nic cringed so deeply his eyes squeezed shut. The little boy snorted, earning a glare from his mama. And Pia? She slapped a hand over her mouth to stop her giggle ripping free. And since when did she giggle? *Ugh.*

Contrite, Nic shrugged those big shoulders and smiled crookedly, almost blushing as he apologised to the staff. Pia honestly didn't know why he bothered, because they were all in love with him and he could have trashed the shop for all they cared. He could buy the place fifty times over and they knew he'd pay his dues.

After discarding a few outfits that she wouldn't be seen dead in, she settled on a sheer white T, a pair of jeans, a glamorous loose-fitting blazer and the softest pair of suede boots that made her feet sing. Then, before she could second-guess herself, she started to pull out the pins in her hair. Would Nic like her hair down? Even when she'd been sick it had stayed pinned back, so he'd never seen it—probably didn't know it was so long. Heck, maybe he wouldn't even care.

What's happening to you, Pia? What is he doing to you?

By the time she'd squashed her self-doubt, pulled the curtain back and stepped out, Nic and his partner in crime were sitting on the floor, leaning against the wall, chattering about the greatest football players of all time.

Pia cleared her throat. 'Are you boys behaving yourselves?'

Two faces jerked up. Two mouths—one big, one small—dropped.

'Wow. She's pretty. Is she your girl?'

Now it was Pia's turn to blush scarlet. Heat spread up her cheeks as Nic just sat there. Blinking. Staring.

Eventually he launched to his feet. 'I would like her to be. Do you think she should?' he asked the boy.

'Totally. You're cool.'

'This is my thinking exactly,' he said, with an arrogant nod that made her roll her eyes.

Pia watched him prowl towards her and covered up her unease by cocking her hip. 'Ta-da! Whadaya think?'

'I think that mouth of yours was made for better things than to speak slang, *querida*.' He walked around her, eyeing every curve, every nip, every inch. 'And I think you look ridiculously young, amazingly cute, a whole world lighter and the most beautiful woman I've ever seen.'

'Oh.'

'Speechless? *Dios*, has the world ended?'

'Sometimes I crave kicking you in the shin.'

From behind, he whispered huskily in her ear. 'Let's not get into cravings. Mine would make your toes curl and they are becoming more and more impossible to ignore.'

At the touch of his palm cupping her behind, she melted into a puddle.

'Your lush derrière was made for jeans—you know that?'

Oh, God. Then she felt him toying with a thick lock of her hair, the tug on her scalp sending her dizzy.

'You've finally unpinned your glorious hair. *Dios*, Pia, what are you trying to do to me?'

I'm not sure. Make you want me for me—not for who I am or what I can give you. Show you I'm more than the siren you want in your bed. Make you see me.

When he'd come full circle she stared at his mouth and he grinned wickedly.

'Want a taste, Pia?' he said, in that luscious, growly voice that made her tummy flip and her heart do a triple-somersault in her chest.

So of course she changed the subject. 'Where did you

learn to play football like that? You could've been a professional.'

It was as if she'd caused a power cut. The lights flickered. Blanked out. Then the stark flare of anguish in his eyes was so strong Pia had to root her feet to the floor to stay upright. What did they say about hidden depths? She'd never seen that kind of pain in him before. That depth of emotion.

'Nic? What did I say?'

Pain morphed into something hard and cold that made her shiver. But as quickly as it had come, it was gone.

'I was a pro. A long time ago.'

Oh, God, no wonder. 'So what happened?' she asked softly.

Turning his back on her, he stalked towards the cashier's desk. 'Injury. Let's go.'

She wanted to ask him how and why and when, but something told her he'd clam up even further because it would be opening a Pandora's box.

How awful that must have been for him. Having his dreams ripped away. And they *had* been dreams—no one could have missed the joyful, almost wistful smile on his face as he'd performed for the little boy.

Nic paid the bill after he'd given her a warning glare not to argue—in truth she'd never had anyone buy her a gift, and today had been so special she didn't want to bicker—and then asked for all the boxes to be delivered to his penthouse at the hotel. There seemed to be far too many, but she was so distracted with thoughts of his shattered aspirations she didn't question it.

When they'd left the store Nic reached for her hand, and this time Pia took it. She'd avoided his hold all day, but she had the distinct impression he was asking for comfort.

His strong, warm grip tightened, as if he were pleased, but once they were sauntering down the tree-lined avenue he flipped back to his jovial rakish self.

'Now we can hit the town,' he said. 'Dinner and a club—our first date.'

Pia stumbled on an invisible crack in the stone. 'Date? Do friends go on dates?' She couldn't even bear to think of her last date. It made her feel physically sick.

He placed his hands on her waist to steady her and cocked an eyebrow knowingly. 'Friends who want nothing more than to rip each other's clothes off? All the time.'

'There'll be no clothes-ripping tonight.'

Absolutely not. Here she'd been, unravelling at the seams, and he'd just reminded her of a time when giving her trust to a man had royally stitched her up.

His whisky eyes sparkled down at her and her stomach did a hot, sultry roll.

'You keep telling yourself that, *querida*.'

She *was*, dammit, and it didn't seem to be working a jot!

CHAPTER TEN

DUSK HAD PUNCHED through the day in a bruised swirl of rouge and the same violet-blue as her eyes, and the air was sharp-edged with salt from the Balearic Sea.

She'd gone quiet, Nic mused, drawn inwards with a small pensive frown, and the only reason he could think of was the way he'd given dinner the innocuous title of a 'date.'

Still, he held her hand in his warm grip, unwilling to let go, knowing full well they were coming off as two inseparable lovers, and ushered her into the best tapas bar in town: a tiny undiscovered hole-in-the-wall discerning locals flocked to.

He leaned in and gave her arm a nudge. 'You have been on a date before, haven't you?'

Dios, she must have. Look at her. Those jeans made the blood rush to his head and his groin, making him simultaneously dizzy and hard.

'Casual' suited her to perfection. While he lusted after the sexy siren in power clothes, this was a softer look that gave her a girl-next-door vibe and made her so approachable that strangers thought nothing of striking up a conversation whenever they paused. A world away from Finnmark, where she'd been the high-class businesswoman in total control, verging on anally retentive, who'd had everyone on tenterhooks trying to anticipate her next move.

'Of course I have,' she scoffed—a tad defensively, in his opinion. Not many dates for Pia, then. Interesting.

While she snapped her spine pin-straight and hiked up her chin Nic laughed inwardly. If she thought those dense ice walls would perturb him she had another think coming.

'Nicandro! It has been too long, *amigo*!'

He grinned at the sight of Tulio Barros, the best chef on the planet, dark, short and sharp, with a wicked taste in art. 'It certainly has, my friend. Glad to see the place hasn't changed.'

The bar's main wall was a pastel canvas of tasteful yet evocative nudes from a bygone era, while the other three remained exposed brick. The rich scents of tapas baking, the dark wood slab tables and heavy chairs, the cream tiled floor—all lent the intimate space the warmth this part of the world was famous for. Nic loved it; somehow it reminded him of home, of Brazil, a place he hadn't visited in twelve long years.

The conversation exploded into a bout of, 'How have you been? How is business? Who is this beautiful lady?' and Nic curled his arm around Pia's waist and made introductions.

He could literally feel the tension ease from her body as Tulio soaked her in his Spanish charm and pointed to a small private table in the corner. 'Go sit at my table and I will bring some Sangria and my best dishes of the day, yes?'

Pia weaved through scattered handbags and chairs and eyed the seating.

Nic gave her another nudge. 'Trying to work out how to sit the farthest away from me?'

She pursed her lips. 'Yes.'

He chuckled darkly, getting a kick out of her blatant honesty. 'Something I will never allow. *Sit.*'

With a gorgeous little glare she slid along the bench and Nic followed, until they sat in the corner at right angles, knees bumping, flesh touching and Nic in his element, with a perfect view of the room and her beautiful face aglow from the intimate lighting.

Tulio poured tall glasses of Sangria—which she sucked through a straw, her full lips working rhythmically—and the man went all-out to tease her out of her shell with creamy squid rings, known as *chocos*, *patatas bravas* with creamy *alioli*, *llonganissa* sausage and *tigres*—stuffed mussels to die for.

Nic wanted to let loose a string of Brazilian curses as his trousers became too tight for comfort. He knew he was staring but, *hell*, she ate as if she was making love to her food. As if she savoured and gloried in every delicious morsel. And it was the most provocative sight he'd ever seen.

Those little licks, the slow, erotic roll of her tongue, watching her cheeks concave as she drank deeply—it all had him in a state of agony, with a hard-on that just wouldn't quit and a craving for her to take him inside the hot cavern of her mouth. It was killing him.

He tried to think of the last time he'd had no-holds-barred sex for hours on end, but all he could remember were some awkward dates and some passable yet mediocre sex. After that he'd told himself it just wasn't worth the hassle.

He'd meant to ask how many dates she'd been on—continuing their earlier conversation—but the nibbles and tentative bites and succulent licks were messing with his brain.

'How many lovers have you had?'

As for that steel band around his chest, tightening as he waited for her answer…? That was *not* jealousy or insecurity or obsessive behaviour. He simply needed to eat. When he ceased being riveted by her.

But this, apparently, had been the wrong thing to ask when her mouth was otherwise engaged.

Choking on a mussel, she lurched forward, and Nic rapped on her back until she could breathe without turning blue.

'Are you trying to kill me? That is none of your business!'

He gave her back a sympathetic rub and leaned closer to murmur in her ear, 'Which means none. Are you a virgin, *bonita*?'

'No!' Half the restaurant's patrons whipped their heads their way and she thumped his thigh under the table with her fist. Then she whispered furiously, 'For pity's sake, have you ever heard of a twenty-eight-year-old virgin?' Snapping upright, back pin-straight, she sniffed—a tad haughtily, if you asked him. 'I've had lovers.' Yeah, definitely defensive.

'Good lovers or mediocre orgasms at best?'

Jaw slack, eyes enormous, she shook her head at him. 'Do you have *any* filter between your brain and your mouth?'

'Mediocre, then. Hmm.' He brushed his fingers over his lips and smiled inwardly when he caught her staring and she licked her own pout. 'Why do you think that is?'

Had to be control. Pure and simple. He didn't believe in any of that garbage about there being 'The One' with whom sex was not just great, or even fantastic, but *life-changing*. How could sex be life-changing? What ludicrous hogwash. As for Pia… Come to think of it, he remembered how she'd frozen on the verge of her climax back in Finnmark. He knew the signs. He'd never left a woman unsatisfied in his life.

'You'll never experience earth-shattering, cosmic, star-realigning pleasure until you give up control. *Always* you have to be in control, Pia. If you let go the power of ecstasy you feel will be fifty-fold. You stopped yourself back in my cabin, didn't you?'

A hot flush slashed across her cheeks. *Busted.*

'I know a woman close to the edge, *querida*. If I had touched you where you were wet and wanting me you would have exploded.'

Darts of pique shot from her eyes, the violet deepening to the colour purple. '*Wow,* Nic, it's a wonder you can get that head of yours through the door. I just don't think I'm made for it. It's nothing to get excited about for me.'

Dios, no wonder she'd resisted him this long. '*"It"* being sex? You *can* say it, Pia. It's not illegal or immoral in this country.'

'Good job, since you'd have been convicted ten times over. Worldwide.'

She stuffed a meatball in her mouth and—call him a masochist—he followed every move.

'Strange that *innocent* would never be a word I'd think of with you but often that is exactly what you seem. You need educating, Pia.'

'And I suppose you'd be the man for the job, right? You'd make it your civic duty to ensure Olympia Merisi experienced a good orgasm?'

His face was a veritable invitation to debauchery in that moment, he knew. 'Ah, *querida*, I promise you there'd be *way* more than one—and "good" wouldn't even come close.' Nic leaned forward, dipped his head and drizzled whisper-soft kisses up the curve of her jaw before murmuring in her ear, 'By the time I was finished with you, you wouldn't know which way was up.'

Those gorgeous breasts began to heave as she struggled to suck in air.

'I think you've been hanging around ego-inflators too much, Nicandro. You really shouldn't believe everything women tell you. Money is the greatest aphrodisiac, and it makes the most expert liars.'

Her voice was more ice than fire, and the cold front washing over him prickled his skin.

Slowly Nic straightened as a lightbulb switched on and flooded his mind, illuminating every aspect of Pia with new meaning. Moreover, he'd have to be blind not to no-

tice the pain that pinched her brow. Hell, he could virtually see her praying that he wouldn't jump on her *faux pas*.

'Let me guess. Some cad broke your heart, Pia?' It was
pure conjecture but she was ripe pickings for anyone who
knew her father. Heiress that she was. 'I imagine men are
either intimidated by you or they're after your father's
money. Is that about right?'

A heart-wrenching combination of reluctance, hurt and
rage darkened her eyes and punched him in the gut.

'You could say that,' she said, in that hard, icy tone he
hadn't heard for days and frankly had never wanted to
hear again.

Now he understood the frozen façade a little better. Once
bitten twice shy. Cliché, but true.

'What happened, Pia?' he asked gently, knowing it was
a bad idea to push but incapable of stopping himself. He
didn't like the idea that some man had damaged her, and
that didn't bode well in light of his grand plan.

She stroked the smooth skin between her eyebrows in
that way she did when she was deliberating. Unsure. Then
she seemed to come to a decision, because she jerked up
her chin and nailed him on the spot.

'I dropped my guard for no more than a minute. I believed every lie that came out of his mouth. I came to trust
him. Then one night we went out on a date and I heard him
telling his friends he was bedding Zeus's daughter to get
into Q Virtus, and she was so easy he could marry her tomorrow and have the world at his feet.'

Nic's stomach took a nose-dive. No wonder she was
holding back, defiant, rebelling against the insane biological chemistry between them. She'd been used, and the
fact was in her eyes Nic was using her too—for a meeting.
Wasn't he? Of course he was.

He tuned back in to her brittle voice. 'And do you know
what my father said to me? He said, "Trust no man, Olym-

pia. They all have an agenda. You want people to take a *woman* seriously? You stop acting like a whore.'"

The way she said *woman*—as if it was something to be ashamed of—rang alarm bells in his head. Hell, no, he wasn't having this—and it had nothing to do with any deal.

'Enjoying making love and being close to a man doesn't make you a whore, Pia. You have so much beauty stored inside you, and if you don't stir it up and let it flow out it will wither and die. Sex—making love—makes you feel alive. There's nothing to be ashamed of about that.'

The delicate curve of her throat convulsed. 'Are you saying this as a man who needs me in his bed to gain an audience with Zeus, or as a *friend*,' she taunted, reminding him of his words. 'A friend without benefits.'

'A friend. I promise you.' Oddly enough, it was the truth. 'Forget who I am or why we're here, sharing one another's company and great food. Do *not* let your past ordeal with a man dictate a future of a cold, solitary life. Was he your last lover?'

'Yes,' she said quietly, distractedly, as she glanced around the room, her gaze bouncing from one loved-up couple to another almost wistfully.

Nic swallowed hard, reached for her hand on the table and wrapped his fingers tight around hers, squeezing until he had her full attention. 'Keeping your distance, holding people away from you, denying yourself affection and a loving touch doesn't make you stronger, Pia. If anything it makes you weaker, because you're doing it out of fear.'

Her blonde brows drew down into intent little Vs, as if what he was telling her was far beyond mentally taxing. That over-active, constantly analysing brain of hers would be her downfall, he was sure.

'You're a beautiful, sensual woman, Pia, not meant to be alone. There's so much fire inside you. No matter what happens between us, promise me you'll remember that.

Be open to trying again. Not all men are dishonest, lying philistines and…' Nic trailed off.

I'm not either, he wanted to say, but that would be a barefaced lie. At least to her. Ironic that the one woman he wasn't being honest with was the one he wanted most.

Suddenly he felt as if someone had just picked him up and torn him clean down the middle. He wanted to crush the fool who'd bruised her heart, but he was about to do the exact same thing. Take advantage of her name, of who she was, exploit her for his own ends, use her just as badly as her last lover had.

Settling back in his seat, Nic closed his eyes, unsure if he could do it. Maybe he could find some other way to get to Zeus. *And what if you can't?* He was so close. After so many years he was now days away from facing the man who'd taken his parents from him, stolen his legacy, ruined his life.

Torn—so damn torn. Why was this tearing him apart? Why did he want her so badly? Why was he even considering her happiness before his own? His father's obsessive compulsions sprang to mind, but he squashed them just as swiftly. He was *not* his father!

Dammit, why was everything going so disastrously wrong?

Pia sat at the glass-topped table in Nic's penthouse, laptop open in front of her, gazing at the stunning sight of nightfall—a swollen waxy moon and a sky bursting with diamond-studded brilliance, its glow shimmering over a town that bustled with cosmopolitan chic glamour and frenetic energy.

Nic was backing off. Had been since the restaurant last night. The big seduction routine had crashed to a halt with the subtlety of a ten-car pile-up.

Often she caught him staring at her intently, with a voracious hunger that made her want to crawl out of her skin, but otherwise he was the perfect gentleman. Nic—*the perfect gentleman?* It was surreal. Maybe he'd been taken over by an alien life force or something. It was worrying to think he had such depth.

She'd half expected him to cancel their trip to the Picasso Museum that morning but, Nic being Nic, the idea hadn't seemed to cross his mind. Nor had cancelling tonight—their last night in Barcelona—and escorting her to his samba club in the old town. If someone had told her a month ago that she'd be sitting like some idiotic schoolgirl with a crush, counting down the hours, she'd have told them they were mentally insane. Yet here she was. Verging on lunacy.

Except no other man had ever looked at her the way Nic did. Predatory. Hungry. Just the heat in his whisky-coloured gaze, running hotly over her skin, their flames dancing in the dark depths like a physical manifestation of the blazing inferno that continued to rise up between them had Pia willing to do anything and everything he desired.

The bing-bong of an incoming e-mail diverted her attention to her mailbox.

No news. Nothing to link Carvalho to the hype at QV. He looks clean. Know more when I've spoken to PI in the morning.

Be careful, Pia.

J.

Careful? Wasn't she always careful? Always playing by the rules, using her head, emotionally barren. But with Nic she felt every sensation as if her senses were torn open and raw. As if she'd been held under the power of sensory deprivation her entire life—and maybe she had.

Her thoughts were severed by the ping of the elevator and the sight of Nic—all sweat and ripped muscle—coming back from his run.

Heaven help her, one look and her body simultaneously sighed in relief and flamed with heat, like some primal animal seeing her mate.

His hair was damp, the thick waves plastered to his brow. Beads of sweat dripped from his temples and clung to his chiselled jaw. And she could just imagine those corded, flexing muscular arms and his thick, powerful thighs moving with athletic grace as he pounded the pavement.

He scratched the hard ridges of his belly absently as he sauntered over, his dark gaze searing, as if he'd missed her face. 'Working again, *querida*?'

'Some problems at the club.' Pia looked at him closely but he didn't flinch at the mention of Q Virtus.

'Let your father deal with it, Pia,' he said, brisk and decisive.

She almost told him she didn't have that option.

'We'll leave in twenty minutes. I'm taking a quick shower.'

Can I be a fly on the wall?

Honest to God, he was sex incarnate, and the thought of another night lying alone in his huge bed in the guest room, thinking of how he'd made love to her mouth, how his thick hardness had nuzzled against the apex of her thighs, was a new form of persecution.

One hand on his hip, he didn't move an inch towards the shower, just stared at something beyond her left shoulder, and as she looked closer she could see stress bracketing his eyes. 'Is everything okay, Nic?'

Finally he met her gaze and his mouth shaped for speech, as if he wanted to tell her something. Something important, if his deep frown and tight jaw were anything to go by, and Pia felt as if she teetered on the edge of a cliff, waiting for a fall. His eyes lingered on her for long moments but he didn't answer her, didn't say a word, and after a frustrated clench of his fists he stalked off to the massive en suite bathroom.

Pia blew out a breath she hadn't known she was holding and slumped against the chair.

'By the way,' he said, loud enough to be heard through the penthouse. 'There's a box on your bed; you'll need it for the club tonight.'

There was?

Pia launched from the seat and tried not to dash through to her room like a child on Christmas morning. There on the pristine white sheets of the enormous four-poster bed was one of the boxes from the designer boutique; signature black, with a huge gold velvet sash tied into a sumptuous bow.

Her breathing grew a little fast and she rubbed her hands down her jeans.

A gift. Nic had bought her a gift. The man she'd watched from afar, the man who'd saved her life, the man who desired her like no other ever had. Surely this shouldn't feel so huge, so momentous, and yet that was exactly how it felt.

Arms wide, she curled her fingers under the lid and lifted, heart pounding with anticipation and excitement and the thrill of him doing something especially for her. Again.

Pia tossed the lid aside, looked down and sucked in air so fast her throat burned and tears stung the back of her eyes.

A red sheath lay on black tissue and with trembling fingers she stroked the embellished silk bodice and low-scooped neck, adoring the hand-stitched beads that tickled her palm. Lifting it from the wide straps, she noticed the fitted waist and the chiffon skirt that would kick out from her hips—a little flirty, a whole lot of fun—and flare out when she spun. It wasn't something she'd have chosen in a million years, but as she dressed in a daze, slipping the fabric over her head, letting the silk whisper over her skin and kiss her cleavage, for the first time in her life she felt like a billion dollars.

Odd how she could have bought hundreds of dresses just like this but had never wanted to—never had the need to dress up for anyone. But this… This dress was worth more than her fortune—at least to Pia—because it was a gift from the heart of a man who had to care. He *had* to.

And it was about time she admitted to herself that she cared right back. Had wanted him before they'd ever met face to face. Question was, did she have the strength to go for it? Surrender to him? Give him her body and reveal who she was? Take the ultimate risk?

Lost in thought, she lifted her left leg like a flamingo, reached down and nudged her foot into one glittering red stiletto. Then the other.

A quick glance in the mirror and she knew exactly what was missing.

Grabbing her jewellery case from the dark wood vanity, she slid the catch and opened the box, her heart doing a little pitter-patter as she spied the large black teardrop diamond and remembered the day her father had given it to her. No affectionate kiss on the cheek or words of love, but she'd known he'd cared for her in his own way and that had been enough. More than she'd ever expected or hoped for.

Lifting the chain from its bed of velvet, she watched the prisms from the chandelier above glint off the smooth black surface and the flash of a memory dimmed her buoyant mood. *Zanzibar.* The pure loathing in Nic's eyes had been strong enough to make her feel genuine fear.

Shivering, she gave a cursory glance towards the door to see if he was out of the shower, wondering if anything had been unearthed about Santos Diamonds. Then, to preserve her fragile optimism, she snapped the case shut. Maybe Nic truly *did* have voodoo suspicions about black jewels, and he was in a strange enough mood as it was.

When she stepped out into the hallway the sound of rushing water lured her towards the open doorway of his wholly masculine en suite bathroom.

Steam poured over the top lip of the towering glass enclosure, pluming in the air with moist heat, and when she took a tentative step closer her heart gave a pang at the sight of him. Ached so badly she could hardly stand it.

Arms braced on the black granite tile, head down as the water poured over him in a hot wet rush, he looked utterly torn. Frustrated. Demoralised.

As if sensing her presence, Nic lifted his head and twisted at the neck until she could see his profile. Water dripped down his nose and he wiped his face over his hard bicep to clear his eyes.

'Pia?'

He was so beautiful. From the hard sculpted lines of his back to the tapering of his waist, the dimples at the base of his spine and the perfect firm curves of his sexy butt.

Moisture dotted in between her breasts as her blood heated.

'Did you buy the dress before or after you smashed the place up?' she asked, her voice thready as she unravelled before him.

'Before I broke a two-thousand-euro vase? Yes. Do you like it? The dress?'

'I love it, Nic. Thank you.'

He gave a small nod. 'You're very welcome.'

She couldn't look away—could only imagine what it would be like to strip off his gift, walk in there and act out any of the various tawdry fantasies she'd conjured up over the past week. And all the while he didn't move a muscle, kept his body averted, and she started to ponder if he was thinking of her in the same way. If he was as turned on as she was.

'You need to leave…*now.*'

Her stomach twisted with pure and painful longing. 'What if I don't want to?'

Tipping forward, he banged his forehead off the wall and ground out, 'I'm not making love to you, Pia.'

The penny dropped. In fact it was as if she'd hit the

jackpot and all the nice shiny coins were pouring out in a gold rush.

He didn't want her to feel used. The way Ethan had made her feel. *Now* she understood. *Now* she wanted him more than ever. He would *never* purposely hurt her.

Pia smiled, but all she said was, 'You keep telling yourself that…*querido*.'

CHAPTER ELEVEN

'I'VE CHANGED MY MIND.'

At Nic's voice, Pia tore her eyes away from the limousine window and the sight of La Catedral, with its richly decorated Gothic façade graced with gargoyles and stone intricacies. Then she cursed inwardly.

One look was all it took tonight. Her lower abdomen clenched with want—empty, so needy she bowed slightly to ease the ache.

Nic put her in mind of a roguish prince in his wicked midnight-blue suit, with his unruly hair black in the dim light and curling seductively at his forehead and nape. He'd eschewed a tie in favour of an open collar and the sight of his smooth tanned throat was making her weak at the knees.

'About what?' she asked, cringing at the quiver in her voice.

'This is the most beautiful I've ever seen you.'

'You say that every time I change clothes.'

One side of his lush mouth kicked up. 'A man's prerogative, *querida*. Are you going to dance with me tonight?'

His voice, she noticed, was still thick and rich, but there was a hesitant tone there too and it matched his manner. As if he was so deep in thought, so conflicted, he was tearing himself apart. Clearly he didn't want to talk about it—she'd asked him often enough—but that didn't mean Pia wasn't listening.

'Yes, I want to dance. But I'll warn you now I have no idea how.'

'I can teach you the samba in five minutes. Or the rumba. Have a little faith—your body was made for dancing.'

The dark interior charged with an electric current that gave a sharp ping when Nic glossed his warm palm over her knee and drew tiny circles with his thumb over and over. A covetous touch that made her pulse spike. She wanted to feel him inside her so badly she could barely sit still. It was getting worse, she realised, this inescapable want. It was as if she just couldn't breathe without him touching her.

Squirming in her seat, she scrambled for something to say. 'This is *your* club we're going to?'

'Yes. Barcelona is one of my favourite cities in the world and a friend of mine—an actor, believe it or not—was bemoaning the lack of good dance clubs when he came into port. Next thing I knew I'd opened one. Una Pasion Hermosa—A Beautiful Passion.'

The car rocked to a stop outside a trendy upmarket nightclub with an endless queue and a dizzying red carpet.

Just like that her sangfroid flew out of the window. 'Good name. Is it a celebrity haunt?'

'Generally. Depends who's in town.'

The car door opened to the excitable cacophony of the crowd and Nic flowed from his seat—all sleek masculine elegance—and held out his hand.

She stared at it like an idiot, trying to ignore the nauseating curl in her stomach.

'Pia?'

Oh, God. Deep breath, hand in his and up she went, swirling into the foyer in a blur of blinking camera lights, ducking her head self-consciously, coming unglued with the idea that people would try and figure out who she was. Nic might be used to the limelight but she wasn't. She chose instead to stay behind the scenes. Very few knew her true identity and she wanted to keep it that way.

'Nic,' she whispered furiously. 'Maybe this isn't such a good idea. Won't people know you? Wonder who I am?'

He shrugged with so much insolence she could have whacked him. 'Only my staff really knows who I am, and they are paid very well not to make a fuss. They're used to high-end clientele and I doubt anyone will look twice at us.'

Nic wrapped his hand around hers tightly, as if sensing she was about to go nuclear with the power of angst-laced adrenaline rushing through her veins, and she felt the flow of tension drift from her body on a slow sweeping wave.

Come on, Pia. You don't want to ruin your last night fretting about things that might never be, do you? No. She wanted to enjoy every second. Live in the moment. Out in the real world. For once not hiding.

Nic led her to one of the private booths set on an elevated dais and Pia slid into the overstuffed velvet bench seat, feeling the seductive bass line of the Brazilian samba pound through her blood.

'What's your poison, Pia?' he said, leaning over, his whisky eyes aflame with heat and desire.

'You choose. I don't want to make any decisions tonight. I want to just...*feel*.' Her voice sounded unreal. Loose. Licentious. As if her body was slowly taking over the power of her analytical mind.

Nic ordered French 75s and they were delivered minutes later, served in champagne tulips. Pia blamed the heat for what she did next: knocked back the first gulp with so much abandon she almost blew her head off.

'Wow. Potent stuff. Someone just shot a flame-thrower down my throat.'

'For a potent lady,' he murmured, lips carved with a devilish smirk. 'A gutsy, lusty blend of gin, champagne, lemon juice and sugar.'

The way he puckered his lips and said *'sugar'*, with a

naughty, intoxicating lilt, sent the delicious tart-sweet cocktail straight to her head. And all she could see was the swar-
thy sexy mess of his dark hair, the lights flickering over
his aristocratic face, the smooth bronzed skin of his throat.

Good God, this sensation of recklessness was like being
on a brutally intense rollercoaster and she wanted the ride
to go harder and faster, way beyond control.

When Nic caught her staring and raised an arrogant
brow she tore her eyes away, more than a little perturbed at
her complete lack of morals. Was she coming off as some
kind of...? *Of what, Pia? Whore?*

No. No, she wasn't going there. What had Nic said?
Being close. Affectionate. Yearning for a lover's touch.
She'd never had that before. That was probably why it had
made her feel so dirty to be used. She'd allowed Ethan to
make her feel worthless. But this give and take, connection and tenderness, had its own kind of beauty and there
was nothing dirty about that—he was right.

Proof of that was in the crush of dancers moving sinu-
ously across the floor to the unique samba beat. Under the
brilliant strobes they were all beautiful arches and lines,
weaving in light and shadow.

She focused on the couples who appeared to be lovers
and picked up the nuances of their behaviour. The man
tucking his lover's hair behind her ear, kissing her jawline, the tip of her nose, nuzzling her collarbone—all fiery
heat, promising dizzying pleasure. More than anything
she wanted to be close and affectionate like that with Nic.

'You're looking at them with such heart-shattering longing, Pia. What is going through that pretty head of yours?'

She didn't answer—couldn't...not with such a great
lump in her throat.

'Maybe you are ready to dance, yes?'

'Now or never.' And she meant that literally. Something
told her tonight was her last chance, her only chance with
him, and if all she ever had was the heady sensation of his

body moving against hers—even fully clothed—then so be it. She'd take it. It would be enough.

Pia stepped onto the pulsing dance floor and before she could think about where to stand or how to move Nic was there, taking control, taking the lead.

Aggressive, dominating, he curled his left arm around the base of her spine and pulled her to him, crushing her breasts against his chest. Then he clasped her right hand tightly in his—a silent declaration that he wouldn't let her fall, wouldn't let go. The moment was achingly wonderful, and as she looked up into his eyes and saw the longing reflected back at her she knew she was done for. Knew she'd never feel this way again.

'That's it, *querida*. Relax. Give all that control over to me.'

She had the notion they were talking about more than dancing, and she was already halfway to coming undone and unravelling quickly.

'Feel the contagious beat in your blood. Let the music move you; let it flow through your body and follow my lead.'

His voice was a giddy narcotic all on its own as he confidently steered her around the whirl of tight bodies and swaying hips.

Pia clutched his strong upper arms, loving the sensation of honed muscle beneath her fingers, and yet he bent them and moved with such masculine grace he was a stunning sight to see. His hands splayed across her lower back, where he gripped her tight and then moved their hips in a figure eight—all sensuality and sin—and then she was twirling like a top as he executed a perfect spin.

Just like that she was dancing, and she'd never felt so connected to another person in her entire life.

A second later she slammed back into his chest, palms flat, panting softly, breasts swollen and heavy, nipples peaking against the lace of her bra, begging to be touched.

Nic gazed down at her, all broody and dark.

It was like dancing with the devil, she realised. His every movement was a wicked invitation to vice, his covetous touch was possessed with danger, his scorching hot body created to spawn lust.

That was when she noticed. Nic wasn't the only one looking at her. Them.

'People are watching us,' she breathed.

'And most are obscenely envious of me, *querida*. Not to mention turned on.'

Well, they weren't the only ones.

His grip was firm but tender, holding her in the way a musician might prise the best from a rare instrument, and with every undulation, every sinuous return of her hips, her body hummed like a piano wire and she felt a hiccup of orgasmic pleasure. Not a full-on climax but a short, sharp, sweet jolt that was gone in an instant. Then another would hit, and suddenly she was shaking with uncontrollable need.

'Nic?' *Oh, God.* This was a whole new level of sexual tension.

Their bodies were so close from the waist up they barely moved. Her cheek now rested against his and the smell of his skin made her head spin, as if he was twirling her round and round the floor. When she inhaled through her mouth she could taste him, and her mind began to wander imagining a scene playing out...

Nic holding her down—wickedly naked—as they danced to an earthly wanton tune in his bed.

Dizziness hit her like a truck and the next thing she knew she was on her tiptoes, pressing her lips to his. *Kiss me, please.*

He hesitated and dread thrashed its monstrous tail, whipping her insides until—*oh, yes*—he thrust his hands into the fall of her hair and coaxed her mouth open with his tongue. Until she was seduced into an erotic play that had her nerves singing as he kissed her with such unrestrained passion she thought she might faint.

Beneath the mastery of his plundering lips the ache between her thighs grew to painful proportions full of emptiness and need. And impatience gathered inside her, right *there*, at the base of her abdomen, its frustrating heat spreading outward.

Pia undulated against him, stroking the thick erection that pushed against his seam over and over.

'*Dios*, Pia. You're killing me,' he groaned into her mouth, his hands unsteady as they moulded to her body.

His touch was electric and it seemed to be everywhere and nowhere all at once. She needed him to do something. To take control. Take *her*.

That was another thing he'd been right about. It was all about control for her, and she didn't like giving hers up. It made her afraid of being hurt. But in giving up her power and control to Nic, in return he'd give her something she needed far more right now. The assurance that what she had to offer of herself was worth giving to someone. That *Pia* was worth it. That her past hadn't tainted her beyond value.

'I want you, Nic. So much…' she whispered as she nuzzled across his jaw, and the last vestiges of doubt dissolved beneath the power of his searing heat. 'Take me back,' she implored. '*Take me.*'

So foolhardy. So reckless. So inevitable.

Emotion roamed across his features, shifting from conflicted to cautious to aroused and everything in between.

Pia watched the war raging inside him…

Then her heart smiled.

The limousine was dark. Streetlamps flashed at regular intervals, flaring through the shadowy black leather interior. And he tried to say no, to hold on, but within seconds of them tumbling into the car she was straddling his lap and gyrating against him. It was biological fireworks and he was only human, right? He'd been desperate for her since the day they'd met.

His agonising erection nudged the mound of her lacy briefs, pressing into her hot wet folds, and his mouth was on hers, ravenous, devouring, stunningly erotic.

For the first time in his life he was incapable of restraining his impulses—his body's carnal urges were stronger than his cast-iron will.

It was all hands and mouths and thrusting hips, murmured begging and endearments that made no sense, but they were both past the need to care about anything but pleasure and release.

The desire, already voluminous, became so acute he thought he was going to have a heart attack. How he was going to last the eight-minute drive was beyond him.

The sound of cloth tearing reached his ears, and when he felt her hungry hands on his chest he let out a low groan.

'Pia, slow down—or I swear you'll be on the floor in ten seconds flat.'

It seemed her version of 'slow' varied widely from his, because her open mouth glossed down his chest and licked over the flat copper disc of his nipple.

Nic hissed, but the sound was cut off when he felt her fingers at his waist, unbuttoning his trousers.

He should stop her, really. But, dammit, he didn't want to. Just wanted to feel her hot hands on him, her fingers wrapped around his pulsing thick length. Just. Like. *That.*

Nic's brain blew a circuit or two, but that didn't stop him from looking down. *Big* mistake. Her tongue snaked out and licked into his belly button before travelling down, down...

'Pia...' he growled with warning.

'I've wanted to do this since I saw you tied to my chair,' she said, in that smoky, sultry voice that drove him wild. Dropping soft, moist kisses down his length, she breathed hotly, 'Did you want me then? Think about me doing this?'

'*Dios*, yes—*yes!*'

Her hot wet tongue flicked and licked around the swollen head of him, the soft sensual pressure spiking his pulse and firing his blood. His every thought fragmented. Then her mouth opened wide and his vision blanked.

'*Pia...*'

He gritted his teeth as her lips slid down his erection on a soft suck, her tongue circling every sensitive nerve-ending.

Nic cried out, then bit his lip to stifle the sound. 'Pia… you need to slow…stop.'

Somehow his hand had taken on a life of its own and he weaved his fingers into her flaxen hair and gently thrust into the slick heat of her mouth, begging her to make love to him harder, faster, and he lost it—let his head fall back onto the cushioned leather and undulated, gasping at the wicked pleasure of it all.

What she was doing to him in the back of a limo…what people could see if the windows weren't tinted—Pia was driving him out of his tiny mind. And without warning it was all suddenly too much. Electricity charged his skin and his hair stood on end as his body tensed, the power rising like an unstoppable wave.

'Pia…too much… I'm going to… You need to move. *Now.*'

But she didn't move, only gave a tiny whimper and a groan of unadulterated pleasure that vibrated down his groin. And that was it. His entire body seized as his orgasm hit him like a crack of thunder, the sensation both unexpected and anticipated, and mind-numbing pleasure reverberated outwards, stealing his breath.

Heart pounding in his ears, his harsh rasping breath filled the stifling air as he scrambled for his brain to kick in.

When he figured he could talk again, or at least try, he swallowed. Hard.

'That was incredible. *You* are incredible.' Nic reached down and hauled her back into his lap, then buried his nose in her hair and clutched her to him. 'I want you naked and in my arms and in my bed. I want to hear your cries echo through the room, and it has nothing to do with any deal or bet or power-play. Screw the meeting, Pia, let us have this night.'

He'd find some other way to get to Zeus—without using her. He couldn't do it. He wanted something honest and real with her, and taking away their deal was the only way.

She eased back and the streetlights flickered over her exquisite face as he watched her confusion morph into a sweet kind of happiness.

'You mean it?' she whispered. Hopeful. Beautiful.

'Every word.'

With a glorious little smile she kissed him, soft and slow. It was almost shy, distinctly vulnerable, the way she needed to keep touching him.

Nic kept a tight hold of her, tasting himself on her tongue, luxuriating in a tender intimacy he'd never known. Especially after an act so sensually erotic. But then he'd known from the first that she would turn any idea in his head upside down and shake it up. She was unpredictable, and that was the one thing he loved and feared most about her.

His revived need was a living, breathing ball of fire, burning his patience to cinders, and he worshipped her, lavishing patient moist affection over every millimetre of soft, scented pearly skin he could reach.

Pia gripped his upper arms—each nail a brilliant half-moon of perfect agony—and just as he tilted sideways and rolled her onto her back across the wide seat the car shuddered to a stop.

'*Gracas a Deus*. Perfect timing.'

Hovering above her, Nic revelled in the way she arched her back and tipped her head in a non-choreographed compulsion of pure obedience. He knew exactly what she wanted—Nic to take control, to show her the kind of earth-shattering pleasure he'd promised.

Reaching up, she cupped his face and confirmed it. 'I want you so much, Nic. I want you to need me, take me, make me feel like you said I would.'

'No pressure, then.'

She laughed, the sound so glorious he knew there was no place he'd rather be—and that wasn't only astounding, it was terrifying.

'Just take it all away. Melt the ice inside me. Make me feel alive, just once.'

I want him. Need him so much. It was laughable, because as if any need this elemental was really a choice.

It was a beautiful, terrible desire—one she'd sworn she'd never let herself feel again. In truth, she could hardly compare what she had with Nic to her past—it was like water to wine—but it was a door that led to heartache. Not the loving kind but the using kind—the kind that made her feel cheap and worthless. So she'd sealed herself off, determined never to reopen herself. Yet here she was, opening up once more.

But he'd said no deal. That this was no game. To forget about tomorrow and live for tonight. If he wanted her that much it must mean something. *Had* to.

Tomorrow she'd give him Zeus and he would trust her. They would talk and together they'd find a way to figure it all out.

Pia was strung so tight the slightest pluck on her strings resonated, and when the elevator doors pinged shut she flinched. But Nic was right there, cinching her waist, lifting her up until she was level with his mouth and kissing her with thrust after languorous thrust of his tongue, licking into her mouth, taking her higher and higher, until she was a floating cloud of sensation.

'Wrap your legs around me, *bonita*, let me feel you.'

She did just that and ground her pelvis against him—the aftershocks sending rippling shivers down her spine—while she kneaded the hard ridges of his upper back.

Nic nuzzled down her throat, across the bare skin of her chest, dropping moist, luscious kisses across the curve of her breast where it swelled above her bodice, breathless in his need.

'I need to see you.'

That was the only warning she got before he lowered her to the ground and pushed the red satin straps off her shoulders.

'I'm so hungry for you I could eat you alive.'

A dizzying pulse of excitement made it difficult to think, but if any doubts lingered his answering passion razed them to the ground.

In a red blur, fabric swished down her body and pooled on the floor. And when Nic took a step back to gaze down at her, displayed under the harsh light, she shook inside, wanting to cover herself up. She wasn't as lithe as his usual conquests, not so toned, not so sculpted, more soft and generous.

'*Dios*, Pia, look at you. You take my breath away.'

Tentatively she lifted her chin, and what she saw in his eyes melted the final shards of ice in her heart. Reverence. Ferocious desire.

With one finger he reached out and drew a line from her collarbone down the deep cleavage of her breasts—*thank you, push-up lacy bra*—and farther still over the slight rise of her stomach to the dip of her panties.

He let out a low rumbling groan. 'You're killing me, here. Those sexy stockings and seams. I am keeping them on, *querida*, and licking up every line. Turn around.'

The command in his voice was unmistakable—wrapped in silk and satin and awe and tenderness, but there none-theless.

Her panties sliced across her cheeks and she gave another little thank-you for bum squats as she gave him what she hoped was a seductive look from beneath her eyelashes and turned, arms spread wide, palms flat to the mirrored wall.

Never had she felt so confident, so provocative, so sexual, so insanely turned on.

'Heaven help me,' he growled. 'I think I've just come again.'

She laughed—she couldn't help it—and watched his reflection, the heat in his eyes, the desire that made her blood thicken in her veins. But there were other emotions there too. Affection, and a pride that made her giddy heart leap to her throat. For a moment she considered that this might mean far more to her than was wise.

Then he was on his knees and fulfilling his promise— kissing up her stocking seams, his lips as soft and teasing as the touch of a feather—and she trembled where she stood.

Her hot panting breaths steamed the mirror and she watched her own eyes grow heavy and slumberous as he went higher, higher…reaching the bare pinch of skin where her thigh met her bottom.

'Nic?' Tremors ran up her legs and gathered at the soft folds of her femininity. Her inner walls clenched with an unbearable need for something inside. Nic inside her. Filling her up. Making her whole. 'Please.'

He nudged her legs wide and she cursed the stilettos making her teeter as his dextrous fingers slipped forward to stroke her where she was hot and wet and— 'Oh, my God, Nic!'

'So close,' he murmured, kissing the nape of her neck. 'But I won't let you come yet, Pia. I forbid it. You have to wait until I'm deep inside you.'

'I hate you,' she whispered adoringly.

His dark chuckle was interrupted by the ping of the elevator doors and the sharp noise was the final pluck on her nerves. Her legs buckled beneath her.

'Whoa, *bonita*. Oh, no, you don't.' Nic swept her into his arms, held her against his chest and strode into the penthouse, down the hall to his bedroom—where he laid her in the centre of his huge satin-drenched bed.

She writhed in pleasure as his gaze soaked up her sumptuous black bra, skimpy chiffon panties and stockings.

'Now, *that* is a picture I will never forget,' he said, his voice thick with passion as he stripped in front of her, shameless in his skin.

Those hot eyes were burning, threatening to incinerate her where she lay breathless, waiting for his muscled physique to come into view.

He was so fabulously tall that from her position on the bed she felt as if she was staring up at the cathedral in the square.

Lascivious and wolfish, the smile on his mouth was as heady and thrilling as the need etched tightly across his gorgeous face. And the last vestige of her sanity went the way of his snug hipsters when he took himself in his hand, circled his fingers and brushed his thumb across the head of his erection in a way that made the air whoosh out of her lungs.

He was winding her up like a musical toy, and the coiling tension became so acute she almost feared the inevitable striking chorus of release.

Softness came up to swallow her back as hardness descended from above and she found herself sandwiched between heaven and hell.

'What am I going to do to you first, *querida*?' He unlaced the ribbon bows of her panties, tied at her hips, and tugged the lace free.

Just the pull of the fabric against her folds tore a whimper from her throat. She didn't care what he did as long as he did *something*.

'I think you are too close for more play, Pia,' he growled as he lavished her with more kisses across her collarbone, up her throat.

Pia twisted, nuzzling his face to find his mouth, and at the first thrust of his tongue between her lips her heart pitched.

She strained towards him, canting her hips, bowing her whole body, while her emotions whiplashed from wanton desire to wholehearted devotion. 'Make love to me like you promised,' she begged. 'Please, Nic. *Please.*'

'*Dios,* Pia, you are on fire. Burning up.'

He pushed her down into the mattress, pinned her beneath his body, his hands forming sweet warm shackles about her upper arms, and pushed inside her in one long, hard, powerful thrust. And—*oh, yes!* She revelled in the wicked slide into oblivion.

Their eyes locked—his stunned whisky depths meeting awestruck violet-blue—as they shared one breath, the moment so profound she wasn't surprised to feel a tear escape the corner of her eye.

Right then it occurred to her that she'd just made a fairly spectacular misjudgement. One night would never be enough and she'd dream of this man always.

Gazing down at her, Nic brushed damp hair back from her forehead and the tenderness of the gesture wrenched her already wide open heart. So she turned her face to hide in the crook of his neck and breathed deeply.

'No, Pia, don't do that. Don't hide from me. Not tonight.'

'I…' *I need you.*

As soon as she obeyed him and glanced back up he began to move—slow and shallow at first, teasing her to a cataclysmic high—until she was writhing beneath him and his thrusts became deeper, harder, more powerful than anything she'd ever known. Until where Nic ended and she began was the ebb and flow of an erotic wave of pleasure.

She wanted to touch his skin, feel the flexing muscle of

his ripped body beneath her palms, but those sweet warm shackles only moved upward to hold her wrists above her head with one of his large hands. The other skimmed down her cheek, farther down her throat and over her chest, to cup her breast and squeeze the aching flesh.

A desperate moan blistered the air—his or hers, she wasn't sure, didn't care—as he rubbed over her nipple, then sucked the tight peak into his hot mouth.

'Nic… Nic…' She chanted his name over and over and it seemed to fuel his inner fire. Not to move faster but to slow, as if he knew she was close and wanted to prolong the agonising pleasure.

'One more minute—then I will let you fly.' His voice shook, his hands were unsteady from holding himself back, and she realised he was in as much pain as she was.

'Nic…*please.*'

'So beautiful,' he murmured, still moving at that maddening pace, keeping her on the edge of a shattering fall.

Pia dipped her chin, silently begging for his mouth, and he gave her what she wanted—*needed*—and simultaneously thrust his tongue into her mouth and slammed his hips forward with a tiny undulation that rubbed her sweet knot of nerves once…twice…

'Nic!'

'Now you may come. *Now.*'

Lightning bolts of sensation gathered in her core like a bright white pinpoint of light—a star about to go supernova—and the cry that tore from her throat felt wrenched from her soul.

Bursts of pleasure shot outward and those streaks of lightning tore down her spine and crackled along her nerves with an almost spiteful ferocity—the sheer intensity stealing her breath and holding her on an erotic plateau that made her vision blank, her mind faze out and life cease to exist for long, endless moments.

She came to as Nic released the shackles from her body

and soul and rose above her, chasing his own nirvana. He captured her lips in a deep kiss that was tinged with desperation. Held her with a reverence she'd only ever dreamed of, making her feel accepted and worthy and wanted beyond reason. So perfectly *herself* that falling was inevitable.

His cries were wrecked and ravaging as his orgasm tore him apart and Pia licked at his lips to taste his pleasure—pleasure *she* had given him—ecstasy he'd found only in her.

His glorious weight descended and she felt safe and cared for, and cherished in the crush. And she knew it was coming—was powerless to stop it.

The overwhelming cacophony of emotions—joy and fear and adoration and amazement—refused to be ignored, and they rose up within her and escaped in a breath suspiciously close to a sob. Nic gathered her in his arms and held her with fierce strength—stronger than a mighty god. Almost devout. It was the culmination of such an amazing night that she wished she could freeze the moment in time for ever.

CHAPTER TWELVE

WHO'D HAVE THOUGHT Nicandro Carvalho was a cuddler?

Pia smiled, reminiscing about the way he'd followed her around the bed like a heat-seeking missile. When he hadn't been making love to her, that was. One minute he could be deeply intense and dominating, his lovemaking so powerful it wrought tears, and the next he was light-hearted and fun, making her laugh out loud with teasing touches and that wicked, incorrigible grin. He thought nothing of saying something outrageous mid-thrust as he took her against the wall or pleasured her on his knees. She'd never imagined couples could make love in so many different ways. But, then again, maybe that was just Nic. Maybe only he could be like that.

The high of the night still rushed through her veins but there was a dark cloud closing around her, obscuring her euphoria, obliterating her joy. It was over. Time to get back to the real world, check on work, unveil the truth and tell Nic exactly who she was.

Pia eased from his hold and slipped from the bed with a slight wince, deliciously sore and tender. She told herself not to look back, only forward. Yet still she couldn't resist one glance at the sheets that held the impression of their lovemaking and the beautiful tall, dark man who'd taken her to heaven.

Heart heavy, she snuggled into a soft fluffy robe and wandered into the kitchen for her early dose of caffeine.

Ten minutes later she sat at the glass-topped table, coffee in hand, her laptop open at the financial section of a Saturday newspaper.

Eros had taken another kicking, she noticed, feeling the punch of it in her stomach and an after-ache of dread.

Pia flipped through the pages to check Merpia. Looked okay. Back to the stock exchange…flick, flick, flicking the pages—

Her fingers stilled on the keys. She backed up—heart thumping—sure she'd seen his name… *Nic's name…there.*

Goldsmith stock climbs as a merger in matrimony with real estate magnate Nicandro Carvalho is revealed.

What?

Fingers now flying, Pia jumped from one site to another through various links, with a sickening fear that instead of being poised for flight into a brave new world, she'd propelled herself well past the edge, no wings in sight, and was about to plunge into a black void that would swallow her whole.

Somehow she ended up in the New York society pages, her throat so tight she couldn't breathe, her heart beating so hard and fast she could barely see, let alone read the words.

Carvalho out and about in Barcelona with a mystery blonde.
Goldsmith heiress leaving the Fortuna mansion under cover. Hiding tears?
Billionaire Nicandro Carvalho at his nightclub in Barcelona with a new playmate. Who could she be?

'Oh, my God,' she breathed, her fingers fluttering over her mouth, the tears scorching the backs of her eyes making the hideous photograph of her and Nic distorted and blurred. She looked like a tramp. She looked like the whore her father had told her she was—and, goddammit, she felt like it!

And that girl—the girl Nic was apparently marrying—looked genuinely devastated as ravenous newshounds circled her, ready to catch her fall on candid camera. Suddenly Pia was grateful for them, because she'd ignored the truth, convinced herself there was more between them. Instead she'd fallen under his spell, surrendered herself to him body and soul during his magnificent last act.

Hadn't she learned *anything*? Had the past taught her *nothing*? She was only good enough to use. Worthless for anything more.

Pia slammed the laptop down, bolted upright, sending the chair screeching across the floor, and stormed through the living room, headed for his bedroom, furiously brushing at her tears because she would *not* cry in front of him—she would not.

The shrill of her phone cast her to stone. The phone she'd been ignoring most of the night. Something she'd never, *ever* done before.

She didn't have to look at the caller. She didn't have to greet Jovan or say a word. Because in that moment she might not know the *why* but she certainly knew the *who*.

'Pia? Tell me you got my message—tell me you are *not* still with him.'

Self-loathing so thick she almost choked on it. Humiliation so sharp she almost cut herself on it. Pain so powerful it almost crushed her bones. Heartbreak so shattering she could hear her soul weep.

She could barely breathe for hating. Herself or Nicandro Carvalho, she wasn't sure.

'Pia, are you there? I still cannot believe he is alive. I was *there*, Pia. At the Santos mansion. I was *there*! Where are you, dammit?'

'In bed with the enemy. Am I not?'

CHAPTER THIRTEEN

Eiffel Tower—Monday six p.m.
Zeus will be there.

THAT HAD BEEN her goodbye. The only lingering tangible evidence to prove she'd been in Barcelona at all and that Nic hadn't lived a dream was the red samba dress, every shoe and scrap of clothing he'd ever gifted her and her black velvet scent on his skin.

Nic stepped out of the glass elevator on the top floor of the Eiffel Tower and walked to the railing, to stare unseeingly at the breathtaking architecture: the Arc de Triomphe, the Champ de Mars—on it went, along with the slow drift of the River Seine, everything that embodied Paris…the city of love.

Knuckles white, he gripped the iron bar as the scathing wind whipped through his hair and pierced his skin with needles of ice. His thick black overcoat with the collar up failed dismally to keep him warm as the shadows of the past had him in a stranglehold.

She'd seen the pictures splashed all over the news. She must have. All the damning articles about his upcoming marriage. A marriage he hadn't even fully committed to. *Yet.* And the way he was feeling right now, Goldsmith could go to hell.

Yeah, right, Nic. You want Santos Diamonds so badly you'd deal with the devil himself.

He squeezed his eyes shut and raked his palm over the hard ridges of his aching stomach, trying to ease the pain of an all-encompassing sadness. One night with Pia and nothing looked the same. Pushing inside her had somehow been the most perfect, most important, most heartbreaking thing he'd ever done.

He'd never pictured a world where his need for revenge would collide with his heart to mingle and smear together, distorting his views, until the future looked vague and devastating.

'Hello, Nicandro.'

His heart stopped.

His first thought: she'd broken her written word. Zeus wasn't coming.

His second thought came hard on the heels of that, because deep down he knew Pia would never break her word. It was sacred to her. So when realisation hit his eyes sprang open to land on her statuesque frame—flaxen hair pinned back, designer powerhouse black suit, long cream cashmere coat, lips coated in armour, eyes glacially cold.

The ice queen was back, and that was more devastating than the implications of what he faced.

Had he been played all along? A first-class double-cross?

Snippets of conversation, visions of business papers and the ultimate feminine power flashed through his mind and, like pieces of a complex conundrum, all slotted into place, fitted together to create a perfect picture of truth.

Dios, he'd been so blind.

The realisation grabbed him by the throat and he found he could barely speak past the iron fist. 'Good evening, Olympia. Or should I say *Zeus*?'

'You may call me anything you desire, Mr Carvalho, while I hear the truth.'

He smiled ruefully as his entire world shifted beneath his feet. 'Is Antonio Merisi dead?'

'Yes, he is.'

Thirteen years. Thirteen years of waiting for his chance to ensure Antonio Merisi felt even a tenth of the pain Nic or his *avô* or indeed his parents had felt gone with three little words and a contingency he'd never have considered in a million years. But why would he have when Zeus's name still lingered on people's lips?

Olympia Merisi. Zeus.

Nic was sure he should feel something. Anger. Rage. Hatred. The need to lash out and scream at the injustice of it all. Except his whole body was devoid of sensation. He was numb. Nic supposed the only saving grace was that the toxic wrangle of emotions Pia had left inside him had been numbed too.

'He died of a heart attack four years ago. I now own and control his companies, as well as my own—and let's not forget Q Virtus.'

Knowing what was coming, he lifted his eyes to hers and locked on to those chips of ice.

'Do I have *you* to thank for the revolt that has brought my club to its knees, Nicandro?'

'Yes.'

'Did *you* manipulate the stocks and shares at Eros International?'

'Yes.'

'Are you trying to annihilate my world, Nicandro?'

'Yes.' No point denying it. Every word was true. 'Except it wasn't *your* world, Pia. Not in my eyes.'

'Oh, but I think it was. You knew I was inextricably linked, regardless. Let's not open the doors to the past just yet. Let us pretend my father is here to answer for his sins. What have *I* ever done to you? What heinous crime could *I* have committed for you to take revenge on my body and on my world?'

'Not you *per se*, Pia. This was not person—'

'Do *not* tell me this was not personal, Nic.' Fire had

obliterated the ice in her eyes until they were a deep violet-blue. 'You made it personal when your mouth touched mine. You made it personal when you held me down and took my body.'

Closing his eyes, he swallowed. Hard. He wanted to deny it, but what good would that do? At the heart of the matter she was right. She was simply laying out the facts in all their stone-cold merciless glory. He could tell her he hadn't known her at the start. He could tell her he'd fought with his conscience. But at the heart of the matter she was still right.

'You're right, of course. The moment I saw you, found out you were his daughter, my mind was set. Destroy him and take from you as he took from me.'

'And what did my father take, Mr Santos?'

'My entire world.'

'Yet here you stand, a new man.'

Right then he realised what she'd said. *Santos.* 'How…?'

'While I was falling into your deceitful practised arms Jovan was digging into your real world. I asked him to check out Santos Diamonds back in Zanzibar. The way you looked at me when I was wearing that necklace…with such vitriol…it wouldn't leave me. Would you believe he actually lied to me too, that day? Something that will take me a long time to get over.'

She'd trusted Jovan implicitly. Had started to trust Nic. Then the bottom had fallen out of her world. So now here she stood, unable to trust a living soul.

The implications of what had happened to her were hitting him as hard as the bullet that had pierced his back all those years ago.

'He said he had no idea what had happened to Santos Diamonds. Turns out he was right there all along.'

Nic frowned deeply. 'At the house? No.' He shook his head vehemently. 'I would have recognised him.'

But would he have? Thirteen years was a long time

to pass without any physical changes. Nic hadn't had the greatest viewpoint of the room back in the Santos mansion, and what was more when they'd met in Zanzibar he'd been too busy fighting Othello's green-eyed monster to see past Jovan's relationship with Pia.

'He was there. He thought you'd died that day.'

Nic thought he'd heard a chink in her icy armour, but when he glanced over she wasn't even looking his way and her cold façade remained unreadable, unreachable. *Dios*, it was heartbreaking. All her laughter, all her smiles, all that fire in her eyes and in her soul gone. Destroyed by him.

Self-loathing sucked his throat dry. When had he become a man he barely recognised? The kind of man who would wreak his revenge on an innocent woman. Had the years of rage and resentment, the obsessive fixation on vengeance, left him so callous, so cold?

'I know my father played dirty with yours. I know your parents died that day, and I am—' Her voice *did* crack then, and he watched her throat convulse. 'Truly sorry for your loss. For all of it. But that's all I know—and considering Jovan was outside until almost the end that's all I ever will know. You have my oath that I will not breathe a word. I only ask that you speak to Jovan for a moment or two. He was under orders to be there and retrieve the debt and I believe what happened has haunted him ever since. He would like to apologise, to explain…'

Her voice didn't just crack—it disintegrated.

And why shouldn't it?

She'd just found out her father had been no more than a greedy, ruthless common crook. A man who'd sent his scapegoats to collect on a bet that he himself had rigged. All because he'd wanted Santos Diamonds. Nic would hazard a guess she didn't even know he'd hailed from the Greek mafia. She was likely standing there wondering if she'd known her father at all. In the space of twenty-four hours Nic had betrayed her, her trust for Jovan had faltered and her father—the man she'd thought she'd known—had died another death in her heart. Was it any wonder she was frozen to the core?

His body flooded with sensation, the agony returning fifty-fold and he reached for her, cupped her beautiful face. 'Pia. *Bonita*, I am so sor—'

She wrenched away, taking a large step back, and he watched her blink furiously. 'Please don't touch me. I don't even know who you are.' She bit down on her lips and closed those stunning violet-blue eyes for a beat or three. 'I have no idea who I shared a bed with. What was deceit and what, if anything, was truth.'

He could taste her misery in his heart and he wanted to choke on it. Could hardly speak past the lump in his throat. 'Pia...*please*, let me explain.'

'No, I... Jovan is waiting in a black limousine at the base of the Tower, if you'd like to speak to him, and I sincerely hope that you find happiness in your...'

Her chest quaked, as if she was holding back a sob, and it tore at his heart.

Then she whispered, 'Goodbye, Nic.'

Head high, she turned her back on him and walked away.

CHAPTER FOURTEEN

DARKNESS HAD FALLEN over Paris.

Glittering with dazzling promise, lit with elegant flair, the Eiffel Tower stood tall and magnificent, the perfect image from a romantic storybook, ignorant of the fact that Pia's heart had shattered on its top floor.

Suitcases stood by the door of her suite and Pia shoved the last of her business papers into her briefcase and pulled the zipper shut.

If she'd thought the aftershocks of her last affair were bad, they were sugar-coated candy compared to this. This bone-deep sorrow. This heart-wrenching pain. This anger and self-hatred that simply wouldn't cease.

She'd been woefully unprepared for the chaos Nic was capable of unleashing, but as she'd torn down the walls and released all the terrifying implications it had become clear that Q Virtus was no more. Her one promise to her father and she'd failed to keep it.

Pia collapsed on the sofa, surrounded by the caliginous gloom.

Ah, yes, her father. The brilliant and unpredictable scion of a long line of Greek *Godfather*-wannabes. That is, phenomenally wealthy, untouchable criminals.

And she hadn't known a damn thing.

How could that be? Yes, he'd been cold, hard, but she'd honestly thought he'd been honourable at his core. He'd taken her in, saved her life, and she'd spent years desperately trying to repay him and earn his pride. Such an arduous pursuit—because nothing she'd achieved, no amount of money she'd amassed, had been good enough. She'd still felt dirty, tainted. And right now that made her furious. How dared he call her trash when he'd lived such a life? At least she had honour, integrity. Wasn't that worth more than dollar signs?

A hard rap at the door yanked her from her ugly pity-fest and she shoved her arms into her coat, picked up her briefcase and went to catch her flight.

In swung the door and Pia swayed on her feet. Had to do a double-take in case her traitorous imagination had conjured him up from her basest fantasies.

No. He was here. At her door. In all his dark, brooding glory, wearing the same black overcoat and the same depth of pain in his eyes.

He seemed so tired. A profound exhaustion of the soul.

It shattered her heart all over again.

She'd never given a thought to the possibility that Nicandro Carvalho could be so damaged. His polish was usually so brilliant and bright; he shone like a guiding star. But now the gloss was rubbed away it had left something so marred and cold she could plainly see the evidence of his mortality in the rigid lines of his body, and it all made a bittersweet kind of sense.

Pia wanted to take him in her arms, stroke his hair and soothe his pain. A glutton for punishment, clearly. All along she'd been a means to an end. She'd let a man use her, play her, for the second and final time in her life.

Lifting her chin in the face of adversity, she found her voice. 'What are you doing here, Nic? I couldn't possibly have anything else you desire.'

Had he even wanted her in the first place? She had no idea. It had all seemed so real. She still couldn't believe how hard and fast she'd fallen under his spell.

'Can I come in for a few minutes, Pia?'

When she hesitated he begged her with his eyes.

'Please let me speak to you, *querida*. I need to explain. About Goldsmith too—you deserve at least that from me.'

Yes. Yes she did.

Leaving the door open, she walked through to the living area, leaned against the vast plate glass windows and crossed her arms to stop herself from reaching out, begging to be held, for him to take the pain and emptiness away. And what did *that* say about her? Not anything she remotely liked.

Through the shadows she watched him enter the room, his footsteps hesitant, vague, as if he was no longer sure of his place in the world. She guessed that might happen to a man who'd been so driven for thirteen years, only to have the rug pulled from beneath his feet at the final hour.

Pia hated her father right then. For ruining Nic's life. Stealing his parents, his dreams. All she had to do was remember the utter joy on his face at that boutique, playing ball with that gorgeous little boy, and she wanted to cry all over again.

Nic mirrored her position a few feet in front of her and leaned against the table.

'Q Virtus,' he said decisively, and it was the very last thing she'd expected.

'Ah, yes. The rumours leading to its downfall. Mostly true I would say—wouldn't you?'

'Yes, but unless we do something the club will fall. You must know that.'

'Of course I do, Nic. You've made it so that the members no longer trust me—and they have no idea who I even am.'

'Exactly. That's the answer, Pia. You have to show yourself. We need to fix it.'

'*We?*' She laughed bitterly. 'There is no "we", Nicandro, and I can't reveal my identity. I'll lose it all. Then again, what does it matter now? You've already made certain of that.'

The acerbity in her tone made her cringe, because if she was being honest she couldn't blame him. To lose so much all in one night. All because of her father's greed.

'The old rules of the club state that only a Merisi male can lead, and my past is such...' She swallowed past the rise of despair. 'It's dirty—you know that well enough. Listen, I don't blame you for this... Or maybe I do, but I don't hate you for it, or fail to understand your motivation. Nor do I want to see you ever again. So if that's all you came for—'

'Pia, *listen* to me.'

There it was. That commanding Carvalho tone that made her shiver.

'The old rules of the club are archaic—who better to change them than the woman who's made it more successful than ever before. *You* are the law, Pia. Change it! Stand in front of them and show yourself. Quash the rumours dead. I guarantee no one in his or her right mind will leave. Worst case scenario: a couple of the troglodytes pack up and go—who cares? I bet you good money that, for some, a woman at the helm they can trust is of far more import than the ghost of a man who is mired in filth.'

'My past isn't much better.'

'*Don't*, Pia.'

His voice turned hard, so dominant her blood fired through her veins.

'Do not lower your worth to his level. I will *not* allow it. Know what I think?'

'I never know what goes on in that head of yours, Nic. You're a closed book.'

'Not any more. Turn any page and I will read you a line.'

'I'm not interested.' *Liar.*

'I think you know you could've approached the members before now. No doubt you've convinced yourself you aren't good enough. You're ashamed of your past. I think your father made you that way instead of telling you to be proud of the woman you've become and to stand tall before them.'

He was truly intimidating when he was this way—brooding and torrid. Even his body was pulsating, telling her he wasn't in total control and that moreover he couldn't give a stuff.

Frowning deeply, she sifted through his words. Or she would have if he'd given her half a chance.

'Don't you see? That damn hypocrite is still controlling you from the grave. Not only do you work to the extreme, as if you're still trying to prove your worth to him, but you're *hiding*, Pia—behind a curtain of shame. When you're probably one of the richest, most successful women in the world.'

Stunned, she blinked over and over. He was right. She never stopped, was always working, and no matter her success it was never enough. Not for her. Why couldn't she just be proud of herself? Forget the past and move on?

'You brought the female members in, didn't you?' he asked, yanking her from her musings.

'Yes. I was trying to drag the place into the twenty-first century. But to say it hasn't been easy is an understatement.'

'It would be if you were a visible power to contend with. You have more strength and honour than most of the men I know. How you run the companies, the club…I have no idea, Pia.' He moved a little closer, out of the shadows and no one could miss the awe written over his face. 'I am so proud of you.'

Oh, God. 'Don't say that,' she said brokenly. *Don't make me think you care. Not again. I can't take it.*

Nic took another step towards her, reached up and cupped her face in his hands. Hands that weren't quite steady as he stroked over her cheeks with the pads of his thumbs.

'Nothing of what I felt about you, how I wanted you,

was a lie. I've never wanted any woman the way I crave you, Pia, and that is the truth. I never want you to believe you were nothing to me. *Ever.*'

Pia caught herself nuzzling into his hand, so skin-hungry, so desperate for his touch, so dangerously wanting to believe him. To trust in the sincerity darkening his eyes. And it was more than she could bear, because distrust lingered as if hope had been violated beyond repair.

'I think you should go.' She tried to steel her voice but heard the deep shift of higher emotion and knew he'd heard it too.

Leave. Please. Just walk away. Her heart was breaking. Why did she have to fall for a man who'd used her every step of the way? Who was apparently marrying another woman in ten days?

'Pia…' He softly kissed her temple, her cheek, and when he pulled back and looked down at her she felt the agony and torment in his expression in her own soul.

Suddenly words were spilling, tumbling, pouring from her mouth. 'I'm sorry you lost your parents that way. I'm sorry your dreams were stolen in the night. I'm sorry he destroyed that life. But I'm glad—*so* glad—you found the strength to stand tall and make another.'

Tears filled his eyes, pooling precariously. 'Pia…'

'Go. Marry your sweet bride. Be happy. As I will be.'

He jerked back as if she'd struck him and thrust his hands into his hair, ravaging the sexy mess. 'I haven't agreed to marry her! *Dios*, Pia. I wouldn't have slept with you if I had! I made Goldsmith retract the statement and say we were in talks, which is the truth.'

She had seen that, but reading it and hearing it from his lips were two entirely different things.

'Talks? A merger? Do you really want something so cold?' It didn't suit him at all. Didn't make sense. Unless…

'Do you love her?' It came out as a whisper, because even asking him hurt so badly.

Then. *Then* she knew. And emerging into the reality that she'd fallen madly in love with him was as stark and cold as being born, leaving her naked and shivering and utterly defenceless. How could she have been so stupid?

'No, I don't love her, Pia. Which is the entire point. I want Santos Diamonds for my grandfather—before I lose him too. I promised him.'

Pia frowned, trying to piece together what he was saying, but before she even had a chance to open her mouth and ask what the hell he was talking about he flung his arms in the air with all that Brazilian flair and passion she loved so much.

'And dammit, I don't want to feel like this!'

'This?' God, the look in his eyes. Torment. Utter torment.

'This…this *agony* when I look at you! This obsession to hold you in my arms. This craving to have you *now*. Like you are air and I can't breathe without you. This unnatural possessiveness that grabs me by the throat and makes my heart want to explode every time I touch you, kiss you, see your smile, hear your laugh and know it will be over any minute now.'

Her heart was beating so fast she was sure she'd pass out at any moment. Unsure what all that really meant.

He vibrated with a torrid combination of possessiveness, violence, sorrow and an almost desperate hunger. It all worked to pull her into a near fatal frenzy as the end of their game came into sight.

'Pia…'

Like a blistering storm he closed the gap between them, thrust his hands into her hair and crashed his mouth over hers, crushing, devouring.

She tried to pull back, she really did, but it was the first time she'd felt anything close to alive since she'd left him.

The salt of his tears exploded on her tongue and in the back of her mind, though she knew he was using her once more in order to feel something other than pain, she let him take and take and take. Bury his sorrow, his anger, deep inside her.

Somehow they made it to the bed, just skin against skin, frantic, desperately trying to soothe. And then he was moving inside her—one minute slow and somehow devout, the next angry and ferocious as he ran through a tumult of emotions and unleashed them all on her body one by one.

Murmurs filled the air—some she could neither hear nor understand, others so heartbreaking she was on the verge of tears.

'It wasn't meant to be this way,' he whispered against her throat, before inhaling her scent deeply.

This wasn't making love or sex; this was Nic ripping her soul out of her body with his goodbye.

'Please tell me I haven't hurt you.'

Then her own tears came, and she clutched him to her so he wouldn't see her own heartache drawing lines down her temples, down her cheeks.

'You haven't hurt me. You could never hurt me,' she breathed, the lies spilling from her as easily as the tears.

'I would die first,' he vowed as his climax raged through his body.

Pia followed him into the light, that supernova burning bright, only for it to flicker and die as if it had never been.

And when she woke he was gone, leaving the cold seeping into her heart once more. Frozen to the core.

CHAPTER FIFTEEN

AVÔ TAPPED HIM on the shoulder and Nic jolted back to the present. Though he'd swear he could still feel her petal-soft skin, taste her rich, evocative scent on his lips.

He'd hoped the craving would have paled by now, ten days on. Lust could burn—Nic knew that. But he'd never felt it threaten to incinerate every rational part of him. Obliterate all the careful shields he'd built to make him a functioning member of society, leaving this savage, beastly Neanderthal filled with need and want.

He spun round and thrust a glass of cognac to Matteo Santos, all the while drinking his own in one powerful mind-numbing shot.

'There is a parcel here for you—just arrived. Open it.'

Nic didn't even glance towards the antique monstrosity of a table in Goldsmith's study. 'No. Let Eloisa open the gifts.' Women liked that kind of thing, and she'd made no bones about the fact that wealth and security were her reasons for marrying him. Nic wasn't interested.

He watched the marquee rise up beyond the leaded windows and for the first time wondered what kind of husband he would be.

Fair? Definitely. Supportive? He'd try his very best. Loving? Honourable? Was it faithful to marry one woman and dream of another? The woman who'd left him suffocating in the smouldering ashes of an incomprehensible wanting. It struck him as a kind of cheating all on its own.

'It is not a wedding gift.'

'Have you suddenly developed psychic abilities, Avô?' He was being as facetious as hell today, but he knew what was coming. Knew he couldn't avoid it any longer. Not when Avô had finally cornered him in the same room.

One grey eyebrow arched. Dark brown eyes glittered with annoyance. 'You are not too old for me to whip your hide, boy.'

As if. Matteo Santos had never done so much as flick his ear.

'I want to know what the blazes we are doing here, because from where I'm standing you look like you have another gun to your head—and I am getting too damn old and cantankerous to pick you up again.'

'I did not ask you to pick me up last time.' Even as he said it he cringed with self-disgust at the disrespect and ingratitude of those words. But, *Dios*, he was dying here. Dying as conflict and turmoil roiled in the darkness of his mind. Spectres of anger and regret were circling like vultures, ready to feed off his soul.

'No, I damned well *made* you. Told you to get up and walk again and not let the bastards win. Told you to find something to live for—'

'And I did.'

'Yes.'

He gave a bitter laugh that raked over Nic's skin like the claws of a feral cat.

'Revenge. I know fine well what drives you, my boy. Always have. And I let you, probably even encouraged it, just so you'd take one step, then two. Then four, then ten.'

Avô's voice cracked and Nic felt it in his bones.

'Just so you'd eat and sleep and wake. So I would not lose you too.'

The old man's eyes started filling up and Nic's heart lurched—the first movement it had made, its first sign of life since he'd left Pia, beautiful and warm and safe in her bed.

'And I am grateful, Avô,' he said brokenly.

'Are you really?' he demanded. 'Because from where I'm standing you're just choosing a different kind of death. A longer torture and a slower suffering. You may as well have died on that floor with my glorious girl and her useless husband.'

One fat tear trickled down Avô's cheek and it broke the dam inside him.

His voice was so thick with pent-up emotion it shook, barely audible even to his own ears. 'I only wanted to give you back what you lost. Santos Diamonds. The lost Santos Empire.'

'Excuses.'

White-hot anger filled him. 'No!'

'Yes! You are *not* your father!'

Nic braced his weight off the stained glass windows and blasted the weather pundits who had lyricised for days about this perfect sun-drenched day, clear and calm and hot enough to fry *huevos* on the pavements. Instead the sky was a bruised swirl of black and grey, the atmosphere sharp with chaos as storm clouds thundered across the New York skyline like the wrath of the gods, ready to beat him with their displeasure.

'I don't want to discuss my father,' he said, loath even to think of that day.

'Maybe I do.'

'Please don't,' Nic begged. *Not now. Not today.*

'I lost my daughter, Nicandro, and you can't get her back. And if you do this I will have lost you too. You really think money and diamonds can redeem souls, mend hearts, replace love?'

Nic's mind gingerly touched the words.

Love? Was love like being in the rapture of heaven and

the torture of hell? No. Love was surely sweet and kind. Not possessive and obsessive madness. Unnatural.

The scepticism in his mind masqueraded as logic and argued vehemently with him.

Being with Pia in Barcelona hadn't felt unnatural. It had felt right. Heart-stoppingly perfect. It was when he was without her that it all went to hell.

Pia...

Her name spun inside him like a key tumbling a lock. Even his skin remembered her touch—like a kiss from a ghost.

Was it possible that he'd just walked away from the only woman he could ever truly love? And was Santos Diamonds worth giving her up for?

'No, I tell you!' Avô hollered across the oppressive stately room. 'It's impossible. So I ask you again—what are we doing here?'

'Goldsmith owns Santos Diamonds and his daughter is a suitable wife.' He sounded like an automated message.

'For many, I am sure. For you? Poppycock! As for Santos Diamonds—who cares? Let it go. You either continue to live in the shadows of the past or you break into a new dawn.'

Nic squeezed his eyes shut and bowed his head.

It suddenly became glaringly obvious that he was clinging to Santos Diamonds like a life raft, still desperately trying to reach the end game he'd worked so hard for. Because otherwise it would have all been for nothing and what did he have left?

Pia...you could have a lifetime of Pia, a little voice whispered. Taunting. Teasing. Coercing his heart to beat again. *If* she'd even consider having him after what he'd done to her. He still couldn't believe he'd taken her like an animal in Paris. He wouldn't be surprised if she never wanted to speak to him again.

'I'm scared,' Nic said, unable to let go of the possibility

he would some day turn into the man his father had become in the end. A monster.

'The other side of fear is freedom, my boy. Only when we are no longer afraid do we begin to live. This is your chance for true happiness. Let me see you happy before I go. Knowing there is someone in the world you cannot bear to lose and that you are not spending every single moment holding her to your heart is an unthinkable tragedy.'

Pia stood in front of the double doors leading to the boardroom, thinking how apt it was that she'd been living—*hiding*—in this darkness for so long.

Q Virtus members were gathered around the seventy-foot conference table. One chair was vacant and for that she was grateful. She was unsure if she would have had the strength to do this if Nic had been here. This morning the front-page headlines had been dominated by photographs of the happy couple at a gala dinner last weekend. They'd looked sweet together, she thought begrudgingly.

She should hate him for dredging up all of her loneliness and rage and feelings of worthlessness. For giving her hope of an unconditional love from someone who accepted her for who she was and where she'd come from. But the fact was, how could he ever love her? She had no breeding, like his wife. Her own father had ruined his family. Nic would never look at her with adoration—only resentment for the power of his desire for her. He'd made that clear in Paris.

And he must care for this woman he was marrying, Pia thought, to go ahead even after she'd sent him the package. It had taken her days, fighting with her conscience and her heart, to make a decision. Her head had told her to let him rot in a miserable marriage that was nothing more than a con. While her heart had loathed the fact that her father's actions had placed him at the altar to start with. In the end her heart had won out and she'd gone to visit his grandfather.

Pia couldn't help but smile at the memory.

Striking even in his seventies, the silver-tongued devil had trounced her at Gin Rummy, told her she had 'spunk' and kissed her goodbye. It would be very easy to love a man like that. More so because of his absolute devotion to Nic. He'd hugged her long and hard with tears in his eyes when she'd lifted her necklace—the Santos Diamonds—from the velvet cushion and given them to him.

The only gift her father had ever given her. Going in there, she'd thought it would wrench her apart to give them up. But it had felt so right—like fate. As if somehow she'd been led—by Nic—to this man to return his legacy and make good on the sins of the past.

Then he'd winked at her when she'd given him a note for Nic. One she'd rewritten over and over to make sure that no emotion lay between the lines. That her love didn't pour from the page. Telling him to ask Goldsmith exactly how much stock he owned in Santos Diamonds.

So as far as she was concerned the past had been put to rights. Now it was time to make good on the future. If Nic had given her anything it was the strength to do this. To be proud of the woman she'd become and stand tall before them.

Chin up, she took a deep breath, then another, trying to fight past the anxiety flurrying inside her as she walked down the hallway, concealed by the shadows. Then the double doors slowly opened before her, luring her forward, guiding her into the light.

Stunned gasps were a susurrus around her head and Pia could hear their surprise, feel their shock. This was tantamount to a revolution. This was their new beginning. And hers too. No more hiding. She'd blasted Nic for his dishonesty, his betrayal, but hadn't she too used subterfuge and chicanery to run this club? Yes, she had.

And now she wanted to draw off this last veil—to bring her whole self to the stage. She didn't want to be Olympia

Merisi, the tainted girl who had been groomed into the son her father had never had. She didn't want to sit in her ivory tower behind a curtain of shame and hide any longer. *And if the club falls?* whispered the little devil on her shoulder. Then she'd have done her utmost to be honest and true to them and to herself, and that was more important than upholding a vow to a man who'd thought nothing of destroying a family to fuel his greed.

Yes, despite everything she'd loved her father. He'd saved her, given her a future, but surely after twelve years her debt had been repaid.

This was for Pia.

She stood in front of a high-backed leather chair—a ludicrous throne she'd toss out at the first opportunity. She wouldn't lord it over anyone. In this room they were equals.

'Good evening, ladies and gentlemen,' she said, her voice strong enough to carry through the room as she looked every single man and woman in the eye, her heart steadying as her inner strength bolstered her will. 'I am Zeus. And I believe we have business to discuss.'

She hadn't seen him. Wouldn't even glance at his empty chair—a chair he'd asked Narciso and Ryzard to leave empty so as not to distract her. And Pia certainly didn't need to borrow his courage, even though he'd gladly give it for eternity, because she had the strength of a lioness all on her own.

What she needed was to be loved. Adored. Cared for and cosseted in the way only a lover could. She needed to laugh and smile, have piggybacks and wear jeans, go dancing and give Nic the power to make her feel alive. She needed *him*. Nic just had to convince her of that.

When he'd walked away from his shambles of a wedding all at once he'd wanted an entire future with her—afraid of nothing, side by side, walking into a new dawn to live their dreams. He wanted them fused and naked and damp between his sheets. And in the morning he wanted to kiss that face, cherish all that heart-stopping endearing beauty so tenderly she wouldn't wake, only turn to seek his lips, trusting him, loving him.

That was what he wanted. That was what he was here to beg for.

Nic watched her work the room, brewing and stirring the crowd like a cauldron until magic bubbled in the air. She declared the old laws null and void in this age of a new day, when women were becoming more powerful in their own right and could bring much to Q Virtus. She mentioned Ryzard's wife, Tiffany, who sat straight and tall beside her husband, a look of shock and awe on her face.

And she wasn't the only one. Every man in the room couldn't take his eyes off her, mesmerised by the power, the determination emanating from her. He only hoped to God *he* was the only one seriously turned on, because he had more important things to do than warn off suitors tonight. *Jealous, Nic?* Yeah, what if he was? Nic was his own man, comfortable in his own skin, and that would never change.

In a move that was simply genius, instead of leaving the way she'd come, exerting her influence and power, Pia made her way around to shake hands. One man. One woman. Equals in every aspect. A show of trust that no matter what had gone before her reign she would run the club with honour and integrity.

From the ashes of despair and the flames of fiasco she rose like a phoenix, and his chest felt crushed by the weight of his pride and love for her.

When the doors finally closed behind her she didn't look up to where he now leaned against the conference table, wood cutting into the base of his spine, aiming for a sexy, insouciant pose and royally messing it up by having a seriously bad case of the shakes.

Nic crossed his arms. To stop himself trembling or pulling her into his arms and demanding a second chance he wasn't sure. But if he had any sense—debatable, considering he'd just come from his own abandoned wedding—he would use a gentle hand to coax and lure.

His resolve was shattered when she slumped against the door, clearly fighting the urge to crash to the floor. But she wouldn't. He knew it.

'You were magnificent, *querida*.'

Up came her head, so quickly it smacked off the door—*ouch*. Then down she went, landing on her lush bottom with a soft thump.

Nic had to grit his teeth against the overpowering compulsion to grin at the effect he had on her, thanking his lucky stars it wasn't one-sided.

'What…what are you doing *here*?' she said, the snippy emphasis on 'here' accompanied by a messy arms-and-legs scramble to her feet.

Nic pushed off the table, let his arms fall to his sides and compared his nervous terror to the day he'd clambered from his bed, glaring at the rails that would teach him to walk again as if they were the devil's pitchforks and taking his very first step. He actually thought this was worse.

'Shouldn't you be…?' She wafted her hand around as if searching for the right words as she clung to the wall and walked around the boardroom, getting as far away from him as she could. 'On your honeymoon? In bed with your wife?'

Barely, he stifled the impulse to run over there and grab her. *Dios*, she was so beautiful she made him ache. 'Where are you going?'

'As far away from *you* as I can get. Are you going to answer my question?'

'People only tend to go on honeymoons when they're married, Pia.'

That stopped her. Barnacle-like, she clutched the hardwood panelling at her back.

And he'd had enough.

Nic strode forward purposefully.

'Stay right where you are, *Lobisomem*.'

'No.' He growled in frustration when she stepped forward and started to skirt around the table—on the opposite side to him. 'I'm going to spank you for that.'

'I'd love to see you try.'

He laughed wickedly and darted to the left.

Pia darted to the right and he growled again.

'Now, now, Nic—be serious.'

'Worried, *querida*?'

'Yes. I mean no. Stay back!'

'Lesson number one,' he said, lowering his voice to a commanding tone that he knew would make her shudder from top to toe. 'You are not the boss of me, Olympia Merisi, and when I tell you to stop, you stop.'

She sneered but it was a dire effort. 'Not in this lifetime. Now, run along to your bride and leave me be!'

'*Dios*, I have no bride!' Not yet, anyway.

'Oh? Realised she was marrying a wolf in sheep's clothing, did she?'

'No, she found out I was in love with someone else.'

'What? Who told her that?'

'I did.'

She blinked the confusion from her violet-blue gaze. 'Oh, I see. When you got my note and realised it was all a con you had to get out of it, right? Poor woman—you probably broke her heart.'

'I did not break her heart! Love was never in the equation. I— Wait a minute. Note? What note? And what do you mean *con*?'

She pursed those lush lips. 'You didn't receive my note this morning?'

'No. You wrote to me, Pia? What did it say? Tell me,' he ordered, his agitation at her avoidance ratcheting into the red zone.

Slowly she shook her blonde head. 'I don't think I will. Not until you tell me why you're here.'

His patience snapped and he launched himself atop the table, skidding over the highly polished surface on his backside and landing in front of her wide-eyed and stupefyingly beautiful face.

Then he backed her up until she slammed into the wall. 'Ah, this is much better. You know I prefer the personal touch.' Palms flat to the wall either side of her head, he buried his face in her neck and inhaled deeply.

Gracie de Deus. Finally.

Pia wriggled and pushed at his chest—quite hard, actually. Not that it moved him. They both knew it was a half-hearted effort. 'Why…why didn't you get married?'

Nic straightened up and cupped her jaw, dropping a tender kiss on her temple. 'Because one day I met an amazing woman I intended to wreak the ultimate revenge upon and she was unlike anything I'd ever known or seen before in my life. She scared me, and I'm a man who doesn't handle fear well, Pia. I told myself she was a means to an end and that I'd seduce her into my bed to reach my end game. What I wouldn't admit, even to myself, was that she was slowly stealing my heart.'

'She was?' Pia breathed.

He dropped another kiss on the tip of her nose. '*Sim.* Minute by minute. Hour by hour. Day by day. Until I didn't know what was up or down. Until every breath I took was for her.'

She gazed up at him with a little pleat in her brow. 'Then why…?'

'Why did I leave you lying in your bed while my heart was breaking?'

'Yes.'

'Because I didn't want the same kind of marriage as my parents. My father was obsessed with my mother. Possessive beyond control. My father fired the first shot in that room, Pia. He killed my mother.'

Shock flared in her eyes. 'Oh, my God.'

'My father lost Santos in a rigged deal at Q Virtus—you know that bit. But what you probably don't know is that it was my mother's money—my mother was the Santos heir. My father even had to change his surname to take control. Which he did without question, because he was obsessed with her. But it was an unhealthy kind of love. He often stalked her when she went out. Flew into jealous rages when they got home if she'd even spoken to another man while they were out together. Screaming matches would last for hours. He even locked her in the attic once so she couldn't go out. But the more he pushed her the more she rebelled—and let me tell you she was a reckless, zesty woman to start with. So volatile, Pia. All of it...'

'Sounds like my childhood,' she said, her gaze dropping to the open collar of his black shirt. 'Volatile.'

'I know, *bonita*,' he said, curling one hand around her nape and holding her close for a long. precious moment. 'Is your mother still alive?'

'No, she died of a drug overdose a couple of years ago. I never saw her again after she left me outside my father's house. He gave her fifty thousand dollars to disappear and in a way I felt as if I owed him.'

Nic could hear the pain of being abandoned and the sorrow in her voice at what might have been if her mother had been a different kind of woman.

'I take it your father never married her?'

Pia shook her head.

'Once a Santos marries that's it. Stuck for life. Which was the problem with my mother and father. There's a myth—a legend based around the necklace. The Heart of the Storm. It says only a true intended Santos can wear the jewels or provoke the wrath of the gods. Same if a Santos union is broken. Superstitious nonsense—that was my

retort. But the moment I saw them around your neck…
Looking back, a tiny part of me—one I had no intention
of acknowledging—had always known you were meant for
me, and I think they led me to you, Pia.'

Lips curved, she beamed up at him and his heart flip-
flopped.

'I think there was more than revenge on your mind back
then, Nic.'

'Yes, I know. Our fathers have a lot to answer for.'

Cinching her waist, he lifted her up and carried her to
a high-backed leather chair, where he sat with Pia straddling his lap. Then he tucked a stray lock of hair behind
her ear and went on.

'When my father lost the empire to your father and
Merisi's men came to take ownership of the mansion—the
necklace—my parents had a huge showdown. I walked in
and didn't know what the hell was going on, but my father
was getting more and more agitated. My mother was yelling, screaming that this was it, she'd had enough, she was
leaving him…' Nic closed his eyes, reliving the memory.
'He snatched the gun out of the pocket of one of Merisi's
men, turned and just…shot her in the heart. Right there in
front of me. Next thing bullets were flying, the room was
steeped in panic, and one of the henchmen killed him. I got
caught in the middle of it all. One bullet in the back and it
took me over a year to walk again.'

'Oh, Nic, I'm so sorry.'

'I needed something to live for, Pia. Finding your father,
making him pay for rigging that deal, for sending thugs
to my home to threaten our lives and pushing my father
to the brink… As far as I was concerned Antonio Merisi
had put the gun in his hand and virtually pulled the trigger.
Revenge was all I had to live for. And after that I wanted
Santos Diamonds. That was all I had to live for. Until you.'

'I wish you'd trusted me—told me all this. Now I understand why you'd marry her.'

'I just didn't want that kind of erratic marriage. Gold-smith's daughter is nice…timid; there'd have been no jeal-ousy, no furious outbursts of possessiveness to shake the foundations of our home. No insanity to take one of our lives. But I was missing something in all this. I'm not my father. I am nothing like him.'

'No, you're not.'

'I am my own man.'

'Yes, you are.'

'And you—you are not my mother. Don't get me wrong, I adored the woman, but to marry a woman like her…?' He shuddered.

Pia smiled and shook her head in that way she did— as if he was past help. Where she was concerned, he was.

'But you know the downsides of a safe marriage, Pia? No passion, no adoration. No heart banging with one look. None of that weird bird-flapping in my chest. No violent tug when you're near that changes into a harrowing emp-tiness when you're gone, as if you're the other half of my soul. *Dios,* I was so proud of you tonight.' He wrapped her hands in his larger palms and kissed her thumb, her knuckle, stroked her hands over his cheeks, craving her touch all over his body. 'I've missed you so much, Pia. Felt I was dying without you.'

'I've missed you too,' she said, the words tremulous and watery as she leaned in to kiss him. Long and slow and deep.

Nic struggled to come up for air. 'That will be enough for me. Maybe you'll grow to feel more when I've gained your trust again, and I'll be grateful for that.'

'And maybe I've loved you from the start.'

He'd swear his heart paused in that moment. 'Maybe or definitely?'

'*Definitely*, definitely.'

Nic grinned as that heart of his floated to the ceiling. There was a God after all—

Hold on a minute…

'And yet,' he growled, suddenly annoyed with her, 'you were willing to let me marry another woman?'

She arched one eyebrow and gave him a load of sass. 'I gave you a choice. Something *I've* never truly had. Until tonight. Until I chose to come out of hiding. To stop living in my father's shadow. Just like you told me to. Ever since he died I've honestly thought I was free. Controlling my own life for the first time ever. But, like you said, he was still controlling me from the grave. I was still carrying the stigma of my past when instead of being ashamed I should've been even prouder of myself for what I've achieved. For coming so far.'

'Damn right you should.'

She leaned forward until the tips of their noses rubbed in an Eskimo kiss. 'You whirled into my life like a hurricane and showed me a taste of life outside the cage I was living in. Just the thought of stepping back into the darkness was more frightening than going forward into the light. So I decided that I'd give you all the facts and the choice was yours to make.'

'What facts?'

'That Goldsmith was trying to pull the wool over your eyes. He only owns forty-two per cent of Santos, Nic.'

'*What?* That dirty louse! I *will* flatten his unfortunate beak of a nose after all. That— Hang on—who owns the remaining shares?'

Her satisfied smile made her eyes sparkle. 'You do.'

'I think I would know this, *querida*.'

'Only if your grandfather told you that I signed my shares—my fifty-eight per cent—over to you at eight this morning. Santos Diamonds is back where it belongs. I gave him the necklace too—laid it right in the palm of his hand.'

Blinking, jaw slack, he stared at her until her words stopped caroming around his head like pinballs and he let them compute. Then she blurred in front of him. 'I don't believe it. You *love* me. To do that you must love me.'

She held his face and kissed away the tear that slipped down his cheek. 'Of course I do. With all my heart. I'm so surprised you didn't realise about the diamonds. You should know the majority shareholder would always keep possession of the jewels, Nic. Didn't you see that in Zanzibar?'

He shrugged helplessly. 'All I could see was you.'

She let loose a half-laugh, half-cry and wrapped her arms around his shoulders, holding him to her, blissfully tight.

'Marry me, Pia. Please,' he begged.

She squeezed him tighter. 'I'll think about it,' she said.

And while her tone was teasing he knew she was asking for some time. Time to learn how to trust him wholly, completely, and after everything he'd done he couldn't blame her for that. It would be torture, but he'd wait.

'And if I say yes I won't want you to take my name, Nic.'

'There is little chance of that, Pia. You'll be taking mine and there will be no arguments. Our power struggles will begin and end in the bedroom, *bonita*. With me in charge!'

She shut him up with another kiss—this one deep and passionate, messy with emotion and unbearable need— until he reluctantly pulled back to dive into her violet eyes.

'This is going to sound ridiculous, but it has been plaguing me and I...'

'What, *querido*? Tell me.'

'What can I give you, Pia, that you don't already have? That you can't buy for yourself?'

Tenderly, lovingly, she ran her fingers through his hair, brushing it back from his brow. 'Your heart, your gorgeous smile and the way you make me laugh. The way you make love to me. Take control.'

Her voice dropped, sultrier than ever, and she licked across the seam of his lips and undulated over his lap with a sinuous serpentine movement that made him hard in seconds.

'I love it when you make me fly. Only you can do that. Only you can take away the loneliness inside me, and when I sway only you can help me stand tall. Don't you see?' she whispered. 'I need you and I'd give it all up to have you always.'

Nic swallowed thickly. 'You would?'

'In a heartbeat. And maybe…one day…you can give me a baby so I can take her to football matches in my stilettos and shout at the referee.'

Nic cupped her lush backside and grinned. He could see her doing exactly that. 'Don't you mean him?'

She arched one flaxen brow. 'Girls can make excellent football players, Nic. There'll be no inequality in my house.'

'God forbid.'

He cinched her small waist, then smoothed upward to cup her perfect breasts. Where he lingered, toying with her through the layers of silk and lace until she flung her head back and moaned. He wanted rid of her shirt. *Now*.

'I can do all of that, Pia,' he promised, unveiling her pearly skin one button at a time and flexing his hips so she could feel his hard desire.

'Oh, you can?' she said, a little breathless, a whole lot turned on.

'*Sim*. Starting right now. I'm going to make you go supernova.'

'In the boardroom?' she asked, aiming for horrified. The flush in her cheeks ruined it. 'I'll never be able to have a meeting in here again.'

'Well, unless you have a bed upstairs, I'm not moving an inch. Ten days I've been without you. Never again.'

'My penthouse is upstairs. Take me there.'

'Oh, I'll take you, Pia. I'll take you to heaven and back. Then do it all over again. Every day of our lives.'

EPILOGUE

One year later...

'DON'T TELL ME…' Narciso smirked as he glanced up at the towering white sails that flapped in the breeze as the super-yacht schooner sliced through the South Pacific. 'Your wife of twenty-four hours *is* Ophion shipping.'

Nic grinned. 'Yep. Nice boat huh?'

'Boat…yeah. It would be very easy to feel emasculated by her power—good job you're the most self-assured, arrogant ass on the planet.'

'Sure is.' And after the best year of his life he was just as obsessed, just as madly in love, and it was the most awesome feeling in the world.

Narciso caught sight of his huge smile. 'I couldn't be happier for you, buddy. It's about time she made an honest man out of you.'

Nic curled his thumb and stroked over his thick platinum wedding band, glorying in the fact that he finally had his ring on her finger.

At first she'd kept him dangling from a great height, but he'd managed to keep the panic at bay, knowing she needed time to believe she could trust in his love. Then they'd been busy juggling corporate balls and building Q Virtus into the phenomenon it was today. No longer simply a gentlemen's club since Pia's unveiling had lured a multitude of highly successful businesswomen into its ranks. No longer steeped in archaic rules and masks of secrecy—at least not inside closed doors. Nic had no doubt the club would go down in history as the most respected of all time. Thanks to Pia and her courageous heart.

So this was the first chance he'd had to insist she became a Santos. Who would have thought the person he'd set out to destroy would become the very reason he lived and breathed?

Which reminded him…

'I believe I owe you something.' Nic delved into the pocket of his sharp black suit, lifted his fist and slowly unfurled his fingers.

One look and Narciso burst out laughing. 'A gold pig. I forgot about that. Well, she certainly brought you to your knees.'

'Who's on their knees?' Pia asked, her arm snaking around his waist as she sneaked up from behind.

Nic nuzzled at the soft skin beneath her ear and inhaled her black velvet scent. 'I will be. Later, *bonita*.' Easing back, before he dragged her below deck to their opulent satin-drenched suite, he took hold of her hand and gave a little tug until she twirled in the air. 'Or should I say Aphrodite?' He whistled long and low, glorying in the soft blush that bloomed in her cheeks.

'If I wasn't married…' Narciso muttered, ribbing him as always.

'I would tie you up below deck,' Nic tossed back. 'And—'

'Hey, that's my job,' Ruby said, joining their little cluster and giving Narciso a soft punch in the gut. 'And you *are* married, mister.'

'Blissfully, madly, deeply, devotedly married.'

Nic didn't miss the way Narciso splayed his hand over the slight swell of Ruby's stomach with an adoring possessive touch.

'Something you want to tell us, there, buddy?'

He winked with devilish satisfaction. 'Twenty-two weeks and counting.'

'Whoa—the next Warlock of Wall Street!'

Backslapping and congratulations lured Ryzard and Tiffany into the mix and the conversation quickly veered into a guessing game of 'Who will our children become?' And since Ryzard's firstborn had already made his introduction to the world Tiffany kicked off. Election-style.

'Early signs indicate Max will be equally predisposed to world domination as his father and grandfather.'

'Ah, yes,' Nic said. 'How is your father liking the White House?'

'More so when he has his grandson in his lap, I think. I'd bet good money that right now Max is crawling over his knee in the Oval Office, or he has the First Lady and her security detail catering to his every whim.'

'That's my boy,' Ryzard quipped, laughing as he tucked Tiffany into his side.

'As for our newlyweds here,' Narciso intoned with a wicked smirk. 'Nic tells me they're planning a football team.'

'What?' Pia spluttered.

Nic did his best to keep a straight face and failed dismally. 'I said no such thing—although it would be fun making one.'

Truth was they'd decided to wait, both of them needing to spend some time just the two of them, but he wasn't blind to the longing in those seductive eyes. She had her heart set on a honeymoon baby, so tonight was the night.

Pia's blush deepened, as if she knew exactly what he was thinking, and he got a smack for his lascivious mind that was basically an excuse for her to feel him up.

'I adore you,' he whispered, kissing the flaxen fall of her hair tucked behind her ear. 'With all my heart.'

'I love you too—so much. Sometimes I'm afraid I'll wake up.'

'No fears, *querida*. I'll always be right here by your side.'

She sought his mouth with her lips and it wasn't until he heard the ladies gasp that he managed to pull away from her addictive taste.

The yacht was manoeuvred into dock and even Nic's eyes widened at the view of the tropical island at dusk, their path lit by flaming torches, wending its way through lush vegetation towards the colossal mansion rising from the earth in palatial splendour.

Ryzard was the first to find his tongue. 'I've never seen anything like it. Welcome to Atlantis.'

Their new venture was based on the lost city—a luxurious ten-star resort steeped in mythology and the latest technology exclusively for members of Q Virtus. Their wedding party was the first to stay, and the yachts lining the harbour told him their guests had already arrived for the reception. Avô and Lily were among them—as healthy and full of life as ever.

Right on time a man with a golden tray appeared and Nic coerced everyone into taking a crystal flute.

Grasping Pia's hand, he raised his glass in a toast. 'To my wife, Mrs Olympia Carvalho Santos, for making me the happiest man alive. And to each and every one of you—thank you for being here to celebrate with us. It's a new dawn, my friends. And I wouldn't want to share it with anyone else.'

A chorus of, 'Hear-hear,' filled the air, and the champagne flowed well into the night as they all danced in their brave new world.

* * * * *

MILLS & BOON®

Why shop at millsandboon.co.uk?

Each year, thousands of romance readers find their perfect read at millsandboon.co.uk. That's because we're passionate about bringing you the very best romantic fiction. Here are some of the advantages of shopping at www.millsandboon.co.uk:

* **Get new books first**—you'll be able to buy your favourite books one month before they hit the shops

* **Get exclusive discounts**—you'll also be able to buy our specially created monthly collections, with up to 50% off the RRP

* **Find your favourite authors**—latest news, interviews and new releases for all your favourite authors and series on our website, plus ideas for what to try next

* **Join in**—once you've bought your favourite books, don't forget to register with us to rate, review and join in the discussions

Visit **www.millsandboon.co.uk**
for all this and more today!